City IN THE Sky

GLYNN STEWART

FAOLAN'S PEN
PUBLISHING
faolanspen.com

This edition published in 2022 by:

Faolan's Pen Publishing Inc.

22 King St. S, Suite 300

Waterloo, Ontario

N2J 1N8 Canada

ISBN-13: 978-1-989674-31-4 (print)

A record of this book is available from Library and Archives Canada.

Printed in the United States of America

1 2 3 4 5 6 7 8 9 10

Second edition

First printing: April 2015

Second printing: May 2022

Illustration © 2017 Jeff Brown Graphics

Faolan's Pen Publishing logo is a trademark of Faolan's Pen Publishing Inc.

Read more books from Glynn Stewart at faolanspen.com

ERIK TARVERRO WAITED SILENTLY in the Guild Hall of the Smiths'
Guild. The hardwood seat and simple decorations, fitting for an arti-
sans' guild, did little to alleviate his tension. Every so often, his hand
drifted down to the sword at his belt and caressed the hilt. His grandfather, recovered now from his long illness, had borne an identical
weapon into the Tribunal Room an hour earlier. Combined with
several other pieces, it was to stand as proof of his readiness to be
qualified as a Master of the Guild.

In a gesture too controlled to be a lunge, Erik came to his feet and
began to pace. He'd tried not to get his hopes up, but surely this time
they'd have to accept that he was, indeed, good enough to be a Master.
He was a better swordsmith than half the Masters in the city.

His pacing brought him to a polished shield hung on the wall, and
he paused, examining himself in it. It was his eyes, he knew. His eyes,
with the slant and dark color that his father's aeraid blood had
bequeathed to him, that marked him as a half-breed. He was short for
a human, but not unreasonably so. It was his eyes and face that marked
him as the child of an aeraid. The jet-black hair that he'd drawn back
into a ponytail only accentuated the difference.

Erik turned away from his image in the shield with a muttered curse. His father had been as good a man as any of them, for all that he was not human. Who were they to decide that his blood made his son less worthy?

The door to the Tribunal Room creaked open and Erik turned to face it. Five men, dressed in the formal robes of Master Smiths, walked out of the room, ignoring Erik as they turned toward the back of the Hall, where no mere journeyman could enter.

That was it, then. If there had been any chance, they'd have invited him in to speak for himself, not simply left. The grim expression on his grandfather's face when old Byron followed them out merely confirmed it. Erik met the old man's gaze, and Byron shook his head.

Three times now, they'd rejected him. Not on the basis of skill—even as a journeyman, people recommended him to those looking for good swords—but merely due to his blood. No matter how many of the city's smiths acknowledged him, it always seemed that his Mastery Tribunals were made up of the ones that held his father's race against him.

"Come on, Erik," Byron said finally. "Let's go home."

Erik nodded sharply and slowly released the handle of his sword.

THE FADING AFTERNOON SUN GLITTERED OFF THE BLADE OF THE sword as Erik ran through his exercises. The sword hummed through a complex series of parries, cuts and thrusts, inflicting unspeakable damage on empty air.

Why wouldn't they just accept him as a Master? He was good enough; there was no argument anywhere about that. At least one of the smiths who'd voted today had sent business his way in the past. He was the most respected journeyman smith in the city, but as long as he remained a journeyman, he couldn't open his own shop. He was left working out of his grandfather's shop.

He snarled and spun, thrusting the sword into the "stomach" of the dummy in the quiet training yard. Even money didn't help. He was good enough that he had enough of that, but bribing the Tribunal was nearly impossible, even if it was likely to do any good.

There were simply too many Masters in the Guild who would not allow a "mere" half-blood to "pollute the purity" of their organization. As long as any Tribunal included at least three of them, and there were enough that that was almost certain, he would never have a chance.

He heard the shop bell ring, but he ignored the noise as he slowly and methodically hacked the dummy into very, very small pieces.

BYRON HURRIED INTO THE FRONT OF THE SHOP, MENTALLY CURSING himself for forgetting that Erik wouldn't be covering the store this afternoon as he normally did. Stepping up to the counter, he shed the heavy leather gloves he'd been wearing in the forge and looked up at the customer.

"How can I help you?" he asked automatically, before the man's appearance truly sank in. Almost as soon as the words were out of his mouth, Byron half-froze at the sight of the man.

The stranger was tall, nearly six feet, unusually tall for a human, but bore the same arched cheekbones that marked the aeradi. He lacked their slanted eyes, however, but both his eyes and hair appeared jet-black. He was clad in a doublet of dark maroon velvet that had probably cost as much as a decent horse. Just about everything about the man screamed first *rich*—and then *draconan*. The eyes and height declared him a member of the mountain-bound race that bred and flew the great dragons.

He smiled, and Byron hid a shudder. That smile looked like it belonged on something with scales and claws, not a man.

"I am in need of some...specialized equipment," the man said softly. "I have been told that you have a journeyman here—your grandson, I believe?—who may be able to make it for me. Is my information correct?"

"My grandson is indeed a journeyman," Byron said. "I am not certain if he will be able to help you, however—he is primarily a swordsmith."

"So I was told," the draconan replied with a nod. "I am in the correct place, then?"

Byron shrugged carefully. "I would suppose so. If you will wait here, I can get him for you."

"That would be satisfactory," the man agreed. He selected a chair and sat on the edge of it, looking as if every nerve and muscle in his body was ready to spring into action, and yet remaining perfectly still.

Byron managed to hide another shudder as he left the shop, heading to the yard where he figured Erik would be. It took only a few steps toward the yard for him to be able to hear the hard thuds of steel on wood. When he stepped out into the open space at the heart of the compound he'd built around his house, smithy and shop, he found that his grandson had completely demolished the straw dummy he normally practiced on, and had proceeded to attack the heavy wooden pole it was attached to.

The pole was six feet high and nearly four inches thick. Normally, Byron wouldn't have thought that you could cut through it with a sword, at least not without having to repeatedly sharpen the blade, but the evidence suggested that Erik hadn't really cared. The top third or so of the pole lay on the hard-packed dirt ground, and the top half of the remainder was scarred by sword strikes.

Erik was sitting on the ground, eyeing the sword, which was now stuck deep into the pole about a foot down from its new top. Sweat dripped from the young man's brow, falling onto the already-soaked fabric of his tunic.

"Enjoying yourself?" Byron asked his grandson.

"Not really," Erik replied, his eyes not leaving the sword. "It did help with my mood, but I think I'm going to need to remake that sword."

"You have four others just like it," Byron observed.

"Three others," Erik corrected, gesturing across the yard.

Byron looked where his grandson pointed and saw another sword, from the case next to the one he'd taken into the Tribunal earlier today. Erik had apparently decided to prove the theory that you could break a sword by stepping on it while holding it at the right angle. He'd succeeded, and the broken pieces of the blade shone dully in the sun.

"Ah" was all Byron said. "Are you recovered enough to be civil? I have a man asking for you in the shop."

Erik considered for a moment. "Who?"

"Not a regular customer," Byron replied. "Draconan, rich."

"Not a regular customer indeed," Erik whispered, his calm voice belying the destruction around him. He rose smoothly to his feet with the grace of the trained swordsman he was. "I'll see him."

ERIK UNBELTED HIS SWORD AND LEFT IT AT THE BACK ENTRANCE into the shop part of the smithy. It was hardly necessary for him to wander around his own home armed, and he felt it seemed threatening to the customers if he spoke to them while wearing a sword. Besides, if he needed a weapon, there were half a dozen swords on the wall in the store—hung there as samples for customers to peruse.

He entered the shop and took a moment to look the customer over. Like Byron had said, he was definitely a draconan. He shared the same darkened eyes and hair, and arched high cheekbones, that Erik himself bore as the legacy of his aeraid father, but stood far taller than his father's race.

At the sound of Erik's entrance, the man came easily to his feet, and Erik changed his last assessment. The draconan *was* taller than Erik, but he was quite short for a draconan. With a little effort, he could likely have passed almost unnoticed among a group of humans.

"I am Erik Tarverro," Erik said quietly. "You said that you were looking for me?"

"You may call me Rade," the stranger replied with a sharp nod. "I am looking to have some very specialized items made for me."

"Whether or not I can help you depends on the items," Erik replied. "I am primarily a swordsmith, and my grandfather would likely be a better person to speak to for general tools."

Rade shook his head. "I am looking for a swordsmith." He reached inside his doublet and removed a package wrapped in dark crimson velvet. He unwrapped the velvet and laid three items on the counter. "Look at these," he instructed.

Erik did. Two of the items were identical, daggers with short and very thin blades. They were stilettos more than daggers, actually. Their handles were small, just enough to be held in a hand, no more.

The third item was broken into two pieces. It had been a rather larger version of the stilettos—a poniard. However, the blade had broken off close to the hilt, rendering the weapon useless. Erik picked up the sheared-off blade and examined it closely. The metal had an odd white tinge to it that he'd rarely seen before.

"This is sky steel," he said flatly.

"Indeed," Rade replied. "I need at least eight more daggers, plus two poniards to replace that one. Also, I would like a smallsword, forged to the customary pattern in this city."

Erik nodded slowly. The last request, at least, made some sense. Smallswords were a style of rapier that had become quite common in the human cities. They were mostly decorative, but a properly made one was a deadly weapon in expert hands. Erik very much doubted that Rade was anything less than a master.

"I would also," Rade finished, "like all of these crystal-forged of sky steel."

Erik snapped his head up to meet the man's gaze. He wasn't entirely surprised—sky steel was *far* superior to any normal steel, but it required the empowered crystals of air magic to forge.

"I do not have a great deal of experience in crystal-forging," he said slowly. Something about both this draconan and the items he wanted made him uncomfortable. "I certainly do not possess the materials, and they are quite expensive."

"You are the only smith in this city with any experience," Rade replied. "Also, unlike every other smith in this city, you have Sky Blood. Without that, the forging would be nearly impossible."

Erik almost unconsciously nodded to himself. The man was correct. Crystal-forging was sky magic, and while the crystals, once empowered, could be used by anyone, it was far easier for those of the Sky Blood. For something as finicky as the crystal-forging of sky steel, that ease made the difference between the work being impossible and it being merely difficult.

And Erik's father had been an aeraid, of the People of Wind and Wave. He had the blood. The very factor that gave him such difficulty in becoming a Master was exactly what this man needed. And yet...the items the man wanted disturbed him. These were not the weapons of a mercenary or a guard.

"As for the price of the materials," Rade continued, disrupting Erik's thoughts, "I am prepared to pay twenty Hellitian gold marks." That was more than a third of what Erik normally made in a month, and Erik spotted a glint in the draconan's eyes and realized the man knew this. Before Erik could speak, the man continued, softly, "Up front. With another twenty on completion."

Erik inhaled involuntarily. While the materials were likely to be expensive, they weren't *that* expensive. He'd likely pay for the materials out of the up-front, with several gold left over. The twenty on completion would be pure profit. He couldn't *afford* to turn the man down.

"Very well," he conceded. "I accept."

From the half-smirk that marked the draconan's face, Erik knew the man had known from the very beginning that Erik couldn't afford to refuse him. The money was good, but there were still many things about this job that worried him.

"WELL?"

Erik started at the question, then looked up at the speaker. He'd been looking at the samples Rade had provided and had missed his grandfather entering the room. The burly old smith was standing next to the counter, looking down at the four items on the red velvet cloth.

"He wants these duplicated," Erik replied softly. "Eight of the daggers, two poniards, and a smallsword."

Byron pursed his lips. "That's a lot of work."

"He's offering a lot of money," Erik replied, still quiet. "He also wants them crystal-forged of sky steel, which is why he came to me."

The old smith's expression was unreadable as he picked up one of the daggers and balanced it. He made a small motion, and the stiletto all but vanished in his hand, unseen and yet still deadly.

"Crystal-forging isn't cheap," Byron said, his eyes on the weapon hidden in his hand.

Erik shrugged and turned the purse the draconan had left on the counter onto its side. Coins spilled out, glinting with the dull yellow of gold. "He paid twenty marks in advance for materials," he said helplessly.

Byron suddenly thrust downward with the hand holding the stiletto. There was no glimpse of metal, but when the smith removed his hand, the knife's entire blade had disappeared into the wooden countertop. "Erik, these aren't normal weapons," he said, his voice strained.

"I *know* that, Grandfather," Erik replied. "The one and only time I ever saw anything like them was when I was in Garria. The duredine smith I was working with had a collection of unusual weapons. He had a weapon like this"—Erik touched the stiletto his grandfather hadn't taken—"that was one of the prides of his collection. According to him, it was an assassin's weapon," he finished.

The old duredine smith he'd worked with in the Garria Forest—a nation ruled and mostly inhabited solely by that people—would have known, too. Like many of that long-lived race, he'd been a soldier in his youth, before turning his hand to the forge.

"Erik, this isn't the sort of job you want to get involved in," Byron told him. "The affairs of spies and assassins are dangerous to meddle in. You could get hurt."

"He gave me twenty gold marks up front, and offered another twenty on completion," Erik said flatly. "Without a Mastership and my own shop, I can't afford to turn down that kind of money, no matter what it gets me involved with."

"Erik..."

"It's done, Grandfather," Erik snapped, cutting Byron off. "I took the man's money. I'll do the job."

The old smith bowed his head in acceptance. "Be careful, Erik," he admonished. "We don't know what you've got yourself into yet."

"I'll be careful," Erik promised. "It's not like he's going to kill me for making weapons for him."

⌒

EVEN THROUGH HIS HEAVY CLOAK, THE COOL AUTUMN AIR OF Vidran's busy streets chilled Erik. Smiths' Row was sparsely crowded compared to the rest of the city, but then, many of the smithies were built into the smiths' homes.

Once into the rest of the city, the population picked up dramatically. People of all six races traveled the streets, though the vast majority were human. Everyone came to Vidran, in the end. It was one of the major ports where the aeradi and mermen came to trade with the rest of Cevran.

The population of nonhumans rose as he crossed the bridge over the great North Selt River, whose immense navigable length was another source of Vidran's wealth. In the moments it took him to cross the bridge, he saw barges from the dwarven North Hold and the duredine's Kingdom of the Garria Forest.

He knew he'd arrived at his destination when he heard the high, trilling roar of the first dragon. The eastern edge of the Trade Quarter housed the pens where the draconans corralled their beasts. Even his current worries couldn't keep Erik from taking a moment to stop and watch the magnificent creatures.

The dragons were immense, sinuous beasts. Their necks stretched out a quarter of their length from their broad, wing-bearing bodies. Long, spiked tails flicked out from between a single pair of stocky legs, the tails' neatly shined spikes gleaming under the sun as they flicked back and forth.

Most of the dragons here were the huge blacks, the ones that carried the traders and goods of the draconan peoples across the length and breadth of Cevran. A small number of lesser beasts were kept in pens near the ones for their larger brethren, which likely meant a caravan had come in recently. The only reason for the lesser dragons, the ones who bore the draconan's elite Skyborne warriors, to be in Vidran was if they'd just escorted a trade caravan in.

The armies of Hellit, the kingdom whose trading lifeblood flowed through Vidran, were quite capable of handling a handful of Skyborne, but no one wanted war-trained dragons stabled in a city. The Skyborne caravan escorts normally encamped well outside the city—but would stable inside for the first night or so after arriving.

The combination of the shrill cries of the greens and browns with the louder and deeper roars of the blacks created a cacophony of noise that pressed in on Erik's ears, and he shuddered, remembering the one time he'd been there and something had roused *every* dragon in the pens.

It was an experience he wouldn't soon forget, and the memory helped him leave the dragons and press on to the store he was seeking. Tucked away just inside the aeradi section of the Trade Quarter, it looked exactly like a hole in the wall until one entered it.

To a large extent, much of what the aeradi traders did was pick up goods from one place and trade them for goods from another. They did trade goods of their own manufacture but were more circumspect about which of those they traded.

This little hole in the wall traded the sort of things they were *very* circumspect about trading. Air Magic involved the creation of empowered crystals, and once empowered, those easily used crystals became both valuable and dangerous.

Those sorts of crystals glinted from every wall and display case in the small store. Despite the nondescript appearance of the outside, the inside of the store was both well-kept and well organized. The crystals were organized by purpose and price, everything clearly labeled.

Erik had been there before, and the proprietor rose from behind the plain wooden counter at the end of the store with a smile. He was pure aeraid, with the same slanted eyes and dusky skin as Erik, but coming in at barely under five feet tall.

"Erik," he greeted the smith. "It's good to see you again. What are you looking for today?"

"I need forge crystals, Jaron," Erik told him. He thought for a moment, counting in his mind. "Three of them," he finished.

"Those aren't safe things to play with, Erik," Jaron warned. "You certain?"

"I worked with them when I was in Garria," Erik told him. "I need them for a job."

Jaron nodded. "All right." He paused, and then added, "They aren't *cheap*, either."

"How much?" Erik asked as the aeraid merchant crossed to a specific shelf.

"Four gold marks each," Jaron replied. He took three black-wrapped shapes from the shelf. "If you're wanting sky steel to go with that, it's a half-gold per stock bar."

"You carry sky steel?" Erik asked, surprised. He needed sky steel, and it was almost pointless to use forge crystals for anything other than sky steel, but he'd figured he'd need to go deeper into the Quarter for it. As far as he knew, Jaron only carried crystals.

"Some. Not much," he admitted, "and I wouldn't normally sell it, but it is you. A half-mark is a tenth less than they'll charge you in the Quarter, too."

Erik nodded slowly. "I need twelve stock bars, if you have them." If everything went right, he'd only need ten, but he was experienced enough to know that he was going to make at least one mistake.

Jaron nodded. Laying the crystals on the counter, he knelt down behind it and opened something, presumably a box. He quickly laid out a dozen of the twelve-inch-long stock bars.

Erik picked one up and ran his fingers along it. It was sky steel, all right. The white tinge was there, and both the weight and feel were right for the crystal-purified metal. "Eighteen marks, then?" he asked, removing his money pouch from his belt.

"Yes," Jaron confirmed, his tone suggesting he hadn't *quite* believed Erik had the money.

Erik counted out the coins and laid them on the counter. Jaron swept them off the counter and into the drawer beneath it, and Erik regarded the significant pile of items on the table for a long moment.

"You'll want these delivered to your grandfather's smithy, I presume?" the storekeeper finally asked into the silence.

His eyes on the metal and his thoughts on Rade's still-disturbing order, Erik merely nodded.

ERIK LAID THE FIRST BAR OF SKY STEEL ON THE ANVIL AND regarded it levelly. The forge he and his grandfather shared was supplied with every amenity of the blacksmith's trade. They could afford the best coals and charcoals for their work. All told, this forge could produce the highest heat possible.

The fires in the forge were cold. It took more than natural heat to make sky steel forgeable. No number of bellows or quality of coal could do more than cause it to heat to the touch.

He removed the first forge crystal from its velvet casing and laid it on the anvil, next to the steel bar. It looked innocuous enough, a piece of crystal about the length of his hand, glowing gently silver. Innocuous-looking or not, that crystal could provide a level of heat the forge's fires couldn't.

Erik picked the crystal up and held it above the bar of sky steel. He concentrated, and the silver glow intensified. Carefully lowering the crystal closer to the bar, he focused on the bar through the crystal. The silver glow intensified even more, then jumped from the crystal to the bar as he brought it close enough.

Even through his thick leather gloves, he could feel the heat radiating from the metal. The crystal, however, remained cool. Encased in the silver glow, the bar of sky steel slowly began to glow red with heat.

The bar's glow edged slowly toward the bright orange of forgeable steel, and Erik removed one of the tools from the thick leather belt he wore over his apron. With a quick and precise strike, he neatly broke the glowing bar. The smaller piece he tossed aside onto a bed of sand by the forge, to cool for later use.

The larger piece he left on the forge, glowing even brighter in the light of the forge crystal. It reached a pure orange hue, and Erik lowered the crystal and took up his hammer. With swift and sure strokes, he began to shape the first of the weapons the draconan had ordered.

IT TOOK ERIK TWO DAYS AND ALMOST ALL THE MATERIALS HE'D purchased to produce the draconan's order. He used up two of the forge crystals entirely, and the glow of the third was faded far from its original hue. A single complete bar and a handful of scraps remained of the sky steel, but Erik had the man's eight stilettos, two poniards and smallsword.

Once he'd finished, he turned to the other orders he'd had in. Almost as soon as he'd fired up the forge, however, the shop bell rang. Taken by a sudden suspicion, he glanced over to the apprentice who stood by the bellows.

"Can you cool the forge down, Jona?" he asked. "I think I need to meet a customer."

The boy nodded and Erik clasped his shoulder as he turned away. Throwing a cloak on to cover the heavy leather apron he was wearing, he hurried across the courtyard of the house to the shop.

He met his grandfather at the door to the shop.

"I was just coming to get you," the older smith said. "Rade is here."

"I'd guessed," Erik replied. "His order is in the rack."

"Be careful," Byron advised with a slow nod.

"I will," Erik promised. "Now go check on Jona; he's watching the forge on his own. I'll be fine."

The older smith hurried across the courtyard, and Erik ducked into the store. Rade was waiting, dressed in the same dark maroon as before. Erik met his eyes, and the draconan quickly jerked his gaze away.

"Is my order finished?" he asked.

Erik had finished the order less than an hour before, and he sincerely doubted the draconan had turned up this quickly by accident. He *knew* Erik had the order finished, and wondering how sent a shiver down the smith's back.

"Yes, it is," Erik replied. He reached under the counter and removed the cloth-wrapped package containing the weapons and slid it across the counter to the draconan.

Rade unwrapped the packaging and laid the weapons, each in a leather sheath made by a leatherworker Byron contracted with, out in quick order. He drew each weapon in turn, starting with the smallsword and poniards, and examined them.

"This is fine work, Tarverro," he complimented. "I've rarely seen better. I believe we agreed on twenty marks on completion?"

"Indeed we did," Erik said with a hidden sign of relief. He hadn't been *too* worried, but he guessed some of Byron's fears had rubbed off on him.

Rade drew a bag of gold from inside his doublet and reached across to drop it on the counter. Erik looked down to examine it, and realized that one of the stiletto sheaths was empty.

Almost as he realized it Rade released the moneybag and lunged across the counter, the glint of metal barely visible in his hand. The knife punched through the cloak Erik had wrapped around himself and into the leather apron he hadn't bothered to take off.

The blade wasn't quite long enough to go deep through the leather, and it scored along his ribs as Erik hissed in pain and knocked the man's hand away. He kicked out as he did and sent the draconan stumbling backward.

Rade regained his balance quickly and had somehow grabbed the smallsword off the counter. With a swift gesture, he drew the weapon and slid into a point-forward combat stance, lunging toward Erik.

Erik dove out of the way, slamming his left shoulder hard into the wall and knocking the half-dozen sample swords off of their holders. They crashed down around him, and he grabbed the nearest weapon, a cavalry saber, before rolling back up to his feet to face the assassin, who was circling back in for another attack.

The heavy saber was not the best weapon to face the lethal swiftness of the point-oriented smallsword, but it was what Erik had. He parried Rade's first lunge and found himself parrying three more attacks in quick succession.

The draconan was *fast*, and Erik was backed up against a wall. He lunged with the saber, trying to buy himself some space, but the assassin only deflected it. The parry turned into a riposte that Erik only barely managed to knock aside with his wrist. Metal scored along his face, but the smallsword had no edge, and it was little more than a scratch.

What little space Erik had gained was quickly lost as the assassin pressed in, forcing him to step back to block the attacks. He parried four times and then lashed out with his foot. He caught Rade in the shin, knocking the draconan off-balance. He slashed at the assassin, but the draconan deflected the strike, preventing Erik from hitting him with the blade. As the blade went up, Erik twisted his wrist to slam the hilt of the heavy sword into Rade's face.

Rade reeled backward, spitting blood from his mouth, and Erik pressed his advantage. The saber was heavy, but he barely felt it as he flicked it out in a series of attacks that drove the assassin, limping from the shin strike, farther back.

"Why?" he demanded as they moved into the clear space in the middle of the room.

"No one can know I'm here," Rade spat. "Now shut up and *die!*" The assassin's muscles bunched as he lunged.

Erik stepped aside, grabbed the edgeless blade with his gloved hand. With a quick jerk, he fatally unbalanced the draconan, sending him stumbling to the ground. Acting on instinct, Erik brought the saber whistling around in a strike no light smallsword could have blocked, and the half-standing assassin crumpled the rest of the way to the ground as the blade took his head from his shoulders.

Instants later, the saber clattered to the ground as the blood spurted out of the corpse's neck and Erik realized just what had happened. He collapsed to his knees as the door banged open and Byron rushed in, a hand-and-a-half bastard sword raised.

Erik barely even realized his grandfather was there before the headless body gave one last spurt of blood, directly before his eyes, and the young smith was violently sick.

ERIK SAT IN THE CORNER OF THE SHOP, IGNORING THE ACTIVITY around him, staring at the blade resting on the floor in front of him. He'd cleaned the blood from it, acting as much by rote as by any thought, but he continued to clean the blade.

The City Guard had responded to the messenger Byron had sent with commendable speed. Four guardsmen stood around the store, examining the scene of the fight, while a fifth questioned Byron. Erik heard his grandfather explaining about how the draconan had first come to them, and knew that he should really be helping explain.

It was hard for him to think, though. The image of Rade's head exploding away from his shoulders kept replaying before his mind's eye. The only reason he'd stopped being sick was because he'd emptied his stomach entirely. He scrubbed harder at the saber's blade, barely even noticing the pain of his scored face and chest as he tried to wash the image out of his mind.

The shop bell rang again, and a new man entered the room. He wore no uniform, just plain gray clothes like those anyone on the street would wear, but the guardsmen immediately snapped to a sharper bearing when they saw him.

The gray-clad man crossed to the corpse and stood above it, looking down. "This is the man?" he asked aloud, looking at Erik.

"Yes," Byron replied. "It is."

The man's gaze flickered to Byron, but he nodded. "I want to see what he had made," he instructed calmly as he knelt by the headless corpse.

"Erik?" Byron asked gently.

"On the counter," Erik replied dully.

His grandfather nodded, gathered up the package on the counter and offered it to the gray man.

The man held up a hand, refusing it for the moment. He leaned closer to the corpse, examining the head that lay next to it as well. Without changing expression, he drew a knife from his belt and cut the dead man's doublet open.

Erik heard the man hiss, but wasn't sure if anyone else did. The man immediately closed the doublet over the corpse's chest and stood, taking the package from Byron.

"Master Byron, Sergeant," he said calmly, "please leave the room. I need to speak to the younger Tarverro in private."

The guardsmen didn't even hesitate before leaving with almost unseemly haste. Byron did hesitate, glancing at his grandson. The man must have caught the glance, as he spoke again. "I mean him no harm, Master Byron," he said gently, "but I must speak to him alone."

Byron nodded and left, closing the back door behind him.

Almost as soon as the door closed, the man stepped over to Erik and gently removed the sword and cleaning cloth from his hands. Erik looked up at him and found the man offering him a canteen of water.

"Rinse," he ordered, and then offered Erik a cloth. "Now spit."

Erik obeyed, cleaning the grunge from his mouth.

"As soon as we're done here, have those wounds seen to," the man instructed him. "They're not dangerous in themselves, but infection is nothing to play games with."

"Who are you?" Erik finally asked.

The gray-clad man smiled. "Captain Toris Mehil, Royal Guard," he offered calmly.

"You don't look like a soldier," Erik replied.

"Good," Mehil said. "If I did, that would be a problem."

"You're a spy."

"No, I'm an agent," Mehil corrected. "I do counterintelligence, do my best to keep tabs on spies in the city and every so often deal with the assassins that some idiot inevitably tries to send after *somebody*. In this case, you've done my job for me."

"What do you mean?" Erik asked.

Mehil stepped back over to the corpse and pulled the sliced doublet open, revealing a tattoo on the man's right breast. "Do you know what this is, Erik Tarverro?" he asked.

The tattoo looked much like the dragons he saw regularly in the Trade Quarter, but it was shaded red. "A dragon."

"A red dragon, yes," Mehil replied. "Red dragons, as in the creatures themselves, are thankfully quite extinct. Unfortunately, their worshippers are *not*, and the Dragon Lords find them quite useful."

At Erik's questioning gaze, the Royal Agent grimaced. "While even among the draconans the worship of the High Cult of Salshar is punishable by death, the Red Dragon Cult doesn't indulge in such...*vigorous* forms of worship as the High Cult. They *do*, however, train the true devotees of the cult as assassins. These assassins serve the Dragon Lords quite willingly."

Mehil allowed the doublet to close again. "There is no business a Red Dragon would have in Vidran that we would like, Tarverro. Worse, I didn't even know he was here. You were very lucky."

Erik eyed the corpse askance. "I killed him," he confessed.

"Exactly," Mehil said gently. "This man was a professional killer and likely a very good one. Other than killing him, there was no way you could have survived." He paused and continued in a more formal tone. "I assure you that the Crown of Vidran will not level criminal charges in this case."

Erik sagged with relief. He'd expected to at least have to face a tribunal and prove self-defense. He was starting to suspect, however, that this plainly dressed man had as much authority as any legal tribunal in the city.

The agent stood. "The guardsmen will clean this up and deal with the body." He glanced around the room. "Keep the money he paid you, you did complete the work. It is possible," he allowed, "that there may be a reward for your actions." He clapped Erik on the shoulder.

"Come on, son," he said gently. "Let's get those scratches of yours seen to."

Brane Kelsdaver, Captain of the Red Dragons and spy for the great and powerful nation of Dracona, read the report and cursed the half-blood Erik Tarverro for being stupid enough to get in the way. Then he cursed Rade for being Fires-burnt fool enough to try to kill the man. Then he cursed the Hellitian spy who'd been clever enough to realize what had happened.

Once he was done cursing, the dark-haired draconan looked out the window of his reservoir-side office in the city of Seije and began to weep. Rade had been an agent of his, yes, but he had also been his younger brother.

Both of the young draconans had been drawn first into the ranks of the Claws of the Dragon, the Draconan army, by an eager desire to serve their nation. From there, however, Brane had fallen into the path of Red Dragons and impressed the spies-cum-assassins of Dracona. Impressed them enough that he'd been initiated into the cult, where his lack of height for a draconan—shared with his brother—made him an asset in their intelligence operations.

Brane had never been prouder than he had been on the day he learned that his younger brother had been initiated into the cult. He'd made no effort to cause it to happen—the Dragons recruited who they willed and were vicious to those who failed to meet their standards after being recruited—but he'd been proud when he learned it had.

Now his pride turned to ashes and hate in his mouth. Their parents were dead, but there was a third brother, the youngest of the three, who had joined the elite Skyborne dragon warriors. It fell to Brane to write and tell him of the fate of their brother.

Before that, however, he had other messages to send. In this instance, both tradition and his personal rage worked together—no one who killed a Red Dragon could be allowed to walk away.

THE ROYAL GUARD CAPTAIN PROVED TRUE TO HIS WORD. A WEEK after the incident, a blandly dressed man, introducing himself merely as a member of the Guard, had turned up and handed Erik a bag of coins.

The man hadn't even stayed long enough for Erik to count the hundred gold coins in the bag but had made swift apologies and left. Partially, Erik was sure, that was due to the press of the King's service, but he'd also seen the man's face when he saw Erik.

Stopping an assassin may have been enough for Captain Mehil to ignore Erik's blood, but it obviously wasn't enough for his man. In a trading city like Vidran, people learned to deal with those of the other Races of Man, but even there, half-bloods drew darker gazes. Many regarded the blending of races as obscene. Some would even go so far as to call it blasphemous.

A hundred Hellitian marks was a lot of money, and it made affairs far easier for Erik and his grandfather in the weeks that followed. Combined with their normal income and the payment for the work for Rade, it meant that they were well ahead of the game on their finances for once.

Nonetheless, Erik threw himself into his work. He had never had any trouble finding work, and now he purposefully found almost too much work. He worked his days through and, once exhausted, collapsed to sleep. Sometimes, he was too exhausted to dream. Most nights, however, his mind insisted on replaying the fight with Rade, in all of its horrific glory.

He worked to hopefully escape the nightmares, but it didn't seem to be doing any real good. Every day, Erik went into the store where he'd killed the draconan, and it seemed that every night he relived the fight.

Finally, one night, about two weeks after the attack, Byron walked into the forge while Erik was working. Erik heard him entering but ignored him as he continued to hammer on the blade on the anvil.

For long minutes, neither spoke, until Erik finished the blade and quenched it. As the hot steel sank into the water, Byron finally spoke.

"Still working, grandson?"

"What else would I be doing?" Erik asked.

"Eating," the older smith replied. "Relaxing. Sleeping. Any of the above, all of which you've not been doing."

"What of it?" Erik demanded. "It's my own concern, not yours." He reached for another steel blank, but Byron's hand locked on to his wrist before he touched it.

"Erik," he said gently, "you're not sleeping and you're barely eating. You're working yourself into a grave, and I didn't spend twenty years raising you to watch you do that."

Erik tried to free his hand, but Byron held him in a grip like iron. "It's none of your concern," he repeated.

"Yes, it is," Byron said. "You are my grandson, the only child of my daughter, and dear to me in your own right. Sit," he ordered, gesturing to the coal boxes against the wall. Pushed by that iron grip, Erik sat.

"You're having nightmares, I know," he stated flatly. "You can't sleep for them. It's not a bad thing, either," Byron added, "I'd not care much for a grandson who'd kill readily and without remorse. It's killing you, though, and that scumbag who came for you isn't worth that."

He raised a hand as Erik opened his mouth to speak. "Hear me out, grandson. Killing a man isn't an easy thing to live with, no matter the cause. Your father was a soldier. It was his duty to kill for his people. I don't know how he managed it, but I know that those he killed haunted him. There's a fighter in you, grandson, and we both know it," he said grimly. "But being a fighter is no bad thing, and the difference between a fighter and a killer is remorse over those you killed."

Erik was silent for a long moment, and then met his grandfather's eyes. "What do I do?" he asked quietly.

"You go on," Byron admitted. "Killing a man was never a demon I had to deal with, thanks be to the gods, but none can deny you'd little choice in the matter. You deal with it and go on. You've a life ahead of you, grandson, and I won't see you throw it away over the death of that sort of scum."

Byron released his grip, and Erik slowly massaged his hand. His grandfather's words made sense; indeed, they repeated what part of his mind had been saying all along. But saying *deal with it* and actually dealing with it were two different things.

"How?" Erik asked quietly.

"You can *start*," Byron observed, "by not trying to work yourself into the grave. Go out and spend some money on your own enjoyment. You've little enough time to yourself as it is, without throwing away what you have."

Erik hesitated. He'd never been inclined to spend money on enter-tainment, mainly because it had always been in short supply. Before he said this aloud, Byron laughed. "Grandson, between the King's reward for that draconan bastard and the way you've overworked yourself these last few weeks, you can afford to do almost anything you want to. You can easily afford a night at a tavern, relaxing. Go."

With a tiny smile on his lips, the first he'd felt in weeks, Erik yielded to his grandfather's demand.

THE IRON HAMMER WAS THE TAVERN VIDRAN'S SMITHS TENDED TO frequent on the occasions where any of them had the time and money to do so. Nestled into the corner at the end of Smiths' Row, the two-story brick-and-wood structure still bore the scars of being one of the few survivors of the fire that had burned through the Row twenty years earlier, killing Erik's parents.

While on the end of Smiths' Row, the Hammer was also conveniently placed on one of the major roads from the harbor to the city's main gates, and the rooms on the second floor were usually full of travelers. The smiths provided steady business, keeping the old tavern afloat, but it was the travelers that made the Hammer's profits.

The main floor of the building was one large taproom, with a large wooden bar stretched along the wall dividing the kitchen from the taproom. An even dozen wooden tables, some of which were as old as the tavern but had weathered the years far worse, were scattered around the room.

The bar was attended by old but still sturdy wooden stools, and it was one of these Erik had taken when he'd entered the tavern. A half-empty stein of ale rested on the bar in front of him as he listened to the bard in the corner.

TWELVE SWORDS, TWELVE DANCES,
    Twelve battles of legend,
    Twelve lords so dire they slew.

TWELVE BEARERS, TWELVE KEEPERS,
    Twelve heroes of Cevran,
    Twelve keys to the dragon-king's cage.

ERIK SNORTED AT THE LYRICS. THE *LAY OF THE DRAGON-KING* WAS quite popular in certain circles—most schoolchildren at least knew the chorus—but only bards knew it all. It was a grand mythic epic of battles and sacrifice and gods, and no one believed a single word of any of it.

"Wings and Sky!" four voices said quietly but together, cutting through the din of the bar. Erik turned almost involuntarily and saw that the table nearest to him had been occupied by four men, none of whom could have been above five feet tall. Slanted eyes, arched cheekbones and the toast they'd just spoken proclaimed them all to be aeradi.

All four were armed, and as Erik watched, one of them pulled his sheathed sword up and tossed it onto the table in disgust. "It had clearly been building for some time," Erik heard him say, apparently continuing an earlier conversation. "Sky steel doesn't just suddenly shear from stress."

"You've carried that thing for twenty years," one of the others commented. "Surely, you've got enough worth out of it to replace it."

The first speaker shrugged. "Maybe, but I won't. You all know why."

The others nodded. "You aren't getting sky steel fixed in *Vidran*; that's for sure," another said flatly. "Hell, I wouldn't lay money on getting it fixed anywhere other than Garria or back home."

"We aren't hitting Garria on this run," the man with the broken sword replied. "I asked the Captain. Just here, Hellit, Seije and then back here to finish up before heading home."

"Just humans?" one of them said with disgust. "They farm well and make good beer, but that's about *all* you can say for them. They sure as hell can't reforge a sky-steel blade."

Figuring that eavesdropping wasn't going to do him any more good, Erik quietly slid his stool out from the bar and crossed over to the aeradi's table. "Excuse me, gentlemen," he interrupted, "but I'm afraid I couldn't help but overhear you talking. I believe you said you had a broken sky-steel blade?"

Three of the four aeradi looked shocked that a human had *dared* speak to them. The one with the broken sword, however, simply looked at Erik. "Yes," he replied. "Do you know of a man in Vidran who can fix it?"

"Yes," Erik told him. "Me."

"You can?" one of the others scoffed. "No human can crystal-forge."

"And many aeradi are blind," the first speaker replied gently. He stood and offered Erik his hand. "My name is Harmon *hept* Ikeras, and unlike my companions, I know Sky Blood when I see it."

That shut the other three up. Erik took the man's hand. "My name is Erik," he introduced himself. "I'm the journeyman at Master Byron's smithy—anyone in here could direct you there. You'll find my rates reasonable."

"The sword has great sentimental value to me," Ikeras said. "I would rather wait and have it repaired perfectly than repaired imperfectly now. I mean no offense, of course," he added belatedly.

Erik grinned thinly. Reaching inside his cloak, he drew the smallsword he'd forged for Rade and laid it on the table. Even in the dim light in the tavern, the white sheen of sky steel was visible on the sword's thin blade.

Ikeras picked up the weapon and ran his finger gently down the blade. He bent it slightly and watched it flick back into position. "This is well forged," he admitted. He looked up at Erik carefully. "Not what I would expect a smith to be carrying, though."

"It is a...sample," Erik answered, evading the unspoken question.

The doubter took the blade and looked at it. "This is excellent work," he observed. "This lad may do almost as good a job as some of the smiths back home."

"I agree," Ikeras said, and turned to Erik. "Would you join us for a drink, young Erik?"

"Thank you for the offer," Erik demurred, "but it is late, and I have work to do in the morning."

"Very well. I will visit your smithy in the morning, then," Ikeras said, inclining his head.

ERIK HAD BARELY OPENED THE STORE THE NEXT MORNING WHEN Ikeras arrived. The sun had only just risen over the horizon and the streets outside the building were completely empty, but the aeraid seemed unbothered by the early hour, entering the smithy with a spring in his step.

"Good morning, milord Ikeras," Erik said calmly as the man entered.

"I am not a lord," Ikeras replied with a smile, "merely a warrior of the Realm of the Sky." He laid the broken blade he'd shown Erik in the tavern on the counter. "So, *can* you fix this?" he asked.

Erik removed the two pieces of the sword from the sheath and laid them down. He examined the break, running his finger along the shear line. The break was clean, a sharp line across the blade, but he could feel stress lines in the sky steel surrounding the break.

"Yes," he replied. "I'm going to have to effectively reforge the entire blade, though. It's *not* going to be cheap."

"How much?" Ikeras asked.

Erik shrugged. "Ten gold marks, half in advance. It will take a day or two for me to get to it, though. I have several contracts underway at the moment."

"I'd pay maybe six back home," Ikeras observed. "And I *leave* in two days."

"I'm the only smith in this city who can do what you want," Erik replied. "Drives the price up. If you want it in two days, it will be even more, as I'll have to delay delivery on several other jobs."

Erik liked the aeraid and was perfectly willing to help him, but there were limits to what he could do. Crystal-forging sky steel was neither easy nor inexpensive for him, and he did have contracts he'd already agreed to. While the delay would be within the limits of the contracts, it *was* a delay, and he could end up cutting the timeframes close if he did this first.

Ikeras sighed. "Five gold marks now, ten more on completion—*if* it is completed by tomorrow."

Erik nodded. "Done." He collected the pieces of the blade. "I will have it for you by tomorrow," he told the aeraid. "Return then."

"Very well. Tomorrow, then," Ikeras confirmed.

ERIK ONLY HAD ONE FORGE-CRYSTAL LEFT, AND HE'D EVEN USED some of that one making Rade's weapons. He examined it in the light shining into the forge from the brisk autumn morning. Its inner glow had faded from the original bright hue, but it was still bright enough that he was confident it would last.

If he did it right, he probably wouldn't need any extra metal, so Erik closed the box he'd kept the sky-steel bar stock and the crystal in and turned back to the forge. Like the last time he'd forged sky steel, none of the fires were burning and he was alone.

The aeraid's sword lay, wrapped in a soft leather case, on the anvil. Beyond his examination of the break, he'd really paid no attention to the blade, but as he unwrapped it, he noted an inscription at the hilt of the blade. That would make re-tempering the blade more difficult, but he could work around it.

Picking up the crystal, Erik slowly raised both of the broken edges to a forgeable heat. As they reached a bright orange shade, he lowered the crystal and grabbed the two pieces by their cool ends. Holding them carefully in a pair of thick leather gloves, he slammed them together with a grunt.

The metal didn't weld instantly, but it fit together nicely and he picked up his hammer to finish the job. Five minutes or so later, the two pieces of the blade had been rejoined into a single blade.

With the pieces joined, Erik still needed to re-temper the blade to prevent it breaking again. The inscription etched into the blade just above the tang would make that difficult, and he examined it to see how he could work around it.

He only barely glanced at the actual text, but what he saw draw his eyes straight back to it. He could have sworn he'd seen the name Tarverro—which was impossible.

But it obviously *wasn't* impossible, for on the tang of the blade, clear as day, was the inscription: *Karn* septi *Tarverro. 2-3-Fire-3-Dorbani. 968 YR. Karn* Tarverro?

Erik's first thought was that it had to be another Karn Tarverro. But it made sense. He knew his father had been a wing lancer before he'd married his mother. That had been twenty-two years before, and six years sounded about right for his father's time in the Wings.

But if this *had* been Karn Tarverro's sword—Erik's *father's* sword— who was the aeraid who'd carried it? How had it ended up in the hands of Harmon *hept* Ikeras? And just what did it mean to a man who'd never met his father?

Erik took a deep breath. They were good questions—questions he'd need answers to. However, the only person that could answer them was Harmon *hept* Ikeras, and the best way to be sure that the aeraid did answer them was to finish fixing the sword.

With another deep breath, he picked up the hammer and the crystal again.

∾

ERIK SAT ON THE EDGE OF THE COUNTER IN THE SMITHY'S SHOP, waiting for Ikeras to arrive. The sun had only just begun to light the street outside and leak under the door to light the dim room. The repaired sky-steel blade lay sheathed across his thighs, both visible and easily reached.

The combination smithy, shop and house was silent. At this hour in the morning, very few, if any, others would be awake. Only Erik took in the slowly rising sun, his fingers tracing the inscription on the blade in its dim light.

Footsteps on the cobblestones were audible for a while in the morning silence before the door opened and Ikeras entered. The aeraid paused in the doorway, blinking against the dark, and then saw Erik.

"You are finished?" he asked.

"Indeed," Erik replied. He slid off the counter and crossed to the aeraid. "I managed to avoid damaging the inscription when I re-tempered it, as well," he continued.

"Thank you," Ikeras replied, inclining his head and taking the sword. "The sword has great meaning to me. It was a gift from a friend, long ago."

Erik nodded slowly. "What was the friend's name?" he asked, his voice distant.

Ikeras looked up at him sharply. "Karn *septi* Tarverro," he said, his tone confused. "He gave the sword to me when he retired from the wing lancers. To be honest, I've never heard from him since." The aeraid paused and shrugged. "I often wonder where he ended up, but the sword is all I have to remember him by. Why do you ask?"

"I had to," Erik said simply. "Once I saw the inscription, I had to *know*." He took a deep breath and turned away from the aeraid. "My family name is Tarverro, Milord Ikeras," he continued softly. "Karn Tarverro was my father and is nigh on twenty years dead."

"*Aris*," Ikeras swore softly. Erik felt the man's gaze on his back and slowly turned back to face him. "Aye, I can see it now," the aeraid continued. "I thought it was only the Sky Blood I recognized, but it was him I saw in your face, wasn't it?"

Erik nodded, saying nothing.

For a moment, the two men looked at each other in silence. Finally, Ikeras spoke into the quiet. "If I may ask, how did he die?"

Erik inhaled sharply but nodded. "There was a fire here, about twenty years ago," he explained swiftly. "You can still see the marks on many of the buildings of the Row if you look. Our house was near the center of the Row. No one had a chance to warn my father what was happening before our house was up in flames."

The smith stared at the walls, remembering not so much the fire itself but the nightmares of flame that had, long before, haunted a young boy. "No one knows what happened. All they know is that when they came searching, my mother and father were dead and I was alive..." Erik trailed off.

He resumed after a moment's breath. "It was impossible for me to be alive. The entire house had been destroyed around me, my parents were dead and somehow I was alive. My grandfather took it as a miracle, but..." Erik trailed into silence finally. Reaching inside his tunic, he withdrew an amulet of crystal that hung around his neck.

Three crystals, all black, splayed out from a central bond to form a triangle which hung from a plain steel chain. There was no adornment anywhere on the amulet, but Erik heard Ikeras exhale sharply in recognition.

"My grandfather's only clue was that this was on me, and he'd once seen it on my father," Erik finished quietly.

"Do you know what it is?" Ikeras asked.

"No. Some form of crystal magic, I think," Erik replied.

"An incredibly powerful form of it," Ikeras told him. "That's a protective amulet. It's Melder work, and difficult at that. It shields the wielder from harm—*any* harm."

Erik was stunned. Air magic crystals came in two types: the single crystals charged by the Aligners, which could occasionally be found in human hands, and the intricate multiple-crystal arrays created by the

Melder masters of the art. The latter were *never* found outside the lands of the races of the Sky Blood.

"It would have protected you from the fire," Ikeras said softly. "But your father would have realized that it could *only* protect one person before dying, and was more likely to succeed in protecting you. He had to choose to save one of the three of you there, and chose his son."

Erik focused on the wall, facing away from Ikeras, concealing his tears from the aeraid. "I'd...suspected," he admitted. "I never expected to *know*."

Ikeras's hand clamped on to Erik's shoulder. "It would be typical of the Karn I knew. He'd never choose his own life over those he cared for. *Never*. He chose to save you because you were his son and he loved you. There is no greater testimony to the man, and few greater for you, his son."

Erik swallowed his tears and slowly raised his head. "You said you knew him, before he came here. What was he like?"

The aeraid was silent for a moment, his eyes distant with memory. "He was a good man," he murmured. "I know that seems like the sort of thing you'd say about anyone to their child, but in Karn's case it was his defining trait. He'd give you the shirt off his back and not think twice about it. He and I came from the same neighborhood, though he was much older than me. Even as a child, he protected those around him, and none of us who knew him were surprised when he joined the Regulars.

"When he became a wing lancer, everyone who knew him was so proud. It was his achievement that caused me to seek the lancers," Ikeras admitted. "I earned my wings shortly before he returned from his last campaign with the lancers. He was wounded, and his roc was dead.

"When a lancer's roc dies, they are offered the chance to leave the lancers, no matter how much of their enlistment remains. Often it's just a formality, but Karn took it to return to a woman he'd met— your mother, I presume. His last act as a wing lancer was to deed me this sword," Ikeras finished, running his hands along the sky-steel blade.

"Thank you," Erik replied after a moment, when it was clear Ikeras had finished. "I don't remember him—or my mother, for that matter—and I couldn't help but wonder."

"He was a man that no one would ever regret having as a friend," Ikeras told him quietly. "Or as a father."

Ikeras laid a bag of coins on the table and picked up the sword. He belted the sword on and turned to look back at Erik. "You do realize that you have family in Newport, right?"

"I do?" Erik asked.

The aeraid smiled. "Yes. You have a grandmother and an aunt. The Tarverro family is fallen from its heights, but they are still both wealthy and respected."

Wealthy and *respected* weren't words that described Erik's family in Vidran, except among and in comparison to the smith community. The words drove home to Erik, in a way he'd never even thought possible, just *how* much his father had given up to be with his mother.

"I haven't spoken with your aunt in years, but the *Septol* Tarverro would certainly welcome you to Newport with open arms if you wanted to come visit," Ikeras said. "Or to stay, for that matter," he continued, his voice soft but heavy with emotion Erik couldn't begin to guess.

The young half-blood stared, unseeing, at the weapons and tools on the walls of the shop, product of his work there. Fine work, but not fine *enough* to convince a Guild obsessed with purity to let a half-breed into its ranks.

"I don't know," he confessed. No matter what his difficulties, Vidran was his *home*, and how could he just up and leave his grandfather like that?

"I didn't expect you to," Ikeras accepted with a nod and a smile. "It was just a thought. But..." He paused for a moment, thinking. "We're leaving on a shipping run through Hellit. We'll be back in fifteen days. If you decide to come, meet me at the Iron Hammer then."

"I will consider it," Erik promised.

"You do that," Ikeras replied. "Aris keep you."

With that, the aeraid walked out of the shop.

THE WIND COMING IN OFF THE NORTHERN SEA HAD A CHILLY BITE to it, portending the winter that would soon encase the city of Vidran in snow and ice. Erik sat on the edge of one of the city's inner walls, looking down upon the harbor. The harbor was sheltered from the cold, and the city's mages would keep it liquid even when ice began to seal the strait to the sea, but soon only the flying ships of the aeradi would call there.

Erik's lips twisted. Vidran was a trading city, and only the aeradi's ships and the draconan's dragons kept it going through the winter—a fact many of the city's residents greatly resented. The city's wealth came from its trade with nonhumans, but even so, nonhumans were unpopular.

Even they were more welcome than those bastard children born of a mix of races, Erik reflected. He didn't know how the other races felt about half-bloods, but the humans of Vidran regarded them as blasphemous insults against the will of the gods.

It had been over a week since the aeraid Ikeras had made his offer, and Erik still had not decided whether or not he would go. Whatever most of Vidran thought of him, he had friends and compatriots among the smiths. He had customers, work—a life. Vidran was his *home*, and he was unsure whether or not he should leave.

As he watched and argued with himself, the sun slowly sank beneath the waves on the horizon, lighting the sea with the red of blood. With no real decision made, he stood and slowly descended to the streets below, headed back to Smiths' Row and his home.

The streets were mostly empty of people as the dark fell. Few areas of Vidran were lit at night, even during the depth of winter, when night was almost all the city saw. Once winter truly fell, the youth of Vidran would make their pocket money as lantern bearers, lighting people's way through the city. Despite the chill, however, it was only mid-autumn, and businesses closed with the sun.

Which meant when he entered the darkened street cutting across the edge of the Trade Quarter, he couldn't see anyone else. So, when a shrill cry cut through the night, followed by the sound of several blows, there was no one else to intervene.

Erik cursed softly to himself and threw his cloak back over his shoulder, freeing the sky-steel smallsword he'd forged for Rade. His quick strides brought him to the edge of the alley the sounds came from, and he paused there, listening.

"*Hold* the pointy-eared bitch," he heard a voice snarl. "Think ya can come flouncing through here, half-blood?" it continued, to someone else. "You must be looking for what your ma found—real men." Several ugly chuckles ran under the voice.

"Well, you found 'em," the speaker continued, "and you're going to get 'em right where your ma did." As the voice finished, the sound of tearing cloth echoed through the alley, which was *more* than enough for Erik.

He drew the sword and stepped into the alleyway. In the dim starlight, it took the men in the alley a moment to realize he was there, and that same moment allowed him to assess the scene.

Six men, dock laborers from their clothes, had pinned a woman clad in a dark cloak to the ground. Her hood had been torn from her cloak, revealing long braids of hair tied back from a pair of long, delicately pointed, ears—the mark of a duredine, rare even in Vidran.

The leader of the bravos had the front of her cloak in his hands, where he had just torn it open, revealing a brighter tunic underneath. The sudden glitter of starlight on steel had dragged his attention away from his victim.

"What the hell?" he demanded.

"Leave her be," Erik barked. His eyesight was better than theirs, and he knew it. Where he could make out most of the details, they would be able to see little more than a shadow with steel in his hand.

Unfortunately, however dark and forbidding he might have looked, there were six of them. The leader surged to his feet, a long dagger materializing out of nowhere.

"Skin the interfering bastard," he hissed. "*Now!*"

As Erik began to slowly walk down the alley, approaching the thugs, five more knives appeared. None of them were that long; even with a smallsword, he had ten inches of blade on any of them. Unfortunately, every single one of the humans was bigger than he was, and there were six of them.

The closest and biggest of the thugs grinned, crooked teeth

flashing in the dim light, as he lunged. Erik's free hand shot out and grabbed the man's knife hand. For a moment, the two men shared a grip on the dagger's hilt, but then Erik brought his weapon into play.

The smallsword had no edge, but that didn't stop it neatly punching through to the back of the man's right leg as Erik dragged him in close. With an audible snap, the sky steel blade severed the man's hamstring. Using his grip on the man's hand as a pivot, Erik spun with him, sending the now-crippled man stumbling across the alley to crumple to the ground, out of the fight.

It was over so fast that the other five barely had time to realize anything was happening before the man was on the ground. As if the first thug's fall was a signal, they all spread out and began to circle in on Erik, providing him with far too many targets to track at once.

At some unspoken signal, three of them rushed forward, with the other two following behind, keeping half an eye on their original prey to be sure she didn't escape. Erik retreated, avoiding the slashing, thrusting knives as best he could.

It wasn't good enough. Fire scored along his collarbone as one of the thugs barely missed their slash at his neck. His cloak went fluttering to the ground. He almost tripped over the thing, overbalancing forward.

One of the thugs tried to take advantage of Erik's imbalance. The tip of the smallsword slammed into his chest, punching into flesh and bone. Erik used the impact to balance himself and then yanked his sword back. The thug dropped his dagger and retreated with his hands pressed to the bloody but relatively minor wound on his chest.

The other four seemed to pause, their eyes locked on Erik. "Another bloody half-breed?" the leader snarled. "Twice the prize today, lads. One for the balls, one for the purse, eh?"

The crudity finally did it for Erik. So far, he'd been trying *not* to kill these thugs, for all that they were attempted rapists. Somehow, the thought that being mixed-blood made him—and the woman on the ground, for that matter—nothing more than *things* to be raped or robbed at will put an end to his charity.

The thugs had long arms and long knives. But the longest knife was shorter than almost any sword, and the smallsword wasn't *that* short a weapon. Erik's lunge crossed the space between him and the thugs' leader in moments, and the sword drove deep into the man's chest.

No bone got in the way this time, and Erik *felt* the tip of the blade punch out the man's back. For a long moment, it was a frozen tableau as the man blinked, a look of complete and utter shock on his face. Then the corpse slowly slid down and off Erik's blade.

Even as the corpse began to move, so did the nearest knifeman. Erik saw the dagger flashing toward him and knew he wasn't going to get his sword out in time. Then an incredibly loud *CRACK* filled the alleyway and the thug's head exploded.

Every head flashed toward the woman who'd been the start of the confrontation. She'd only managed to get herself up to one knee, but the heavy dwarven fire-pistol she held leveled over her left forearm didn't *need* her to stand. The barrel twisted onto the remaining thugs.

"Between his blade and this gun, you're dead," she hissed softly, her voice hoarse. "Fuck off or die."

As the footsteps of the would-be rapists vanished off into the distance, Erik slowly wiped his sword clean and faced her, wordlessly. She'd just saved his life, but if he hadn't turned up, she'd been facing worse than knives.

"Thank you," she said quietly, gesturing at the gun. "This thing only has one shot. If you hadn't been here, they'd have succeeded in their plans."

"I couldn't just walk by," Erik told her.

"Perhaps not," she said enigmatically. She reached inside her cloak and removed something. "Give me your hand," she instructed. Erik hesitated, and she shook her head. "I'm not going to hurt you," she promised. "Give me your hand."

He did, and she pressed something into it. "If you ever find yourself in Garria," she told him, "show this to any Ranger or Priest of Edril and tell them Ariana gave it to you."

"Ariana," he repeated, rolling the syllables over his tongue. "I am Erik Tarverro."

"I know," she replied with an enigmatic smile. "And I know we will meet again. Gods keep you till that time."

With that, she bowed to him and started to walk away, heading out of the darkened alley.

"Wait!" he called after her.

She kept walking, as if she hadn't heard him. Erik started after her but stopped. If she didn't want to speak to him, that was her right. A tingle in his hand reminded him of her gift, and he looked down at it.

It was a pair of crystals, dark enough to seem black even to his eyes in the dim starlight. They were formed into two interlocking circles. It was a symbol of some kind, but Erik didn't recognize it.

The groan of the man he'd crippled brought him back to where he was and to what he'd just done. He stumbled to the side of the alley and was violently sick, emptying his guts and continuing to heave even after there was nothing left. He'd just killed a man and crippled another for life. With a shove, he moved away from the wall, wiping his mouth and surveying the alley. It was time and past time for him to get out of there.

Which, he realized, applied to far more than just this alley. Ariana, whoever she was, had been far too short to be the pure duredine her ears had suggested. The thugs had been correct in their estimate of her as a half-blood. Like him.

She'd been attacked for that "sin." Attacked for the "crime" of being a mix of races. That sort of attack boded ill for his continued safety in Vidran. He knew little to nothing of the realm of the aeradi, but he could presume, for now at least, that half-bloods were at least not *attacked* there for being what they were.

It was time for him to find his father's people.

IN THE END, IT WASN'T DIFFICULT FOR ERIK TO CONVERT HIS decision into action. He hadn't taken any new contracts since Ikeras had made his offer, and a few days' effort cleared most of his old ones, leaving him with nothing legally binding him to Vidran.

Other bonds, of course, were not so easily cleared. While his grandfather had told him to make his own decision and supported the one he'd made, he knew the old man was unhappy to see him go.

Nonetheless, Byron had helped him clear out his accounts, dispose of most of his effects and sum up his funds. He'd also pressed a significant sum on Erik as his share of the shop's profits over the last few years. Once it was all told, Erik found himself in possession of nearly two *thousand* gold marks—over thirty pounds of gold—a small fortune by any standards. A lot of the money came from the sale of his collection of weapons, which he saw no way to take to Newport.

He kept the sky-steel rapier he'd originally forged for Rade, but that was the only one of his extensive collection of weapons and other "sample wares" that he kept. He'd never been much of one for large numbers of clothes or bric-a-brac, and once he'd packed everything up, all of it fit in one small ironbound chest for the money and one largish trunk for his things.

They seemed a very small space to contain everything he'd acquired in twenty-one years of life and work, but he'd traveled with even less during his early days as a journeyman, when he'd actually journeyed. Of course, he'd left a great deal of it at home then.

It took him all of the week he had to make the arrangements, but they were made. The night that Ikeras was supposed to be back in town, he returned to the Iron Hammer.

The lights of the tavern spilled out onto the street, and Erik paused at the edge of the shadow, watching the revelers. Most of the men in the tavern were smiths, and he knew many of them. There were few of them he'd count as friends, but he did know them.

Tomorrow, he'd leave them all behind. He'd already made the decision, but he still hesitated at the edge of the light. Once he'd entered the tavern, he could not go back. He'd be giving up everything on the hope of a better life somewhere else.

Not that "everything" was all that much there. His lips twisted in disgust. Not even the nostalgia of being about to leave it behind could make his life in Vidran look good. His grandfather had been the only one who'd truly supported him. All of his skill had got him nowhere in the guild of his craft. No, there was nothing there for him. Nothing at all.

With a deep breath, Erik stepped into the light spilling out from the tavern and entered the old building. He stopped on the threshold, blinking in the bright light from the lamps lighting the inside of the tavern, and searched for Ikeras.

He was easy enough to find. The aeraid was sitting at the exact same table he'd been at last time, but this time, his only companion was an older, gray-haired aeraid. They spotted him at the same time as he saw them, and Ikeras gestured him over.

Erik joined them, silently taking a seat at the table and regarding the two aeradi levelly. Ikeras returned the gaze calmly, but his companion's gaze seemed to have a measuring edge to it.

"Have you made up your mind?" Ikeras finally asked.

"Yes," Erik confirmed. "I'm coming with you."

Ikeras nodded and gestured to the man with him. "Erik Tarverro, be known to Miki Halare, captain of the *Blue Ascendance*, our ship."

Halare inclined his head. "It is an honor to finally meet you. I knew your father long ago—hell, he saved my life once. I'd be pleased to give you a ride to Newport."

"I can pay," Erik told him.

The aeradi captain waved away the thought. "As I said, your father saved my life. I won't take a penny from his son for this. Though I will"—he raised a finger to emphasize the point—"expect you to help out aboard the ship."

Erik looked at the captain for a moment, assessing the man's words. "Thank you," he said finally. "Perhaps someday you can tell me of my father."

"I'll do so gladly, son, once we're underway," Halare told him. "I presume you have baggage?"

"Two trunks, at my grandfather's house," Erik replied.

"We'll deal with those in the morning," the captain said calmly, and gestured to the barmaid, who set three mugs of ale on the table before them. "For now, let us toast the memory of your father and the hope of your future among the People of the Sky."

ERIK'S LAST DAY IN VIDRAN PASSED IN A BLUR OF ACTIVITY. CAPTAIN Halare lent him two porters and a wagon they used for offloading cargo, and he'd collected his pair of trunks from his grandfather's house. His grandfather hadn't been there—unwilling, Erik suspected, to really accept that his grandson was truly leaving.

They'd offloaded his trunks onto the *Blue Ascendance*, and then the porters had left for other duties. Ikeras had then promptly arrived and handed Erik a list of items he would need for the voyage. The aeraid had then taken Erik into the dock section of the Trade Quarter to find them.

Hours later, Erik found himself carrying a new trunk aboard the ship. Its contents were mainly new waterproof garments he would have rarely—if ever—required in Vidran, and a metal lantern designed to prevent oil spills, highly dangerous on a wooden ship.

Finally, as the sun sank below the horizon, Erik sat on the prow of the *Blue Ascendance* watching the last light on the waves. The ship rocked gently to the waves in a cold breeze. Shivering against the cold, he wrapped his new oilskin cloak around himself.

He'd made his choice and there was no turning back now. In the morning, they'd leave with the early tide and he'd likely never come back to Vidran. He could only hope that he would find a place for himself in Newport.

The ship's gentle motion lulled him, and Erik rested there for a long time.

BRANE STARED AT HIS AGENT IN SHOCK. HE'D COME TO VIDRAN, TO this cursed port town on the northern edge of the continent where the blood seemed to freeze in one's veins, to oversee the elimination of his brother's killer.

"How could you *lose* him?" he demanded. "He was a smith. He had a shop. Where did he *go?*"

"We don't know," the agent, a tall draconan named Dairn, admitted. "One day he suddenly stopped taking orders, and a week and a half later, he was *gone.*"

"Find him," Brane snarled. "Track him to the ends of the world if need be, but find me the bastard who murdered my brother!"

"All that can be done is being done," Dairn protested. At Brane's ice-cold gaze, the agent wilted. "We know where his grandfather is," he offered, as a sop of some kind.

"No," Brane told him. "I do not believe in justice by proxy. Leave the old fart alone. It's Tarverro I want."

"Well, sir, it is possible..." The agent, whose cover job was as a trader, trailed off.

"What?" Brane demanded.

"If he *is* a Tarverro—we know where that line is from."

"He's a half-blood. Would he return there?" Brane asked.

"Where else could he have gone?"

"Where else indeed?" Brane repeated. "Where else indeed?" His eyes were cold. "Burn the man if he has."

"Sir?" Dairn queried. "We have men there."

"They cannot be exposed," Brane replied. "Not even for this. Not even for Rade." He raised his hand and pointed a finger at the agent. "Find the man. Even if he hides among his father's people, find him. We may not be able to touch him there, but if he leaves that city in the sky..."

2

FIVE DAYS OUT OF VIDRAN, Erik was reminded why the aeradi ships were called *sky*ships. He stood on the deck, helping the crew deal with the sails as best as he could—mainly a matter of standing still and holding a rope. Short for a human, Erik still towered over the *Blue Ascendance*'s aeradi crew. Combined with a blacksmith's muscles, he was the best anchor they had.

He was looking out along the ship's course and spotted what looked like a huge gray cloud on the horizon, stretching from the ocean into the sky. Just as he noticed it, the bosun's pipes twittered in a signal he hadn't heard before, and every man on the sails tied up what they were working on and slid down to the deck.

In less than a minute, they went from having nearly twenty men aloft to every single member of the crew standing on the deck. Erik opened his mouth to ask what was going on but was gestured to quiet by a member of the crew.

Moments later, a crystal embedded in the mainmast began to glow a bright white. Similar crystals in the fore and aft masts, positioned at a lesser height, followed it. Then, to Erik's consternation, the ship began to lift out of the water.

The crystals held a steady brightness as the ship rose, and Erik could *hear* the water sluicing off the hull and scattering across the waves, and then the thump of water rushing together as the bottom of the keel lifted out of the water.

"All right, you slackers," the bosun announced, "we're skyborne. Which means you lot can get to cleaning the decks and hull. I want this ship to *shine* when we reach port!"

Erik slowly walked over to the edge of the ship and looked over it. The ship was now easily a hundred feet into the air, and still rapidly rising, leaving the water far beneath. It was both stunning and terrifying.

"Impressive, isn't it?" Ikeras said from behind him. "I asked the crew not to warn you—I wanted to see your face the first time we went skyborne. Tells you a lot about a man, how he reacts to being a thousand feet in the air."

"It's incredible," Erik murmured, awestruck. "How is it done?"

"The most complex piece of air magic anyone not a Melder is likely to see," Ikeras replied. "If you wander down into the hull, there's a long room in the center containing the primary lift crystals. There's about six relay crystals positioned around the hull, and those three"—he pointed out the glowing crystals above their heads—"in the masts."

"How high can we go?" Erik asked.

"Higher than you can breathe," Ikeras replied drily. "There's a few specialized ships with crystals to provide some kind of air supply and pressure, but they're few and far between, and honestly, there isn't much use for them." He shrugged. "The crystals only last so long until they need to be replaced. That's why we sailed most of the way."

"Why aren't we sailing now, then?"

Ikeras snorted. "How exactly do you think you enter a *sky city* without flying, son?" he answered with a grin.

Erik had no answer.

As the hours drew by, Erik watched the sky city of Newport slowly grow into visibility. The main portion of what he'd thought was a cloud turned out to be the massive floating island on which the aeradi had built most of their city.

Erik had no inclination to even guess the diameter of the island, but the city built on its back was substantial. Eerily tall crystal spires marked the center of the city, the only structures visible over the heavy, tower-studded stone walls that encircled the edge of the island.

Beneath the crystal- and stone-adorned floating island, three immense pillars of crystal and stone descended in majestically imposing grace to a second city below. Each of the pillars had to be at least a thousand feet across, and as they drew closer, Erik saw the lights of some sort of buildings *inside* the pillars.

The second city, the lower one, was built on massive floating wooden platforms. Where the structures above were made of stone and crystal, and surrounded by heavy walls to boot, these were built mostly of wood, with only a handful of crystal and almost no stone or brick structures.

The sun was already dimming toward sunset, and in the fading light, the city *glowed* in its own lights. Erik could see almost all of the lower city, and even there, streetlights marked broad avenues where the wood appeared to be covered by some stone-like material. The higher city was mostly hidden by its walls, but even before the skyship rose high enough to see over them, Erik could see a corona of glowing lights glittering over the city and tracing paths up the sides of the crystal spires.

The *Blue Ascendance* swept above and around the city, to where Erik saw a huge set of docks, glittering in crystal and sky steel, extending out nearly a mile from the western edge of the island.

The ship slowly flew in toward the docks, and the crew turned out on deck once more, coiling ropes and preparing to anchor the ship. As they approached an empty dock, the *Blue Ascendance* slowed even more and gently slid up between the doubled pier of the aeradi-style dock. The crew immediately got to work, slinging ropes out around heavy pylons and securing the ship as strongly as possible.

As they finished, a group of dockhands arrived, led by a man in dark blue robes who Erik guessed to be the Aligner responsible for the crystal magic of the dock. The Aligner stepped up to the pylons and touched them in certain patterns. Erik watched carefully and saw beams of a dark blue light slide out from hexagonal crystals placed in the center of the pylons. Twelve beams touched the edge of the ship's hull and then seemed to somehow solidify. When they did, all motion of the ship—which, even with the lift crystals active and the ropes, had been shaking gently in the wind—stopped.

Erik was stunned from his reverie by Ikeras clapping him on the shoulder. "That's that," he said calmly. "Get your things, and I'll take you to meet your grandmother."

The young smith blanched. Between the busy activity of the journey and then his awe at the sheer size and glory of the city, Erik had completely forgotten that he was supposed to be meeting his father's family.

THE NEIGHBORHOOD IKERAS TOOK HIM TO WAS LOCATED CLOSE enough to the docks that they walked rather than hiring one of the horse-drawn carriages that had seemed to materialize out of nowhere when the ship had been secured. Despite its proximity to the docks, it was clear that *this*, unlike most of the areas nearby, was not where the ship crews lived. This was a neighborhood for ships' officers and captains, and for merchants who wanted to keep in touch with the source of their wealth.

The trees lining even the poorer streets in this entirely artificial environment were new to Erik—Vidran had parks, and the single dure-dine city he'd visited had been built *in* trees, but that many trees—all of which had to have been imported to the floating island—were still amazing to him.

This neighborhood's street was something else again, even beyond that. Where even in Garria, roads had simply been divided by a simple guide rope, this street was fully split into two parts by an earthen divider lined with oak trees that were easily two or three hundred years old.

The houses themselves, while seemingly smaller than many of the ones outside the cul-de-sac, were set back from the road behind well-groomed lines of bushes unlike anything he'd seen before. Similar bushes appeared to divide the houses from each other.

All of the greenery, combined with the imposing stone edifices of the houses, gave a strong impression of wealth and arrogance. Unfortunately, for that impression, a group of children ranging in age from almost-toddlers clear up to teenagers was engaged in a rambunctious game involving large amounts of screaming, running and tree-climbing.

One of the older teens nearly ran clear into Erik but managed to pull herself to a stop in time, grinning up at the half-blood, and froze as she saw Ikeras.

"Uncle Harmon!" she shouted. Moments later, the doughty aeraid found himself covered in excited kids demanding to know where he'd been, when he'd got back and if he had anything for them.

It took Ikeras a few minutes to detach himself, but he then produced a bag of sweets and handed them out, being careful to equitably distribute them before shooing the children on their way.

Four of the older teens remained, looking strangely at Erik. Finally, the girl who'd first seen Ikeras spoke up. "Who's your friend, Uncle Ikeras?"

Ikeras grinned. "Erik, be known to Shelli Norit, Bran Norit, Liki Shelt and Kir *hept* Dralon. All of their families are *kep* to *sept* Tarverro. As," he added with a shrug, "is my own, for that matter." He turned back to the children. "This is Erik Tarverro, kids."

"*Tarverro?*" the boy introduced as Kir questioned. When Ikeras nodded, he turned to Erik and bowed deeply. The others, to Erik's consternation, followed suit. "Well come, my lord. Well come indeed."

Before Erik could reply, the four teens finished their bows and scampered off to try to bring the younger children under control.

"What did you mean by '*kep* to *sept* Tarverro'?" Erik asked softly.

"It's not my place to tell you," Ikeras replied with a shrug. "Like I said, Arien deserves to see you first, and she's the one to explain all that."

"Arien?" Erik asked.

"Your grandmother."

~

WHEN ERIK SPOTTED THE BUILDING AT THE END OF THE CUL-DE-SAC, he had figured that that massive, brooding edifice of crystal and stone was their destination. However, shortly before they reached the mansion, Ikeras stopped and turned onto a side path, leading to a small stone house set well back in the trees.

"Who lives in the mansion?" Erik had to ask.

"No one," Ikeras replied. "Well, that's not true. There's a small maintenance staff that keeps the place up, but no one really *lives* there anymore. It's the Tarverro family seat, but your grandmother's refused to live there since your grandfather died—said it was too empty without him."

Taking a glance back at the building—*his* family's seat?—Erik could understand that sentiment. Living alone in that house would have been a recipe for insanity. A *fast* recipe.

His preoccupation with the mansion distracted Erik until he was at the doorstep of the house Ikeras had brought him to. Ikeras's using the heavy doorknocker on the door brought his attention back to this house. An odd symbol decorated the doorknocker—three crystals splaying downward, forming a triangle. The symbol was familiar, but Erik couldn't place it.

"This was the guest house, "Ikeras told him quietly, "until Arien moved out of the main house. Now this is her place."

Erik swallowed hard as the door opened, and a young aeraid woman dressed in green and black appeared. "Yes?" she said calmly, and then caught sight of Ikeras. "Harmon!" she exclaimed. "Come in, come in. When did you get back?"

"About two hours ago, Shel," the older aeraid told the girl. "Is Her Ladyship in?"

The girl—Shel—nodded. "She doesn't go out much these days. She says there's no reason."

"Can you tell her I'm here to see her?" he asked.

"Of course!" Shel replied, looking at Erik with an odd expression on her face. "Do I know you?" she asked.

Erik inclined his head slightly. "I'm afraid not, miss."

"I'll explain later, Shel," Ikeras told the girl. "But do me a favor and don't mention him to Her Ladyship, hmm?"

"Certainly," the girl replied with an impish grin. "Head through to the waiting room; I'll go find Lady Arien."

Ikeras led Erik through to a plushly decorated room with neatly arranged furniture in deep green cloth and dark wood. He then seated Erik with a courtier's grace, adding to Erik's suspicions that Ikeras had a higher place in this odd little community than he'd stated.

The sound of footsteps caused Erik's gaze to turn to the entrance toward the rest of the house, which meant he received his first look at Lady Arien *septol* Tarverro. His first impression of her was her height and elegance—even for an aeradi, she was short, three inches or more under five feet. Her silver hair swept halfway down the back of her dark green dress, bound back by simple silver bands. She seemed the perfectly poised aristocrat, and Erik could not even begin to conceive that *this* woman was his grandmother.

Then she located Ikeras in the room, and Erik began to believe. The tiny woman almost seemed to fly across the room to drag the bigger man into her arms. "Harmon! When did you get back, you silly sailor?"

"About two hours ago," Ikeras admitted wryly, carefully setting her back on her feet.

Arien tilted her head. "Why did you come here so quickly?" she asked.

The older aeraid took her shoulders in his hands and turned her to face Erik. "My Lady Arien *septol* Tarverro," he said formally, "meet Erik Tarverro." He paused, allowing his words to sink in. "Karn's son," he finished, gently.

Erik met his grandmother's gaze as the old woman froze. For a long moment, the two of them just stared at each other. Erik could see, now, the similarities between this woman's features and his own.

"Karn's son?" she questioned. Erik nodded. "Harmon?"

"Yes, my lady?" Ikeras replied immediately.

"Leave us." The tone of command was completely different from her comfortable familiarity of a moment before.

The aeraid bowed. "Understood. This is *sept* business, not mine."

Silence reigned in the room as Ikeras let himself out, and then Erik found his gaze locked by Arien's again. "I can see a resemblance," she whispered, almost to herself, "and I do not believe Ikeras would intentionally deceive me. Nonetheless, this is hard to believe."

"How do you think I feel?" Erik asked, his voice equally soft. "My father died years ago—I never even knew the man, let alone that I had family on his side."

"Dead?" Arien said, lowering herself into a chair. "I feared as much when my efforts to find him, when your grandfather died eight years ago, failed."

"Eight years ago?" Erik whispered. "He was twelve years dead by then."

"Tell me," Arien instructed. "*Please*, tell me...how my son died."

He shook his head, realizing it was the wrong question. "I'll tell you how he lived," he promised.

～

ERIK KNEW NOTHING FIRSTHAND OF HIS FATHER'S LIFE IN VIDRAN, but his grandfather had told him much of his parents and their love for each other. Everything he knew, he told his grandmother. He told her of the whirlwind courtship, the marriage, of the love they'd held that had never seemed to diminish.

And he told her of the fire, and the choice his father must have made among the flames and smoke. He told of the man who, realizing that he could only save one person, chose to save his child rather than living without his wife.

He told his grandmother all that he knew of his father in life, and watched her tears fall slowly, gently, the tears of a mother for the son she should never have outlived. By the time he finished, the sun was down and the maid had lit soft oil lamps to light the living room.

They sat in silence for a time, and Arian spoke first in the end. "I do not believe that you lie, but I must have proof. Show me the amulet."

Without a word, Erik removed the crystals on their chain and passed them to her. The old woman raised it, allowing the drained crystals to reflect the lamplight, for a moment seeming to glow like they'd never been touched. As the crystals turned in the light, Erik realized where he'd recognized the symbol on the outside of the house —the crystals on the amulet were formed in the same pattern.

"Harmon would not know the significance of this," Arien said finally. "His family may be *hepti*, but it is a tradition only the *sept* follow, and not one we speak of much."

"Which tradition?" Erik asked. "And who are the '*sept*'? And the '*hept*,' for that matter?"

She smiled, her eyes tired. "The *sept* and *hept* are the noble families of the aeradi. I will instruct you more in their nature as time goes by, but only one thing is important now. These amulets"—she twisted it in her fingers and it shone in the light again— "are given to the *septons*— the family patriarchs—and their heirs."

"Heirs?" Erik could not imagine his father being the heir to *anything*. "To what?"

"To the authority, wealth, powers and ancient rights of their *sept*," Arien replied. "Your father felt he could leave because I was pregnant with a younger brother for him—a replacement heir so to speak. But that child died," she continued, old grief adding to the new in her face, "and both your grandfather and father are dead."

Erik looked at her, confused. "So?"

"Some *sept* have many members, side families and so forth," Arien explained, "but the *sept* Tarverro has only the direct line. Your father and grandfather are gone, and a female can only hold the authority in trust for a male." The glimmer of the crystals vanished as Arien clenched it in her fist. "Which means, my grandson, that we must find you a replacement for this amulet, as it would never do for Lord Erik *septon* Tarverro, heir to and master of the most ancient and respected *sept* in the city of Newport, to wear a discharged protective amulet."

Erik stared at her in shock. *He* was a lord? The descendant of an ancient and powerful line?

"It can't be," he said aloud.

"It is," Arien said simply. A grin, a small one under the grief he'd brought her, appeared on her face. "And aren't some of our fellow *ept* going to just *piss* themselves at the thought of a half-blood *septon*!"

Arien refused to tell him any more that night, simply arranging for him to be put up in a room, with a comment of "Now that you're here, we can justify opening up the main house."

The room was as comfortable as he could imagine, but sleep refused to come to him. In the course of a handful of hours, everything seemed to have changed. A few hours before, he'd been a poor smith seeking his father's family. Now he was apparently the lord of a noble clan.

It was hard to accept, and the thought kept him tossing and turning all night. When the maid knocked on his door in the morning, he was already awake, up and shaving.

"Come in," he answered, and stepped out of the small bathroom attached to the room, toweling off his face.

The aeradi maid curtsied shakily to him, clearly made nervous by this huge stranger. Conceiving of himself as large and intimidating—the last thing he'd been among humans—was enough to bring a smile to his lips, which seemed to help the girl relax.

"Milord *septon*," she addressed him, "your lady grandmother sent me to fetch you. She's presenting you to the *kep* this morning."

Erik still wasn't entirely clear on just who the *kep* were, but he also knew that, official authority or no official authority, Arien *septol* Tarverro would rule this sept in reality until she died. Which meant that if she wanted Erik Tarverro, the official *septon* of said clan, to turn up to be presented to the *kep*, Erik *septon* Tarverro was bloody well going to turn up.

"Thank you," he told her gently. "I will be down shortly."

The girl curtsied again and fled the room. With her absence, Erik began to sort through his trunks, looking for his formal tunic. He doubted it was aeradi style, but it was all he had.

In the end, the charcoal-gray tunic and doublet appeared to pass Arien's inspection. When he came down, she looked him over, straightened the doublet and nodded cordially to him.

"It's not what they'll expect," she murmured, "but that's all to the good."

"Oh?" Erik asked.

"By now," she told him, "the rumor that there is a new *septon* Tarverro is beginning to percolate around the city. Without any intervention on our part, it will be all over the city by afternoon. By tomorrow morning, the fact that you're a half-blood will begin to spread. That will take longer to spread, as people will find it difficult to believe." The old aeradi woman shrugged. "I don't intend to let that happen.

"We'll introduce you to the *kep* this morning. That's important—technically, you're not *septon* until they approve you. There won't be an issue, though," she assured him. "You're Karn's son and have my support. They'll accept you."

"Good to know," Erik replied, still nervous over the sudden change in his status and life.

"Later, we'll take you to the tailors and get you fitted out in the *sept* colors," she added.

"Didn't you just say the clothes were fine?" Erik asked.

"They're fine for being presented to the *kep*," Arien replied. "They won't do, however, for your presentation to the King and the Court tonight. We'll also need to get you a sky-steel sword, but that may take too long to have it for tonight."

"I have one," Erik told her. "The story behind it is...complicated."

Arien looked at him. "I think I may want that story—indeed, I believe I will want *all* your stories, grandson—but for now, it's good that you have the blade. Only the *septon*s and wing lancers can bear a sky-steel sword into the King's presence. Carrying it will drive home your status to those who doubt."

"How many will doubt?" he had to ask.

She shrugged. "There will be some. Most won't object, but those who do will object strongly." Arien paused and glanced at the crystal clock on the wall. "But instructing you in the intricacies of our politics, and why some will hate you and some won't, must wait. The *kep* will be here now."

~

His grandmother led Erik to the main house and into a large meeting hall off the main corridor. Clearly, the house staff had spent the early hours of the morning clearing the room until it gleamed. The wood of the furniture and the stone of the pillars and walls had been polished until they shone, and the cushions of the furniture had been cleaned and dusted.

Scattered on the chairs throughout the room were about thirty or so older men. Erik noted that they practically ignored him, their eyes solely for Arien. Despite her small stature, even for an aeradi, and advanced age, it was clear who was the power there.

Only one man noticed Erik. Harmon *hept* Ikeras sat next to a man who had to be his older brother. He met Erik's eyes and winked. Somehow, the gesture made him feel better.

Arien directed him to a seat by the dark wooden podium at the head of the room and then stepped to the podium herself.

"Gentlemen," she greeted them, and Erik noted that the tracery of crystal he could see on the top of the podium appeared to function as a projector. Arien didn't speak loudly, and her voice didn't sound loud, but it did fill every corner of the room.

"You're wondering why you're here," she continued. It wasn't a question; it was a statement. She had likely known every man in there since they were born. "You are here because it is my solemn duty to inform you that what we believed is true: my son, Karn *sept* Tarverro, the man who should have been your *septon*, is dead."

A rustle surged through the room, but Arien silenced it with a gesture. "However, along with this discovery, I have learned something else. Something that means that I will no longer be your *septol*."

She let the moment of quiet that answered that hang for a moment, as the heads of the *kep* families of the *sept* Tarverro considered what she meant, and then gestured Erik forward.

"*Kep* of Tarverro, Karn had a son," she said flatly. "I present to you Erik *septi* Tarverro, son of Karn and grandson of Emil. He is my grandson and your *septon* by right of blood."

Erik stood and stepped forward to join her at the podium. Dead silence reigned in the room as the *kep* took him in. He made an intimidating figure standing there. The formal tunic and doublet of Vidran style were tight enough to make clear the heavy muscles of the smith he'd been to make his living and the swordsman he'd been as a hobby. If the muscles weren't enough, he overtopped the next tallest man in the room by a good three inches. While he'd been short for a human, he was toweringly tall for an aeradi.

Erik saw Harmon nudge his brother, who then stood, quietly, and met his eyes. "The *hept* Ikeras, *kep* Tarverro, accepts this man as the *septon* Tarverro," he said formally.

A moment later, another man stood. "The Adera family, *kep* Tarverro, accepts this man as *septon* Tarverro," he also stated.

Another man stood, and another, until every one of thirty men in the room had stood and proclaimed their new allegiance to Erik *septon* Tarverro, now in law and fact their lord and liege.

THE REST OF THE DAY PASSED IN A WHIRLWIND AS THE NEW *SEPTON* Tarverro gained a great deal of respect for his grandmother's organizational abilities. She took him to the tailor she'd mentioned, got him sized and fitted for formal court clothes and paid the tailor to jump the effort ahead of his other contracts to have it done for that night.

She then took him to the *sept* accountant, where Erik received his greatest shock of the day.

"*How* much?" he demanded of the man.

"You are heir to the full *sept* accounts and authorities," the banker, a small, even for an aeraid, man named Kilos Rader, *kep* Tarverro, repeated. "Except for a fund set aside in your grandfather's will to maintain his wife and daughter, you have full authority on all accounts and estates of the *sept*."

Erik shook his head. "Firstly, I don't think that the fund will be necessary. Give Lady Arien complete access to all maintenance funds and liquid assets of the *sept*." That, he thought, should be enough for her to effectively run the estate until he'd felt his way into the position. "Lady Arien will also function as my deputy on all other matters if I am not present," he added. Then he glanced over at his grandmother, who gave him a small smile. Not really surprised, but approving. "Also," he continued, "give my aunt limited access to the funds—how much should she need a month?"

"Limit it to about two or three hundred crowns," Arien advised. "Or she'll spend us out of house and home."

"Three hundred crowns," Erik agreed quickly, almost choking on the concept of that as a *monthly* figure. A Newport crown was a quarter-ounce gold coin, effectively identical in value to the Hellitian mark —and one mark was the normal *weekly* wage for many of Vidran's laborers. "Now, as to my original question. *How* much?"

"The total, including estate and liquid assets, has an estimated value of two and a half million gold crowns. The actual value is uncertain, as large portions of the estate—such as the *sept* seat and surrounding areas rented to the *kep* families—have never been evaluated for sale." The banker paused, eyeing Arien, who nodded for him to continue.

"The estate maintains a reserve of one hundred thousand crowns in cash coin," he told Erik, who couldn't help staring at the man at that figure. "The estate also holds one million crowns' worth of shares in roughly one hundred fifty trade ships. Those shares, combined with the rental properties, provide the estate with an income averaging ten thousand gold crowns."

"Ten thousand a *year*?" Erik asked, stunned. The entire smithy back home, not counting cost of materials and living expenses, had barely made five thousand marks a year between a master, two journeymen, including himself, and half a dozen apprentices.

Kilos shook his head with a pained expression. "No, milord. Ten thousand crowns a month."

"A month?" Erik repeated.

The banker nodded. "The Tarverros are not the wealthiest *sept*, but we are certainly not the poorest."

Erik signed the document put in front of him in a haze. When they left the banker's office, Arien looked at him with a small smile.

"Surprised?"

"Very," Erik replied. "I hadn't realized just how much my father gave up."

She looked at him oddly. "Your father made the choice I expected from my son—he pursued his heart, as he always had. Don't disvalue your heart, grandson. It can easily be worth a mere two or three million crowns."

"And we're not the richest?" he asked.

"No. The *sept* Tarverro is far fallen from its heights, but when your heights are as high as ours were, even your fall leaves you higher than many."

"Our heights?"

She looked at him and shook her head. "Of course you wouldn't know."

"Know what?" he demanded.

"The *sept* Tarverro was the main founding family of Newport. For five generations, men of our *sept* were the Kings of Newport. Your great-great-grandfather was the last Tarverro King, but we are still both wealthy and powerful. By your ancestors' blood, you are a player in our politics whether you want it or not."

THE FORMAL TUNIC WORN BY THE *SEPTONS* OF THE AERADI WAS VERY nearly a uniform, and Erik found it highly uncomfortable. It was long, stretching down to his knees, and high-collared. Each *septon* wore it in his *sept*'s colors; in Erik's case, dark green and silver. On the shorter aeradi he'd seen heading into the Great Hall in front of them, the various colors and their lines looked neatly elegant, but he suspected his extra inches had given the tailor difficulty. As far as he could tell, his tunic didn't fit.

He stopped fussing over his tunic as he and Arien reached the entrance to the Great Hall of the Palace of Newport. He hadn't actually believed her when she'd said she'd present him to the King tonight. Then, however, he hadn't known that the *septons* and their families had an automatic right to be at this sort of affair.

Arien guided him to the doors into the Hall and up to the herald standing next to it. She leaned over next to the herald and gave him their names quietly, so quietly even Erik couldn't hear what she said.

The man's face shifted through surprise to pure shock to an outright grin. "I see, my lady," he told her.

"Oh, and Jamie," she finished as she pulled back from the herald, "indulge yourself."

The grin turned downright feral as the herald turned into the hall, and Erik looked at his grandmother questioningly. Before he could say anything, Jamie, the herald, announced them.

"The Lady Arien *septel* Tarverro," he boomed, and then paused for a long moment to let what he'd said sink in. Erik could hear the room rustling in shock. They'd be shocked first that she was even *there*— from what she'd told him, Arien had not attended these affairs in years —and then the title would sink in.

As Erik understood it, a *septol* was the senior woman of a *sept*, either the *septon's* wife or—as Arien had been—holder of the *sept's* estates in trust. The *septel*, however, was the senior woman who was *not* married to the *septon*.

The *septel* was, by and large, the *septon's* mother...or grandmother, in this case.

Jamie left it a long moment, until the sound shifted from surprise that she was there to questioning the new title. As the rustle of surprise turned to a murmur of surprised conversation, the herald waved them forward and continued his announcement. "...and the Lord Erik *septon* Tarverro."

Erik and Arien stepped into the hall together and paused, allowing the whole hall to see the new *septon* Tarverro. Erik couldn't help acquiring a feral grin of his own at the utter shock he could see on some of the nearer faces.

He offered Arien his arm and they swept down into the crowd. As they did, Arien leaned over and whispered in his ear. "Jamie has a horrible taste for melodrama. Normally, we get him to suppress it, but a little melodrama was *just* what we needed tonight."

Erik nodded slightly, and swallowed as he realized where she was taking him: the end of the room, where the thrones of the King and Queen of Newport occupied a raised dais. The thrones were unoccupied, but it didn't take a genius to realize who the man wearing a simple gold circlet and dressed in a black-and-green *sept* uniform standing at the foot of the dais was.

His Majesty Lokar *septon* Adelnis, King of Newport and member of the Council of the Realm of the Sky, was tall for an aeradi, at nearly three inches over five feet. Erik *still* had an inch and a half on the dark-haired, muscular man.

Guiding him with an iron grip on his arm, Arien stopped him a traditional three paces from the King. "Bow," she instructed, murmuring.

Somehow, in the hectic hours of the day preceding this meeting, his grandmother had found time to instruct Erik in the proper bow of a *septon* to his King. His bow was not as graceful or as polished as his grandmother's or the other men around, but it was, at least, the proper bow.

King Adelnis responded to the bow with an equally proper inclination of his head. "*Septon* Tarverro," he greeted Erik. "You have been too long from your proper place." He offered Erik his hand, something only done among friends and relatives among the aeradi.

"I am pleased to welcome the son of my friend to the halls of his fathers," he continued as Erik clasped his hand in the greeting, "and am *most* pleased to confirm you in the rights and titles of *septon* Tarverro."

Erik released an imperceptible sigh. The right of the King to approve a *septon* was nothing more than a formality, but his position as a half-blood *septon* was tenuous enough with royal approval. If Adelnis had refused it, he may as well have packed his bags and gone back to Vidran.

The King embraced him as if he were a close friend. "We must speak again, of your father," he whispered. "Not tonight, but soon."

Erik nodded imperceptibly. "Your will, my King."

THE MEETING WITH THE KING DONE, THE OTHER NOBLES BEGAN TO converge on Erik. The ones who were already around the King were the first to reach Erik, and they passed him by in a blur of names and faces that he *knew* he would never remember. Once they were clear of the hectic mob around the throne, he realized he probably wouldn't need to remember anyone for a while yet.

As the first party approached him, Arien began to whisper their names and positions into his ear. "That's Hiri *septon* Rakeus, *the* richest of the *septi*," she told Erik, gesturing with her chin at a very fat aeraid, accompanied by two young men, one of whom had stretched the *sept* uniform as far as it would go toward looking like a peacock, and a young woman. "Don't let his bulk or his wealth fool you, he is neither greedy nor stupid. He is both a very smart man and a very *good* man, which is rare this high among the *ept*."

"The fop is his biological son, Kels," Arien continued. "He's deadly with a blade, and that's his sole 'virtue.' The other boy is his adopted nephew, Letir. The boy's parents died young and Hiri's brother adopted him. When *he* died, Hiri effectively adopted the lad.

"The girl is Hiri's daughter, Deria, the antithesis of her brother. She and Letir are lovers, which Hiri turns a blind eye to. They'd marry, but for Letir, a commoner, to marry the daughter of a *septon*, he needs a *septon* sponsor."

"Why not Hiri?" Erik asked.

"She's *his* daughter," Arien replied simply. "Another *septon* has to sponsor him." She looked at him significantly.

"Such as me," Erik murmured, stating her meaning aloud.

"Such as you," Arien agreed. "Except that the marriage would almost certainly result in Letir being declared Hiri's heir. Rumor has it that Kels has sworn to challenge and kill any man sponsoring Letir."

"Why is it worth it to me?" Erik asked softly.

"Hiri is a major player in our politics," Arien told him. "He controls the faction that believes in open and free trade, which is in the ascendant in Newport right now. His alliance could go a long way to easing your acceptance here." She paused, and Erik felt her gaze on him. "And because those poor kids deserve a break, and that ass deserves a lesson."

Erik eyed Kels carefully. Despite his clothes, the man did move with the grace of a swordsman, and yet... The arrogant tilt to his face and the apparent argument he was carrying on with his father suggested other things.

"My father gave up everything for love," he said quietly.

"That he did," his grandmother agreed, equally quietly.

"We'll see what we can do," Erik said finally as the *septon* and his children reached him. Just before they did, Kels gave up whatever argument he was having with his father and stalked away.

Rakeus spent one look after his son and then turned to Erik. "*Septon* Tarverro," he greeted him with the carefully measured bow of *septon* to *septon*. "Well come and well met. I am Hiri *septon* Rakeus."

Erik returned the bow, with as much grace and measure as he could, and the greeting. "A pleasure, *septon* Rakeus. I have heard many things of you."

"Good things, I hope," Rakeus replied. He gestured to the two youths still with him. "May I introduce my daughter Deria and my nephew Letir?"

Erik turned to the pair and inclined his head. "Deria, Letir," he greeted them. "I may be able to aid you. Speak with me later," he instructed.

The two youths shared a long, meaningful look, and then both bowed in an eerie synchronicity before Deria met his eyes and spoke. "Thank you," she murmured. "We will."

Rakeus arched one eyebrow at Erik as the two youths drifted away, their eyes suddenly alive. "If you do as you say, Lord Erik," he said softly, so no one else could hear him, "I will be indebted."

"I seek no debtors," Erik told him, just as softly. "Only friends and allies."

"Those you shall have if you make possible our shared hearts' desire," the *septon* told him. "I see the crowd gathers to speak with our newest *septon*," he continued, causing Erik to glance around the Hall. "I will detain you no further."

As Hiri and his children drew away, Arien guided Erik away from the crowd for the moment. "Hiri is leader of only one of the three political factions in Newport," she whispered. "He represents the merchants and the *septs* that dabble in trade. There are two other major factions, and their leaders are the only men you *must* meet tonight. I would not call the rest inconsequential, but those two you must meet, if no one else."

Erik nodded wordlessly, and then the crowd caught up with them, and he was lost in a flood of carefully measured bows and even more carefully measured words and greetings.

Even through the swarm of hangers-on and in the middle of the conversations, he spotted the second of his grandmother's faction leaders at quite a distance. Where the vast majority of the men in the room wore *sept* uniform, he wore the blue-on-black of the aeradi Sky Fleet, and was trailed by four men in odd yellow-and-white uniforms.

He nudged his grandmother slightly and pointed at the uniformed officer wending his way through the crowd toward them. "That is Bor *septon* Alraeis," she whispered. "He's a Squadron Admiral in Sky Fleet— he commands the Second Squadron—and heads what's often referred to as the paranoid faction. They believe war with the draconans is inevitable, and they don't mean the little skirmishes over trading rights and basing stations that go on every few years."

"Who are the men with him?" Erik asked.

"Wing lancers," Arien replied. "Your father wore that uniform once, long ago." She paused. "Be careful, Erik. Politically, Alraeis will want to be allies with you. On a personal basis, however..."

"He doesn't like half-bloods," Erik finished for her. "He isn't alone in that. I'll deal with it."

He turned toward Alraeis, meeting the aeraid's gaze. The Admiral increased his pace, pushing through the crowd with consummate ease. He broke through the crowd and Erik got his first look at him.

Alraeis was short, even for an aeraid, easily a foot shorter than Erik. His hair was graying, but he was still quite trim. The two little golden ships on his collar marked him as a Squadron Admiral of the fleet.

Erik bowed to him and Alraeis returned the bow, after a moment's hesitation. "*Septon* Tarverro," he greeted Erik. "Welcome to Newport. I am Squadron Admiral Bor *septon* Alraeis."

"Well met, Admiral," Erik replied. "How fares the Second Squadron, my lord Admiral? While I know little of our sky fleets just yet, I understand that I have much to learn!"

He'd meant the question as a courtesy, but from the way Alraeis jerked, he realized he'd surprised the man. Clearly, he hadn't thought that Erik would know what squadron he commanded, or care about its well-being—or want to know more at all.

"The Second fares well, *septon*," Alraeis replied. From the small smile of a man pleased with his own work, Erik realized that his unthinking question had put him more on the officer's good side than anything else he could have done or said. "Any attack against our city will find us more than a handful to deal with."

"Is such an attack likely?" Erik asked, trying to feel out just how strong the paranoia of the "paranoids" stretched.

"Not truly," the Admiral admitted. "Even if the current round of negotiations falls through, the draconans are unlikely to attack without warning."

"Forgive my ignorance, but which negotiations?" Erik asked.

"The usual," Alraeis answered with a shrug. "The draconans have been trying to open access for their traders to sky cities other than Newport for years. As long as we continue to deny it, the chances for war grow with each passing year."

Erik was stunned. He'd known that trade with the Sky Cities was limited. He hadn't realized it was forbidden outside Newport. No wonder the paranoid faction expected war!

"If they do attack, I am sure you and all of our sailors are ready to do your duty," Erik said crisply.

"We do our best, *septon* Tarverro," Alraeis replied. He bowed, giving Erik the full gradation due a *septon*. "If you will excuse me, I see Lord Beldar. There are matters I must speak with him about." Rising from his bow, he met Erik's gaze. "It has been a pleasure."

"Likewise, *septon* Alraeis," Erik replied, returning the bow. He nodded to the four wing lancers, who bowed in return before sweeping off after Alraeis.

"Det *septon* Beldar is the Councilor for the Treasury," Arien said calmly. "Alraeis is lobbying him for increased Fleet funding." Erik turned to her and found her regarding him oddly.

"Well done, by the way. You turned someone I hoped to make at most neutral into a favorable neutral and possible ally, with one simple question."

"Is the trade as restricted as he implied?" Erik asked.

"Worse, actually," Arien replied. "Only two Sky Cities other than Newport allow *any* traders into their environs, and they both limit them to the lower cities. One of *them*, to top it off, specifically forbids dragons on the grounds that the lower city is too flammable for them."

Erik winced. "I begin to understand the paranoids' viewpoint."

"There's a reason I call them the war hawks, personally," Arien admitted. "Really, all they are is realists. They have a major bone to pick with the purists, obviously, and are in close alliance with the merchants. Unfortunately, that's only in Newport. The purists and their allies seem to dominate every Royal Council *except* Newport."

"The purists?" Erik asked.

Arien didn't reply for a moment, and then hissed, "Men like *him*."

Erik followed her gaze and found the man he thought she referred to. He was so perfectly aeraid, it was hard to see him as anything else. *Sept* uniform in perfect condition, hair cropped short in the traditional aeraid seaman's style. If there'd been any doubt, Kels *septi* Rakeus followed in his wake as he headed for Erik.

"Korand *septon* Jaras," Arien warned. "He hated your father and, if that wasn't enough, you're an affront to everything he believes in. Watch your step."

She had no time for any further words, as Jaras had reached them. Erik carefully gave the man the proper gradation of *septon* to *septon*. There was, after all, no point in giving the aeraid unnecessary insult.

Jaras did not return the bow at all, merely giving Erik a sneer as perfect and practiced as the rest of his appearance. "And just what do *you* think you are doing, aping the manners of your betters in this city?" he snapped. "You should return to your hovel in the fishing slum from where you came."

Erik rose from the bow, carefully controlling his features. "It seems," he said loudly, "that even among the aeradi, there are those who chose pigs for their role models instead of men."

"You *dare* insult me, you insolent filth?" Jaras demanded.

"I merely return favor for favor," Erik replied. "Aping, as you say, the manner of my supposed betters. I would guess that it's the smell of your own bullshit that keeps your nose turned up so high," he added.

"I suppose we should suspect no better from the child of a madman and a human whore," Jaras snarled.

The growing anger with which Erik had replied to the man's insults vanished to be replaced with pure rage. Only Arien's fingers, driving hard into his bicep before he could do anything foolish, prevented him from drawing his sword and running the smirking fop through in the middle of the King's Hall.

Jaras clearly realized he'd hit a nerve, but the aeraid had also seen Erik's hand drop to the hilt of his sword before Arien stopped him. His smirk was tinged with a degree of worry, and he'd changed his stance. With one step he would now be behind Kels, whose hand was also on his sword hilt.

"You're making a grave mistake," Erik told Jaras flatly. Before the man could reply, he drove on. "I am not your enemy, but you seem bound and determined to make yourself mine."

He locked eyes with the aeraid. "Because I am not your enemy, I will make this offer *once*. Walk away," he instructed. "Walk away and never bother me again, and I will return the favor.

"But," Erik continued, releasing his sword and raising a finger on his sword hand, "if you touch me or mine, I will challenge you and take you out onto the field with a sword in my hand. And on that field, *I will break you!*" he finished in a snarl.

He turned on his heel and walked away, leaving Jaras to stand, stunned and deprived of his prey, in the center of the hall.

ERIK HEADED DIRECTLY FOR THE DOOR, DRAGGING HIS grandmother in his wake. Finally, nearly at the exit from the hall, he turned back to the older woman, his anger over Jaras's comments still raging. From his grandmother's expression, it showed on his face as well.

"Can we go now?" he demanded. "Or must I stay and listen to more men insult my parents?"

"Erik, believe me, Jaras is the worst we have to offer," Arien told him. "Most of those who knew your father respected him, and even those who didn't will mostly give you the benefit of the doubt. It's merely a few with more earth than water in their brains who'll cause you problems."

Erik's face was a mask as he tried to control his anger. "Be that as it may, I believe I have been insulted enough for one night, *Grandmother*," he replied.

The old aeraid woman sighed. "Very well," she murmured. "I'll have them bring the carriage around."

The carriage ride back to the Tarverro seat was quiet, both Erik and his grandmother lost in their own thoughts. The horses drew the vehicle down the lamp-lit concourses of the city toward the docks, then up the cul-de-sac to the house.

Exiting the carriage, Arien took Erik's arm and guided him, not to the small guesthouse where she'd lived but to the massive mansion that had been dark and cold for years upon years.

"I thought you'd only opened up the house for the meeting this morning," Erik said as they approached the now brightly lit building.

"With a *septon* Tarverro finally here," his grandmother replied, "we need to have the seat fully open and ready to receive visitors. Unless you object, of course," she added.

Erik shook his head. The mansion was far more house than he really needed, but he was a stranger in a strange land, suddenly thrust into a position of authority. He'd listen to his grandmother and cling, almost, to her advice. She was his only guide and advisor among these his father's people. Without her, he would quickly find himself lost and confused among a strange people. When she advised, he'd listen.

THE NEXT MORNING, ERIK DISCOVERED THAT TELLING YOUNG lovers to meet him in the morning was a bad idea. He was in the middle of his breakfast when Shel came in and looked at him.

"There's a young couple at the door, milord," she told him, seeming uncomfortable to be reporting to him and not to his grandmother, who shared the table with him. "They say that you invited them."

"Did they give their names?" Erik asked, lowering his full fork to his plate. He was pretty sure he knew who they were, but he figured he should still check.

"Letir and Deria, milord," Shel replied.

"Let them in," he instructed. "For that matter, tell Meria to set two more places for breakfast. I'm not going to stop my breakfast for this, and if they're here this early, I doubt they ate first."

His grandmother smiled at him as Shel left the room. "They're young yet," she murmured.

"So am I," he reminded her. "Letir is *older* than I am."

She nodded softly. "Be careful with this, Erik," she warned. "Kels is not joking about challenging the man who sponsors Letir, and he's killed two men with swords on the field."

"I've killed men with swords in alleys and shops," Erik admitted. "I can't imagine fighting on the field of 'honor' to be any more difficult."

Arien met his gaze, a strange look in her eyes. "I didn't know that," she replied.

"I know," Erik said flatly, looking away.

"Still," she continued softly, "be careful. Please. There is no *septi* Tarverro. We can't afford to lose you so soon."

Erik said nothing, merely nodding as the two youths were shown in. "Have a seat," he instructed them, gesturing at the two places that had been set out at the table. "Have you eaten?"

Letir looked almost shamefaced as he shook his head. Erik smiled gently and waved to Meria. "Meria, can we manage to feed two more hungry mouths?"

The cook, a plump matronly woman he'd been told had three sons, just smiled and vanished back into the kitchen. She returned momentarily with two plates loaded with food that she placed in front of the two youths.

"Eat up," Erik told them. "Meria is an extraordinary cook, and it's a shame to waste any of her food."

The two took him at his word, tucking into the breakfast like they'd never seen food before. Erik regarded them for several moments, noting how even while eating, the two seemed to be in constant physical contact, touching and brushing each other.

"Now," he said after their initial rush at the food had abated, "I am told that you two wish to marry. Is this correct?"

The two exchanged a glance, and Erik caught a small gesture from Letir to Deria.

"Yes," she murmured. "We've known each other our whole lives. There's never been anyone else for either of us, but..."

"The law says no commoner can marry a *sept* without *sept* sponsorship," Erik finished.

"And tradition says the sponsor has to be of equal rank to the *sept's* parent," Letir added. "Which for us means a *septon*, and there are none who are prepared to risk Kels' challenge and Jaras's displeasure."

"I acquired Jaras's displeasure by being born," Erik observed. "As for the other"—he shrugged—"I am prepared to risk it, given sufficient reason. Tell me, Letir, why I should sponsor you to this marriage."

Letir looked over at Deria. Clearly, he was used to letting her take the lead in these conversations. Erik saw her squeeze Letir's hand, and the youth took a deep breath and spoke. "Like Deria said, milord, we've always loved each other. There's never been anyone else. I can support her, even in the style to which she's become accustomed. I've worked several ships and bought shares in others. I've been offered a master's berth on the *Equatrix*, which would provide more than sufficient money to support us both." He paused. "I love her, sir. I can't think of any real reason other than that," he finished in a rush.

Erik smiled gently. "I see."

He eyed the two lovers for a long, long moment. While his grandmother had proposed this, her own fear for his safety seemed to be changing her mind about the wisdom of it. The danger was there; there was no avoiding it. And yet...he could see their hands touching as they drew strength from each other, hoping against hope that he would help them.

His father's son could *not* refuse them.

After a moment or so of thought, he looked over at Deria. "And you wish this as well?"

"I do, milord *septon*," she confirmed.

"Then may I impose upon you to set up a meeting with your father so the four of us can sit down and discuss this?" he asked. "If he has no objections, which I don't believe he will, then you will have your sponsor, Letir."

"Thank you, sir!" Deria said for them both, starting to stand as if to go find her father immediately.

Erik couldn't help but laugh. "Sit down, both of you," he ordered. "Finish your breakfast. You'll need the energy."

HIRI SENT ERIK A MESSENGER LATER THAT MORNING, ASKING HIM TO meet with him and the couple that very afternoon. Erik sent the messenger back immediately, confirming that he would meet with the other *septon* at the Rakeus estate.

The Rakeus seat was surprisingly modest. The residence of the undeniably richest man in Newport, the stone mansion was actually smaller than the Tarverro seat and not much farther from the docks. Of course, where the houses of the *kep* families surrounded the Tarverro seat, the Rakeus seat was surrounded by crystal spires housing the offices necessary to run the widespread Rakeus business empire.

Two men in the Rakeus *sept's* uniform, *kep* retainer guards, met Erik and the accompanying pair of his own *kep*, at the entrance to the estate. They guided him through the business offices to the house.

At the entrance to the seat itself, Erik sent his own guards off with the *kep* Rakeus. Entering the house of another *septon* with no guards was a sign of great trust, but he did trust Hiri *septon* Rakeus and was willing to prove it.

Deria met him inside the entrance and guided him to the room where her father waited, a glowing smile on her lips. She was obviously quite certain of how the meeting was going to go. For that matter, Erik didn't blame her.

"*Septon* Tarverro," Hiri greeted him, offering his hand in the clasp of close friends.

Erik took the man's hand. "*Septon* Rakeus. Well met."

"Well come," Hiri replied. "Please, sit down. I understand from my daughter that you have something you wish to speak to me about."

"Indeed," Erik said. Despite their admirable formality, both he and Hiri were grinning widely. "Letir here has spoken to me of his desire to wed your daughter, Deria."

"He has spoken of such desire to me as well," Hiri replied. "However, he is a commoner and cannot marry the daughter of a *septon* without a sponsor of a suitable class."

"He has proven to me his good nature and suitability for the match," Erik returned gravely. "I would be prepared to sponsor the lad for the marriage."

"If that is the case, then I have no objection," Hiri said formally. "We may then proceed with the plans for the betrothal."

"Indeed we may," Erik said, then gave up on the formality and grinned at the two lovers. "I believe that between us, we *should* be able to afford to see you two publicly betrothed."

"Thank you," Deria told him. "A thousand thanks."

"It was and is my pleasure," Erik told her with a smile. "All of our pleasures," he added, glancing at the girl's father.

Hiri was about to speak when the door slammed open and Kels stalked in.

"What's going on here?" he demanded.

"A private meeting in what, last time I checked, was still *my* house," Hiri replied. "You have no right to barge in here."

Kels ignored his father, locking eyes with Erik. "*You!* You've sponsored that scum Letir to marry my whore of a sister!"

Erik came to his feet in a rush, sending his chair clattering back to the ground. With the same motion, he locked his hand onto Letir's shoulder and drove the youth back into his seat. "I do not agree with your descriptions, but yes, I have sponsored Letir to marry Deria. I see no reason to prevent the match."

"How about this for a reason?" Kels spat. "I formally challenge your right to sponsor him. Hell, I formally challenge the right of a half-blood bastard to be *septon* of one of our most ancient bloodlines."

"*Kels!*" Hiri bellowed, silencing Erik before he could speak. "You do this, I am *done* with you."

"What does it matter?" Kels spat back. "You'll name precious Letir your heir as soon as he weds my whore of a sister—you know, the one he's been *bedding* for the last year as you turn a blind eye." He turned back to Erik. "I'll have your blood for this, you half-blood *scum*."

"I am not your enemy," Erik assured Kels, the same words he'd used to Jaras. "But for this, I may choose to become so. If you are so insistent, I will meet you. Blade to blade. For your slighted ego and *your sister's* right to happiness."

For an instant, it seemed almost as if Kels would back down, then he jerked his head in a nod. "Tomorrow. The Square of the Gods at dawn."

"I'll be there," Erik replied flatly, and watched as calmly as he could as Kels stalked from the room.

Silence reigned for a long moment, and then Hiri's hand came down on Erik's shoulder, and Erik turned to look at the shorter aeraid.

"There's no changing it, lad," the *septon* Rakeus told him. "This has been coming for a long time. The gods themselves couldn't have stopped it."

"I don't want to have to kill your son," Erik half-whispered.

"As of today," Hiri said sadly, "I don't believe I have a son."

THE WHETSTONE SCRAPED ON THE SKY STEEL OF ERIK'S RAPIER, loud in the silence of the small atrium at the back of the Tarverro seat. While the atrium was under glass, focusing sunlight to keep the plants alive even in the middle of winter, it was still cold in the small indoor garden.

The absence of any wind contributed to the lack of any sound except Erik's stone on his sword. The sky-steel weapon didn't really need sharpening, as the smallsword had no edge, merely a point. While making the point sharper would help against armor, Kels would not be wearing armor the next day. It was simply a method of controlling his tension, and it wasn't as if the sky steel's legendarily hard surface could be damaged by the effort.

Footsteps sounded behind him, but Erik ignored them, continuing in his pointless ministration to the blade. The footsteps continued until they were directly behind him, and a voice broke the silence.

"You've been barely three days among your people, and already you want to risk your life?" Arien asked. "Even Hiri's alliance can't help you if you're *dead*, you know."

"I do not fear Kels," Erik told her.

"Then you're a fool," his grandmother replied. "You are *septon* Tarverro—a *septon* with no heir, the sole male of your line. If he kills you, we return to being an heirless line, with no prospect of survival except by bringing another male in."

"Men marry into *septs*," Erik replied. "Such a marriage would not destroy the *sept*."

"Men seek such a marriage," Arien told him. "Your aunt is pursued for them. If you die, I fear one will marry her solely for the *sept*. If you die, all that your grandfather and I rebuilt from the faded ashes of our line goes to waste. Would you see that happen?"

"You encouraged me to this course," Erik reminded her.

"I didn't expect you to throw his oath in his teeth and meet him blade-to-blade on your fourth day in the city," Arien replied exasperatedly. "We could have worked slowly, pulled it off before he realized it was happening and handed Kels a done deal. He couldn't challenge you if it was already *done*."

"Could we have?" Erik asked. "Really?"

"We could have *tried*," his grandmother snapped.

"And we may have failed, and he seems impetuous enough that it would likely have changed nothing," Erik replied. "To fulfill this task, I would have had to fight him anyway. It's better this way."

His grandmother laid his hand on his shoulder, and he heard her take a deep breath and sigh. "I'm sorry, Erik," she told him. "I shouldn't snap at you, but I'm worried. You are my grandson, and I've only just found you. Do you blame an old lady for my fear of losing you?"

"You are not old," Erik told her, covering her hand with his own.

"And you need not fear. I have fought worse battles, and with less warning."

They sat there for a long time after that, and neither of them said a word.

～

ERIK STOOD ON THE WIDE AVENUE LEADING INTO THE SQUARE OF the Gods and simply looked at it. He'd seen it already, but today, when it could easily be his last sight, he took the moments to drink it in.

The massive plaza lay just short of the innermost portions of the city. The wide, spacious boulevard he stood on led from the main docks directly to the palace, and the Square of the Gods was the last clear space before it reached the palace. It was, in fact, the sole access point between the inner and outer portions of the High City, the single gate through the inner fortifications being on the inside of the square.

Of course, he reflected, the inner fortifications of the city were regarded as an unnecessary paranoia in this day and age. While the massive stone walls were undiminished by time, the stone forts, though still surrounding the Palace with dwarven cannon and aeradi crystal bows with full magazines and charged crystals, were unmanned. The gates stood open, and even from this distance, his cursory examination suggested that they were rusted in that position.

Nonetheless, the gates and walls made an impressive backdrop to the square. The stone-paved boulevard opened out onto an expanse of stone and marble pavement, marked with lines of trees, sweeping terraces of grass and flowers, kept clear of snow even in winter, and dozens of marble statues of the four gods in assorted poses.

"Erik," Hiri said into the silence.

"It's beautiful, isn't it?" Erik replied quietly. "All of it."

"We have to go," the older *septon* reminded him.

Erik nodded silently and turned to the far eastern side of the square, where a cleared expanse of pure white sand, surrounded by carefully groomed evergreen trees, marked the dueling grounds.

Erik and his party walked through the trees that hid it from normal view, to find that the dueling ground itself was fenced off. A clear area between the trees and the fence was provided for combatants to prepare themselves and for the dueling ground's judge to speak to them.

Kels was already standing next to the judge, and Hiri gestured for Erik to join the pair.

"Gentlemen," the judge said to the two duelists as Erik took his place before the man. "You meet here this morning under the Dueling Code of the City of Newport and the Realm of the Sky. I am required by law to request that you seek a peaceful solution to the quarrel between you."

Kels looked at Erik and shrugged. "Withdraw your sponsorship, and this becomes unnecessary."

"You have no right to dictate their lives," Erik replied. "Walk away, Kels. I do not wish to hurt you."

Kels sneered and turned to the judge. "No, there can be no resolution."

"Very well," the judge conceded. "You each have ten minutes to prepare, and may the gods judge fairly in this quarrel between you."

Erik returned to his side of the sands, where Hiri and the young couple waited for him. Letir was carrying Erik's sword, the sky-steel smallsword he'd forged for Rade, half a year, half a world and an entire lifetime away.

With a shrug, he removed the jacket he wore over the simple white tunic he would fight in. He met Hiri's gaze and shook his head helplessly. "He won't back down."

"I didn't expect him to," the *septon* replied.

"I don't want to kill him," Erik told him.

"Do what you have to," Hiri replied coldly. "I lost my son a long time ago. Today is simply the formality." He offered his hand in the clasp of friends.

Erik returned the handclasp and then watched helplessly as the *septon* walked to the side of the field. He turned to Deria and Letir. He made a gesture with his hand, and Letir drew the rapier and extended it hilt-first to him.

He took the sword and looked at the sister of the man he was about to fight. "I'll try not to kill him if I can," he promised.

"Thank you," Deria replied quietly. "He's been a stranger to us for forever, it seems, and no matter what happens today, my father will disown him. He'll be dead to us in law, but it would pain us—even my father, who refuses to show it—if he was dead in truth."

Erik turned to the sands but stopped as Deria's hand settled onto his shoulder. "All that said," she continued softly, "you're worth more to us now than him. Try all you want, but come back to us alive."

He nodded choppily and then stepped through the fence onto the sands of the dueling ground.

~

THE AERADI DUELING CODE ALLOWED NEITHER ARMOR NOR SHIELDS, limiting the combatants to light clothing and their swords. The nature of the sword was left to the combatants' discretion, but it was the only thing a combatant could carry onto the dueling grounds.

Of course, the code also enshrined the concept of duel to first blood, but Erik doubted that Kels would accept defeat after a single cut. He was probably going to have to seriously injure the aeraid to force him to admit defeat.

He shook his head, ridding his head of thought, and raised his sword. Kels met him at the center of the grounds, wielding the traditional ancient aeradi weapon, the tachi: a long, slightly curved sword only sharpened on the outer edge. Like Erik, his blade was forged of sky steel.

At a signal from the judge, Erik and Kels crossed blades in the formal gesture of readiness. The judge eyed them both and raised a red cloth.

"Begin," he ordered, dropping the cloth and stepping back.

Kels attacked even before the cloth hit the ground, yanking his sword away from the crossed blades and launching a spinning slash at Erik's neck. Erik ducked the strike and stepped back out of the smaller man's reach.

A second slash came in almost before Erik adjusted, but a flick of his rapier sent it careening off into the air. The defensive flick easily turned into a riposte as Erik lunged toward Kels.

The aeraid blocked the blow with the back of his free forearm, smacking it against the edgeless length of the smallsword and knocking it aside. Jarred, perhaps, by the opening he'd left, his next attack was a perfectly controlled lunge at Erik.

Erik hit it with the base of his smallsword, knocking the heavier sword aside. Before Erik could make a move of his own, Kels demonstrated just why he was feared as a swordsman. Using a strength of wrist that Erik knew *he* just barely possessed but that few *humans*, let alone aeradi, could even dream of, Kels turned the deflected lunge into a deadly slash at Erik's midsection.

Erik barely managed to interpose the smallsword against the slash, hammering the blades together in a hilt-on-hilt crash of metal. For a moment, the hilts of the two weapons locked, but Kels' weapon's heavier blade weight told. The smallsword's blade slowly bent away from the contact point.

The heavier tachi slid down the rapier's more flexible blade, and Erik had to dodge back to avoid its deadly sharp edge. The tachi kept going and slid off the smallsword onto the ground, unbalancing its wielder. For a moment, Kels was unguarded, and Erik slipped in.

The smallsword had no edge, but that didn't mean it couldn't cut. The deadly sharp tip sliced a line across Kels' cheek, leaving blood to leak out onto the other man's face.

"First blood," Erik told Kels. "Yield. I don't want to have to hurt you."

"Go fuck a dragon," Kels told him flatly, and attacked. He sent a flurry of blows at Erik's chest and head, forcing Erik back, as he couldn't meet those blows with the flimsy blade of the smallsword.

"I need a heavier sword," he muttered as Kels brought his tachi whistling around in an unstoppable blow that would have been head-height on any other aeraid—chest height on Erik. He threw himself sideways, onto the ground, barely avoiding the glitter of sun on steel.

He heard the spectators gasp as he hit the ground, and gritted his teeth. He rolled across the sand and came back up, his free hand spinning around to throw a handful of the sand into Kels' eyes.

The aeraid tried to prevent Erik from taking advantage of his sudden distraction by slashing heavily at the taller man, but it was too late. Even as the sand hit Kels' eyes, the tip of Erik's sword drove deep into Kels' sword shoulder.

Kels then demonstrated the *other* reason he was feared. Even as his sword began to slip from his swordhand's fingers, his off hand grabbed the blade. He spun the sword in his fingers, aligning the blade so he could use it in that hand. The man was ambidextrous!

Erik leapt backward with an oath, evading the blow he hadn't expected to come. For the first time, he failed, and fire burned along *his* off arm as sky steel gashed the flesh open.

Another cut opened Erik's forehead, then another slashed across his chest as he stepped back again and brought his sword up, parrying a thrust that would have run him through.

For a moment, the two combatants paused, both panting and bleeding, swords held in hands now slippery with sweat. Then Kels snarled and charged, his tachi lancing out in front of him.

Erik sidestepped the lunge and stabbed downward. The point of the rapier laid Kels' entire upper thigh open with a horrific tearing sound, and the aeradi swordsman went down with a thud.

The sand shifted underfoot as Erik stepped to his fallen opponent and laid the tip of his smallsword against Kels' neck. "One blow," he warned. "One blow, and you're finished. It's over."

"Finish it," Kels snarled. "Finish it, you coward!"

Erik let the point slip downward, pressing into the other man's skin and piercing it, then released the pressure. "No. This was your will, not mine. I have no desire to kill you." He looked up at the judge, standing three full paces away. "This duel is over," he said flatly.

The judge nodded. "Agreed," he said, looking down at Kels. "Kels *septi* Rakeus, it is my judgment that you have been defeated. This judgment is not to be appealed." The judge's eyes were cold. "Go home, lad, and be grateful for your life."

Erik turned away, leaving it to the judge to see that Kels' wounds were cared for and that the man was properly dealt with. As far as he was concerned, he was done with the man.

Kels, however, had other ideas. Erik never heard the shifting of the sands as the aeraid managed, somehow, to stand despite the gaping wound in his leg. All he ever heard was Hiri's shout of warning.

"Erik! Behind you!"

Erik spun, extending his sword so he could parry whatever blow was coming. He caught a glimpse of Kels lunging toward him, his tachi held high to deliver a blow no rapier could have stopped.

The blow never landed. Erik's smallsword lunged out, an unthinking continuation of the extension that came with the turn, and punched into the aeraid's chest. It grated between the man's ribs and out his back, sliding neatly through his heart on the way.

Kels froze as the steel slid through him. For an instant of eternity, the aeraid simply stood there, Erik's sword through his chest, his own sword held above his head like a vengeful bolt of lightning. Then he fell, the heavy sword sliding from his hands to thump onto the sand as he fell forward, landing at Erik's feet.

Erik hit his knees almost as Kels hit the ground, but he was too late to even catch the man's last breath. Kels had been dead before he'd reached the sands.

DAIRN'S ENTRANCE INTO BRANE'S OFFICE INTERRUPTED THE SPY practicing one of the more the ancient and venerable arts of the draconans. He was quietly folding a single sheet of paper into the shape of a small dragon. Since the paper the agent was distractedly destroying was actually a report on the Hellitian ministry of trade's internal politics, his immediate release of the paper and baleful glare at the other Red Dragon were perhaps understandable.

"We have news from Newport, Captain," Dairn reported. "They've located Tarverro."

"That was quick," Brane replied. From what he knew, his own message asking his agents to look for the man should only have arrived a day or two before. He certainly shouldn't have received any reply.

"It was sent before they got our message," Dairn replied, his mouth twisting. "They won't have to look too hard when they get ours."

"What?" Brane demanded, suddenly straightening.

"It seems one Erik Tarverro, the half-blood son of Karn Tarverro, was presented to the King of Newport five days ago...as the new *septon* Tarverro," Dairn reported.

Brane whistled. "I hadn't realized he was one of *those* Tarverros."

"If he was *sept*, he'd have had to be," Dairn replied. "It didn't occur to me, either."

Brane waved that away. Dairn operated among humans; he couldn't be expected to really follow the internal affairs of the aeradi. Brane, on the other hand, was one of the senior operatives in the whole of north-western Cevran. He was fully up to date on the internal affairs of the aeradi and of the draconan operations among them.

"It should have occurred to me," he admitted. "No matter, however." He grimaced. "Unfortunately, this makes him even more untouchable. A *septon*, in Newport, may as well be among the stars for all that we can touch him. Yet."

"What about..." Dairn trailed off, apparently suddenly remembering he wasn't supposed to know about the draconan plans in Newport.

Brane simply smiled. He *expected* his agents to be inquisitive bastards. It was what made them useful. It was occasionally annoying, as they discovered things they weren't supposed to know, but Red Dragons were too well trained to speak of things outside the order.

"You know nothing about that," he said drily. "Nonetheless, when 'that' comes to pass, many things will change. Many things will change," he repeated, his hand caressing the hilt of the dagger at his waist.

"I WANT TO SPEAK TO THE MAN!"

Erik paused at the entrance to his grandmother's study in the Tarverro seat at the sound of the angry voice, a sheaf of papers under his arm. He'd been looking for her to ask her about the papers, a financial analysis of some of the new industrial opportunities in the city that were looking for investors, but the shouting caused him to pause at the door.

"He's quite busy, dear," he heard Arien reply. "He is, after all, *septon* and still newly confirmed. He has a great deal to do."

"I have as much right to see him as anyone," the voice snapped. "I am, after all, *sept* Tarverro. Unless you've decided to take that from me, too?"

"Hella, I have no idea what you're angry about," Erik heard his grandmother snap back. "You're receiving as much—if not *more*—of the *sept's* money since he took over. What are you complaining about?"

Hella was his aunt's name, Erik had been told. Which meant that the upset woman in the other room was his father's sister. He really should go in, he realized, but the conversation was quite interesting.

"They've all left, Mother," the voice told Arien, cracking toward the end. "All of them. Since *he* turned up, I haven't had a single suitor."

Erik's conscience finally won the battle with his curiosity, and he stepped calmly into the office.

"I don't know about you," he said calmly, "but that doesn't sound like they were all that interested in *you* and not your money."

Hella spun, and Erik found himself facing a quite attractive aeraid woman in her mid thirties. He wondered why she was only now receiving suitors, but then noticed the brass-and-gold ring on her right middle finger. The ring marked a member in good standing of the First Society, the organization of academics that all teachers of higher learning belonged to. Such a ring meant she was qualified to teach students at the highest level, and such rings would *take* until thirty or so to acquire, even with a *sept's* money backing you.

"What would you know?" she demanded hotly.

"Not much," Erik admitted with a smile and a shrug, "it just seemed obvious."

The woman paused before responding, eyeing Erik's face. She seemed to swallow an angry reply, and said instead, "You're Erik, aren't you?"

"Indeed, Aunt Hella," he replied politely. "I regret the loss of your suitors," he continued, "but surely, those you've lost sought only your position. I doubt, for that matter, that you've lost *all* of them," he finished.

The woman sighed. "Hori asked me to dine with him, now that I'm back, but...it's *Hori*."

Erik raised an eyebrow at his grandmother, who chuckled quietly. "Hori was one of her fellow students when she decided to go for the Society as a mathematic. He's a mage," she added, parenthetically.

Despite his aunt's poor showing so far, Erik was impressed by that. To achieve Society standing, or so he was told, was hard enough in any discipline, but math stood up along with magic as the hardest, and, unlike magic, couldn't be made easier by any natural talent beyond the ability and willingness to learn and think.

"And what's wrong with Hori?" Erik asked his aunt. "After all, he doesn't seem put off by my existence."

"It's *Hori*," Hella replied. "I've known him my whole life. He's boring."

"What does he do?" Erik asked.

"He's an experimental mage," she told him. "Works on new battle magic. Half the time when I see him, he's regrowing eyebrows."

Erik's eyebrow arched again, almost on its own. "That's *boring*?" he asked.

Hella paused for a moment, considering. "But it's *Hori*," she burst out.

Arien shook her head. "If that's how you feel, that's how you feel," she told her daughter. "Feel free to turn him down and look for others —even without the entire *sept* as your dowry, you're a wealthy and attractive member of the Society. You'll find some more suitors soon enough."

"Don't be hasty," Erik's aunt replied, her tone thoughtful. She looked at Erik strangely. "I hadn't thought about that, really," she admitted. "I've just known him for so long, it's hard to remember what he does."

"Give him a chance," Erik advised. "If it doesn't work out"—he shrugged—"tell me and I'll have some of the burlier *kep* discourage his interest."

"Don't you *dare*!" Hella snapped, and then stopped mid-breath, realizing how thoroughly she'd been had. "Maybe I will give him a chance, then," she told Erik, then flounced out, bestowing a small smile on her nephew as she did.

"Phew," Erik exhaled as she left, turning back to his grandmother. "That's my aunt Hella?"

"That's your aunt Hella," Arien confirmed. "She should have married Hori *years* ago—the two of them were head over heels when they first went for their rings, but the studies got in the way, and then Emil died and all those beautiful young men started trying to woo her for the chance to inherit the *sept*." The tiny old woman shrugged. "It went to her head, I think. Hori's not given up—any experimental mage *has* to be persistent, thankfully—and she really does like him when she thinks about it."

Erik's grandmother brushed her hands off, as if leaving her daughter to her own affairs. "Now, I'm sure you had some other reason for coming to see me," she said briskly.

~

AERADI CUSTOM WAS TO KEEP THE PERIOD OF BETROTHAL QUITE short. That custom, as far as Erik could tell, was mainly designed so that sailors could get betrothed and then marry before their ship left. Certainly, since Letir had received the master's berth he'd been expecting, that was the reason for it in this case.

One week to the day after Erik's duel with Kels, he found himself in the Square of the Gods again. This time, however, he was standing as patron to Letir at their open-air wedding.

The wedding party was quite small, as *sept* Rakeus was in official mourning for Kels. A group of *kep* Rakeus in full ceremonial armor surrounded Deria, and Hiri stood at their head as Erik, with two of his own *kep* in armor, escorted Letir to them.

"Who comes to the house of *sept* Rakeus?" Hiri demanded, beginning the ritual.

"A man to wed the daughter of the *sept*," Letir replied.

"Harrumph," Hiri replied. "Who would vouch for this man, that I will know he is worthy of my kinship?" he demanded.

Erik stepped forward. "I, Erik *septon* Tarverro, vouch for this man, that he is honest and of good standing, a worthy husband to any daughter, a worthy son to any father."

"Then I am satisfied," Hiri replied. He stepped aside, and the circle of *kep* opened, allowing Letir to walk to his bride.

Erik and his *kep* filled the gap in the circle, leaving the two youths standing alone in the middle of a circle of armored men. Every man took a single step back, opening a space between them, and the wives and other female guests stepped into the gaps, laying a circle of flowers around the couple.

As the circle of flowers was closed, Letir took Deria's hands in his and went to one knee. "I ask the right to take your hands in marriage," he began, "to hold your heart and guard your thoughts as my own. I ask the right to be the father of your children, the provider of your home and the bringer of your dreams."

Deria sank to her own knees—the reason that even the bride's wedding clothes were trousers in aeradi custom—and pressed his hands to her heart. "My heart you hold already," she told him, only barely audible to the circle around them. The words weren't part of the ritual, but none of the broadly smiling men or sniffling women saw any reason to object.

"Those are the rights of a husband," she said loudly, stepping back into the ritual. "They are not the rights of a day but the tasks of a life-time. Are you prepared to keep to these tasks and these vows through fire and rain, through earth and air, to the ends of the world and until the end of our lives?"

"I am prepared," Letir replied.

"Then I am also," she said, rising with him, their hands still linked. "I swear that I will keep your home, your heart and your children. I swear to be the guardian of your dreams, your thoughts and your love. I will do you good and no harm all my days. I am your wife."

"I swear that I will guard you and keep you, through fire and rain, through earth and air, to the ends of the world and until the ends of our lives," he replied. "I will do you good and no harm all my days. I am your husband."

Erik and Hiri stepped forward and broke the circle of flowers, opening a path for the newly wedded couple to come out of the circle.

Behind them, the *kep* left the circle and formed a path coming out from the gap, raising their swords to create an arch.

As the couple passed each pair of *kep*, they lowered the swords behind them, until the couple had passed out of the arch of swords, and the ceremony was over. Letir was now a member of *sept* Rakeus and married to the woman he loved.

Erik smiled at the young couple—neither of them was much older than him—and considered life's little ironies. He'd made the offer to sponsor Letir as a political move, an attempt to gain an ally to help him survive the hazardous shoals of the system he'd suddenly found himself in, but he'd discovered that he honestly liked the young man. His sponsorship of Letir, in the end, had become more than a political move. He'd have done it anyway, even if he hadn't been gaining a strong ally in Newport's games of power.

His smile faded as he caught the faces of several of Hiri's *kep*. Three or four of them had formed a little knot, and were glaring at Erik. Kels had not been popular with his father's *kep*, but he had been *septi* Rakeus, and some of the *kep* Rakeus believed that Erik had no right to sponsor a man to marry the sister of a man he'd killed.

They weren't the only ones who thought so, either. Erik had been drawing sidelong looks from people ever since the duel. He was starting to think he needed a break from Newport.

"They're idiots, and you know it," Hiri said sadly into the silence of Erik's thoughts. "They never even liked Kels, but he was *sept*. I don't blame you for what happened. Don't blame yourself."

Erik shook his head. "It's hard not to," he replied. "I keep thinking there had to have been some way I could have beaten him without killing him."

"You tried," the father of the man Erik had killed replied. "Gods, man, you nearly let him kill *you*, you tried so hard."

"I failed."

"Yes, you did," Hiri replied. "Part of me hates that. He was my son, for all our problems, and I mourn him. But you *tried*, and no one ever even said you should."

Erik turned away, his eyes falling onto the crowds drifting through the square. "Maybe," he admitted, "but I grow tired of being the target of dark looks." He shook his head again. "I think I need some time away from here."

"How long?" Hiri asked.

"I don't know," Erik replied softly. "Why?"

The older man shrugged. "It was a thought I'd had," he told Erik. "Most of the *septis* and *septons* are reserve officers in the guard. It doesn't require much effort of us, though I fear if ever called upon, many of them will fail in their responsibilities. It is, however, a symbol of our service to the city. However, to become an officer in the guard, you need two things: a sponsoring officer from the guard, who I'm sure that between you, me and your grandmother, we could come up with, and service experience. What's preferred is a tour as either a noncom or a junior officer on a trade ship."

"Which would get me out of Newport," Erik murmured thoughtfully.

"And give you a close introduction to the true source of the aeradi's power," Hiri continued. "That is not something to disregard. I can probably arrange such a tour aboard a ship of mine, if you wished."

Erik considered. He could arrange the tour himself, but inevitably, if he arranged it himself, he would end up on a Tarverro-owned ship. Being the owner of the ship might cause certain issues in chains of command and so forth. Shipping out on a Rakeus-owned ship should manage to avoid those.

"Yes, I would like that," he replied.

"Is it true?"

Arien's voice caused Erik to look up from the solid wooden desk in his office—once his grandfather's office—in the heart of the Tarverro seat.

"Is what true?" he asked mildly.

His grandmother pulled up a chair, hardly seeming to look. That wasn't surprising, as this had been her husband's office for decades and Erik hadn't got around to shifting the furniture yet.

"Are you leaving?" she asked bluntly.

"Ah, that," Erik conceded. "I'm planning on taking a tour on one of the trade ships—I'm told that it's expected of someone in my position."

"It's expected of *septi*," Arien replied. "Not *septons*. It's a foolish risk, Erik. And an unnecessary one."

"Foolish?" Erik asked. "Maybe. Unnecessary? Not really. I killed Kels, Grandmother. I make no distinctions about that, and people are holding it against me."

"It will fade in time, Erik," she replied. "The duel was legal, and everyone knows he challenged you."

"I am a newcomer here," he said, not bitter but coming close to it. He'd so hoped things would be different in Newport. "A newcomer and a half-blood. I am inevitably seen as a villain by those who knew him."

"That *will* change, Erik," Arien insisted. "They don't know you yet. Give them time."

"That's the point of this, Grandmother," Erik objected. "To give them time. To give it time to fade from people's memories. Besides"— he shrugged—"it is one of the rites of passage of *septi*. I never knew I *was septi*—not until I was *septon*—but this, at least, I can do to try to fit in among them."

His grandmother shook her head. "The *septons* are a bunch of cantankerous, inbred lunatics. You don't *need* to 'fit in' among them, for Hydra's sake. They'll grow to accept you, no matter what. We've had *septons* who were *professional* duelists!"

Erik shook his head. "I need to get away, Grandmother," he told her firmly. "Nothing really counts besides that."

She sighed and looked at him. "You've made up your mind, haven't you?" she guessed. "There was no changing your father's mind, either, once he'd made it up. It's why he ended up in Vidran with your mother."

"I know," Erik said, half-turning away from her.

"It's not a bad thing, grandson," Arien told him. "Go, then, if you need to. But promise me one thing—no, two things."

"What?" Erik asked.

"First, you'll talk to Harmon about this," she said. "Not to convince you otherwise, just to get an idea of what you're walking into and to find out what you should bring."

"Done," he agreed. "I intended to speak to him anyway. The other?"

"Promise me, by Water and Air and your mother's Earth, that you will come back to me," Arien asked. "I have buried a husband and a son, and learned of another son's death twenty years too late to bury him. I *don't* want to lose my grandson."

Wordlessly, Erik crossed to her and wrapped the tiny old woman in his arms. "I promise," he swore. "By the Gods, by the Elements, by waves and sky and earth, I promise I will come back."

THE NEXT DAY, THE MAID INTERRUPTED ERIK PORING OVER A LIST of things he'd want to take with him. He didn't know what ship he'd be sailing on yet—for that matter, he didn't even know how long the voyage would last—but he remembered the voyage to Newport from Vidran. That gave him some idea of what he'd need.

Of course, he had far more funds to pick things out with now, which meant that there were things on the list—for example, sky-steel chain mail—that he would never have *dreamed* of as a mere smith from Vidran.

"Milord," the maid said, breaking into his deliberations.

"Yes, Shel?" Erik asked, smiling gently at the girl. His height intimidated the household staff, but he'd been doing his best to win them over. He hadn't been entirely successful so far, but at least they'd stopped looking at him like he was about to eat them.

"Your *kep* Harmon *hept* Ikeras is here to see you, milord," she told him.

Erik's smile broadened. "Thank you, Shel. Can you bring him up here?" he asked, gesturing at the papers on his desk. "I asked him to come, and he may have some thoughts on things I've missed."

The girl curtsied, something he *still* hadn't grown used to being directed at him. "Yes, milord," she said before vanishing out the door.

Clearly, Ikeras hadn't been waiting at the front door, as Erik was still smiling and shaking his head at the maid's antics when the older aeradi stepped through the door, bearing a long package wrapped in cloth.

"Good morning, milord," Ikeras said.

"Ikeras, sit down, and lose the *milord*s," Erik told him. "I'm growing to hate the formality."

"Good," the old wing lancer replied, settling onto a spare chair across from Erik's desk, his package across his knees. "If I was worried about anything, it was that it would all go to your head."

Erik's smile faded to a bleak expression. "The dark mutters about abominations and murderers would help deal with that worry, I think," he said bitterly.

Ikeras shook his head. "Telling you not to let them bother you would be pointless," he observed. "What you're doing is *probably* the next best thing, so I can't advise against it. How goes the planning?"

"All right," Erik replied. "Mostly just an expansion of what you had me bring for the voyage here. Mainly, I just added a suit of armor, a shield and a bow, though I think I need a different style of sword for this."

"You do," Ikeras told him with a grin. "Which does bring to me why I'm here, besides your asking me to come, that is." He offered Erik the cloth-wrapped package. "This is for you."

Erik took it, eyeing the older aeraid warily. He carefully unwrapped the package, exposing a sky-steel sword that glittered in the sunlight streaming through the window.

He took the sword in his hand and shifted it. The balance was excellent—nearly perfect, in fact, and he inhaled sharply. The shape was just *slightly* wrong for being a normal tachi. He twisted the sword over and saw the inscription he knew would be there.

"My father's sword," he said quietly. "He gave this to you," he objected, extending it back to Ikeras.

"And now I'm giving it to you," Ikeras replied. "I don't really need a sky-steel blade—not since I left the lancers. Besides, the lancers *did* issue me my own short-blade—carrying this was an affectation and a way of remembering an incredible man." He reached out and wrapped

Erik's fingers around the hilt, and pressed the sword back on the younger man.

"There is no better memorial for Karn than his son wielding his sword," Ikeras told him. "He would have wanted you to have it. Almost as important, perhaps, *I* want you to have it."

Erik said nothing, silently running his fingers down the flat of the blade. Then he looked up at Ikeras, and he knew that there were tears in the corners of his eyes.

"Thank you," he whispered. "Thank you."

"I think you're worthy of it," the older man replied. "Prove me right."

"I will," Erik promised.

$\text{❦} \quad 3 \quad \text{❧}$

THE *CLOUDRUNNER* WAS a standard aeradi skyship. She was a hundred yards long, with a maximum beam of about fifteen. In water, she displaced about a thousand tons and could sail at the better part of ten knots. In the air, she ran on three primary lift crystals and could fly at just over eleven knots. Four dwarven built fire-cannon and two aeradi crystal bows were mounted on each broadside, providing a defense that would be ably assisted in real conflict by the sixty marines the trader carried.

In many respects, she was identical to the hundreds of ships that sailed out of Newport or any other sky city. Of course, none of the other ships had a *septon* aboard as a marine sergeant. However, as Erik had discovered, several ships had *septi*—the *sept* heirs—aboard in similar positions, and most carried *sept* of some standing. As Hiri had said, it was a tradition among the aeradi.

In the week since he'd decided to leave Newport, Erik had managed to acquire a simple but extremely well-made set of light chain mail—made of sky steel, so its strength defied its looks—and an aeradi bow to go with his father's sword.

The bow was an unusual weapon. Matched to the aeradi height, it was only about four feet tall, but it was made of a wood he'd never seen anywhere else—he'd been told it only grew on the sky cities—and had an incredible draw for its size. Practicing with it, he'd begun to understand why aeradi archers were feared.

He wore the bow slung over his shoulder and the sword at his waist as he approached the ship, carrying a single bag containing as many sets of clothing as Erik figured he would need and the chain mail. He expected the sea to be hard on his clothes, so he'd brought simple, sturdy garments. Both the bag and the cloak he wore over everything were the oilskins Ikeras had helped him pick out in Vidran, proof against anything short of outright immersion.

"Tarverro!" a voice called out from the ship, and Erik turned to find a dark-haired aeraid, wearing much the same style of clothes as he was, only lacking the oilskins for now and wearing a simple silver star on his collar.

"That's me," he confirmed. "And you would be Lieutenant Albiers, correct?"

Despite the junior-sounding rank, the Lieutenant aboard an aeradi trader was the commander of all of her marines, and second in authority only to the Captain if it came to a fight, though he'd answer to the bosun as well the rest of the time.

Albiers nodded and extended a hand. "Joran Albiers, to be exact: Lieutenant of marines aboard the trader ship *Cloudrunner*. Welcome aboard, Sergeant Tarverro."

Erik inclined his head, acknowledging the new rank. "Thank you, sir," he replied, acknowledging the man's authority as well.

Albiers shook his head at Erik with a smile. "Tarverro," he said calmly, "there are only one hundred and twenty-five sailors and sixty marines on this ship. If we stick to formality, we'll all go insane. Call me Albiers."

"All right, Albiers," Erik replied evenly.

"That all your luggage?" the Lieutenant asked, gesturing at the oilskin bag.

"Yes," Erik replied. "Why?" The question seemed to have an odd tinge.

The aeraid laughed aloud. "Because you're about the twentieth aristocrat I've hauled on these 'blooding' tours of yours," he told Erik, "and only about the third to pack sensibly."

"I see," Erik said gravely.

Albiers laughed again. "I think I might be going to like you, Tarver-ro," he told Erik. "Don't let that go to your head, though."

~

"WE HAVE SIXTY MARINES ABOARD," ALBIERS TOLD ERIK LATER, after they'd settled him in and found a seat in the ship's wardroom. "Six squads of ten, split into two platoons. One stays aboard ship, one goes shoreside to escort the cargo. All of our men are double trained—tachi-and shield as well as bows."

The Lieutenant stood, pouring both of them a drink. "Now, I'm putting you in charge of Third Squad in my First Platoon." He eyed Erik for a moment, and then shrugged as if deciding something. "The sole reason for that is that the squad's Corporal, one Enviers by name, is the best I have. Listen to him and you'll be fine."

"Give the unknown factor to the best man you've got, huh?" Erik murmured. "What did he do to deserve that?"

"It's usually the last test before we make a man a sergeant in his own right, actually," Albiers told him with a wicked grin. "No offense, but *none* of the aristocrats we get can run a squad when they arrive. Less than half can do it when they leave, either."

"I'll be careful to listen to Enviers," Erik promised. Anything else he might have said was interrupted by the arrival of two men dressed in oilskins and the same sort of utilitarian clothing as Erik and Albiers.

"Ah, speak of the sea," Albiers said with another grin, leaving Erik to conclude that the arrival of the two men was not an accident.

"This," he told Erik, gesturing at the younger of the two men, "is Corporal Enviers. For some reason, he doesn't want to join Fleet Marines or the Regulars, so we get to keep his lazy ass around. He'll be the second-in-command of your squad."

Erik inclined his head in respect to Enviers. "I look forward to working with you, Corporal Enviers."

"Call me Ennie, sir," the aeraid replied. "Every other sonbitch on this tub does."

"Very well, Ennie, then," Erik said, hiding a smile at the man's coarse words.

"This," Albiers continued, gesturing to the second man, "is Sergeant Tolars, the commander of my First Platoon. You'll be reporting to him, as well as to me, obviously, for the duration of your stay aboard *Cloudrunner*. Clear?"

"Yes, Lieutenant," Erik replied.

"Now," Albiers told him, a truly evil look stealing over his face, "it's time for you to meet the Captain."

THE LIEUTENANT LED ERIK BACK TO THE CAPTAIN'S QUARTERS BUT stopped at the ironbound door. He knocked on it and gestured for Erik to proceed.

"Go on in," he instructed.

"Aren't you coming?" Erik asked.

"No," Albiers replied. "I have other duties, I'm afraid. Don't worry; the Captain doesn't bite."

Erik took a deep breath, remembering all of a sudden that he was still only twenty-one, and stepped through the door. He heard Albiers close the door behind him, and began to silently examine the room.

Like the rest of the ship, the Captain's day room was built of heavy oak from the Sky Isles, the original homeland of the aeradi. It was completely undecorated and contained only a large desk and several chairs.

The stark austerity of the room drew the eye inevitably to the room's sole occupant, sitting at the desk. The aeraid looked about average height, though it was difficult to tell with him sitting down. The arched cheekbones of the aeradi were slightly muted in him, leaving him with a somehow feminine look for one of his kind. He was dressed in a neatly fitted dark-blue-and-green uniform, the colors of *sept* Rakeus.

"Erik *septon* Tarverro," the Captain greeted him, "have a seat."

Erik took a chair and remained silent. For a long moment, the small room was quiet, and then the Captain chuckled.

"You are a cool one, aren't you?" The man's gaze met Erik's across the table. "My name is Demond *sept* Rakeus."

Erik couldn't conceal a slight start, and Demond smiled. "Yes, Hiri is my *septon*. He is also my second cousin on my mother's side. He trusts me, which is why you're on my ship."

"I see," Erik replied calmly.

"While you're on this ship, you answer to the chain of command," Demond told him. "That said, my beloved cousin also made it quite clear that if I didn't bring you home in one piece, there'd be blood to pay."

"I have no intention of coming back in any great number of pieces," Erik replied softly. "So, I think we can work together on that."

Demond nodded and gestured to the desk. "It shouldn't be a concern, in any case. This is an ordinary trip, nothing especially dangerous."

Erik looked at the desk and saw it was covered by a map of Cevran under a glass sheet. Green markers, stuck somehow to the glass, marked four cities on the northern side of the continent.

"We're running a pretty small circle, actually," Demond admitted. "I've done the long-range runs—I ran weapons into Met for my cousin during the war there—but I stick pretty close to home these days." The Captain, who Erik judged to be easily fifty years old, ran his fingers along a jagged white scar on his cheek. "I'll leave the risks—and the profits—to the younger generation."

Erik nodded. "Where are we going?"

Demond traced a path between the four green markers. "We leave Newport at dawn tomorrow and splash down by noon. We'll have to leave the water a week or so later, and several days after that, we'll land in Seije Reservoir. The cargo for there is from here: crystal lights and heaters, a small amount of Sky Isle oak on a specific consignment, crystal-forged sky-steel weapons and assorted miscellany shipped from around the world."

The Captain tapped the marker, then moved his fingers to the next one. "We'll load a cargo of pure grain at Seije and ship to Yun. We'll follow the Selt River, though it isn't big enough for us to actually sail on. We'll trade half the grain at Yun, trading it in for wine, grapes and brandy. We'll take that, plus the other half of the grain, on to North Hold, where we'll trade it all to the dwarves."

"From the dwarves we'll pick up a few hundred tons of alignable crystal and fill the rest of the hold with firepowder and iron ore." His finger touched the last marker. "We'll sell most of the firepowder and ore to the draconans at Black Mountain, and load up with alignable crystal to fill the hold. In the final numbers, we'll bring about six hundred tons of alignable crystal and a couple hundred tons each of firepowder and iron ore back to Newport from there."

Erik eyed the four markers, digesting the Captain's lightning-quick summary of the plan. "How long will it take us?" he asked.

Demond shrugged. "Depends on too many factors to really predict. If the wind works in our favor, which it should this time of year, and the cargos are all ready as promised..." He shrugged again. "At least six weeks. Could be two months."

"I see," Erik replied. "Looks like we're certainly going to see a good chunk of northern Cevran."

"Hellit, Ell, Dvar, Dracona," Demond listed. "Four cities, four countries, three species and it *still* isn't that much of even northern Cevran, kid. The world's a big place."

Erik nodded his understanding. "Anywhere specific we need to watch for extra trouble?" he asked.

Demond shrugged. "Black Mountain, to a certain extent. There's *always* trouble between us and the draconans, though nothing really major right now. There's always a chance that some idiot is going to try to hold us up, though, and peace is subject to change with them, anyway. That said—keep your eyes open everywhere. We never know where we'll have trouble."

With a nod, Erik stood. "Understood. With your permission, I'll return to my quarters and get my things stored."

"Indeed," Demond waved lazily. "We'll have the trip to Seije for you to get to know your squad. If I remember Albiers correctly, drill will be on the deck at nine bells. I would recommend being there," he finished drily.

"Of course, sir," Erik replied, saluting roughly before exiting the dayroom.

~

NINE BELLS FOUND ERIK ON THE SHIP'S MAIN DECK, SWORD AND shield in hand, watching as Albiers mustered the two platoons of the *Cloudrunner*'s marines into their files. Erik stood at the head of his file of ten men, with Enviers right behind him. Six files stood on the deck, occupying almost the entirety of the free space available.

Albiers stood facing the sixty men, with his two platoon sergeants at his side. "Gentlemen," he said loudly and clearly, "welcome aboard the *Cloudrunner*. Of the sixty men on this deck, eighteen of you have not served aboard this ship before. I have spoken with each of you in the previous few days, and I have a few final instructions, which will serve as reminders to our old hands.

"Look around you," he instructed. "There are sixty aeradi on this deck. Six squads, two platoons. These men, for the duration of this voyage, are your brothers-in-arms. You will get to know them well—far better than you'd like, all considered," he added with a grin. "Their lives will be as dear to you as your own, because if they aren't, we're screwed.

"We're going to be traveling into areas that are well traveled by aeradi ships, but it's still possible that we'll end up the only skyship in port. Which *means*, gentlemen, that *we* will be the primary military force defending aeradi interests in a given city, and the local factors and embassies may need to call upon us to serve in that capacity.

"That, however," Albiers continued, "is unlikely. What *is* true, however, is that we *will* be the only defense this ship has. We will have no backup except each other. No aid, except each other and the weapons of the *Cloudrunner* herself. We stand together, or we die."

The Lieutenant eyed the men in front of him for a moment. "Understood?" he suddenly barked.

"Understood, sir!" all sixty men chorused back, Erik among them.

"Good," Albiers said with a grin. "Now, obviously, the deck is too small for all of us to drill. Actually, from past experience, it's too small for even a single platoon to drill, so only two squads will drill at any one time. Sergeants!" he barked again, and Erik, like the other file leaders, snapped to even stiffer attention and paid close attention.

"*You* will find the drill schedule pinned to the barracks door. If there is a problem, you will speak with your platoon sergeant. If there is not, your squad *will* be on the deck for your two-hour training period each and every day. Understood?"

"Understood, sir!" Erik chorused back, with the other five sergeants.

"We have ten days until we splash down in Seije Reservoir," Albiers said finally. "While I don't expect miracles, I expect every squad to be capable of holding up their portion of the guard duty when we do. Sergeants, meet in my day room at ten bells. Dismissed!"

AN HOUR LATER, ERIK JOINED THE OTHER FIVE SQUAD LEADERS IN Albiers' day room, just off the marine barracks toward the rear of the ship. Albiers and the two platoon sergeants were waiting for them, and Tolars gestured the six men to chairs facing the desk the three senior men stood behind.

"Gentlemen, at ease," Albiers ordered. "Now, two of you are new aboard the *Cloudrunner*, but it's a rare run when we have no new squad leaders aboard. We all know our duties; this is just the final brush-up before we leave."

The Lieutenant eyed the squad leaders. "Firstly, are there any issues any of you have noted that should be dealt with?" He waited for a moment, but none of the sergeants said anything. "Good. It always helps to start a voyage off on the right foot.

"Now," he continued, "as all of you know, we're hitting four cities on this run: Seije, Yun, North Hold and Black Mountain. None of these require any special precautions, except for Black Mountain. We will maintain a normal procedure of one squad aboard ship in armor at all times, and no more than a platoon off ship under any circumstances."

"While off ship, you will make certain that your men are armored and carry their swords, no matter where we are," Albiers told them. "Shields aren't necessary except when on specific tasks, such as escorting goods or coin chests to traders, where you will turn your men out in full gear."

"In Black Mountain, however," the Lieutenant said grimly, "we'll work under stricter conditions. There will be no shore leave in the citadel, I'm afraid. We will go off ship only to escort, and only in full gear. We will maintain two squads in full gear aboard ship at all times. The rota for this, as well as security operations and shore leave in the other cities, will be arranged before we splash down at each location."

He laid a sheet of paper on the desk. "This is the training schedule. Look it over now," he instructed, and one of the squad leaders grabbed it.

It slowly made its way to Erik as Albiers continued to detail the nature of the training schedule. Basically, two squads practiced at a time, with most of one platoon in the morning, most of the other in the afternoon, and the remaining squads would do cross-platoon drill at noon.

"That's for the troops, though," Albiers finished. "The rest of the time, while we're out of port, the grunts are assigned to assist around the ship. *You*, on the other hand, will be joining me for sand-table tactical exercises every evening. With the division of drill, all of a platoon's Sergeants will be free in either the morning or the afternoon, and you will do platoon-level exercises with your platoon sergeant"— he gestured to Tolars and the other platoon sergeant—"in that time frame.

"When we're done, the troops are going to be good, and *you* will all know exactly what to do with them," the Lieutenant told them. "Even those of you who've served before can still use the polish, and Tarverro and Ellis can use it even more."

Erik nodded for himself, glancing over at the other new sergeant, who apparently had Second Platoon's Third Squad. He met the man's gaze and Ellis nodded at him. From the man's age, he guessed that Ellis was a veteran of the trade ships, only just taking up the senior noncom's role, probably either in lieu of, or in preparation for, transferring to a Regular or Sky Fleet marine position.

"In any case," Albiers continued, ignoring the byplay, "we have ten days until we splash down in Seije. The schedule covers all of those days. We are in port for three days, for which I will post the rota before we land. Expect a reasonable amount of shore leave, folks—Seije is friendly territory with an embassy and permanent presence."

Erik nodded his understanding along with the others. He was actually eager to get to the task of learning how to handle the squad—he'd trained to fight for himself, but commanding other men wasn't something he'd learned before.

Which, he reflected, was probably exactly why the Militia insisted on these sorts of tours for its officer wannabes.

TEN DAYS LATER, THE *CLOUDRUNNER* BEGAN TO SLOWLY DROP OUT OF the sky toward Seije Reservoir. Once, a long time before, Erik had visited the city as a junior journeyman smith. At the time, he'd thought the massive reservoir, fed from the Selt River via an aqueduct, was solely for water storage.

Now he saw the other use of it, the one that explained why there was a dock on a purely artificial and landlocked lake. The skyship slowly drifted down out of the sky and splashed down in the middle of the reservoir. The gentle breeze drifting across the northern plains was more than sufficient to slowly carry the ship into the dock, where a single other skyship already rested.

Just off from the dock on the reservoir Erik could see the cleared landing areas and pens for the draconan traders. A handful of greens and a pair of black dragons were the only lizards in the pens today, which likely meant that there were traders around but no major caravans.

"Tarverro!" Tolars exclaimed, coming up behind Erik and clapping him on the shoulder. "You saw the rota, right?"

"Yes, Sergeant," Erik replied. "My squad is escorting our oak consignment to its destination."

"Why aren't you in armor?" the platoon sergeant asked.

Erik grinned and slid his thick oilskin cloak off his shoulders, revealing the light sky-steel chain mail he wore concealed underneath it. "I'm supposed to be joining Ennie and the others in a minute," he said calmly. "My shield is there."

The older Sergeant snorted. "Not bad, youngster," he replied. "You almost had me going there, thinking you'd forgotten."

"Not today, at least," Erik replied. He glanced out over the city stretching out beyond the reservoir. "It's been a few years since I've been here, but it shouldn't be too much of a stretch to find my way around."

"Good," Tolars replied. His serious tone drew Erik's gaze, and he faced the *septon* Tarverro squarely. "I'm going to give you a warning the rest of the men don't really need, Tarverro," the Sergeant told him. "Aeradi are tolerated, even welcome in some places, in the city. But..."

"Some people have an issue with half-bloods no matter where you are," Erik finished for him. "Like I said, I've been here before. I'll deal."

"Good," Tolars repeated. "Now, why aren't you with your squad?" he demanded.

Erik grinned at the older man and went to join his marines.

EVEN SPIES DID PAPERWORK. IN CAPTAIN BRANE'S OPINION, Dracona's Red Dragon spies-cum-assassins did far *too* much paperwork. Officially, the office he worked in belonged to a trade factor that dealt heavily with the draconans. Officially, Brane Kelsdaver *was* that trade factor and a Hellitian subject.

He knew better, however, and a raid by the Hellitian Royal Guard on the office would have turned up a lot of incriminating evidence to prove that belief wrong. However, his superiors insisted on written reports, so he, and his men, wrote reports. Brane collated those reports and then shipped them home hidden in various crates of trade goods.

Nonetheless, the draconan *hated* paperwork, so when his door burst open, he almost welcomed the interruption. On the other hand, *no one* was supposed to burst into his room like that, so by the time

Dairn stumbled to a stop, Brane had the crystal rod out and aimed at the agent.

The tiny rod of crystal didn't look like much, but it was a deadly weapon. Functioning on a similar principle as the much larger crysbows used by the aeradi and some draconans, it unleashed a bolt of lightning when used. Of course, unlike the larger weapons, it didn't recharge and was useful for only a handful of bolts—rarely more than three—but it was deadly and easily hidden.

It was the weapon of an assassin or a spy, and Brane Kelsdaver was both. So was Dairn, who should have *known* better. The agent froze at the sight of the tiny weapon and raised his hands.

"Peace, sir, I didn't mean to interrupt," he said apologetically.

The rod vanished back into its wrist sheath, and Brane locked his glare—almost as deadly a weapon—on the agent. "What was so Firesburnt important?" he demanded.

"We've found Tarverro, sir!" Dairn reported.

Brane shook his head at the agent, remembering their previous problem with the half-aeraid. He wanted the man dead, but he'd left Vidran months earlier, and an aeradi *septon* was far beyond their reach. "We found him months ago," he observed pointedly.

"I mean we've found him *here*," Dairn replied.

"*What?*" the Red Dragon commander demanded.

"He's aboard the skyship that landed this morning," Dairn told him. "Working as a marine sergeant—one of their blooding tours, it seems. One of our agents—Korian—spotted him leaving the ship escorting a consignment in town. The agent was one of the men who tracked what happened to Rade, so he recognized the man."

"Where is Tarverro now?" Brane asked.

"Still heading in-town, so far as we know," the junior agent replied. "Korian came back here—he needs authorization to do anything more than observe, and he figures he can intercept Tarverro on the way back."

Brane grabbed a piece of paper and dipped his pen into the inkwell. He scribbled an authorization on the paper and handed it to Dairn.

"Korian is cleared to carry out the kill," he said firmly. "Tell him to do it as quietly as possible but to make certain of the kill."

"Understood!"

The merchant who had, for whatever reason, ordered twenty tons of seasoned Sky Isle oak, had sent ox-drawn wagons and several of his own guards to collect it. Nonetheless, Erik and his men had been assigned to escort it to the man's warehouse.

Though Erik didn't really think anyone was going to try to steal four wagons full of logs, he did understand why his men were being sent despite the merchant's guards: there were only two locals. Neither of them was armored, and they were only armed with batons. No one might be inclined to steal wood, but just the sixteen oxen pulling the wagons were worth more protection than that.

Street protection duty was straightforward. Erik split his squad into its two lances and put one on each side of the wagons, with the two locals out in front. His men marched in good order, with their swords sheathed but their shields held firmly against their bodies.

The journey through the city passed without any major event. Even non-casual thieves were going to be deterred by the sight of ten professional soldiers, and casual thieves had no interest in oxen and loads of lumber.

Seije was a human city and, as such, one would have thought would have had taller buildings than an aeradi city, if only since the *people* were taller. The facts were quite to the contrary, however. The only good thing to be said for the city was that it had good sanitation, which was true of most human cities, at least. It lacked the crystal towers of the sky cities, and even the stone buildings that made up most of the city seemed to rarely rise above two stories.

When they reached the merchant's warehouse and offices, and Erik found himself expecting the offices to be in a crystal tower, he realized just how thoroughly he'd fallen into aeradi perceptions, even with his short time among them. The three-story stone-and-plaster building that held the offices would have been quite impressive to him before he'd gone to Newport.

Shortly after they arrived and men began offloading the cargo, a short-ish—for a human—man came bustling out of the offices. He was wearing what looked like normal working clothes, but an ermine cloak swirled around them, providing a workable combination of comfort and elegance.

"You escorted the cargo here?" the man asked without preamble.

"Yes, sir," Erik replied. "That is Captain Demond's policy."

"So I see, Sergeant..." The man trailed off, leaving Erik a space to fill.

"Tarverro, sir," Erik gave him. "We didn't really expect someone to try to steal lumber, but it's better safe than sorry."

"Indeed, Sergeant," the merchant agreed. "My name is Harrin Dolst. If you're prepared to wait a few moments, the payment is ready, and it makes more sense for you to escort it back now than return later, doesn't it?"

Erik inclined his head. "Of course, Master Dolst."

The merchant quickly returned with a small chest. "The agreed-upon price," he told Erik, "plus a fifty-mark payment for the escort."

"That's not necessary, sir," Erik told him, quite truthfully.

"Nevertheless, it's been added," Dolst told him. "It would be *such* an effort to count it back out again, so save me the effort and take it, eh?" he finished with a wink.

Erik shrugged and nodded. "If you insist, sir."

"Oh, I do, I do," Dolst replied. "Pass my regards on to Captain Rakeus, Lord Tarverro."

Erik, who was turning to leave, snapped back around to meet the merchant's gaze as the man gave him the courtesy title due a high-ranking member of the *epti*. All Dolst did was grin at him and gesture him on his way.

RETURNING TO THE SHIP WITH A CHEST CONTAINING THE BETTER part of a thousand gold coins made Erik far more nervous than traveling out with twenty tons of wood had. He had two of the men sling their shields and carry the chest, and surrounded them with a wall of ready shields.

They made it through the main city without incident, however, and Erik began to relax. As they approached the dock, a beggar hailed them, asking for a coin. Erik eyed the man, noting that he was missing an arm.

Checking his men to be sure he wouldn't be missed, Erik chose to give in to his charitable impulse. He crossed the street and took several small silver coins from his purse.

"Here, friend," he told the beggar, dropping the coins into the man's bowl. "Get yourself a room and a hot meal."

The beggar looked up at him and nodded quickly. "Thank you, sir, thank you," he said, his voice hoarse.

Erik nodded and turned away from the man, half-embarrassed by the man's grateful response to his small gift. He was halfway to his men when a hoarse shout rang out from behind him.

"Look out!" The beggar's shout reacted directly with Erik's instincts, and he dove to the ground, barely dodging the crossbow bolt that shot through where his chest had been and skittered across the cobblestones.

Erik surged back to his feet, his shield unslung and sword half-drawn, searching for any further attack. None came, and he turned to the beggar to thank the man.

The man was gone, which wasn't surprising. He'd done more than Erik could have expected in warning him. He slowly re-sheathed his sword and looked up at Enviers as the Corporal approached him, holding the bolt in his hand.

"Just the one shot, sir," Ennie told him. "But see the head?"

Erik did. The steel of the tip was discolored, a dull bluish color. "What is it?"

"I can't be rightly sure," the Corporal admitted, "but..."

"It's poison," Tolars said flatly, eyeing the bolt sitting on the table. "Heartsbane is the name of the stuff, though I've no idea where it comes from. You can find it almost anywhere if you know where to look and who to speak to."

"How bad is it?" Erik asked.

"Bad," the platoon sergeant said, looking up at the Lieutenant who sat silently at the other side of the table. "A crossbow bolt would probably manage to nick you, even through that fancy sky-steel mail of yours."

"And just a nick would have killed you," Albiers said flatly. "I saw it once, a long time ago." He didn't elaborate.

"It wasn't a robbery attempt," Erik said questioningly. "They wouldn't have shot at just me and wouldn't have fled after one shot."

"No, the pattern is wrong," Tolars agreed. "So, tell me, Tarverro, who'd you piss off badly enough to want to kill you the last time you were in Seije?"

"Nobody," Erik protested.

Albiers raised his hand, forestalling any further comments. "Tolars isn't implying anything, Tarverro; he's just playing fun." He glared at the platoon sergeant. "Not everyone is in the mood for your humor, Jola, after they've been shot at."

"Sorry, sir," Tolars replied. "Sorry, Sergeant," he repeated to Erik, who realized that Jola must be the platoon sergeant's first name.

"For whatever reason, somebody just took a shot at you with a poisoned arrow, Tarverro," Albiers said grimly. "I don't know why, but I'm afraid I'm going to have to suggest that you stay aboard ship while we're in Seije."

"No complaint from me," Erik replied. "What about the bolt?"

"Tolars?" Albiers asked.

"I'll take it ashore with me and burn it," the platoon sergeant replied. "Only way I know of to deal with this crap."

"Only way I know of as well," Albiers admitted. "Do it." He turned to Erik. "Tarverro..."

"I'll stay on the ship, don't worry," Erik promised. "I *like* breathing, thanks."

"Good. I don't need the death of one of my sergeants on my hands, let alone a bloody *septon*," Albiers told him.

∿

WHEN BRANE EXITED HIS OFFICE THAT EVENING, HE FOUND KORIAN sitting at the table in the antechamber, a crossbow lying on the table in front of him. The junior agent, only recently initiated into the ranks of the Red Dragon cult, looked annoyed.

"Well?" Brane demanded.

"Someone spotted me as I took the shot," Korian admitted, disgruntled. "He had just enough warning to dodge."

The Red Dragon Captain nodded slowly. He'd suspected as much. The agent had failed, so he'd been unwilling to come in and tell Brane, but he knew Brane needed to know, so he'd procrastinated out there until Brane arrived. Harmless, if rather annoying.

"Complete failure?" he asked, quietly. Korian was junior, new, and young. Overly harsh criticism could do a great deal of damage.

"Complete," the agent said flatly. "I used heartsbane, so even a *touch* should have done it, but I didn't even get that."

"What's done is done, Korian," Brane told him. "You did well in spotting him."

The agent nodded slightly, accepting the slight reduction of his failure. Brane eyed him for a moment, then decided with a jerk of his head.

"Since you know which ship he's on, find its schedule," the Captain ordered. "If he comes off the ship again, tell us, and we'll arrange a warmer welcome for him."

Korian inclined his head and vanished. Brane looked up from where the youth had been sitting and found Dairn standing against the wall.

"If I'd failed like that, you'd have ripped my head off," Dairn observed.

"*You* are a veteran agent with over a dozen kills behind you," Brane told him. "Korian was initiated a bare year ago and has only been given kill orders twice—he succeeded quite well the first time, and coming down on him hard would have ruined the potential."

Dairn shrugged. "Do you really think Tarverro'll come off the ship?" he asked.

"He should," Brane replied. "He has duties, and he'll want his shore leave. He doesn't know we're hunting him, so he has no reason to expect a repeat." The Red Dragon Captain paused, examining the crossbow sitting on the table. "We rushed the attack this time, as he was headed back aboard ship. Next time, we won't be so foolish."

AFTER SPENDING THEIR REMAINING TWO DAYS IN SEIJE COOPED UP aboard the ship, Erik wasn't so sure that it had been a good idea. Nonetheless, he kept his promise and stayed aboard, taking the time to hone his skill with his new bow, which was still almost entirely unfamiliar to him.

Finally, on the third day, the last of the thousand or so tons of grain they were loading there had come aboard, and the *Cloudrunner* lifted off from the reservoir. The skyship followed the Seije Aqueduct south to the Selt River, then turned west along the river, headed to Yun, the second city of the Kingdom of Ell.

On the second day out of Seije, Albiers called a Sergeants' meeting just before the first of their evening exercises. He gave no reason for it until all eight of the ship's noncoms were settled into his office, watching him expectantly.

"Gentlemen, thank you for coming," he told them. Coming early to the exercises had meant that first platoon's Sergeants, who had afternoon exercises that day, had had to eat quickly. "However, there is an issue we need to raise.

"As you all know by now, Sergeant Tarverro was attacked in Seije," he said grimly. "While I would like to presume that this was due to some action of his in his previous time in the city, that appears unlikely. Which means whoever attacked him either had sufficient reach to know that he was on this ship and where it was going, or was generally attacking this ship."

Erik grimaced. He'd been trying not to really think about the implications of the attack, as they were grim. Either someone with a long arm was hunting *him*, specifically, or someone with a somewhat shorter arm was hunting people of this ship.

"In either case, it's *possible* that we may be attacked in the remaining cities of the voyage," Albiers said grimly. "While there isn't much we can really do to be more prepared than we are, we do need to be aware of the possibility. I will emphasize this again: *no one* goes off the ship unarmed. Yun and North Hold are friendly territory, but nonetheless. Consider nowhere safe until we're back at dock in Newport, clear?"

The Sergeants, including Erik, all nodded their acquiescence. Albiers eyed them grimly and returned the nod. "Hopefully, I'm being unnecessarily paranoid, but I'd rather be paranoid and wrong than optimistic and dead."

"It's confirmed, sir," Dairn admitted unwillingly. "The *Cloudrunner* sailed this morning."

"Salshar curse him," Brane swore. "What is the man, a Fires-burnt turtle? He pulled his head in and we never even burning *saw* him."

The junior agent, wisely, said nothing, and Brane's tirade faded to silence as he regarded the view out of his window. Finally, the Red Dragon reached down onto his desk and picked up a single piece of paper.

He glanced down the simple list of numbers and names—dates and cities. "They're headed to Yun next," Brane said flatly.

"Yes, sir," Dairn said solidly.

"Send a message..." Brane began to say, and then trailed off. "Burn that," he suddenly snarled. "Talk to the Skyborne detachment that's in town. I need a dragon and a rider."

"You're pursuing him, sir?" Dairn asked.

"The only way to be certain it's done right is to do it myself," the Red Dragon Captain replied. "You're in command until I get back, understood?"

"Yes, sir," Dairn replied, his face a mask.

The trip west along the Selt to Yun took five days. Five days in which Erik trained with his squad and worried about what awaited them in the city. Realizing that his archery wasn't up to the standard of the rest of the ship's marines, he dragooned Enviers into providing him with extra training outside the normal time frame of the squad's drill.

When they landed in the riverside reservoir at Yun, however, Albiers informed the men that the merchant they were dealing with was providing guards for the wagons carrying the goods into the city. The *Cloudrunner* would be providing a single squad to help supervise loading and unloading and maintaining its own security, but that left a full platoon free for shore leave.

First Platoon had the first day's duty, and there was some good-natured grumbling among Erik's squad, assigned to babysit the stevedores off-loading the cargo, as the men of Second Platoon scrambled past them into the city.

Erik and Ennie reminded the grumblers that they'd have their own chance tomorrow, and made sure the men were paying attention to their duties. Then Erik took the time to go meet his counterpart, the man commanding the platoon of men from Yun.

The men were well turned out, he noted. All forty of the men were apparently light infantry, skirmishers. While their main weapons appeared to be the draconan-style shortswords at their waists, each man had a small buckler—quite unlike the draconan shield—and a bundle of javelins slung over their shoulder.

"You would be Sergeant Tarverro, I presume?" the commander of the platoon greeted him, offering a hand in the human greeting. "Lieutenant Hiakhan, Royal Skirmishers."

Erik took the man's hand and returned the handshake. "You're royal troops?" he asked, surprised.

Hiakhan nodded. "The grain's being purchased for the royal granaries," he admitted. "The last harvest was terrible, and the King had to open the war reserves to make certain there was enough food to go around. Now the merchants are screaming at the cost of replenishing the reserves," he added bitterly. "I think they'd have rather we'd let the people starve than make them pay the bill for replenishing the reserves."

"They may not have thought it through that far," Erik told him with a throwaway gesture. "Or maybe they think that 'war reserves' should only be built up when war is expected," he added with a grin.

The Ellian officer shrugged. "War is rarely expected," he grunted. "And even when it isn't, the reserves are also *meant* for things like feeding the people when the harvests fail."

"True," Erik admitted, glancing across at the grunting men unloading the cargo. "We're just here to make sure nobody makes off with a wagon or three of grain, though."

Hiakhan gave a grin of his own. "They'd have to make it by both of our men, and yours don't seem too bad for a bunch of little boys."

Erik gave the man a cautioning glance. "I wouldn't let them hear that, if I were you," he warned. "They may not like it."

The officer raised his hands defensively. "No insult intended, *Sergeant*," he said, his voice adding a slight edge to the last word.

"None taken," Erik said, his voice slipping a notch. "I'll go make sure my 'little boys' prevent anyone slipping by yours," he finished, turning away from the officer.

BRANE ARRIVED IN YUN STRAPPED IN BEHIND A COURIER FLYER ON A smallish brown dragon. While smallish, the brown was still bigger than a green and could manage to carry two men with ease.

He slid off the dragon clumsily. While he'd flown dragonback before, he hadn't done so in quite a while, and he lacked the calluses to prevent saddle sores. He winced as he landed, and surveyed the dragon yard. There was no one there to meet him, but that wasn't a surprise.

"Thanks for the lift, Skyborne," Brane said to the young flyer who was dismounting with the bags of messages. The Skyborne, he noticed enviously, had no problems dismounting the beast.

"Not a worry, sir," the youth replied. "That's why they use browns for this duty."

Brane nodded his farewell to the flyer and walked out of the yard. While he knew where the Red Dragon headquarters in Yun were, it would be bad tradecraft for him to head right there.

Besides, he didn't need to. Perhaps a minute had passed after he'd left the yard before a voice spoke from behind his shoulder.

"Welcome to Yun, Captain Brane," the stranger said to him. "We have located the ship as you requested and have been watching it. Would you care to explain why?"

From the sound of the voice, Captain Delk, the Yun commander, had come personally. Brane was senior to the man, but they fell into different chains of command—different nations, to be exact.

"There's a man aboard the ship who was responsible for the death of a Red Dragon," Brane whispered, knowing without even looking that Delk was close enough to hear what he said.

"I see," Delk replied. "Kill authorization?"

"Mine," Brane said simply. "It is policy," he added.

"Indeed" was all Delk said.

"Do you have the resources?" Brane asked.

"We have a group we've been cultivating," Delk told him. "Street gang, but we've taught them a few tricks—enough for them to cover one of ours as he makes the kill."

"Reliable?"

"Enough," the Yun officer replied. "By gold, if nothing else."

"Very well."

"The target?" Delk asked.

"Half-aeraid named Erik *septon* Tarverro," Brane told him. "Marine Sergeant aboard the *Cloudrunner*."

"So, aeraid features but taller?"

"He should be in uniform with rank insignia, which will make identification easier," Brane told him.

"It should at that," Delk agreed. "Done. We'll make the kill."

DESPITE THE MAN'S CAREFULLY HIDDEN PREJUDICE, ERIK WAS forced to admit by the end of the day that Hiakhan was both competent and had no intention of letting his men slide just because their duty seemed light. Half of his platoon accompanied each group of grain wagons out, and then brought them back.

By the time night fell and Erik's squad returned aboard ship, most of the cargo for Yun had been off-loaded. He estimated that by noon the next day, they'd start loading the cargo for North Hold, but, fortunately, his men had the day off.

"Hey, Sarge," Ennie called out as he was standing to leave the mess hall. "You know much 'bout Yun?"

"Not really," Erik was forced to admit.

"How about I show you 'round the city tommorrer?" the Corporal asked. "I've spent a lot of time on runs coming through here; I know most of the sights to hit."

Erik hesitated. Whoever had attacked him in Seije might take him wandering around Yun as an open opportunity to take a second shot, and he didn't really want to put anyone else in the target zone. On the other hand, he really didn't know Yun at all.

"You can't let the sonbitches keep you down, Sarge," Ennie told him. "You need to get out; you can't spend all your time on this boat."

Erik hesitated for a moment more and then nodded. "Sure, why not?"

Whatever else being toured around the city by Ennie might be, he doubted it would be boring, and he'd had enough boredom stuck aboard ship for three days in Seije.

To Erik's surprise—he'd been half-expecting a tour of the brothels and taverns of the city—Ennie took him to the main district of the city, where government buildings, merchant-house offices and temples to the gods competed to be the most extravagant structure in sight.

The Corporal took Erik down the main street, pointing out various features of the marble and stone buildings in his pithy dialect and demonstrating an in-depth knowledge of architecture that would have astounded most of those who knew the aeradi noncom. *Erik* was certainly surprised when Ennie pointed out the difference between the "draconan-style" pillars on a temple to Fiehr, and the "Elmatian-style" pillars on the offices of a merchant who dealt with the southwest corner of Cevran.

From the small smile underneath Ennie's near-constant stream of information that would have done any professional tour guide proud, the Corporal knew just how much he was surprising his noble superior.

As they drew even with the massive temples of Edril and Hydra that faced each other across the street, just short of the city's Council Hall, Erik finally gave in to his temptation.

"How do you know all this?" he asked the non-com.

Ennie shrugged. "You go through every sonbitch city on Cevran, Sarge, you see every sonbitch thing they build. Listen to the sonbitch tour guides, 'member what they say and think about it, and you'll be surprised what you learn." He eyed Erik and grinned. "And me dad was an architect, which helps," he admitted.

"I see," Erik replied. "I think I'm *still* impressed," he added.

"Thankee, Sarge," Ennie said, stopping and looking over at the temple to Hydra, the god of water. The major gods of the humans, who claimed the blood of earth and water as some mystics reckoned things, were Hydra, god of water, and Edril, god of earth. Hence, those two temples were the biggest in the city and, while matching each other in size, clearly tried to outdo each other in opulence.

"I know a woman who stays in 'ere," Ennie told Erik, gesturing toward the water god's temple. "She's a priestess, a blind one, and some say crazy as they come, but she sees the future, or so it's said." The noncom shrugged. "I don't believe in no fate, but it's decent fun anyways."

Erik considered for a moment, and then shrugged. "Sure, why not? Let's see what she has to say."

Ennie grinned, leading the way through the massive pillars topped with stone carved to resemble waves, into the temple. Just inside the huge wooden doors, which looked like they'd never been closed and probably couldn't be, a blue-robed priest met them.

"Can I help you gentlemen?" he asked them, his voice pitched softly against the gentle tinkling of the fountains inside the temple.

"We're looking fer Eselda," Ennie told him.

"The prophetess does not see just anyone," the priest told them in a lofty tone, looking down his nose at the aeradi noncom.

Erik laid his hand on the shorter man's shoulder, preventing him from acting, and stepped forward to look the priest in the eye. Among humans, he was short, but somehow that didn't stop the priest taking a step backward.

"My name," he said softly, "is Lord Erik *septon* Tarverro of Newport. Is that sufficiently 'someone' for me to meet the prophetess?"

The priest obviously recognized the title *septon*, from how he blanched horribly. "I will see if she's available," the man squeaked, and vanished back into the temple.

"See, Ennie?" Erik murmured. "There are uses for noble titles after all."

"I'll not argue with you, Sarge," the noncom admitted.

The priest returned shortly. "The priestess Eselda will see you," he said, gesturing for them to follow him.

The pair of aeradi noncoms followed the priest through the pure white corridors of the temple, many of which had small waterways tinkling down along the sides. The path they followed took them deep into the heart of the temple to a single, unadorned door.

The priest stopped at the door. "Go in," he told them. "I will wait here to guide you back out."

Erik nodded to the priest and opened the door. The other side seemed quite opulently decorated for a moment, but then he realized that the wall hangings and vast numbers of cushions covering every piece of stonework were probably necessary for a blind woman. Her fellow priests clearly didn't want her hurting herself.

The woman at the center of the room looked odd to Erik's eyes. Her hair was long and white, and drawn into a long braid that exposed ears that were very clearly pointed. Despite the ears, she was short, no taller than the aeradi at his side.

"Welcome, Lord Tarverro," she whispered, her voice gravelly with age, and turned to face him. She bore the arched cheekbones of a draconan or aeradi, and that made no sense. To serve there she had to be human, yet she had the marks of every race he'd ever met.

His confusion at her appearance became meaningless as her eyes met his. They were milky white, some sort of substance having covered them long ago, yet they seemed to hold his gaze for a long moment.

Then the moment ended, and her smile of greeting turned to a snarl. "*You!*" she hissed, spitting at him in fury.

"*Get out,*" she snarled. "Father of shadows, harbinger of dark fates!"

Erik backed away. "I'm sorry, I don't know what I've done."

"Nothing to me, but to my children and my children's children," Eselda snarled. "Hero and conqueror, *your seed shall break the earth and set Him free.*"

The ancient priestess grabbed a cushion and threw it across the room. Showing a surprisingly good aim and throw for a blind old woman, it hit him in the face, hard, and he beat a hasty retreat, quickly followed by Ennie.

The priest met them outside the door. "What did you do?" he demanded, glaring at Erik.

"I don't know," the half-aeraid snapped back. "She just looked at me and started screaming."

The priest swallowed. "She saw something in your future, then," he said simply. "Something she didn't like."

Erik looked back at the simple door, deep in the heart of a temple. "Nothing she said made sense," he replied. "I'm barely a soldier, let alone a 'hero and conqueror.' I have no children, no wife. How am I a 'father of shadow'?"

"The words of prophecy are rarely clear," the priest told him. "You have been blessed—and cursed—beyond many men. Few are those whose futures Eselda sees in any detail. Few indeed."

With a final glance at the door, Erik gestured the priest to lead them out. If only a few had futures the priestess saw in detail and that was her reaction when she did, he could have quite happily avoided being one of them.

WONDERING JUST WHAT THE PROPHETESS HAD MEANT BY HER WORDS distracted Erik as they left the temple. Ennie attempted to cheer him up by continuing his litany about the architecture and buildings surrounding them, but failed miserably.

Bare minutes after they left the temple, however, a commotion in front of them managed to penetrate even Erik's distraction, especially when he realized the men at the heart of it were aeradi.

"What the hell?" Erik demanded aloud, and broke into a run for the knot of aeradi soldiers gathered in the middle of the street with drawn blades.

On reaching them, he found half a dozen aeradi, several of them with blood on their drawn swords, gathered around a seventh on the floor. The seventh was wearing Sergeant's bars—was, in fact, Sergeant Gared, the commander of First Platoon's Third Squad. The aeradi were all *Cloudrunner* men.

"What the hell is this?" he repeated as he took in the scene. Then he got a closer look at Gared and realized why the man was on the ground: several nasty wounds gaped across his chest and left arm.

Before anyone else could respond, Erik took a glance around the street. He didn't see anyone who could have attacked them, but the way the men were gathered around, an attack could get through. "This isn't a street party, men," he snapped before any of them could begin to reply. "Perimeter, close. Slope arms, Fires burn it!"

Perimeter, close was a specific formation that had been trained into the men. Despite their shock, the men quickly fell into it, sloping their drawn swords back against their shoulders as they faced outward, watching the crowd.

Erik knelt by Gared, joining the man's squad corporal, who was dressing the wounds with cloth torn from Gared's uniform. None of the wounds looked immediately life-threatening, but the aeraid had lost a lot of blood.

Worse, as Erik knelt, Gared started coughing, a horrible fit that spewed blood across his hands. *None* of the wounds touched his lungs, which made that bad. *Very* bad.

"Ennie, get to the Temple of Edril," Erik said distractedly. The temple was just across from the Temple of Hydra they'd just left. "Bring a healer. At sword-point, if necessary."

"Yes, sir," the Corporal replied, and took off at a run.

Erik turned to Gared's Corporal. "What happened?" he demanded.

"Some kind of street thugs, gang of them jumped us," Gared told him between coughing fits, overriding his man. "I'm not that bad hurt, just flesh wounds," he continued trying to rise.

"*Flesh wounds* aren't causing him to cough up blood, Sarge," the Corporal told Erik softly.

"I agree," Erik said, helping the man press Gared back to the ground. "There's a healer on the way; stay down, you Fires-burnt fool," he hissed at the older sergeant. "You've probably been poisoned, and if you move, you'll only help it spread."

The Corporal had done all that could be done to bind the wounds. Erik left the man to it, standing and looking for the healer.

As he did so, Ennie returned with a brown-robed man with a shaved head. The priest took one look at the aeradi soldiers and snapped, "I'm a healer; let me through."

"Let him through," Erik repeated, his tone an order, and the soldiers opened a gap for the priest.

The healer brusquely pushed Erik aside and knelt by the man. "How recent?" he asked.

"Fifteen minutes, maybe," the Corporal replied. "He keeps coughing, but none of the wounds touched his lung."

The priest touched Gared's chest and closed his eyes. "*Dragonshit*," he swore. "Cathnicket."

"What?" Erik asked.

"Poison," he said grimly. "A nasty one—not the worst, not by far—but bad. Kills the lungs, slow for a poison, *fast* by any other standard." The priest glanced at the Corporal, Erik and the half-dozen armed men. "I need space," he said firmly. "This man may yet die, for all that I can do."

"Open the perimeter," Erik ordered. "Give the healer room."

The aeradi spread out, leaving the healer room to work while still keeping a clear space open around their sergeant. Their dark looks and bare steel kept passersby at bay but drew more official attention. The healer had barely closed his eyes and gone to work when a squad of the City Guard arrived.

The Guards eyed the aeradi troopers warily. They had twice the marines' numbers, but they were only lightly armed and armored. The aeradi marines looked far more dangerous than they were being paid to tangle with.

Leaving Gared to the healer and the two Corporals, Erik strode to meet the Guards. "I am Sergeant Erik *septon* Tarverro, off the *Cloudrunner*," he told them.

"Sergeant Lors Dhan," the squad commander introduced himself. "We received word of an altercation here. Do you know what's going on?"

"One of my fellow sergeants was set upon by thugs," Erik told the man. "Fortunately, several of his squad members were with him and the gang was driven off. However, Sergeant Gared was wounded, and at least one of the knives was poisoned. Cathnicket, according to the healer."

"*Cathnicket?*" the sergeant demanded, his face growing cold as stone.

"That's what he says," Erik confirmed.

The Guard nodded slowly and turned to his men. "Sweep the street," he ordered. "If there's *any* trail, find them."

He turned back to Erik as his men spread out, his face grim. "Cathnicket, Sergeant Tarverro, is a plant that grows *only* up near the northern coast of Ell," he said flatly. "We grow it for medicinal purposes, but it is very, *very* controlled, as while the seeds are medicinal, the *leaves* can be used to make a deadly poison. There shouldn't be *any* of it in circulation, even in the criminal community."

"I see," Erik said. "That is what the priest said, though."

"I don't disbelieve you," Dhan replied. "It simply makes things far more complicated. Did you see which way they fled?"

Erik shook his head. "I wasn't here, but you're welcome to question Gared's men. The healer gave the impression he'd be a while."

Unfortunately, Dahn and Erik's questioning of the men turned up nothing. The attackers had apparently just appeared out of the crowd. As soon as Gared went down, they'd grabbed their wounded and vanished back into it.

Clearly, they'd been after the sergeant. Which was a disturbing thought in Erik's head. Either someone was systematically trying—and so far, failing—to take out the *Cloudrunner*'s marine sergeants, or someone was specifically after one of them.

If someone had been after the squad leaders in general, Erik was sure there would have been more attacks. There was a specific target, and he couldn't help noticing that Gared was wearing his Sergeant's triple chevrons. If the thugs had simply been told that their target was, say, a tall aeradi sergeant, they would likely have targeted the other aeraid.

It could easily be a case of mistaken identity, with the real target someone else. Given that someone had *already* tried to kill him on the voyage, Erik couldn't help but feel that the target was probably him.

"We have nothing," Dhan told Erik finally. "Someone is attacked in the middle of *my* city, and I have *nothing*," he snarled.

Erik raised a hand, forestalling further comment from the Guard as the priest-healer approached.

"Your man will be fine," he told Erik. "He was lucky—only one of the daggers that cut him was poisoned. If the rest had been"—the healer shrugged fatalistically—"I would never have been able to save him."

"Thank you," Erik told the man softly, pressing a handful of gold crowns—*sept* Tarverro's money, really, but well worth it—into his palm.

"I can't take this," the priest replied, offering the coins back. "It was my duty to Edril to heal those in need."

Erik shook his head. "Consider it a donation to the temple, then," he replied. "Gared's life is worth it and more." He paused. "What is your name?" he asked, finally.

"Edelnor Katel," the priest replied, bowing his head. "I have dealt with the poison and his wounds," he told Erik, "but he should rest for at least several days, more if possible."

Erik nodded. "We will be leaving here tomorrow. We'll make certain he rests on our voyage west."

"Good," Edelnor replied. "I take my leave of you now. May Lord Edril keep you and bless you."

Erik bowed his head to the man in response and watched him leave. As the priest continued down the street back to his temple, Erik turned to the Guard.

"I regret that we cannot help you," he told the man.

"You should not apologize," Dhan growled. "It is *we* who should be concerned. It is our duty to prevent attacks like this happening."

"You do all you can," Erik replied calmly. "The gods and the Fates decide the rest."

"Aye, that's true enough," Dhan returned, "but I am still concerned. We shall do the best we can to track these thugs down so that they bother no one else."

"I'd thank you for that," Erik told him. "If you have no more questions for the men, though, may we return to our ship? We need to get Gared into a bed, I believe."

"Yes, of course," Dhan agreed. "Good luck, Sergeant."

"And to you."

THE MEN OF GARED'S SQUAD WERE JUSTIFIABLY PARANOID AFTER THE attack on their sergeant, which suited Erik just fine. He quite happily ignored the drawn blades of the half-dozen marines and their effect on the crowd around them. He preferred terrifying innocent people to being caught unawares again.

The arrival at the loading dock gate of eight aeradi, half of them carrying a wounded ninth and the other half with drawn blades, caused a problem. The royal troops, Hiakhan's men, swarmed around the squad and reacted the way trained soldiers react to drawn blades: they drew their own.

Erik, however, was not in the mood to deal with Hiakhan's men's offended sensibilities. "Back, Fires burn you!" he snapped. "We have a wounded man we need to get to the ship."

The Ellian men, many of whom recognized Erik from his guard duty the day before, drew back. The squad commander appeared about to wave Erik through, drawn blades or no drawn blades, when Hiakhan himself arrived.

"What is the meaning of this?" the officer demanded, drawing himself up furiously. "Carrying drawn blades in my city? Put up those blades *now*, or we'll put them up for you."

"Don't be stupider than the gods made you, Hiakhan," Erik snapped back. "I have a wounded man—wounded in your *precious* city —and I'm taking him to the ship. Get out of our way."

"Like Fires I will," the human officer replied. "Put your blades up and keep a Fires-burnt civil tongue in your mouth, half-blood."

"I'll put my blade up when I feel I can trust *your* city to guard my men," Erik snapped. "Since I've seen no sign of *that*, get out of my way."

"Why, you stinking little half-breed," Hiakhan snarled, his hand dropping to his sword.

Before the Ellian could do more than touch the hilt, Erik had crossed the intervening space, and his sword rested against Hiakhan's neck.

"Don't you bleeding *dare*," he hissed. "I have neither time nor patience for your games. Get your men out of our way!"

Hiakhan's men had reacted to Erik's move by drawing their own swords once more, and for a long moment, the air was filled with a lethal tension. Then Tolars, who had thankfully been checking on the squad currently guarding the dock, arrived.

"What in fire is going on here?" he demanded. "Erik, release him! The rest of you, sheathe your fucking swords!"

Unlike Hiakhan, Tolars, firstly, was the aeradi marines' superior and, secondly, had half a squad of aeradi troops behind him. Relaxing, slightly, in the presence of their fellows, the men slowly lowered their swords.

Erik merely released Hiakhan without sheathing his sword. "Sergeant, Sergeant Gared was wounded on the streets—and poisoned, with a drug I'm told is under *sole* control of the Ellian Royal Army. I am unprepared to trust his safety to anyone other than our own men."

"Well, our men are here now," Tolars told him bluntly. "Sheathe your sword."

Slowly, Erik obeyed the command. Tolars watched him until he did, and then turned his glare on Hiakhan.

"Get out of my sight," the aeradi platoon sergeant snapped. "Do your fucking job; don't get in the way of men doing theirs."

The Ellian officer looked like he was going to reply, clearly scandalized by being addressed like that by a noncom. Then his gaze flicked toward the heavily armored and armed aeradi marines behind Tolars, and the men with Erik. With a stiff nod, he turned and stalked away.

Once the Ellian troops were out of immediate earshot, Tolars turned back to his men. "Enviers, Yelt, Sorn," he said firmly, gathering the attention of the three Corporals, including the one commanding the men with him, "take the men and get Gared aboard ship. Erik," he continued before Erik could pretend that also applied to him, "stay here. You have some explaining to do."

Erik watched the men leave almost forlornly, knowing that he was going to get it.

Indeed, as soon as the aeradi men were also out of earshot, Tolars fixed him with a steely glare. "Congratulations," he said sardonically, "you just very nearly started a fight with our employer's men, not to mention that they're the Ellian *Royal fucking Army*. Care to explain yourself?"

"Lieutenant Hiakhan is a prejudiced prick," Erik said. It wasn't so much an excuse or an explanation as an observation.

"Yes, he is," the platoon sergeant agreed. "That doesn't mean taking off his head is a good idea, nor was that the reason you were so touchy. Full explanation, please. *Now*."

THOUGH BRANE HAD FOUND ROOMS IN THE CITY, HE WAS SPENDING most of his time at Captain Delk's safe house. He was there when the Red Dragon tasked with killing Tarverro was carried in by four of the thugs he'd recruited.

"He's wounded," the leader of the thugs said calmly as a half dozen Red Dragons went for weapons at their arrival. "I presumed you'd want to help him."

"Indeed," Delk said coldly. He jerked his head at his men. Two of them quickly took custody of the wounded Dragon and carried him deeper into the house.

"Your mission?" Brane demanded of the thugs.

"Your friend there," the thug replied, pointing his chin at where the wounded Dragon had gone, "got the *Sergeant* with his little knife—you know, the one with poison on it?"

"And?"

"One of my boys stuck around to watch, just to make sure," the thug told Brane, a smile of some sort hovering around his lips. "Someone *else* matching your description—without the Sergeant's bars—turned up and found a healer for the first. Dunno which of 'em was your man, but you didn't get neither of 'em."

"You *fools*," Brane hissed, his hand falling to the sword at his belt.

The thug turned to Delk, half-ignoring Brane. "Control your dog there, Delk," he said flatly. "I've got four dead and six wounded over this fight of yours. I *hope* you can pay up."

"You failed and you want your money?" Brane demanded, infuriated. "Whistle for it, *thug*."

"My name is Jair Temas," the human replied. "I may be a criminal, a murderer and a thief, but that wouldn't stop the Guard at least investigating if I told them the Dragons had a bunch of assassins here, would it?"

"Jair, we've dealt well together in the past," Delk said, with a warning glance at Brane. Brane may have been the man's senior, but Delk was the senior Dragon for Yun. "You don't mean that."

"If you don't find the gold for my men to see healers, I'll have no choice but to hope the Guard's feeling generous in their rewards," Jair replied.

Brane glared at the thug, but Delk merely nodded. "Very well." He gestured for one of his Dragons to pay the man.

"I have a better solution," Brane snarled, and before the other Red Dragon could react, snapped the crystal rod from his wrist sheath. Four blasts of lightning flashed out, and the humans collapsed, the stench of burning flesh filling the tavern.

Delk turned on Brane, but Brane caught the Red Dragon's hand with his sword half-drawn.

"They fucked up and quite possibly got the wrong man," he snarled. "That is the punishment for failing the Red Dragons. *You* know this."

"That he was healed was not their fault," Delk said, his voice calm as his hand struggled against Brane's iron grip.

"And it would have mattered if they'd attacked the right man!" Brane snarled.

"We didn't have enough information," Delk replied, his voice still somehow calm. "We expected the man to be in uniform—if he wasn't, we start to run short of ways of identifying him."

Brane said nothing, wordlessly snarling as he released the other draconan's hand, turning away.

"We should get another shot at him before he leaves," Delk told him. "If I can find any more tools," he added, eyeing the smoking corpses on his floor.

"Last time we took a shot at him, he vanished aboard ship," Brane replied. "The *bastard* seems to have a strong sense of self-preservation. Even if he comes off ship, he likely won't leave the area around their ship, and we can't touch him there."

"What now, Captain?" Delk asked, suddenly reasonable as he gestured for his men to remove the bodies, a slight sneer of distaste the last sign of any concern for their deaths.

"I find the next courier dragon to North Hold," Brane replied. "The sooner I get to North Hold, the more likely I can have an appropriate welcome prepared," he explained. "If you get the opportunity to take him, try," the Captain added, "but I doubt you will."

"Understood," Delk said flatly.

In the end, Erik explained events, as he knew them, three times. After hearing him, Tolars took him to Albiers, who promptly took both men to Captain Demond. The *Cloudrunner*'s Captain simply sat there as Erik explained both this attack and, at his superiors' suggestion, the previous attack in Seije.

Demond sat in silence for a long moment after the explanation was complete, and then looked up at Erik. "You know what the most likely target of these attacks is," he said calmly, a statement, not a question.

"The heirless *septon* Tarverro," Erik acknowledged. "But that would be a political goal of someone in Newport. Who there would have the reach for this?"

The Captain shrugged, glancing over at the other marines. "There are others who would rather *sept* Tarverro not rise again. Your grandfather's political foes, yes, but there are those external to the Realm as well."

"Your father, for example," Albiers noted, "distinguished himself in the last war against the draconans. Your ancestors have traditionally been advocates of a less...compromise-prone foreign policy. There are those who would not object to the turmoil caused by the death of a *septon*, either."

"I am the most junior *septon*, with neither great influence nor strong opinions yet," Erik objected. "Even if I died, my grandmother would just go back to running the *sept's* affairs."

"And when she died, *sept* Tarverro would end," Demond told him. "There are those, even outside Newport, who would see that happen, for old vengeance's sake if nothing else."

Erik said nothing, accepting their arguments if not their point. "What can we do?" he asked. "Assuming we're not going to just lock me up aboard ship, that is," he added, sardonically.

"Don't think for a second I'm not tempted," Albiers replied. "But really, there isn't that much more we can do. I'd say cancel all shore leaves, but..."

"We can't," Demond said flatly. "The crew would mutiny. I'm going to issue orders for all of our people to stick together. But you, Erik," he said firmly, "you only go off ship for duty purposes, with your squad. That's it. Understood?"

"Don't cut my squad out of the duty roster for my sake," Erik warned. "But yes, understood."

"We can't cut your squad out, worse luck," Tolars told him. "We're in North Hold next, and you *don't* move firepowder without a platoon escort. Not unless you're crazy, anyway."

Albiers nodded. "You should be safe moving in a platoon, but I don't want you going off the ship unless you're on duty—and with the whole platoon, preferably."

With a snort, Erik rose, but nodded his acceptance. "Very well. In any case, I should check that my squad has all made it back in one piece."

"Indeed," the Lieutenant replied. "Your squad is on deck guard duty tomorrow. We'll be leaving around noon, so it shouldn't be too hard on you."

"Understood, sir." He turned to Demond. "With your permission, Captain?"

"Yes, yes, dismissed," Demond told him.

THE MORNING DECK GUARD, LEANING AGAINST THE SHIP'S RAIL WITH bow, sword and shield to hand, went quickly. The only major point of interest Erik noted was that Hiakhan's part in their altercation seemed to have met with even less approval than his own: a different Royal platoon, under a different officer, supervised the loading of the ship.

The casks of wine, brandy and grapes were quickly loaded, and Erik's men watched as the aeradi crew and soldiers filed aboard. Finally, as the sun reached its zenith, the crew and the marines cast off the ropes binding the ship to the docks, and Captain Demond activated the crystals, raising the ship out of the water.

The journey to North Hold lasted eight days. For the first five, the skyship followed the westward line of the Selt River, wending its way along the southern border of the Kingdom of Ell.

Finally, on the evening of the fifth day, the ship's straight-line path left the river behind and began to cut across the northern plains. Beneath them it was mid-autumn, and the vast expanses of plain on which the Ellians raised both grain and horses were a patchwork of light brown mud and the dirty white of snow mixed with mud.

The few villages they saw were bundled up, preparing for northern Cevran's lethal winter storms to lock them in for the season. Those storms were one of the defining concerns of aeradi voyages, but the

Cloudrunner was sailing just early enough to avoid the worst of the winter blizzards.

For three days they sailed northwest across the plains, until they reached the foothills of the mountain chain known as the Spine of Cevran. They reached the foothills just after dawn on the eighth day, and by noon they were into the mountains.

Erik was on deck, finishing up with his squad's exercises, when the ship drew past the first set of mountains and into the mouth of the river valley. He stopped in place, the exercise forgotten as he stared off the front of the ship at the view in front of him.

The entire valley was cultivated, steep hills turned into functioning farmland by massive terracing earthworks. A road, ribbon-thin from this height but probably wide enough for four or five wagons abreast, wound its way up the valley, occasionally bridging the river that, over the millennia, had carved this slot into the ground.

Toward the end of the valley, the river split into a pair of canals that fed two artificial lakes, one on either side of the road, and then fed back into the river. The artificial lakes held the docks for the aeradi skyships.

The causeway through the lakes held the first set of defenses, a medium-sized fort set across it to bar passage, but clearly the designers hadn't expected it to hold against an enemy on its own. Just beyond the lakes, a massive curtain wall marked the edge of the surface portion of the dwarven city.

Behind the wall, the city crawled up narrower terraces built for houses instead of farms, until it reached the cliff face, where the river flowed out of a deep and narrow gorge through the mountains.

Where the city reached the mountains, it was clear that, whatever the original shape of the mountains, they'd been shaped by years—centuries—of dwarven work. The mountains on either side of the river had been cut flat, to create sheer vertical surfaces. Fortifications were cut into those sheer walls, providing defenders with nearly invulnerable positions.

Beneath the slits for the forts, each of the two mountain faces had a massive gate, both of them visible from the end of the valley, dug into it. Clearly, a large portion, if not the majority, of the hold was inside those mountains, buried underneath millions of tons of stone.

Between the lakes and the outer walls was what appeared to be the traders' section of the city, a vast sweep of tents and pens for both dragons and lesser beasts of burden. Large buildings that Erik presumed to be warehouses lined neat avenues through the throng of tents.

At the eastern end of the traders' area, half a dozen skyships bobbed at rest at stone docks built on the artificial lakes. The docks were easily capable of holding five times as many ships, but it was the end of autumn, and even the aeradi hesitated to sail with the storms coming.

The vast sweep of North Hold grew in their gaze as the *Cloudrunner* floated down the valley, slowly drifting down toward the more southern of the two lakes, where her sisters—and the men who'd paid for her cargo—awaited it.

BRANE WAS SURPRISED TO FIND HIMSELF MET AT THE COURIER PEN BY a uniformed draconan. If that was his contact, it was *horrible* trade-craft, and the dwarves disliked Dracona well enough without giving them additional reasons to do so.

Further inspection, however, revealed that the uniform bore the olive branch of the draconan diplomatic corps—presumably a mark of assignment to the embassy there. That meant the man might even have a legitimate reason to be meeting a supposed trader.

"Captain Brane, I presume," the draconan greeted him.

"I am," Brane replied. "You are?"

"Deris," the man said in his turn. "Trade attaché to the Black Mountain embassy in North Hold. Red Dragon," he added, more quietly.

So, the man did have a viable reason for meeting Brane. It was *still* horrible tradecraft. "Where are we heading?" Brane asked as the junior Dragon gestured for him to follow.

"The embassy," Deris replied. "Dwarven law insists that all draconans staying in the city for more than one night have to be put up there."

Brane had forgotten. He'd assumed he'd either find lodgings or be put up in a safe house. But... "Won't they watch our comings and goings?"

"That's the idea," Deris confirmed. "Of course, we've made... arrangements since then."

The Red Dragon Captain relaxed slightly. "You know my mission, I presume? Do you have any agents in place to carry it out?"

Deris nodded, slightly, as they turned a corner onto a broad avenue. "I know your mission. However, I don't have any agents to lend you."

"What do you mean?" Brane demanded, adding a touch of ice to his voice.

"I have no agents at all," Deris replied starkly. "Our kind stick out too much among the dwarves, and the short Fires-burnt bastards hate our guts."

With plenty of reason, at that, Brane reflected. The dwarves did not like the fact that the draconans had settled into the mountains they arrogantly claimed as "theirs," and a series of wars had been fought over it. Absolutely none of them had been even remotely decisive, other than the dwarves burning out every settlement beyond the citadels themselves. Draconan dragons prevented the dwarves taking the citadels, but dwarven troops and tunnels prevented the draconans expanding.

"You have *no* agents?" Brane repeated.

"I have exactly two men," Deris replied. "Their primary purpose is to provide an unexpected edge to the guards if we're forced to defend our embassy."

Such a defense had been required more than once in the long, bloody history between dwarf and draconan.

"How, exactly, do you intend to assist me with my mission, then?" Brane asked, his voice dangerous. If he had to deal with Tarverro himself, he would, but in that case, Deris should never have risked meeting him.

"I have no *draconan* troops," Deris replied after a pause. "I *do* have a network of informers, and contacts with one of the local gangs, a group known as the Blood Axes, or just the Bloods. Given enough money, they'll be prepared to help you out."

"And the money?" Brane asked.

"Including myself, I have three men," Deris told him with something resembling a grin. "But our superiors chose to give me the same budget as any other chapter. I can provide the money."

THE BACK EXIT OF THE DRACONAN EMBASSY ACTUALLY CAME OUT underground, in the vast expanses of city underneath the mountain. Brane was intrigued and had to wonder just how whichever of Deris's predecessors had had this dug had managed to sneak it by the dwarves.

However it had been done, some dwarves clearly knew it existed. Two, dressed in coal-black leathers studded with nasty-looking spikes, waited for him. Neither topped five feet or was less than four or so across the shoulders. The leathers were an affectation, and a rather stupid one—most dwarves regarded leather as rather pointless, preferring the easier-to-wash linens and cottons. Dust, after all, was a rather constant theme of their lives.

One dwarf, slightly shorter and broader than the other one, stepped forward, swinging an axe whose handle was painted dark red from her—from the swelling under the thick leathers, he *presumed* it was a her—wrist by a leather thong.

"You Brane?" she demanded in a surly voice.

"I am," Brane admitted. "Who are you?"

"Kelt," she told him, in the same tone of voice. "Blood Axe. Come."

That appeared to exhaust her conversational ability, and she and her companion took off into the caves. Brane, with little choice, followed them deeper into the mountain.

The path they took involved a great many turns and changes of direction, highly unusual in the usually neatly ordered and straight-lined dwarven caverns. Given that none of the tunnels they followed were especially curved or twisted, he assumed that either they were going around something or trying to disorient him. Or both, of course.

Finally, after an interminable tour through the tunnels, the two dwarves stopped and turned back to him. Kelt removed a strip of thick black cloth from somewhere and proffered it to Brane.

"You wear. Cover eyes," she instructed.

"Why?" Brane demanded.

The click of the other dwarf cocking the small arquebus that seemed to appear out of nowhere was nearly deafening. The Red Dragon's gaze met that of the gunner.

"You wear," Kelt insisted.

"So even if you can find this place, you cannot open the door, stone-head," the other dwarf said, the first words he'd spoken since Brane had met the pair. His voice was low and hoarse, as if he'd taken a throat wound.

Brane took the cloth and wrapped it around his head. As he began to do so, the second dwarf made the arquebus vanish again. Finally, the cloth was completely wrapped around his head, and the Dragon couldn't see anything.

He could hear the grating of stone on stone as something opened, and then felt a tug on his sleeve. Without a word, he followed the pull on his arm through what he assumed to be some kind of tunnel that twisted on for a several-minute walk.

Finally, they stopped. Brane reached up to remove the blindfold, but one of the dwarves knocked his hand away.

"No touch," Kelt ordered. "You stay. No look."

Footsteps receded into the distance, presumably his escort leaving. He waited for what had to have been several minutes, and was about to lose his patience and remove the blindfold when it was suddenly pulled off his head.

Brane found himself looking down at a dwarf dressed in deep-red-dyed leathers. Either he'd been in the room when the Red Dragon entered—in which case, Brane hadn't even heard him *breathe*—or he'd managed to walk in without Brane hearing him. Both were quite impressive feats.

"Welcome to the home of the Blood Axes, draconan," the dwarf told him. Unlike his escort, the gang leader spoke quite smoothly. "I think it is best if you know me only as the Red, hmm?"

"Perhaps," Brane admitted. "You'll excuse me if I do not provide my name either."

The Red waved away the thought. "That is not important. I deal with your Captain Deris—his name I know, if you betray us. He said you would pay for a 'task.'"

Brane eyed the thug. The Red was supposed to be nothing more than a street-gang leader, but he gave off the impression of something... more. The Red Dragon shrugged. He doubted it would be important.

"Indeed," he told the dwarf. "I need a man eliminated."

"What do you want me for, then?" the Red asked calmly. "You are an assassin, and so too is your Captain Deris. I cannot see a single man stopping your type."

The Dragon barely managed to suppress a snarl. "Unfortunately, the target is guarded. At least a squad of aeradi soldiers, possibly a full platoon."

"Aeradi?" the Red said. He turned away from Brane, and turned back with two pipes in his hands. "Smoke?" he asked.

"No, thank you," Brane said stiffly. The dwarf grinned at him and lit his own pipe.

"A platoon of aeradi is tough work," he said between puffs. "I have ways to deal, but they are expensive. How much?"

"Four thousand gold marks. Hellitian mint."

The Red was a very good negotiator, Brane noted. His only sign of surprise was a slight pause in the movement of his pipe. "That...may be enough," he allowed. "What has the target done?"

"How's that your business?" Brane demanded. "Is the money good or not?"

The Red grinned around his pipe. "The money is good. I still want to know—it is good to know what one is getting into."

"Fine. He killed one of ours. We're returning the favor," Brane told him.

"I see. Can you identify him?" the Red asked.

Memories of the debacle at Yun in his mind, Brane nodded. "I can give a complete description and tell you where he will be. I'd prefer if the entire platoon were wiped out, just to be sure."

A puff on the pipe, and the Red shook his head. "Not good enough. You come with us," he said flatly.

"What?!" Brane exclaimed.

"It is this dwarf thing called a 'work ethic,' dragon-boy," the Red told him, holding his pipe out of his mouth. "You pay me to do a job, I make certain it gets done right. Only way I see to do that is to have you around to make sure we get the man. Clear?"

The Red Dragon eyed the dwarf, the acrid smoke from the pipe burning his eyes, and considered. It would, at least, prevent another debacle like Yun.

"Clear," he grated out.

~

ERIK'S SQUAD, ALONG WITH THE REST OF FIRST PLATOON, WAS detailed to escort the wagons of firepowder from the mill, up on the side of the northern mountain, down to the docks. In full armor, with shields and swords, thirty aeradi marched up the mountain.

Unlike the other two cities the aeradi had visited, they weren't short by local standards. The dwarves were mostly about the same height as the marines, which meant that Erik was once again comparatively tall.

Of course, there were differences between the aeradi and the locals, and when the guards at the main wall stopped them to check their papers, Erik took advantage of the lull as Tolars dealt with their leader to study the soldiers.

A single platoon of forty men was policing the traffic into and out of the outer portion of the Hold. The dwarven soldiers looked quite competent and definitely dangerous. They might have only been the same height as the aeradi soldiers, but they were far broader, and the soldiers bore their chain mail and axes with the ease of long practice.

The greater heft of the dwarves was the major difference between them and the aeradi, but as the dwarven platoon commander made his way down the aeradi platoon, checking that the numbers matched the document, Erik got a good look at the man's unhelmeted face. The dwarf lacked both the slanted eyes and the high-arching cheekbones that the aeradi shared with their draconan rivals.

Erik's observation of the dwarves was cut short by the officer finishing his inspection and standing back to wave them through. Erik, like the other two squad sergeants, gave the dwarf a salute as they passed by. While the dwarf didn't lose his stone-like expression, he nodded in return to each salute.

Even having seen the city from the air, North Hold impressed Erik and the other first-time visitors. A massive avenue, the continuation of the highway that made its way up the valley, led directly through the city, splitting in the center to head to each of the two entrances into the underground.

They didn't follow the main road for long before turning right onto a road that led them up the north side of the valley. They passed through several terraces of homes and shops, and then into a terrace that was just trees and grass, a buffer, Erik realized, between the homes and the outside factories.

Past the park terrace, the aeradi passed into a set of terraces where the air quality seemed to plummet. Massive foundries and powder mills lay out in the open air, linked through small gates to massive underground warehouses and steam lines. The quality of the air around the factories explained better than any words why the dwarves left these factories outside—the cannon foundries and powder mills produced vast quantities of noxious fumes that, if released into the controlled air system of the underground caverns, would poison the entire population.

It left them vulnerable, but Erik also noted that the mountain just *above* the industrial terraces had the sheered flat look of dwarven fortifications built into the stone.

"Cannon above the terraces," he observed softly to Ennie, who nodded.

"Dozens of 'em," the Corporal told him. "They may leave the stinkers outside, but they won't let people attack 'em freely."

Erik nodded his silent agreement as they wound their way deeper into the open-air industrial zone.

~

THE BLOOD AXES LED BRANE ON A ROUTE OUT OF THEIR HOME DEEP in the caverns that was just as complicated as the one he'd followed in. About the only thing the combination of the two routes allowed him to be certain of was that they were higher up than he had been originally.

They passed into sunshine through what appeared to be an industrial entrance, where rails allowed dozens of carts to be pulled into and out of the mountain by dwarven steam engines.

"Is this safe?" Brane asked the Red.

"No, of course not," the dwarf replied with a laugh. The thug hadn't bothered to change out of his leathers, which meant he was far more neatly turned out than the scruffy majority of his gang. He was also all but unarmored, and swung a deadly-looking jagged-edged axe from his right hand by a thong.

"If one of the cart trains turns up, we will all be turned into wheel grease," the Red continued cheerfully, "but the main mines are on their lunch break—there should not be any trains for a few hours yet."

At least partially mollified by the Red's response, Brane followed the dwarves through the tunnel with its iron rails into the outdoors. They stood high up in the industrial terraces on the north side of the North Hold valley.

"Now, where are they supposed to be?" the Red demanded.

"They're headed to the Derian powder mill," Brane replied. Along with the *Cloudrunner*'s itinerary, he'd managed to learn who the ship's customers were.

"They will be coming up that road, then," the Red said with a grunt, gesturing at one of the paths cutting its way up the terraces. "Move."

The dwarves moved surprisingly swiftly and with little notice through the factories and smelters on the terraces, ignoring the smog in the air. Finally, as they came down a terrace, they spotted a solid bloc of people moving up the side of the mountain.

"That them?" the Red asked.

Wordlessly, Brane removed a small telescope from his belt and looked through it. The group was definitely aeradi, moving in good order with shields and armor. His lips turned upward in a slight smile at the sign of their ready paranoia.

He focused the telescope on each face in turn, and found the one he was looking for about halfway back through the ranks.

"Yes," he said shortly. "Tarverro is there."

"Good," the Red replied. He turned back to his men and eyed them. His gaze fell upon one of them, the quieter of the two who'd accompanied Erik to their base. "Bors, you keep ten of the boys here, just in case."

Brane blinked. If ten of the dwarves remained behind, that left only a few more than thirty to attack the aeradi.

"How do you plan to pull this off?" he asked, not quite questioning the dwarf's decision.

The Red grinned at him and reached inside his leathers, pulling out a pair of small iron cylinders. He hooked one to his axe's thong and bounced the other in his hand.

"Tell me, draconan," he said with a grin, "have you ever heard of grenades?"

THE POWDER MILL WAS STILL A GOOD TWO BLOCKS AWAY WHEN AN explosion on the street tore through the relative peace of North Hold's northern industrial district, bare yards away from the aeradi marines.

Several of the aeradi went down, and then Erik spotted a small iron canister arc over a fence into the middle of the formation. He didn't have time to even shout a warning before the second grenade detonated.

The explosion hammered the entire platoon into the ground, leaving half a dozen men badly wounded and most of the rest scratched and dazed. Erik, who'd merely been knocked off his feet by the blast, had barely stood up when he heard pounding feet, and looked up.

Thirty or so dwarves, scruffy and unkempt except for the apparently *very* well-maintained swords and axes in their hands, came around the corner and charged the aeradi platoon.

"Up!" Erik shouted. "It's an ambush! Up!"

The blast had shattered the marines' cohesion, and there were barely ten men on their feet with Erik. With a curse, Erik raised his shield and drew his sword, gesturing the other men into line with him, protecting their wounded.

The dwarven attackers hit the improvised shield wall hard. Axes slammed into Erik's shield, and he grunted as the impacts traveled up his arm. For a moment, all the marines could do was hold the shield wall.

Then one of the dwarves got an axe over the shield of the marine next to Erik and the man went down, bleeding profusely from a horrific wound to his shoulder. Erik turned, warding off the men in front of him with his shield, and lashed out with his tachi.

None of the dwarves were carrying shields or wearing armor, and his target had been leaping forward to take advantage of the gap created by the fallen marine. The long sky-steel blade punched in through the dwarf's side and then ripped out, spilling both the man and his guts onto the cobbled streets.

Erik's turn, however, had destabilized the already weak shield line, and it broke apart into a melee with two or three attackers focusing on each marine. As Erik realized this, he spun away from the man he'd just killed, only to find three dwarves closing in on him.

One of them came in close, a draconan-style shortsword flickering out in front of him. The other two, armed with long-handled axes, stayed slightly farther back but spread out, leaving Erik to face multiple angles of attack.

He desperately parried the swordsman, blocking one axe with his shield and ducking under the other. They forced him back a step, then another. Erik's shield covered one half of his body, and his tachi wove a complex pattern in the air as it parried each attack.

Finally, he blocked a sword strike with his shield and then parried the shaft of the right-hand axe. The axe head dropped to the stones with a clanging noise, and Erik smoothly carried through to drive the tip of his blade into the dwarf's throat.

One of his three attackers dropped to the ground, but the swordsman drove in as Erik killed the first dwarf, his blade skittering over Erik's shield. It hit his armored shoulder and just barely slid off the chain mail links. Unbalanced, the swordsman stumbled forward, and Erik slammed the metal edge of his shield into the man's throat.

With a horrible crunching noise, the second of his attackers fell, and Erik spun lightly on his feet to face the last axeman. The dwarf looked nervous for a moment until two of his friends appeared through the chaos to join him.

Erik took advantage of the pause as his attackers sorted themselves out to glance around. More of the platoon had recovered from the grenade blasts, but most of the marines who'd originally been up were now down, and another ten or so dwarves had arrived, adding to the attackers' numbers.

Even with the losses the first marines had inflicted, the ones still on their feet were easily outnumbered three to one. Erik snarled at his attackers. They might manage to take him and his men, but they were going to bleed for the privilege.

The three dwarves, all armed with axes, met his snarl with answering snarls of their own and charged. Erik stepped into their charge, hammering two of the axe strikes aside with his shield and stopping the last attack by parrying the dwarf instead of the weapon. With a reach none of the dwarves could match, he slammed the tachi into the smaller man's side with a strength few aeradi could claim.

The dwarf crumpled to the side, his torso ripped open by the blow, and Erik turned to the survivors. So far, he'd laid out four of the thugs for not even a scratch of his own, and they were starting to get nervous.

As he turned back to his attackers, however, he spotted something else. At the end of the street, behind the attacker's backs, a squad of dwarven soldiers had just rounded the corner, presumably having been drawn by the sound of the explosions. There may only have been twelve of them, but they were armored and their cohesion unbroken.

Emboldened by the sight, Erik drove forward against his attackers. Neither of their strikes got past his interposed shield, and his strike slid under the curved lower edge of his sword to rip the closer dwarf's leg open, collapsing him to the ground.

Then the thugs finally realized that the soldiers were there, due to the distinctive—and loud—sound of twelve men in heavy chain mail double-timing it down a cobbled street. They broke and ran, leaving their dead and their wounded on the streets.

Stunned by explosions and the sudden attack, the aeradi let them go. Erik stood among the marines, watching them run but lacking the energy to do anything about it. His gaze followed them down the street and paused as he saw another man vanishing around a corner, as if he'd been watching the battle.

The man had looked completely out of place in North Hold's industrial area. He'd looked, in fact, like someone Erik *knew* to be long dead, but that was likely just distance. What Erik was sure of, however, was that he'd just seen a draconan, and that draconan had been watching men try to kill him.

THE INITIAL STRIKE OF THE GRENADES HAD FILLED BRANE WITH exultation, but the aeradi had reacted quickly and well—too quickly, and too well. Even as Bors and his reinforcements went charging to try to turn the tide, Brane was beginning to fade off to the side.

When the soldiers came around the corner, presumably drawn by the sound of explosions, Brane pressed himself against the wall, suppressing pointless curses. Clearly, the attack had become a failure.

Even as he began to look for a way to get away, the Blood Axes broke and fled. Brane had no choice now and quickly stepped out, moving through the running dwarves like he belonged on the street.

He quickly glanced backward as he reached the corner, and nearly froze as his eyes met the gaze of the man he'd come to kill. For a silent moment, Brane found himself staring at his brother's killer before, with a muttered curse, he stepped around the corner.

Brane barely had time to start to breathe a sigh of relief before something hard and metal socketed itself to his chest. For a long moment, the Red Dragon Captain simply stood there in silence, and then he looked down at the dwarf whose arquebus was drilled against his chest.

"So like a draconan," Bors said in his hoarse voice. "So like your sniveling kind to run away when it goes balls-up." The click of the dwarf priming the cocking lever was somehow deafeningly loud, even over the noise of the smelters around them.

"Look, you people were paid in advance," Brane said flatly. "Take the money and run."

"I would rather kill you," Bors said flatly.

The dwarf's momentary distraction, however, had allowed Brane to move his wrist. The crystal rod in his wrist-sheath slid into his hand as he gestured, and he brought his hand up as the dwarf spoke.

Lightning blasted in near-silence, smothered by the sound of industry around them. Bors stopped reaching for the firing lever, the arquebus falling from his suddenly convulsing fingers as he crumpled backward.

A sickening stench of burnt meat rose from the charred and burned wound where the lightning bolt had entered underneath Bors' right shoulder and burned the insides of the man's chest to ash.

Brane re-sheathed the rod and stepped over the crumpled body. He needed a better plan than throwing street thugs at the aeradi. Or, at the very least, he needed a better variety of street thug.

THE DWARVEN SERGEANT SENT HIS MEN TO PURSUE THE THUGS, AND stopped to check on the aeradi. He approached Erik, who was standing dazedly in the center of the impromptu battleground.

"Are you in charge here?" he asked.

"No," Erik replied, looking about for Tolars. Then he realized that the platoon sergeant was down—from the look of the wounds on the older man, from one of the grenade blasts. "He is," he told the dwarf softly, and looked at the shorter man. "Which means I guess I am."

"You need a healer," the dwarf told him. It was not a question. He turned to the one man he'd kept with him. "Delds, run to the patrol house. Grab the Captain, the healer, and"—he pursed his lips in thought—"another squad for security."

The younger dwarf nodded and took off, taking his superior's command to "run" at face value.

"I am afraid I will have to ask you to remain here," the Sergeant told Erik, "at least until my superiors arrive. The healer will come with them, though."

"I can live with that," Erik allowed, eyeing the marines around him. Most of them were still moving, if weakly, and the survivors and the walking wounded were doing their best to tend to the injured.

Four of the aeradi, two thrown by the grenade blast and two bearing horrible axe wounds, weren't moving, however. They lay where they had fallen, mute testimony to the attack.

"I can live with that," Erik repeated, and turned away to aid his men in dealing with the wounded.

Too many of the wounds were beyond any ability they had to help. Erik found himself stripping away armor and slicing up uniforms to bandage wounds and make tourniquets. He was aware, in the back of his mind, of the dwarven soldiers returning and beginning to deal with the wounded of the attackers that hadn't run away.

The dwarves' first aid to the thugs was rough and ready but would keep them alive. Most of their attention went to helping the aeradi deal with their own wounded.

Finally, after what seemed like an eternity, more dwarven soldiers arrived, accompanied by not one but two healers. Erik had never been happier to see anyone than he was to see the two brown-robed healers: two more of the aeradi had died while their comrades strove to save them.

With the arrival of the healers and more soldiers to help with the simpler forms of first aid, Erik was freed to speak with the commander of the dwarves. Dressed in identical chain mail to his men, the only way to identify him was by the simple crossed silver axes emblazoned on his helmet.

"Captain Held Eeroin," the dwarf introduced himself. "Commander, Sword Company, Third North Hold Security Battalion." He surveyed the remnants of the aeradi platoon, many of its men simply sitting or lying on the ground and being ministered to by either the healers or the dwarven soldiers.

"What happened to you?" he asked softly.

"We were attacked," Erik said flatly. "A group of... I don't know—assassins? Thugs? Footpads? There were thirty or forty of them, at least. They used some kind of thrown explosive to lead their attack."

"Gods," the dwarf cursed softly. "Sergeant, I promise you that this will be fully and completely investigated, and we *will* find out the cause of this! In the meantime, what aid we can extend to you, we will."

Erik nodded. "Thank you," he told the other man. "Once our men have been healed, we must return to our ship—I hesitate to continue to pick up our cargo after this, especially with our platoon commander wounded."

"You have papers for this cargo?" Eeroin asked.

Erik nodded.

"Give them to me," he ordered. "It will be brought to your ship."

Erik gave the dwarf the papers, and he handed them to another dwarf whose armor bore a single silver axe, a Lieutenant.

Eeroin spoke to the man in a rapid stream of guttural syllables, of which Erik managed to understand about a word in ten. While most of Cevran spoke very similar languages, and while if it was spoken slowly, Erik understood dwarven almost as well as he understood the aeradi or his own native Hellitian dialect, the thick dwarven dialect rendered the language unintelligible at full speed.

Whatever Eeroin told the junior officer, he took the papers Erik had given the senior dwarf and left shortly thereafter. Eeroin turned back to Erik.

"These squads and I will accompany you back to your ship, as will the healers," he told Erik. "We will make absolutely certain no further attack takes place."

Erik murmured his thanks but also knew that no amount of determination after the fact would bring back to life the six bodies the dwarves were now covering in sheets.

～

IN THE END, EEROIN'S ENTIRE COMPANY ESCORTED BOTH THE
platoon and the wagons of firepowder back to the docks. Messengers
had gone on ahead, and the *Cloudrunner*'s Second Platoon was turned
out on the dock in front of the ship.

At the head of the platoon, Demond and Albiers stood together,
their faces like stone as the dwarves carried the severely wounded, and
Erik's squad carried the dead, past them and onto the ship.

Except for the stretcher party, the dwarves stopped at the edge of
the dock, leaving the aeradi to themselves for this moment. The
survivors of the platoon who weren't wounded or detailed with
carrying the dead drew up in front of their commanders, exactly ten of
them.

Six men were dead, ten were detailed with carrying their bodies,
and four men, including Tolars, had been wounded beyond the immediate ability of the healers to fix. Ten men, a single squad, out of thirty,
remained.

Erik saluted wearily. "Sir, First Platoon reporting."

"At ease," Demond ordered. "By the gods, at ease."

The men of First Platoon seemed to sag in place, as if they'd been
held up solely by the force of discipline. Albiers stepped forward and
surveyed them.

"Marines, you've done us proud," he declared. "Go get some rest.
That's an order."

Erik waited in silence as the rest of the men were dismissed, and
his commanders turned to him.

"That goes for you as well," the Lieutenant murmured. "I've heard
what the dwarves have to say, and according to their prisoners, you
were the only reason they didn't run right over the platoon."

"Do their prisoners know why they attacked?" Erik asked. He knew
the dwarves had taken the attackers' wounded away to be interrogated,
but none of the information from that had reached him yet.

"They were all too junior," a voice said behind him. Erik turned to
see that Eeroin had arrived. "It was, apparently, a street gang of long
standing," the dwarf continued grimly. "We have such, but most don't
come into this sort of area. All any of those we captured knew was that
they'd been paid in gold to make the attack."

Erik nodded acknowledgement, but his face was cold. "So, we know nothing."

"Nothing certain," Eeroin replied. "One of them said he had seen the man who hired them, but it was in the dark and at a distance—all he could say for certain was that he was tall. Not just human tall, though—*very* tall."

"Draconan," Demond said flatly.

"Indeed," the dwarf agreed, nodding. "It would not surprise us, either."

"Why not?" Erik asked.

"They have been buying cannon and firepowder in huge quantities recently," Eeroin told them. "It is making us suspicious, but we cannot claim Adaeran's Edict without them actually attacking somebody."

Adaeran's Edict was an order issued by the Stone King Adaeran a century and a half earlier. It said, quite simply, that the dwarves would not trade cannon or firepowder to an aggressor nation.

"You think they're stockpiling," Demond guessed.

"Yes," Eeroin replied. "Not just that—I do not know how recently you left Newport, but there have been several incidents in the last few weeks. Dragons burned a skyship off the Ellian coast a week or so ago —they claimed it was smuggling drugs, but all evidence suggests otherwise. Relations between your folks and the draconans are starting to get nervous."

"Our next stop is Black Mountain," Albiers told Demond. "Maybe we should think about aborting and heading straight home. We do have our dead and wounded to consider."

"I am afraid that I cannot make any recommendations," Eeroin told the aeradi. "I have probably already overstepped my bounds by telling you what I have, but somebody attacked you in our city. We owe you that, at least."

Demond nodded. "We thank you, Captain."

"Least we can do," Eeroin replied. "My company will also be guarding your ship until you leave, just in case."

"Again, our thanks," Demond told him.

The dwarf saluted and left, returning to where his company was taking over the security of this part of the dock area.

Demond turned back to Albiers. "We *can't* miss the Black Mountain leg," he told him. "We've already loaded the cargo *for* there, and we need the cargo *from* there. We have contracts to meet."

"We're delivering firepowder to a nation that appears to be preparing for war against us," Albiers objected.

"Nonetheless, we have a contract and we *will* fulfill it," Demond replied. He looked at the two marines. "We don't have a choice. We do, however, have five days until we land at Black Mountain. I want whatever arrangements you have to make to adjust for the losses here made, and the platoons drilled as fine as you can. If things are as bad as the good Captain suggests, we may end up having to fight our way out."

Albiers nodded stiffly. "In that case, Captain, I should get to it."

The marine commander left, leaving Erik and Demond alone.

"Sir," Erik said hesitantly.

"What?" Demond asked, his voice portraying his weariness after the day.

"I think I saw the draconan the prisoners mentioned," Erik told him. "At a distance, but close enough. He was dressed in red—all in red."

Demond looked at him oddly. "You're sure?"

"I'm sure," Erik replied. "I saw a draconan dressed like that, once. He was an assassin. He bought weapons from me when I was a smith, then tried to kill me. I killed him instead."

"That's not good," the older aeradi said. "Do you know what a draconan who dresses like that probably is?"

"A Red Dragon on a mission," Erik guessed.

"They're bad news," Demond agreed. "Very bad news. They're what the Dragon Lords use to deal with problems. And they're noted for hunting down those who kill their own."

"Wonderful," Erik concluded drily. "You mean the draconan rulers' personal assassins are after me?"

"You have a talent for making friends, don't you, Sergeant?" Demond said, shaking his head. "Go talk to Albiers, then get some rest. Don't tell him about the Red," he added. "He has enough worries as it is."

"So do the rest of us," Erik replied.

~

ERIK FOUND THE COMMANDER OF THE *CLOUDRUNNER*'S MARINES sitting next to Tolars' bed. Healers could fix almost any injury, but often their cures for more serious wounds simply involved bringing the patient back from the edge of death, and then encouraging the rest of the healing process to speed up.

At least the healers *could* help the survivors, unlike the six bodies who had been carefully laid in a room lined with preserving crystals, but their methods could leave men who were badly wounded in bed for weeks, even after the healers had dealt with them.

The platoon sergeant had been almost on top of the second grenade and had been quite badly wounded. Erik was surprised to see him awake at all, let alone talking with Albiers.

"Sir, Sergeant," Erik greeted them quietly.

"Have a seat, Tarverro," Albiers told him. "Tolars was just giving me his own assessment of what happened out there."

"Sir?" Erik replied, questioningly.

"I think you're the only reason any of us are left," Tolars told him gently, his voice scratchy with the aftereffects of his wounds. "I've not met many men who could have realized what was going on and gathered even the men you did. That's why I recommended what I did."

Clearly exhausted by the effort of talking, the platoon sergeant leaned back in the bed in the barracks.

"What did you recommend?" Erik asked.

"Jola won't be able to command First Platoon like this," Albiers told him. "He probably won't be fit to command until after we make it home." The Lieutenant shrugged. "We're going to need First Platoon in North Hold, which means it needs at least a temporary commander. Tolars"—he gestured toward the sergeant lying silently in the bed—"has recommended you. Want the job?"

Erik was quiet for a moment. With the casualties and the wounded, the platoon was down to only two squads, but even so, it was a lot of responsibility.

"Not really," he admitted.

"Good," Albiers replied. "You've got it. Your first task is to reorganize your men into two squads—put Ennie in charge of one, leave Sergeant Kalt in charge of the other."

Erik stared at his superior for a moment, and Tolars started laughing but stopped as he started coughing.

Once the Sergeant had recovered, he grinned at Erik. "Anybody who wants to command a military unit probably shouldn't be allowed to, kid," he told Erik in that scratchy voice. "You'll do, lad. You'll do."

Brane caught Deris, literally, napping. The junior Red Dragon was leaned back in his chair, his eyes closed. Brane shook his head and proceeded to slam his sword into the desk directly in front of Deris.

The speed with which the agent had a crystal rod out and trained on Brane's head was impressive but wouldn't have saved him had Brane really been out to kill him.

"You," Deris said disgustedly, allowing the rod to slide back into its sheath. "What do you want?"

"Your locals failed," Brane said flatly. "The Hold Guard is going to be busy dealing with a pile of dead thugs."

"It happens," Deris replied with a shrug. "No loss to us."

"Except that they *failed*, and the man who killed one of ours still walks free," Brane snarled. "You have *no* resources for this?"

"Captain Brane, I have the resources necessary to carry out intelligence operations and protect the embassy," Deris told him coldly. "I was not provided with the resources to carry out assassination operations. What resources I have, I provided to you. If they failed, that is *not* my responsibility."

Only a lifetime of self-control kept Brane from drawing his sword again and removing the insufferable little bastard's head.

"Very well, then," he grated out. "Can you at least manage to prepare me a dragon? If we are out of resources here, then we must strike in Black Mountain."

THE FIVE-DAY VOYAGE TO BLACK MOUNTAIN PASSED IN A BLUR FOR Erik. Entirely out of the blue, his responsibilities had been doubled, and he found himself busy organizing and taking care of twenty soldiers. It left him very little time for worry or introspection.

When they drew into sight of the citadel, however, Erik found time to watch the approach. Where North Hold had been settled into a valley between mountains and dug into the rock on both sides, the draconan citadel of Black Mountain was built on and into a single mountain.

The mountain, whose black basalt stones gave the citadel its name, rose up like the unyielding patriarch of the foothills and lesser mountains around it. Its lower slopes, and the valleys and foothills around it, were cultivated, providing the grain necessary to feed a city of some hundreds of thousands.

Above the cultivated fields, however, the citadel spread along the slopes of the mountain. Nine concentric sets of walls divided the city up along the line of the slopes and guarded the high palace and the entrances to the dragon crèches at the very top of the mountain.

In the first ring, the lowest and largest portion of the city, a reservoir covered the western portion of the walled area, lapping against the outer walls themselves in places. The rest of the lowest city was mostly warehouses and boulevards, statues and barracks.

The outermost ring of the city was not, Erik realized as the ship descended toward the water, a place for people to live. It was a showcase of the draconans' wealth and power, a meeting place for merchants and a contained zone in which the aeradi and their skyships could be carefully watched.

As they drifted over the wall, Erik noted vast batteries of dwarven cannon and crys-bows. Like the aeradi and the duredine, the draconans had the Sky Blood and produced Melders and Aligners of their own, and the latter weapons were their own production.

For this citadel, however, the walls and cannon and crys-bows were the last defense. The first defense was their vast hosts of dragons. Four greens represented those hosts, escorting the *Cloudrunner* to her berth.

According to Enviers, who stood next to Erik at the front of the ship, the normal escort for a ship during peace was one dragon, *maybe* two. Four was a wartime escort.

Which, in and of itself, told Erik that all the warnings they'd had were perfectly true.

~

IN BLACK MOUNTAIN, THE COURIER DRAGON DIDN'T LAND IN A TINY pen designed to hold two, maybe three dragons at a time. Here, in one of the draconans' own citadels, the dragon landed on a section of packed earth in the Fourth Circle, large enough for two or three dragons to *land* at once. Attached to the landing ground were the stables for dozens of courier dragons.

The sight of that sign of power and strength—a reminder that his city could afford to turn dozens of dragons into little more than messenger boys—reassured Brane. Surely here, in his own city and with all its resources, he could not fail to eliminate the man who'd killed his brother.

He thanked the rider who'd brought him there, and turned to leave, heading for the Red Dragons' headquarters. The sight of who stood waiting for him, however, caused him to freeze in place.

Five men, dressed in a deep red version of a Claw officer's dress uniform, stood just inside the gate to the landing compound, waiting for him. At the distance, it was hard to be certain, but the glint of red off one man's collar suggested that he was wearing the dragon ruby— an insignia only worn by the commander of the Red Dragons.

As Brane drew closer, his eyes confirmed his suspicion. The center man was General Tel Machieava, the leader, high priest, and commander of the Red Dragons. The four men with him were a cross between staff and bodyguards.

The hundred or so yards Brane walked across the yard seemed like miles, but he reached his commander soon enough and sank to one knee.

"My lord," he said simply. The Dragon Lords, the city of Black

Mountain and the nation of Dracona held Brane's *loyalty*, but *this* was the man who *commanded* him.

"Welcome home, Captain Kelsdaver," Machieava said calmly. "Rise."

Brane did, brushing dirt from his knee. "What does my commander wish of me?" he asked.

"To speak, Captain," Machieava told him. "Walk with us."

The Red Dragon Captain fell into step besides his commander. For several blocks as the group traveled up toward the inner circles, Machieava was silent. Finally, he spoke again.

"I am sorry to hear about your brother, Captain," he said, his voice as calm and emotionless as ever. "He was one of our most promising agents."

"Men die, my lord," Brane said flatly. "All that remains to us to see that justice is done."

"Justice," Machieava snorted. "Justice, we do not pursue. The pursuit of fear—that is why we kill those who kill our own. The pursuit of fear, and the pursuit of *vengeance* in the case of those who carry out that policy." He said nothing directly against Brane, but that made the accusation all the sharper.

"It is policy," Brane replied. He refused to make excuses, as he knew his commander was right. It *was* for vengeance that he pursued Tarverro, but it was a vengeance the Dragons' policy supported.

"So it is," Machieava agreed. "But so far, we have spent money and blood like water on this. The blood is not our own—*so far*—and money we have plenty of, but there comes a point at which we must limit ourselves."

"Are you commanding me to give this up?" Brane asked carefully.

"Not yet," Machieava told him. "But I will have other tasks for you soon, Captain Brane Kelsdaver. You are running out of time to deal with this man."

"He is coming here," Brane said flatly.

"I know," the commander of the Red Dragons replied. "That is the sole reason why I will permit this. I will allow one last strike, Captain Brane. If you fail again, there will be no more."

"What resources will I have?"

Machieava shrugged and gestured to one of his men. "Captain Doren will assist you." For a moment, the commander's face showed a single sign of emotion, a slight hardening of his eyes in anger as he spoke. "Strike hard, Brane. For both our policy and *our* vengeance, Tarverro must die."

~

AS SOON AS THE SHIP HAD TOUCHED DOWN IN THE WATER, ERIK turned First Platoon out on the deck. All the marines stood on the deck, watching as Albiers and Demond discussed something at the front of the deck.

Finally, the two seemed to come to an agreement and walked back to the marines. Albiers nodded to the two platoon sergeants, a group Erik was still uncomfortable to be included in.

"All right, people," he said loudly. "Second Platoon is going to remain aboard ship as security detail with me. First Platoon is going to escort Captain Demond to meet the merchant here."

The marine Lieutenant looked Erik in the eye before glancing on to the men. "Remember, gentlemen, the draconans don't seem to be very welcoming right now. We've heard some of what's gone on, but we don't know everything. Stay on your toes; we don't know how they're going to react."

His short speech done, Albiers gestured for the men of Second Platoon to break up, and Demond walked over to join Erik.

"Is this a good idea, sir?" Erik asked him in an undertone. "I hesitate to seem afraid, but if the draconans are after me specifically..."

"They're unlikely to openly attack you in their own city," Demond replied. "An assault on a *septon* in draconan streets? That would be an act of war. As long as you stay in the First Circle, you'll be fine."

"Where's the merchant we're meeting?" Erik asked, more loudly.

"In the First Circle," the Captain answered with a grin. "We aeradi, treacherous bastards that we are, aren't allowed higher in the citadel, so all the merchants who deal with us keep their offices down here."

Demond shrugged. "His name is Alast Teller. He's a good man, as draconans go, but we'll still watch our step. Understood?"

"Yes, sir," Erik acknowledged.

～

BRANE KELSDAVER STARED AT THE ARROGANT INFANTRY OFFICER IN complete shock.

"What do you mean, you cannot help me?" the Red Dragon demanded. He gestured at the papers in the Claw of the Dragon Major's hand. "You have orders from General Machieava and a warrant for Erik Tarverro's arrest in your hand. What more do you need?"

The officer on duty for sky port security in Black Citadel, Major Jodias Kale, laid the papers down and looked at Brane with unreadable black eyes.

"Yes, a warrant," he said slowly. "For the arrest of a non-citizen of Dracona for a crime committed outside Dracona. I'm familiar with that type of warrant, *Captain* Kelsdaver."

Brane's wrist half-completed the motion that would bring his crys-rod into his hand before swallowing as much of his anger as he could. As the Major had so *subtly* pointed out, he was junior to the Claw. Even being a Red Dragon wouldn't keep his head on his shoulders if he murdered a superior officer.

"My *orders*," Brane said slowly, "are to bring Tarverro in. We both answer to the General, Major."

The Claw shrugged.

"And the General answers to the Lords," he replied calmly. "And they, in their munificent wisdom, have commandeered the majority of the soldiers assigned to sky port security for a large-scale assault exercise. This desk is normally manned by a Colonel, Captain, with an entire regiment on standby.

"I have little more than a company," the Major concluded. He looked at the papers Brane had handed him again and grimaced.

"The General's orders are to provide any aid I require," Brane told him coldly. "I don't care about your problems—the sky port hardly requires thousands of troops to secure it. You can spare the men."

The officer tapped the warrant again and gave Brane another unreadable look.

"Fine," he finally spat. "You can have my two spare squads—I'm keeping my damn company together, *Captain*, because there are real issues that come up in this Circle."

Brane considered arguing for more troops for a moment. He even considered going back to the General's office and getting higher-ranked support. The General, however, had made it clear that there was a limit to the resources Brane could commandeer to end Tarverro.

There weren't many forces in the world that could stop twenty fully equipped Claws of the Dragon. It would have to be enough.

MAYBE IT WAS THE KNOWLEDGE THAT THERE WAS PROBABLY someone in the city that wanted to kill him, but the First Circle of Black Mountain made Erik nervous. Even in Vidran, the Trade Quarter had been precisely laid out with straight avenues and neat lines of buildings.

The First Circle wasn't. It looked far older than any city Erik had ever seen before, and the roads through it looked like they'd been laid out by the random paths of somebody's cow. They twisted and turned, with alleys and new roads seeming to appear at random intervals.

The close quarters and lack of sight made the rest of the marines nervous as well. First Platoon's perimeter around Demond was tight, and the men marched with their shields on their arms and their hands on their swords.

The first warning they had was a slight smell of smoke and ash upon the breeze, then they turned the corner of one of the twisting roads and beheld a horrifying sight. An entire block of warehouses and offices had burned to the ground in a fire. The primarily stone outer shells of the buildings were still mostly intact, but windows, shutters, interior walls and doors had all been burned away.

It was clearly recent, less than a day old. The smell of smoke was still in the air, and the draconans' fire services were still there, laying out the bodies under white linen wraps. The buildings at either end of the burnt-out block still dripped water, showing how the fire had eventually been contained.

The platoon stopped at the sight, but as Erik stepped forward to tell them to keep moving, Demond raised a hand.

"There's no point, Sergeant," he warned softly. "Those were Teller's offices. His home, too, for that matter."

"We should still check if he's alive," Erik replied, equally quietly.

Demond slowly nodded and stepped forward again. At a quick gesture from Erik, the platoon moved as well. The aeraid Captain crossed to where a man in a black-and-red uniform seemed to be directing things, and then gestured for the marines to stay behind as he approached him.

Erik accompanied Demond and eyed the draconan. Much taller than even the humans Erik had grown up among, the draconan had high, arched cheekbones like most aeradi but lacked the slanted eyes that caused Erik's father's people to stand out.

"I'm looking for Alast Teller," Demond told the man. "Do you know if he's all right?"

"Not unless you have an unusual definition," the fire warden replied, his voice hoarse as if he'd recently inhaled smoke. He gestured toward the neat row of white-covered bodies. "He's over there. He was the last one we pulled out—he'd apparently tried to get his family out first." The draconan shrugged. "He didn't manage it. We were too late," he added, his face turning dark.

Demond shook his head softly. "He was a good man. I'm sorry to hear about this. Do you know what caused the fire?"

Erik wished his Captain hadn't asked that. He wished with all his heart, but Demond had, so he listened to the answer.

"We're not sure yet, but there didn't seem to be any spilt lamps or anything, and they certainly didn't have enough warning to escape," the warden replied. "I don't know, but I can't see any natural reason."

Arson was the word, Erik knew. Someone had intentionally set the fire, and he'd bet he knew why.

As if his thoughts had triggered it, the draconan fire warden finally turned around and really *looked* at the man whose questions he'd been answering. The draconan and aeradi dialects had both been shaped by similar concerns and philosophies. This had left them close enough that even a native speaker could mistake them for each other if he was distracted.

"What does one of your kind want to know, anyway?" he demanded, realizing he was speaking to an aeraid. "Be off with you; you'll do no business with the dead!"

"No, I fear I won't," Demond replied, his voice growing cold. "Pass the regrets of the *sept* Rakeus on to his surviving family," he added before turning away.

"I will," Erik heard the draconan warden admit, grudgingly, before Demond led him back to the platoon.

The Captain looked nervous and gestured Erik to come closer as the marines closed around them again.

"This is bad," he told Erik quietly. "If someone on their side is killing *draconan* merchants for trading with us..." the Captain shook his head. "This is far worse than I've ever seen."

"Then I suggest we get back to the ship," Erik replied. "Before we drown in deeper waters than we thought we faced."

THE AERADI NOW WANTED ONLY TO RETURN TO THEIR SHIP AS quickly as possible, but the twisting avenues of the lowest district of the draconan citadel made that difficult. Even though Demond knew the route, the way it twisted and turned made it difficult to move quickly.

Finally, just a handful of turns away from finally reaching the docks, the platoon turned a corner and found the road blocked. A line of draconan heavy infantry, the fancifully titled Claws of the Dragon, blocked the road.

At the sight of the aeradi, the draconan unit, about twenty men, stepped forward, rapidly approaching Erik's men. Erik gestured his marines to halt, allowing the soldiers to approach them.

The Claws reached the platoon and re-formed into a double line, concentrating their numbers. Erik's marines, without his doing anything, seemed to drift around to bulk up the front of their formation, the part facing the draconans.

For a long moment, the two groups of armed men faced each other in the street, then three men stepped out of the formation. Erik wondered how he hadn't noticed them before, as they were dressed completely differently from the soldiers. Where the soldiers were heavily armored, bore their shoulder-high half-cylindrical shields and had their deadly dragonclaw shortswords out, these men were in red cloaks and appeared unarmed.

The leader of the three men was unusually short for a draconan, short enough to blend into the crowd in any human city. The distinctive features of the draconans were recognizable but muted. The man seemed oddly familiar to Erik, but he couldn't place why.

"Who leads here?" the draconan demanded.

Demond gestured for Erik to remain hidden among his men and stepped out. He was silent for a moment, and Erik saw the draconan eye him up and down coldly.

"I am Captain Demond *sept* Rakeus of the aeradi skyship *Cloudrunner*," Demond told the man. "Who seeks to know and why?"

"My name is Brane," the draconan replied. "I am looking for a man known as Erik Tarverro, and I am informed he is in your service."

Demond looked about to deny this, but before he could say a word, Brane's gaze met Erik's. For a moment, the two men held each other's eyes, and Erik suddenly knew where he recognized the man from.

The assassin Rade had shared the same features, height and dress. This wasn't just one of the assassin's brothers in the Red Dragon cult—this was quite possibly the man's *real* brother.

Erik knew, now, who had been pursuing him across northern Cevran with even greater zeal than the Red Dragons normally pursued those who killed their own. Other men may have actually attacked him, but *this* was the architect of his pursuit.

"And I see my information is correct," Brane declared, his gaze still on Erik's face. "You may as well come out here."

Erik moved slowly, his eyes holding the draconan's as his hand fell to the hilt of his father's sword. Finally, he stood beside Demond, just in front of his men, still close enough for them to protect him if something went wrong.

"Erik Tarverro," the draconan said formally, "it is my duty to inform you that you are under arrest for the unprovoked murder of the Red Dragon Rade, while he was working in the service of Dracona. You will come with me."

"And if I refuse?" Erik asked softly.

"You, your men and your ship will be interred," Brane replied. His eyes flicked to Demond. "Surely, Captain, you will not risk such a fate for the sake of a man who killed another in cold blood?"

"I have heard two stories of the fate of the *assassin* Rade," Demond told Brane softly. As he spoke, he placed a hand on Erik's arm and took a step backward. The men behind them parted, allowing them into the line of aeradi marines.

"I know which I believe," the Captain continued. He drew his own sword, and the skittering sound of steel on leather was repeated as every one of the aeradi marines drew their blades.

"You will take a man of my crew—*any* man of my crew," Demond said flatly, "over the dead bodies of *all* of my crew."

The three red-cloaked draconans had barely seemed to move, but long and lethal-looking blades now glittered in their hands, and the Claws behind them had taken a step forward.

"Very well, then," Brane told Demond calmly. "I see no reason to object to your condition."

AT BRANE'S WORDS, THE TWENTY CLAWS IMMEDIATELY HEFTED their shields and advanced in step, splitting to allow the Red Dragons to drop behind their formation. The aeradi marines did much the same, and two shield walls clashed together in the center of the citadel street.

The draconans used a much heavier shield than the aeradi, a half-cylindrical structure that covered a man from ankle to neck. Pressing against the lighter aeradi shields, and the simply smaller and weaker aeradi, it pushed the aeradi back. Normally, the aeradi would try to break Claw formations with archers, but this fight had started from too close.

Erik was still in the front line, but he knew that his men couldn't fight this kind of battle. He carefully judged the gap between the lower curve of his shield and the curve of the shield to his right, then thrust forward with his sword.

The sky steel of the blade punched clean through the shield of the Claw in front of him and into the man's thigh. Erik ripped the blade out, and the man crumpled, a spurting flow of arterial blood marking his probable demise.

Erik used his weight and strength, greater than most of the draconans due to his years as a smith, to push into the gap. The marines next to him followed, their flickering tachis dropping the men to either side of the Claw he'd killed.

The draconan line broke. Not completely, not the breaking and running that would have made the battle easy, just the disintegration of the battle into pure melee—a type of fight where the aeradi's lighter shields and longer blades gave them at least a chance.

For the first moments after pushing into their line, Erik simply used his shield and weight to drive the gap further open. Pushing men back with his shield, he didn't bother to use his blade.

Once the draconans accepted the change to melee, however, he couldn't pull that off anymore. While the Claws trained mostly for the heavy shield wall tactics they'd just tried to use, they also knew how to fight in messier environments. Despite the numerical equality, they did their best to focus two of their men on each of his, and the aeradi were smaller and weaker to begin with.

Recognizing that his size made him the greatest threat and that he was the man they'd been sent after, three of the Claws came at Erik. They stayed back, somewhat, wary of the reach his longer blade gave him, but they pressed in, using their shields to cover themselves.

Uninclined to stretch things out, Erik slammed his shield into that of the Claw who came close enough first, hard. The Claw stumbled, slightly, and for a moment he was distracted.

A moment was enough, and Erik's sky-steel sword ran neatly through the plywood of his shield, the iron of his armor and the flesh of the Claw's chest in short succession. The man choked and crumpled, allowing Erik to yank his sword back out, just in time to parry a thrust attempted by another Claw.

The thrust parried, Erik followed through with his shield. The tall oval of the aeradi shield also carried a heavy metal boss at its center. This chunk of metal slammed into the top of the draconan's shield, splintering it and sending shards of wood back into the man's face.

He stumbled back, leaving Erik free to pivot and thrust toward the third Claw. The draconan had been launching an attack of his own but found that, unlike most aeradi, Erik's arms weren't short enough to cost any of the reach advantage of the longer sword.

The draconan's dragonclaw sword skittered off Erik's sky-steel mail, slicing his cloak, but Erik's sword embedded itself in the man's stomach. Erik yanked it out and turned to the other Claw, only to find that one of his marines had run the man through while he was falling back from Erik.

Before Erik could move to aid any of his men, he caught a flash of motion out of the corner of his eye. He spun in place, barely managing to interpose his shield against the strike.

One of the Red Dragons snarled at him as he knocked the strike aside with his shield. It wasn't Brane, but that made things no better, as the Dragon launched another devastatingly quick strike.

Erik blocked with his shield again, but this time, the blow sheared off a good chunk of his shield. Before he could even think of reacting, another blow came slicing in. Again, Erik blocked with his shield, and again part of the wood scattered off onto the ground.

The Dragon managed to strike a fourth time, but this time Erik reacted faster. The metal boss of his shield, like the rest of his armor and weaponry, was sky steel. He interposed it against the strike.

The impact vibrated clear along his arm, but it clearly did much the same to the draconan. It was quite possible the draconan's sword was sky steel, as few weapons forged of lesser materials could have withstood that impact, but the vibration had nearly knocked it out of the Red Dragon's hand regardless.

In the moment of distraction as the Dragon tried to recover, Erik ran his sword through the draconan's throat. With a choking gurgle, the draconan slipped to the dirt, his red cloak pooling around him like blood.

Somehow, Erik was not surprised to find Brane stepping over the corpse of his compatriot.

"*Septon* Tarverro," he hissed, "time for justice."

Erik didn't bother to respond, except to lunge forward with his sword. Brane parried the strike and unleashed one of his own, slashing at Erik's head.

Dropping under the blow, Erik released his much-battered shield. There wasn't enough left of it to really help, and he was going to need the freedom of maneuver.

Using the impetus of the shield's release, Erik bounced back up to his feet, causing another blow to go awry. He grinned tauntingly as Brane missed, and unleashed a stroke of his own.

Brane parried it aside, forcing Erik to take a step sideways as well. He didn't look as he did, and his foot came down on a blood-slicked dragonclaw sword. With a screech of metal on stone, the sword slid out from under him, and his foot slid with it. Suddenly off-balance, Erik found himself dropping to one knee.

The draconan snarled at him and launched a devastating slash. Down on one knee, Erik had no way of evading the blow and threw his own sword up with all his strength. The two swords met with a horrible keening sound, and Erik's sword, reforged by his own hand less than six months before, sliced clean through the draconan's weapon.

For a long moment, Brane stared down at Erik and at the stump of his sword. Then he glanced around at the ruin of the Claws he'd brought with him and snarled wordlessly.

"This isn't over, Tarverro," he told Erik. He threw the useless hilt of his sword at Erik, the still-sharp broken piece of the blade gashing Erik's cheek open as the impact drove Erik back on his heels, and fled.

For a long moment, Erik did nothing, merely staring at the shattered pieces of Brane's sword. Finally, he heard footsteps near him, and looked up to find Demond looking at him.

"He's gone to get others, lad," the *Cloudrunner's* Captain told him. "Bind that up; we need to get back to the ship."

Demond's words finally brought Erik back to reality. He gazed around the street as he opened the bandage-roll pouch he, like the rest of the soldiers, wore at his waist. Breaking the draconans' line and leaving them to face the aeradi marines, already veterans of a similar street brawl, had doomed the Claws, but they hadn't gone down lightly.

Most of the aeradi were binding wounds, and five aeradi bodies lay unmoving in the streets among the dozen or so draconan corpses. His men had performed magnificently, but it hadn't been enough to prevent more deaths in the already-battered platoon.

The wound in his face bound, the bandage covering the left half of his face up to his eye, Erik surveyed his men. It broke his heart to make them move, but he didn't have a choice.

"We carry the dead and those too wounded to walk," he told them quietly. "We aren't safe until the *Cloudrunner* is in the air, so we better start moving."

None of the marines were unwounded, and those who had no problems walking were pulled down by the weight of the dead and the more severely wounded. Erik himself supported Enviers, who'd taken a draconan thrust deep into his upper thigh. The Corporal's injury had been bound, but it would take a healer to be certain there was no infection or permanent damage.

Despite the hobbling pace of the aeradi, they'd been close to the docks already, and they reached them quickly. Erik was at the lead of the group, and stopped dead in his tracks as he came around the corner.

Over a hundred Claws of the Dragon, a full battle company, were drawn up on the dock in front of the *Cloudrunner*. Erik could see no red cloaks among them, so there were no Red Dragons, but he had no doubt why they were there.

Nonetheless, they had no choice. He started moving again, leading his battered and bloodied platoon to the dock where their ship rested. Before they could get close enough to call to the ship, the Captain of the Claws, accompanied by his colors group, came to meet them.

"I am Major Jodias Kale, of the Black of Twelfth," he told Erik, giving his battalion and regiment. "You are all under arrest and will come with me."

Erik eyed the man coldly. "Go to your Fires, lizard-licker," he hissed. "Go to them and *burn* there."

Kale jerked as if struck. Apparently, despite—or perhaps, because of—the battle-worn state of the platoon, he'd clearly expected them to surrender without a fight. Erik had no intentions of doing anything of the sort.

The half-aeraid Sergeant smiled coldly as the draconan officer went for his sword, and drew his own blade. He did nothing overtly threatening, simply holding the blade in his hands.

"You *will* come with me," Kale insisted.

"When all Fires darken and all Waters freeze," Erik told him contemptuously, and looked over at the *Cloudrunner*. "Hello, the ship!" he shouted, using all the breath he still had.

Kale stared at him for a moment, but Erik gestured for him to look. A head had popped up over the railing and surveyed the scene on the dock. A moment later, thirty aeradi suddenly rose over the railing and nocked arrows to bows. At the same time, sailors appeared out of nowhere to man the ship's weapons.

To drive home the message, the rear fire-cannon in the broadside facing the dock, the only one that didn't bear directly upon the draconan infantry, fired. The stone ball, propelled by the explosion of the dwarves' firepowder, flashed across the dock and splashed into the water.

"Ten, maybe twelve seconds or so for your men to reach us," Erik told Kale conversationally, gauging the distance to the soldiers behind the draconan officer. "Thirty good aeradi archers—and believe me, those ones up there are pretty burnt good—will get off at least sixty shafts between them. Likely ninety, really.

"Three cannon and two crys-bows as well. Not nearly enough time for them to reload the cannon or recharge the crystals," Erik reflected, his voice still conversational, "but I suspect my friends over there have the cannon loaded with grapeshot. Just how many of your company do you think will survive to reach us?"

The draconan Captain stared at him in silence for a long, long moment, his sword in his hand. He looked as if he was tempted to order the attack anyway, in the hope that he might get his sword into this half-blood in front of him.

"Let us through, Major Kale," Erik told the man, almost gently. "No one else needs to die today. Let us through," he repeated.

Slowly, ever so slowly, the draconan company commander sheathed his sword and stepped back. He glared at Erik, and then his gaze shifted to Demond, who'd joined Erik without the half-blood ever realizing it.

"Go," he hissed. "But neither you, your ship nor any other ship of your Fires-cursed kind will *ever* be welcome here again. Understand?"

"We understand," Demond told him flatly. "Now get out of our way."

A FULL STRIKE REGIMENT OF DRAGONS, BLACKS, GREENS AND browns, was kept on ready status at all times, to guard Black Mountain's skies, rendering fixed anti-air defenses redundant. The headquarters of that regiment, for ease of communication, was in the First Circle.

Nonetheless, by the time Brane reached them, he could see the *Cloudrunner* beginning to rise out of the artificial lake below. Unless something was done, and done quickly, they were going to escape. Despite all the effort, Tarverro was going to *escape*.

"I need to speak to the duty officer *immediately*," he snarled at a youngish draconan just inside the headquarters.

The man, wearing the uniform of a Skyborne Lieutenant, looked at him. "I am the duty officer," he said drily. "Most of the senior officers are on exercises."

"Oh." Brane paused for a moment, and then physically shook himself. "I need a pursuit launched of a skyship—they have a convicted murderer on board, and one of their marine platoons just chopped up a Claw unit that tried to apprehend him."

Brane watched in satisfaction as the Lieutenant's eyes widened in shock. "I see," he said, admirably calm. "I think we can do that."

The Skyborne officer turned to a man sitting at a desk. "Get a runner to the Brown's Third Company; they're on active. Tell Captain Holis we have a skyship that needs to be brought in or burnt down."

"Hold that order," a calm, emotionless voice cut through the chatter of the Ninth Strike Regiment's headquarters. "Let them go."

Brane turned around slowly, already almost certain of what he would see. Machieava stood directly behind him, two Red Dragons at his back.

"Let him go," the commander of the Red Dragons repeated more quietly, so only Brane could hear him.

"Why, sir?" Brane asked. The order was inside Machieava's authority to give, but he still wanted to know *why* Tarverro had to walk away.

"Look," Machieava snapped, and pointed. At the edge of Brane's vision, perhaps a third of the way into its descent, was a second skyship.

"If we burn down a skyship, here, in front of another aeradi vessel and with a *septon* aboard," Machieava growled, "we may as well declare war on the aeradi. We *cannot* afford open war with them now. Not yet. We are too close to completing our plans to have the war start before *we* are *ready*. Do you understand me, Captain Brane?"

Brane nodded silent, if unwilling, acquiescence.

"Good," his commander said. "Now come. I have another mission for you. One that I think you will find...acceptable."

Some hesitation must have shown on Brane's face, for Machieava's voice suddenly hardened into a tone of sheer *command*. "Come, Brane," he snapped.

ERIK STOOD SILENTLY AT THE STERN OF THE *CLOUDRUNNER*, watching the citadel shrink behind them. He knew they weren't quite home free yet. Dragons could still intercept them and burn the skyship down, killing all aboard. He could still die for the "crime" of defending himself against an assassin.

Only when the last fortifications of the citadel passed out of his view did the half-blooded aeraid slowly begin to relax. By some miracle, they'd escaped.

Not all of them, though, he knew. The wounded and the dead alike now lay under the decks of the *Cloudrunner*, being tended to by the ship's healer, a now much-overworked man. The healer was human, a necessity as no aeraid could wield the earth magic of healing.

Footsteps sounded behind him, and Erik slowly turned to find Albiers standing behind him. The commander of *Cloudrunner*'s marines stood there watching him for a moment and then gestured to Erik's face.

"Are you going to get that seen to?" he asked.

"There are still men who need attention more than I," Erik replied.

"True enough," Albiers admitted softly. "Decorian died," he added, even more quietly.

"Gods take him," Erik said, his voice twisted. Decorian had been the worst wounded of the men they'd borne down to the ship. He'd hoped the aeraid would live, but he'd feared it would be otherwise. The marine's death meant that six men had died there, for his folly, and that twelve had died on the journey simply because he had been with them.

"Too many have died for me," Erik whispered, his voice still twisted.

"I've spoken to the others," Albiers told him. "According to them, you're the reason *any* of them made it back—most aeradi simply don't have the size and strength to knock the Claws back like that. You saved the others' lives."

"Twelve men are dead," Erik said flatly. "As many more, at least, will be weeks recovering. All this because the draconans were after *me*."

Albiers shrugged. "At least partly," he admitted. "But there were other causes of the tensions, Erik. The balance is shifting—something is changing. More men lived, as it happened, than may have had you traveled aboard a different ship. They would still have pursued you and still have harassed us."

Erik said nothing.

The Lieutenant shrugged again. "You do not believe. You will, as time passes. For now"—he laid his hand on Erik's shoulder—"go see the Healer."

Finally, Erik nodded. As he walked away, headed toward the hatch down into the ship, he saw Albiers take his place at the stern of the ship.

"Erik?" the Lieutenant said, stopping Erik before he left.

"Sir?" Erik replied.

"It has been an honor and a privilege to serve with you," Albiers told him, watching the mountains behind them. "When we return to the city, *septon* Tarverro, you will have my recommendation for the Militia."

What with one thing and another, Erik had completely forgotten why he'd undertaken the voyage aboard the *Cloudrunner*.

"Thank you" was all he could think of to say, and he thanked Albiers far more for his words than for the recommendation.

"Don't mention it," the Lieutenant replied, and Erik knew that he had understood what he *hadn't* said as much as what he had.

❧ 4 ❧

FORTY-NINE DAYS after she'd left, the *Cloudrunner* slowly drifted back into the skydock at Newport. Most of her wounded had recovered, but too many of her crew were dead, victims of the draconan pursuit.

A pair of wing lancers had met them a full hour out of the city, the six-yard golden wingspans of their huge rocs making better signals than any flags. They'd flown close enough for the crew to get a good look at the razor-sharp talons and the black beaks of the horse-sized birds as they shouted instructions for the ship to divert to the military docks.

The lancers had escorted them in, and almost as soon as they'd docked, a blue-robed man with the lightning-bolt insignia of a mage had boarded the *Cloudrunner*. Erik stood at the rear of the ship, with Albiers and the other platoon sergeant, watching the man speak to Demond.

Finally, Demond shook his head at the man and led him back to where Erik and the other marines stood.

"Gentlemen, this is Mage Kirian Norst," Demond told them, gesturing at the robed mage. "He works for the King, and he has some questions he'd like to ask us about our tour."

"Why?" Erik asked bluntly. He didn't know about the rest of the crew, but he just wanted to get off the ship and go home.

"Because the draconans have blocked our ships from their ports," Norst said calmly, "and they specifically named this ship as the cause of this action."

"Did they?" Erik murmured. "And just *what* are we accused of doing?"

"Disturbing the peace, threatening a port official and slaughtering a platoon of the Claws of the Dragon," Norst replied. "Now, while we are uninclined to take the draconans' word at face value, we still need to investigate their accusations. Did these events occur?"

"Did we disturb the peace, threaten to fire on a company of draconan port guards, engage and defeat a platoon of Claws?" Erik asked.

Norst nodded, looking as if he was embarrassed to even be asking. Demond, looking over Norst's shoulder, met Erik's gaze and shrugged.

"Yes, I rather think we did," the Captain said calmly. "Oh, we also killed a couple of Red Dragons. *However*, given that they wanted us to surrender one of our men to their justice, for supposedly killing one of their assassins in a completely different country, I don't see how we could have done differently."

Demond winced, and Norst inhaled sharply. "I see," the mage replied, his voice admirably calm. "Perhaps you would care to elaborate on the exact sequence of events?"

It appeared that *none* of the *Cloudrunner*'s crew were going to get off until Norst had his questions answered, so Erik sighed, and explained the series of events that had led to the eventual ugly showdown on the docks of Black Mountain.

Norst took notes, writing everything down on a small clipboard he'd produced from somewhere inside his robes. Finally, once Erik was done, he returned the clipboard to its pocket and looked at the *Cloudrunner*'s officers.

"I agree with your opinion, *septon* Tarverro," he noted in the end. With the *Cloudrunner*'s return to port, Erik's authority and rank as a member of her crew had expired, reducing him to "only" his blood title. "There was nothing else you could have done. I assure you that I will pass that opinion on to my superiors." He shrugged. "As far as His Majesty is concerned, you need have no worries."

"What about the port blockade?" Erik asked.

Norst shrugged. "They seal their ports to us every three or four years. It rarely lasts more than a few months before they get over their snit—they can't *afford* to seal them forever."

Erik nodded slowly. In comparison, most of the Sky Cities were sealed to draconan trade permanently. It was a disturbing thought.

"In any case," the mage continued, "I have no more reason to detain you gentlemen or your crew. A detail from the port battalion will be arranged to move the bodies of your fallen to the city morgue until the families can make arrangements."

"Thank you," Albiers murmured.

"It's our job," Norst replied. With a salute, he left the marines behind, standing at the front of the skyship and staring into the city.

"That's that, I guess," Erik said.

"Yeah," Demond replied, equally quietly. "I'd suggest that those of us with homes ashore go to them and rest up." He offered Erik his hand. "*Septon* Tarverro, it has been an honor and a privilege to have you under my command. I will speak to the Militia Commissions Board on the morrow on your behalf, you may be assured."

"As will I," Albiers said, offering his hand as Erik finished shaking Demond's. For the aeradi, it was a gesture between close friends, but these men had become that, and Erik shook the Lieutenant's hand as well.

"Thank you," Erik replied. "Both of you. It has been an honor for me as well."

By the time Erik made it back to the Tarverro house, it was well past dark. Crystal lights, held off the ground on metal supports, lit the sky city's streets with a soft bluish glow. Neither as bright nor as harsh as daylight, they were still more than enough to allow Erik to find his way home.

It was late enough that the staff—a laughable description of what, when he left at least, was made up of two maids and a cook—had clearly gone to bed, and the house was mostly dark.

Unwilling to activate the crystal-light chandelier that hung over the east wing—the public areas—of the house—it, after all, had a limited number of hours of use before it needed to be realigned—Erik found a lantern in the cloakroom. A flick of the lever on its side brought the two crystals inside the device into contact, and they began to glow with the same soft bluish glow of the outside lights.

Using the lantern to light his way, Erik entered the west wing, the private areas of the house, to find the one light that was still on. It was a lantern, identical to the one in his hand, resting on a table in the front living area of the wing. The table was positioned right next to the large chair in which his grandmother sat, fast asleep.

A book rested on her hands, sign of her sole "vice." While the carefully maintained industrial and decorative forests of the Sky Isles and the sky cities themselves produced significant quantities of wood, most of it went to either the ships or trade. Paper for books was expensive in the Realm of the Sky, though dwarven-made printing presses made the manufacture of the books themselves a cheap-enough proposition.

With a smile, Erik gently reached out and shook Arien's shoulder. She started awake and looked up at him with sleepy eyes.

"All right, I'm headed to be... Erik?" Her voice went from sleepy to awake as she realized it wasn't one of the servants waking her. "When did you get back, grandson?"

"Earlier today," Erik told her softly. "We got tied up at the port—they had some questions about the events on our trip."

Arien looked at him sharply, belying her state of moments before. "They don't hold crews for questioning unless something..."

"Worry about it in the morning," Erik said, softly but firmly cutting her off. "For now, you really should go to bed." He offered her his arm. "Here, let me help you."

Instead of using his arm to support herself, Arien pulled him into a tight hug. After a moment, she released him and eyed him. "You could have taken the armor off, you know?"

Despite his worries and the weariness left by the trip, Erik couldn't help himself. He started to laugh. His grandmother glared at him for a moment, and then her face faded to a grin as she joined him, her giggles echoing around the room.

~

ERIK'S AUNT HELLA ARRIVED IN THE SMALL DINING ROOM WHERE HE and his grandmother were eating breakfast as he finished explaining the events of the *Cloudrunner*'s voyage. She came in quietly, picked up a plate from the side table and sat down, serving herself from the still-steaming dishes the cook had put in the center of the table.

"Someone's trying to kill you, nephew?" she asked Erik. "What did you do, open your mouth twice?"

While Erik *thought* she was trying to make light of the situation, probably trying to make up for their last meeting, he didn't find it very funny. Before he could work up a good glare at the woman, though, his grandmother laid her hand on her daughter's sleeve.

"It's not exactly funny, dear," she warned gently.

"A lot of good men are dead because those *bastards* are after me," Erik hissed, his hand clenching his cutlery.

Hella recoiled. She turned her attention to her plate. "I'm sorry," she half-muttered. "I hadn't realized."

Erik took a deep breath, trying to calm himself. "No, you couldn't have," he told her—only somewhat reassuringly, he knew. "Remembering the rumor mill in this city, however, everyone will have by tomorrow," he added.

"Sooner," Arien replied. "Something that fascinating is going to spread fast. I'm afraid people are going to talk."

"Gods curse it," Erik swore wearily. Trying to put the situation out of his mind, he then attacked his food with a will. Taking their cue from their *septon*, his two female relatives followed suit.

Erik's plate was clear, and he was eyeing the still partially full dishes in the center of the room when there was a knock on the door. He glanced up to see Shel standing just inside the room.

"Milord?" she said questioningly.

"Yes, Shel?" he asked.

"There's a man here to see you," she told him. "Militia uniform."

"Send him in, dear," Arien told the maid before the girl's last words had sunk into Erik's mind.

Militia uniform could mean anything—most of the men he knew here were members of the Militia, but no one wore the uniform when off-duty. Why would an on-duty Militiaman come to see him...?

The young aeraid who followed Shel back into the room, exchanging glances with the attractive young maid, did wear a Militia uniform. However, unless Erik was mistaken—and Arien's etiquette lessons had been quite thorough—the small shield on the man's collar, quite separate from the shoulder stripe of his Corporal's rank, marked him as a Regular seconded to the Militia.

At the sight of Erik, he came to attention and saluted. Erik returned the salute, confused. While *septons* traditionally had the right to take salutes from any soldier of the city, that was mainly at formal ceremonies.

"Erik *septon* Tarverro, sir?" the man asked.

"I am," Erik replied. "At ease, soldier."

The Corporal remained at attention and offered Erik a plain brown envelope. Curious, Erik took it.

"What is this, Corporal?" he asked.

"You are summoned to speak before the Militia Commissions Board, on the eleventh bell of the day," the soldier replied.

"I...see," Erik said. The eleventh bell was late afternoon, this late in the year. "I will be there."

"Understood, sir," the soldier replied. "Permission to bear that message to the board, sir?"

"Granted," Erik replied, hiding a smile. He realized that the soldier had *never* dealt with a *septon* before and had decided to treat him the same way he'd treat a very senior officer. "Thank you for delivering the message, Corporal."

Another salute, and Shel escorted the soldier out. Leaving his maid and the soldier to their flirtation, Erik turned his attention back to the envelope in his hand. Opening it revealed a single sheet of paper.

The message's prose was far more flowery than the soldier's simple statement, but it carried the same message: appear before the Commissions Board at the eleventh bell. Simple enough, but it also carried an unspoken message—this letter *had* to have been sent before any of the *Cloudrunner*'s crew had made their recommendations.

Indeed, it had to have been sent as soon as the news that the skyship had made port reached the Board.

It was unlikely to be a *bad* sign, but it still made Erik nervous.

ERIK REACHED THE BOARD'S OFFICES, JUST EAST OF THE SQUARE OF the Gods, five minutes before the eleventh bell. Two soldiers in Militia uniform were waiting for him outside the squat stone building.

"Erik *septon* Tarverro?" the Corporal greeted him.

"I am," Erik replied.

"If you will come with us, sir," the Militiaman said calmly. "The Board is dealing with another issue at the moment but will be free shortly."

Erik nodded calmly and followed the two soldiers. They led him into a small chamber where a handful of loose chairs faced a long table with six chairs behind it. Once inside the chamber, the two soldiers took up position just outside the door and left Erik to study the room.

Like the rest of the Board's offices, the room was plain stone and undecorated. The chairs were solid wood, long-enduring but unadorned. The emphasis throughout the entire building had been function first, cost second and aesthetics last.

He had perhaps ten minutes to contemplate the room and why he was there before the Board arrived, all six members filing into the room without a word to Erik. Several of them, who he vaguely recalled meeting at various affairs, nodded to him as all six took their seats.

The man on the left-hand end of the table, the end the aeradi reserved for the senior member of a group, finally spoke into the silence.

"You are Erik *septon* Tarverro, son of Karn *septi* Tarverro?" he asked, his voice firm but clear.

"Yes," Erik answered, nodding as he eyed the man. They'd never met before, but the leader of the board looked oddly familiar. He was of only medium height, even for an aeradi, and quite bulky. The bulk, however, appeared to only be partially fat, and the man had shoulders almost as broad as Erik's own.

"I am Akeis *sept* Dedria," the aeraid told him calmly. "These are my fellow members of the board," he added, gesturing down the table, "Del *hept* Ormani, Jorg Ketrin, Hader *sept* Delts, Mekil *hept* Dorian and Deslir *sept* Jaras."

Erik controlled his features at the last man's name but couldn't help his gaze from flicking to him. The *septon* Jaras and he had met, and the meeting had been pleasant for neither of them. From the disgusted glare Deslir sent Erik's way, he seemed to agree with his clan patriarch's opinions.

"Your application was delivered to us, by proxy, three days ago," Akeis continued. "Of course, assessment beyond the most minimal of the application was impossible while the *Cloudrunner* was out of port." He paused, looking down at Erik.

Erik nodded wordlessly, acknowledging what the Board's head had said. That did partially explain the speed with which they'd apparently moved, though Erik wasn't entirely certain who the proxy had *been*.

"Those more-complete investigations, including interviewing Captain Demond *sept* Rakeus and Lieutenant Joran Albiers, were carried out this morning," Akeis told him. "Based on those interviews and other information we have gathered, this board has made its decision. Are you prepared to hear it?"

For a moment, Erik didn't say anything. He'd thought he was going to be given a chance to state his case, not just hear their decision. Finally, he managed to nod his assent.

"Very well," Akeis said calmly. "The Board was highly impressed by your actions and the level of ability and dedication you showed over the course of the *Cloudrunner*'s voyage. The circumstances were exceptional, and you performed exceptionally."

Erik found himself holding his breath as the Board's head paused, and he was *sure* he saw a small smile flickering around the old aeraid's lips.

"However, at this point in time," Akeis continued, "there are no Lieutenants' commissions available in the Militia battalions."

A combination of disappointment and sheer incandescent rage flashed through Erik for an instant at those words, and he began to rise to his feet, intending to leave.

"Take your seat, *septon* Tarverro," Del *hept* Ormani, the second most senior member of the Board, ordered as Akeis stopped in shock.

Erik said nothing, merely completing his rise and glaring at the man who'd spoken. A long moment endured as he and Del locked gazes, and then the Militia officer laughed aloud. "Take a seat, Erik," he repeated. "We're not done yet."

Torn between anger at their flippancy and curiosity, Erik slowly sank back into his chair. When he was finally seated, Akeis shook his head at him and smiled. No—the man outright *grinned* at Erik.

"Since there are no junior commissions available," he told Erik, taking up the thread of his speech, "we have no choice but to consider other methods of inducting such outstanding potential into our forces. It helps," he added thoughtfully, "that your voyage aboard the *Cloudrunner* included more combat experience than many of our *Regular* officers ever see."

"In two days," Akeis told Erik, "Captain Deril *hept* Orian will be retiring from the Militia battalions to accept a commission in the Regular Marines. Unfortunately, none of his Lieutenants are sufficiently experienced to take over the company.

"You, however, *have* sufficient experience—specifically *combat* experience—to do so. Therefore, at the party in two days when Captain Deril retires, we will officially announce that command of Fire Company, Third Newport Militia, will be assumed by you, *Captain* Erik *septon* Tarverro."

"Does that satisfactorily meet your application?" Akeis asked.

Erik stared at the man in silence. "You're serious," he said flatly.

"Yes," Del said for his superior. "We would prefer if you kept the news secret until we make the announcement, and you won't be *publicly* commissioned until then, but you are, as of this moment, officially a Captain in the Militia of the sky city of Newport."

"Gods help you," Akeis finished.

Erik was speechless. It was *far* more than he'd expected or even hoped for. Even as the elation began to catch up with him, he glanced once more to the right-hand end of the table, where Deslir *sept* Jaras sat.

The man's gaze on Erik had moved from disgusted to something far worse, and Erik was shaken to his core by the sheer and utter loathing in the man's gaze.

〜

ERIK ARRIVED AT CAPTAIN ORIAN'S HOUSE SEVERAL HOURS EARLY, hoping to meet the man who he would be succeeding to command of Fire Company, Third Newport Militia. The house, located in one of the upper-middle-class districts of the city, was plain but well looked-after. An open gate, through which Erik could hear talking and the clatter of furniture, suggested where the party would be held later.

He, however, approached the main door and knocked on it. After a minute or so, he raised his hand to knock again, only to have the door opened just before he did. A young aeradi woman, perhaps three or four years older than him, stood in the door.

"Can I help you?" she asked. "We're rather busy at the moment, so I hope it's quick."

"I'm Erik *septon* Tarverro, ma'am," Erik said politely. "I'd like to speak to Captain Orian."

The young woman's face instantly lit up in a smile. "Of course, *septon*," she replied. "I'll inform my husband that you're here. Come in."

Orian's wife led Erik firmly into the sitting area, where she directed him to a chair before sweeping out of the room. He stared after her for a moment, bemused by her seemingly boundless energy, and then turned his gaze to the room.

Like the house itself, the furniture in the sitting room was plain but well-kept. Two couches and a half-dozen chairs formed a semicircle around a large fire, all decorated in a delicate mix of dark and pale green. The chairs, Erik soon realized, were almost sinfully comfortable despite their plain appearance, and he almost didn't want to rise from his when Captain Orian finally returned with his wife.

"Captain Tarverro!" he greeted Erik with a broad grin. "It's a pleasure to meet you at last."

"Likewise, Captain," Erik replied, inclining his head in a slight bow.

"I was hoping to speak with you about the company before the transfer of command."

"Of course," Orian replied. He turned to his wife. "Leila, dear, do you think you could take care of the arrangements for me? Captain Tarverro and I will likely be a while."

Leila answered her husband with a dazzling smile that Erik found himself half-wishing was directed at him, and swept out of the room with a confident air. Orian watched after her with a small smile on his face.

"You're a lucky man," Erik murmured.

"That I am," Orian agreed, and gestured back toward the chairs. "Please, Captain, have a seat."

"Technically, I'm not a Captain yet," Erik replied, sinking back into the chair as Orian took his own seat.

The Militia Captain, who appeared to be the same age as his wife, shook away the concern. "You and I both know what is happening tonight. No need for games. I'm actually quite pleased that my company will be in good hands."

Erik smiled weakly. "I'll admit to not being so certain of that myself," he admitted.

"Nonsense!" Orian replied firmly. "I'll admit I didn't expect you to be so...so..."

"Tall?" Erik prompted. It was the major mark of his mixed blood there and drew most eyes and a lot of attention, both good and bad.

"Young, actually," Orian confessed. "I received my Militia Captaincy quite young—I'm receiving a Regular Captaincy right now, when most career soldiers are either Regular Lieutenants or just getting Militia Captaincies—but you're, what? Twenty?"

"Twenty-one," Erik replied. "I fear that it won't help with the men."

Orian shook his head. "I know Albiers, Erik," he noted. "If he made you a platoon commander on a seven-week voyage, then I have little hesitancy giving my company to you. As for the men"—he shrugged—"two of Fire Company's Lieutenants are *kep* to your *sept*. That should at least help defuse any seniority issues."

Erik looked at his predecessor with surprise. "They are? I didn't know that."

With a grin, the aeraid nodded. "They didn't pick my company for you out of thin air, Captain Tarverro."

"So I see," Erik agreed. "What about the company do you feel I should know?"

The older man considered. "Well, all four of your platoon Lieutenants are very junior. They're good, don't mistake me, but they're junior. The company command sergeant, however, is a twenty-year veteran of the wing lancers who works as a ship's marine commander in his day job. I believe you know Harmon *hept* Ikeras?"

For a moment, Erik simply looked at Orian, and then laughed. "I've been completely set up, haven't I?"

"I refuse to comment," Orian said virtuously. "I know that there was some worry about bumping you up, especially given, well, that you're a half-blood. So, they picked the company you'd have the least issues with."

"And you?" Erik asked.

"I suspect His Majesty leaned on the Regulars for us," Orion guessed. "I don't object, and neither should you!" He stood, crossed to a sidebar and removed two glasses, half-filling them with a pale amber liquid.

He turned back to Erik and offered him one of the glasses. "Metian brandy," he explained. "Some of the best stuff you'll find on all of Cevran." He raised his glass in a toast.

"To the Captains of Fire Company, Third Newport, past, present and future."

THE TWO MEN SPENT ANOTHER HOUR OR SO DISCUSSING THE company before Leila returned to the room. "Your guests are arriving, gentlemen," she told them. "You two should get out back and start greeting them."

Despite three glasses of Orian's excellent brandy, Erik still managed to rise smoothly to his feet and bow slightly to his fellow Captain's wife. "Thank you, my lady," he replied.

Exchanging a nod with Orian, Erik followed the couple out to the garden at the back of the house. Only a handful of guests had arrived so far, including both Harmon *hept* Ikeras and the head of the Militia Commissions Board, Akeis *sept* Dedria.

Eight-foot-tall hedges that towered over the aeradi bound the edges of the garden. Erik himself could look across the entire space, over the heads of the guests, but he'd grown used to that in the company of his father's people.

Ikeras spotted the two Captains as they entered and crossed to them. He saluted Orian, who returned the salute. "Captains," he greeted them. "It's good to see you."

"I see the rumor mill moves apace," Orian said with a smile.

"In this case, the Board told me," Ikeras replied. "I think they wanted me to prepare the officers and men for the change."

"Understandable," Erik replied. "It's good to see you too, Harmon."

Orian glanced from Erik to the former wing lancer. "I'll leave you two to catch up. I have other guests to speak to," he told them, and then strode off, arm-in-arm with his wife.

"A good man," Erik said quietly, watching Orian leave.

"He is that," Ikeras agreed. "How was your voyage, Erik?"

"Like walking through the Fires," Erik told him. "The draconans seem to want my head, specifically."

"So Albiers said," the old soldier said, equally quiet. "He also said that you were incredible."

"A lot of people died," Erik replied.

"That's war," Ikeras said flatly. "The thing to remember is that more might have died if someone else had commanded."

Erik was silent for a moment, considering what Ikeras had said. Would more men have died if someone else had led those troops? He didn't know. If he'd been there and they'd attacked anyway but someone else had commanded? Perhaps.

"It's not war yet," he objected, ignoring the thought for now.

Ikeras shrugged. "Between us and the draconans? It's always war," he observed drily. "Just different levels of the beast."

"The blockade?" Erik asked.

"It'll pass," the older man told him. "They block their ports to us every so often. It rarely lasts more than a few months—it hurts us, but we can survive. It hurts them more."

"Of course, most of our ports are always closed," Erik observed softly.

"That's the way of it," Ikeras replied. "There's some too paranoid to open the ports to anyone and not paranoid enough to think a real fight's coming."

"Are you two dooming and glooming?" a female voice cut into their quiet conversation. Erik looked up and found Arien standing just there. His grandmother has dressed up for the occasion and appeared quite the elegant aeradi lady in a dark green satin dress.

"This is supposed to be a party, not politics," she continued.

"What's the difference?" Erik asked.

"You *enjoy* yourself at a party," Arien replied. "Ikeras, shoo!"

The older man—*kep* to Erik's *sept*—bowed slightly. "As my *septel* and *septon* command," he murmured.

Once Ikeras had left Arien turned back to Erik. "You heard me, Erik," she said firmly. "You've been moping about one thing or another since that Gods-be-cursed duel. Go! Have fun!"

As Ikeras, Erik bowed. "As my lady grandmother commands," he replied.

Arien smiled at him. "Good. Now shoo yourself!" she ordered.

ERIK HAD BARELY WALKED AWAY FROM HIS GRANDMOTHER BEFORE A man dressed in the uniform of the *sept* Rakeus intercepted him, a man he knew quite well. He smiled at the sight of Letir and his wife Deria coming toward him.

"Letir, Deria, good to see you," he greeted them with a slight inclination of his head.

"No one told us you were back," Deria told him, her lips twisting into a half-faked pout. "I don't think even *Father* knew."

Erik blinked. He hadn't even *thought* of contacting the *septon* Rakeus—he'd assumed Demond would have told him.

"I assumed Captain Demond would have told you," he said aloud, only to have Letir laugh at him and poke his wife gently.

"He did," the young shipmaster replied. "Deria was just having her fun. Hiri is looking for you," he added. "Matters of great importance, one presumes." His tone made the words far less serious than they appeared.

"Thank you for telling me," Erik said. "He is here?"

"Yes, I am," a familiar voice said from behind him. Erik turned to find Hiri *septon* Rakeus standing behind him. The corpulent aeraid offered his arm, and Erik clasped it gratefully for support before releasing his friend.

"It is good to see you, Hiri," he told the older *septon*.

"And good to have you back, Erik," Hiri replied. He turned to his daughter and his son-in-law. "I'm sure there are some of the supposedly noble rapscallions you two hang around with here somewhere. Go enjoy yourselves."

"We want to hear all about your trip," Deria told Erik sternly before taking her husband's arm and leading him off into the crowd.

"They seem happy," Erik murmured, watching them go.

"They are," Hiri replied. "You did a better deed than you knew. All of my men now see that. Some people here still hold Kels' death against you, but most accept that he chose his own fate."

Erik nodded wordlessly, and the older man eyed him.

"And you?" he asked. "Have you come to peace with it?"

"I do not know," the younger man admitted. "So much has happened, I almost forgot until I returned. I seem to be haunted by battle."

"Demond explained it to me," Hiri told him. "Given what seems to have happened to those who came up against you, I'd say they were more haunted by you than the other way around. You can't change it, Erik."

"I'll live. It's good to be home," he admitted. "Some surprises were waiting for me, though."

"I had nothing to do with it," Hiri replied. "Mostly His Majesty, Adelnis, with a little help from Ikeras and your grandmother."

"Turning it down was never an option," Erik said, a statement more than a question.

"True." Hiri glanced around them, seeming to note the space that had grown around the two *septons*. "We do have other business, Erik," he told him, lowering his voice.

Erik eyed him warily. "What?"

"This year's Council of *Septons* is four days from now," Hiri told him. "Since you're back, you will have to attend. No one was sure whether you'd return in time."

"I see," Erik said calmly. "Anything specific I should worry about?" He knew about the Council, though he admittedly hadn't known the date for this year's.

"Nothing I know of," the far more experienced *septon* replied. "The usual halfway-important decisions the King puts to us. You'll have to be presented to the Council, but it's just a presentation, not a chance for them to refuse you."

"That's always good," Erik said drily. His experience with other *septons* was mixed and suggested that a lot of them hated his guts for being a half-blood.

Hiri said nothing to that, merely snorting eloquently. "Your lady grandmother will most likely run you through the attendees. *I* will make sure that a copy of the agenda is delivered to your house— they're not *officially* distributed, but everyone will have one."

"Thank you," the younger man replied gratefully. The thought of walking into a room full of the other *septons* was going to be bad enough even knowing what he'd have to discuss.

"You're welcome," the *septon* Rakeus replied. He chuckled slightly, and Erik looked at him askance. "It seems I've monopolized enough of your time, *septon* Tarverro."

Erik turned to see what Hiri was referring to and found his aunt Hella, along with a man in the sea-deep blue robes of a mage, coming toward him. The pair came up, and Hella gave Erik the slight bow of close *sept* relations to their *septon*.

"Erik," she said, her voice warm, "it's good to have you back."

"Everybody seems to be saying that," Erik observed, and glanced over at Hiri.

"Our business is done for now," the other *septon* said calmly. "We'll speak again before the Council, of course?"

"Of course," Erik confirmed. Hiri bowed, it looking awkward on his tubby form, and strode off into the crowd.

"Aunt Hella," Erik finally greeted his aunt as Hiri left. "It's good to see you, too." He glanced at the mage beside her, noting that the man wore the two silver rings of a full mage on his right hand. "And this is?" he prompted her.

"Erik, this is Hori *sept* Kelsa," she told him, her voice softening even more.

Erik smiled at both of them. So, this was the experimental mage who'd apparently pursued his aunt both before and after the time in which her husband would be the father of the next *septon* Tarverro. He took a moment to silently examine the man, and liked what he saw. Hori was tall for an aeraid, only an inch or two short of Erik's own height, and broad with it. The aeraid was no dwarf, as broad across as tall, but his shoulders held a promise of strength and power.

Despite all this, the man wore the robes of a highly non-physical calling, and the doubled rings of a full mage guaranteed respect in every nation on Cevran. All in all, Erik was quite impressed.

He inclined his head. "It is good to meet you, Hori," he told the mage, who was probably ten years his senior. "My aunt has spoken highly of you," he added, with a wicked glance at Hella.

She blushed and showed Erik her left hand. A simple gold ring, unmarked by the runes of a Society profession, circled her ring finger. "Hori just asked me to marry him," she said happily. "I said yes," she added, unnecessarily.

Erik glanced over at Hori, who was eyeing him nervously. Technically, Erik had the right to refuse any man marrying a woman of his *sept*, but he had no inclination to do so in this case.

"That is good news," he said with unfeigned delight. "Very good news. You have my blessing." The last words were a necessary formality, and he could *see* Hori almost sag in relief at hearing them.

Before Hori could say anything, someone bumped into Erik from behind. Erik turned around just in time to prevent the young woman who'd hit him from falling over. He did *not*, however, manage to catch her glass as well.

Red wine sloshed out onto the front of his *sept* uniform, staining its subdued colors even darker. Erik quickly released the blonde girl he'd grabbed and tried futilely to brush it off.

"Oh, gods, I'm sorry!" the young lady exclaimed, blushing furiously, and Erik turned his gaze from the front of his tunic to her.

She was tall for an aeradi woman but not incredibly so, only an inch or so over five feet, and slim with it. Her blond hair stretched down her back in a neatly done braid.

"It's all right," Erik said, frozen for a moment as he met her eyes but recovering quickly.

"No, really, let me help," the girl insisted. Before Erik could say a word, she ran her fingers down the front of his tunic, muttering something under her breath. The wine vanished under her touch, leaving the tunic pristinely clean. "There," she said firmly. "Much better."

Then, and only then, did Erik realize that she too wore the blue robes of a mage, though only one silver ring adorned her right hand. Hori's chuckle burst into the two youths' private little world, and Erik looked up at his aunt's new fiancé.

"Lord Erik *septon* Tarverro, may I present my apprentice and personal demon, Lady the Mage Elysia *sept* Kirmon," he said to the pair, smiling at them.

Erik bowed slightly to the girl—and girl she was, she was at least two years younger than him. Young to be a mage, even an apprentice one. "A pleasure, my lady," he murmured.

"Likewise, my lord," Elysia replied, dropping a perfect curtsy. "You're the new *septon* Tarverro?" she asked with frank curiosity.

"Last time I checked, yes," Erik replied.

"You're not what I expected," she told him.

"And what *did* you expect?" he asked.

"From my father and his *friends*"—the last word was nearly hissed —"conversation, some sort of foul demonic abomination, out to corrupt and devour all of our people."

Erik froze and opened his mouth to speak, only to be interrupted *again*.

"Elysia, what are you doing over here? Father is looking for you," a voice from behind Erik said to her. The voice was masculine but young, probably an older brother.

The girl rolled her eyes to the heavens, which only Erik saw, then turned. "I came looking for Hori, Korin," she said calmly. "I met Lord Erik here with him."

Erik turned to find a man who was Elysia's twin to the inch. At the sight of Erik, the youth paused and then bowed slightly.

"My lord *septon*," he greeted Erik softly. "I am Korin *septi* Kirmon. We should be going, sister," he said to Elysia, and turned back to Erik. "My apologies, my lord," he murmured. "I am not my father. Nonetheless, it would be better if this meeting never happened in his eyes."

Erik bowed his head in acquiescence, and watched as the twins strode away, his eyes lingering on Elysia for far longer than they should have.

"Their father is Lord the Storm Doldan *septon* Kirmon," Hori explained softly, and Erik started. He'd forgotten that his aunt and Hori were there at all. "He is a close friend of the *septon* Jaras."

Erik nodded slowly. Jaras was a purist and hated Erik's guts. "A Storm?" he asked, almost as softly. Storms were a level up from mages, far more powerful. Far more dangerous.

"Yes. No friend of yours," Hori told him quietly. "The twins are good people, gods alone know how with him for a father, but they are."

"I'll keep that in mind."

"If you two are done plotting and conspiring," Hella said into the silence following that, "it appears that the announcements we're here for are about to be made, which means *you*"—she pointed at Erik—"should be getting over there, doesn't it?"

Erik grinned, for a moment looking his barely twenty-one years of age, and nodded.

THE CROWD SLOWLY QUIETED DOWN AS ORIAN STOOD UP ON THE platform at the end of the garden. Something like two or three hundred people had attended the party, including three *septon*s other than Erik, as well as most of *hept* Orian and all of Fire Company's officers and noncoms.

"Quiet down, folks," Deril ordered in the parade-ground voice most officers learned quickly. "You all know that I don't hold parties like this at random—for obvious reasons!" A chuckle ran through the crowd. Orian was the nephew of the current *hepton* Orian, and stood reasonably high in the aristocratic society of Newport, but his house was only medium-sized. The guests barely managed to fit into the garden behind it.

"So, you're here for a reason, hence the speech," he told them. "I'll keep this short and sweet, though, so you don't get unduly bored. The gist of it is this: I've been offered a commission in the Newport Regular Marines."

Applause cut Orian off for a moment or two, but he raised his hands for quiet. "I'm taking it, but this means I have to step down as Captain of Fire Company of the Third. It's been a good four years with you gentlemen, but good things come to an end." The Militia Captain eyed the crowd, especially his former officers and men, who were silent to the man.

"However, I know that I am leaving you in good hands," Deril continued after a few seconds. "The Militia Board has seen fit to replace me with one of our *sept* leaders, Lord Erik *septon* Tarverro!"

This time, the applause was quieter. Some of those present had no enthusiasm for half-breeds and refused to even pretend to applaud this announcement.

Erik didn't have much time to examine the crowd, as Deril gestured to him. "Come on up here, Erik. Give you a good chance to introduce yourself to the leaders of the Third."

Lacking any real choice, Erik mounted the platform himself and faced the crowd. The officers and noncoms from the Third stood out, as most of them were in uniform at their commander's party.

"Captain Orian did an excellent job running the Third," Erik told them, ignoring the other guests for the moment. "He'll do an equally excellent job running whatever company of Regulars is lucky enough to get him. I can't hope to be his better, but I promise you I will do all I can to be his equal."

He met the eyes of each of his new Lieutenants in turn and gave them a firm nod, and then he and Orian stepped down to loud applause, loudest from the men who now served under Erik's command.

∼

BRANE KELSDAVER STOOD ON THE BATTLEMENTS OF THE FOURTH Circle in the late-evening wind across Black Mountain. The valley spread out beneath him, with its farms and its dragon pens, its armories and foundries. It was a sight that usually filled him with confidence in the power and might of his citadel, but tonight he was blind to it.

Other Red Dragon agents had confirmed that Tarverro had now returned to Newport, which meant he was far beyond Brane's reach. He had failed to avenge his brother, and the attempt had cost the Dragons both men and resources they could ill afford to lose.

There were rumors of a new mission, the one Machieava had told him he was supposed to be assigned to, but he'd heard nothing *more* than rumors. He'd been given a group of new-blooded Red Dragons, thirty of them only just pulled from the Claws of the Dragon, and told to train them as quickly as he could. No reasons, no explanation, just orders.

He'd operated on missions with minimal information before, but that was because they hadn't had it. Now he operated without information because it hadn't been *given* to him, and that was most unusual for the Red Dragons.

Brane knew something was coming. Machieava himself, commander of the Red Dragons, had told the Captain there would be a new mission for him, but so far, all he'd done was train a platoon of soldiers how to be infiltrators and assassins.

The scuff of a boot on stone woke him from his reverie, and he spun in place, his crystal rod out and trained on the figure behind him. Instead of being threatened, however, the figure chuckled.

"So, you are still aware," General Machieava chuckled. Despite his chuckles, his voice remained flat and emotionless. Brane had *never* heard the high priest-cum-general's voice be anything but. "Good. I'd wondered."

"What do you want?" Brane demanded. He knew being so brash to Machieava was dangerous, but he wasn't on duty, and he'd come out there to be alone.

"Well, I was considering telling you what your mission was going to be, but if you're going to act the child about it, perhaps I'll pull you from it," his commander said flatly.

Brane's fingers tightened on the rod, then returned it to its sheath and snapped to full attention. "I am ready and yours to command, General, sir!" he snapped, cadet-like.

"Good. Very good," Machieava replied. "How is your infiltrator platoon?"

"As good as they can get without a lot more time to practice or blooding," Brane admitted. "Unless our mission will take more than another six months to get ready, we're not going to get any appreciable further gains from training."

"It won't," the General replied firmly, stepping up to the battlements to join Brane. "How do you feel about the aeradi, Captain? I don't mean just the propaganda we *say* but how you *feel*."

Brane hesitated. Honesty on that sort of level was dangerous, but his commander had ordered it. "They're arrogant and hypocritical, sir. They trade everywhere and get angry if we close our ports, but theirs are always closed to us."

"Indeed." Machieava eyed the fields below them. "Do you think we could win an all-out war with them, Captain Kelsdaver?"

"All-out war?" Brane breathed, stunned. The though was horrific. The draconans held their own in the constant low-level sparring and occasional minor war, but they lacked the resources—most specifically, the launch bases—to prosecute a real long-range campaign. "It would be close to suicide, sir. We can't touch any of the sky cities—dragons are simply exhausted by the time they reach them."

"We need bases," Machieava confirmed. "How to get those bases has been the primary project of our general staff for over a decade, and we've come up with two plans. One involves a long, drawn-out ground war across northern Cevran. We'd have to seize Ell and Hellit, and probably Garria and quite possibly North Hold to prevent the dwarves interfering. Then we could use the Hellitian ports to launch an air and sea campaign on the northern sky cities."

Brane was silent, considering the cost—in time, money and blood —to fight such a campaign. "Could we do it?" he asked

Machieava laughed. "If the aeradi didn't realize why we were doing it and intervene, maybe. The odds don't favor it, though. That's why it hasn't been done."

"What *are* we doing, then?"

"It is *possible* to get dragons to Newport, at least," the General observed. "But they're too tired to fight when they get there, correct?"

Brane nodded, uncertain where this was going.

"To take the city, they'd need to rest before fighting. Which means that the defenses would have to be suppressed *before* the assault arrived," Machieava said calmly, and Brane swallowed as he began to understand. "Sometime in the next two months, Captain, two-thirds of the Newport Sky Fleet will be in Sky Hame, carrying out the yearly war games. At that point, we intend to use infiltrated troops to shatter the external defenses and break the Militia chain of command. This will allow our assault force to take the city with minimal losses.

"Faced with intact strike regiments sitting on Newport, and an entire army of the Claws of the Dragon in the city, the aeradi will either accept our control of it or fight. If they fight, the city will provide us with a base from which we can hit two more of their cities —the only ones we deal with—and the Sky Isles themselves."

Brane stared at Machieava, stunned. The plan was *insane*. By that very token, it might just work. He also began to understand why he'd been training his platoon of infiltrators.

"What is our mission?" he asked.

"Your platoon will be posing as traders," Machieava told him. "You'll be leaving in a week, and you'll settle in with the trade factors in the city. Your first mission is to learn when the fleet has left. Given that even Newport restricts our travel within the city, that will not be easy, but it is the most important part. Once that's done and the attack has begun, you will use explosives that we'll smuggle in to you to destroy the exterior defenses, and then you will take and hold choke points to prevent the Regulars and Militia forming up. Elimination of officers from both groups is a high priority."

"I see," Brane said thoughtfully, his head spinning with thoughts and plans.

"It's not complex, but neither is it simple," Machieava told him. "It's deadly dangerous, and I won't order you to do it."

"I volunteer, sir!" Brane replied promptly, and Machieava grinned.

"Good. I'll pass that on to the organizers." With a nod, the commander of the Red Dragons began to turn away, but stopped on the steps down from the battlements. "One last thing, Brane."

"Yes, sir?"

"Our intelligence confirms that Erik *septon* Tarverro now has a Militia commission," Machieava told him. "When the time comes, killing him will be in your mission description. I'm sure you'll be willing to take care of it, correct?"

"Yes, *sir!*"

ERIK'S FIRST DUTY WITH HIS COMPANY WAS A TRAINING SESSION THE very next day. Dressed in a brand-new uniform in the Militia's light blue and white, marked with the paired silver stars insignia of his new rank, he found himself standing on one of the Militia training fields on the northern edge of the inner city.

The training field was designed to host a single company at a time and had just enough archery butts, training dummies and other tools for the one hundred and thirty-eight men of an aeradi infantry company. The men of Fire Company, Third Newport Militia, were straggling onto the field as Erik arrived, all in uniform with their Militia-issued weapons and armor.

Two men waited for Erik at the edge of the field and saluted as he approached. One, Erik recognized easily. Ikeras marred his perfect salute with a wide smile at the sight of his *septon* and gestured toward the blond aeraid beside him.

"Captain *septon* Tarverro," he greeted Erik, "may I present Lieutenant Jel Meday, *kep* Tarverro, senior Lieutenant of the Fire Company of the Third Newport Milita?"

"Lieutenant," Erik greeted Meday, inclining his head to the man. "It's good to meet you."

"Likewise, my lord," Meday replied. Shortish for an aeraid and almost blindingly blond, Jel looked familiar to Erik, but then he'd almost certainly been at the meeting where the *kep* acclaimed Erik, all those months before.

"Where are the other Lieutenants?" Erik asked.

"Koren, Telt and Jenar are settling the men into the training before they come meet you, sir," Meday replied. "We figured it would be better to continue with our normal routine before taking the time out of it to speak with you."

Erik nodded approval. "Good. Maintenance of the routine should help ease the transition of command."

"That was our belief as well, sir," Meday replied, his sigh of relief *almost* inaudible.

"Any specific problems I should know about today, Lieutenant, Sergeant?" Erik asked.

"Nothing I know of," Meday replied.

Ikeras opened his mouth to speak and then paused with his mouth hanging open. He closed it to swallow and raised his arm to gesture. "*They* might be a problem, sir," he warned.

Erik turned to see where Ikeras was pointing, to find neat files of men in heavy armor—*far* heavier than that issued to most aeradi infantry—moving onto the training field, pushing his men before them with a brusque indifference.

"Who the hell are *they*?" Erik demanded. He'd never seen *any* aeradi heavy infantry—his father's people just didn't have the mass or strength to carry that kind of armor normally.

"Wind Guard," Ikeras said flatly. "I'm not sure, but I think that's the Air Company of their Second Battalion. Their commander is Captain Dekker *sept* Corens, whose family are allies of *sept* Jaras."

"Wonderful," Erik hissed. He didn't know what the Guardsmen, the elite of the Sky Cities' armies and the men designated to protect the King himself, were doing on a Militia training field, but it was causing havoc among his men, and their commander was apparently among those who'd hate Erik just for his blood.

With a sigh, the newly commissioned Militia Captain led his command staff over to where the Wind Guard had slowed to a stop in parade formation in the middle of the field, blocking off any possible training.

"What is the meaning of this?" he demanded.

"We're carrying out our training here today," a sergeant in the front rank blandly informed Erik.

"This is a Militia field and assigned to the Fire of Third today," Erik replied furiously.

"Well-a-now, variety is the spice of life that helps the men keep their edge in, don't you know?" a voice said in a languid drawl.

A soldier with Captain's insignia stepped through the ranks. His armor shone to the point where it was nearly painful to look at, even in the dull-gray light of the misty spring morning.

"As for the other, well, it's not like a company led by a half-blood waste of air is going to need the training, eh?" Captain Dekker *sept* Corens continued. "You'll just get all the lads killed anyway, so no point in wasting the effort."

Erik's hand drifted across and grabbed Ikeras's wrist just as the ex-wing lancer's hand closed onto the hilt of his sword.

"I see," he said, as calmly as he could manage. "Unfortunately, I'm afraid that my oaths and duty to the King of Newport require me to train my men, and not to waste them either, for that matter. So, I suggest you take your men back to your own training fields."

"Well a now, I'm figuring that since we're here already, we may as well use the space," Dekker drawled. "After all, your men don't seem to be using it much, don't you know?" he added, gesturing at the Fire of Third, which had now been pretty much entirely pushed off the field by his men.

"Well, if a certain overgrown and under-brained group of overly polished metal men would clear the field, I'm sure they would be," Erik hissed through his teeth. Moments later, he regained control of his temper and regretted the words, but it was already too late.

"You *dare* insult me, you half-blood abomination?" Dekker hissed, his drawl sharpening. "I'm not thinking that can be taken." The Wind Guard's hand dropped onto the hilt of his sword, and Erik felt his mouth shape into a snarl, almost against his will.

"This is not your men's place of training. It is mine," he said flatly. "I request that you leave, and I *will* be lodging a complaint with your superiors."

In the blink of an eye, Dekker switched from deadly rage to smooth condescension. "I don't think there's a need for that, eh? Since we're here, why don't we do a little cross-training, eh?"

"Perhaps another time, Captain Corens," Erik told the man coldly. "I have little time for games today."

"How about just you and me, then?" Dekker replied. "One-on-one practice duel, just to see who's best, don't you know?"

Erik tried to resist the urge. It was unprofessional and would be giving in to the man's goads. On the other hand, the man's arrogance was wearing, and Erik very much wanted to wipe the smirk from his overbred face.

"Very well," he said flatly. "Ikeras, training swords, please."

The noncom produced the two heavy, lead-cored wooden practice swords with a disapproving look. He handed one to Dekker, then walked with Erik the regulatory ten paces away.

"This is stupid, sir," he hissed. "That said, kick his ass. For the company's sake, sir," he added piously.

Erik smiled humorlessly and hefted the sword. It weighed a bit more than his normal sky-steel blade, but he still had most of the muscles he'd acquired as a blacksmith. The difference was negligible.

He faced Dekker across the training field, fully aware that both of their companies, nearly three hundred men all told, were watching. For both his honor and the Fire of Third's, he couldn't afford to lose.

Ikeras looked at both men and sighed audibly. "Begin."

THE WORD WAS BARELY OUT OF IKERAS'S MOUTH BEFORE DEKKER attacked, charging across the densely packed sand of the training field, sword held high. As Erik moved to take advantage of the apparent opening, Dekker shifted. His sword dropped from above his head into a textbook-perfect under-arm lunge.

Somehow, Erik managed to twist his sword from his carefully controlled thrust into a parry that knocked the other man's sword aside, leaving Dekker off-balance. Trying to finish the fight quickly, Erik stabbed at the man's chest, only to have the aeraid knock the sword aside with his shield arm.

Now it was *Erik's* turn to be off-balance, and Dekker launched an attack of his own. The heavy practice sword came swinging in at Erik in a blow that could easily break his neck. Erik dropped to one knee, allowing the sword to whistle harmlessly overhead before he lunged up from his kneeling position at Dekker.

The aeraid danced nimbly back out of reach of Erik's blade, and the two men paused for a moment, circling each other under strengthening spring sun.

"You're good," Erik complimented Dekker. "I'm *almost* impressed," he added, trying to goad the man.

He succeeded. With a wordless snarl, Dekker charged in again, launching a whipping series of blows, handling the heavy practice tachi like a much lighter sword. Erik lost himself for a moment in the shift of the blades, concentrating on nothing more than where the next blow was coming from and blocking it.

For a moment, the two men stood like that, Dekker striking and Erik parrying each blow in turn. In the space of moments, the heavy wooden swords clacked together a dozen times, and then Erik shifted.

Instead of blocking the blow, he riposted off it, bouncing Dekker's blade out of the way while he drove for the man's chest. He felt his eyes widen involuntarily as the smaller aeraid managed to dance far enough to give him both room and time to block the strike with the hilt of his own weapon.

Again, the two men began to circle each other, just outside of reach. The two companies of soldiers, one elite and one Militia, were almost dead silent as they watched the two combatants circle.

Finally, Dekker's patience failed and he lunged in again. This time, Erik was almost taken by surprise, and the Wind Guard Captain's attack was perfect. The blow came drifting, almost lazily, in from Dekker's lower right, and Erik was completely out of place to block it.

Nonetheless, Erik managed to interpose his blade against the strike. Hilt met hilt, with Erik's greater mass and strength nearly useless against the angle of the attack. The half-aeraid stumbled once, then twice, and then fell to one knee involuntarily.

An evil grin crossed Dekker's face as he drew his sword back for a final blow, but Erik wasn't done just yet. He grabbed a handful of sand and threw it into Dekker's face as he rose once more. His sword drove perfectly in, aimed directly at the aeraid's sternum.

Then the world seemed to end. He *felt* his sword drive into Dekker's chest, but he *also* felt the impact of Dekker's sword, wildly waved as the man clawed at his face with his free hand, against the side of his helm.

Dekker collapsed backward, gasping for breath as Erik's blow, only barely pulled, drove the air from his lungs. The aeraid hit the sand with a thud even as the effect of his own blow drove Erik to his knees.

"Draw," Erik heard Ikeras say, as if from a very long way away.

"Draw," another voice, presumably Dekker's first sergeant, agreed.

"What do you mean, *draw?!*" the Wind Guard Captain demanded as both officers returned to their feet. "He cheated! You saw him."

"One trains as one intends to fight," Erik said mildly, driving past his aching head. "There is no such thing as cheating in war."

"Justify it however you want, *half-blood*," Dekker spat, his drawl submerged into the snarl of his rage. "You are a cheater, and everyone here saw it." He gestured around the assembled companies. The Wind Guard's face tightened even further as he listened and realized from the tone of the murmurs that even his *own* men didn't agree with him.

"This isn't over, half-blood," he growled, his drawl returning. "It sure as Water isn't over!"

With that, however, he stalked away, gesturing for his company to leave with him.

THE TWO DAYS BEFORE THE COUNCIL MEETING PASSED IN QUIET. Erik met with his squad and platoon leaders on the second day, finally meeting his other three Lieutenants. The men all seemed quietly competent, if rather inexperienced. He suspected they were as good as you got in the Militia.

The men had worked hard, and Erik was both surprised and pleased by their efforts. However, somehow, he got the impression that something was off with them. He wasn't certain what it was, and Ikeras had blown off the thought when Erik had mentioned it.

Erik wasn't so easily deterred, however, and he fully intended to pin his *kep* and senior noncom to a wall and force him to disgorge what was going on, *after* the Council meeting. For now, names and affiliations of every one of thirty-one *septons* as well as details of several trade agreements and taxation laws echoed their way around Erik's head as he waited in the anteroom to the Council Chamber, dressed in his neatly pressed *sept* uniform and wearing his father's sword.

Two men waited with him. One was Jel Meday *kep* Tarverro, who had agreed to stand with Erik for this, in lieu of Ikeras, whose brother had fallen ill the day before. The other was a Royal Armsman, a soldier of the First Wind Guard battalion, the King's personal guard. That was mandated by tradition.

The other *septons* had passed through as Erik waited. Most of those Erik had met previously had exchanged polite nods. The *septon* Jaras, however, had simply pretended that Erik hadn't existed, and Erik had gladly returned the favor.

Finally, the last of the thirty-one *septons* of the sky city of Newport, including the King himself, had entered the Chamber, and Erik's wait was over. The Armsman stepped to the doors and flung them open.

"My lords," he said in a ringing stentorian voice, "I present his lordship Erik *septon* Tarverro!"

Erik gave the man a firm nod and stepped into the room, trailed by Meday. Adelnis sat at the head of the table, near the entrance, and rose to meet him.

"Welcome, *septon* Tarverro," he said, his voice firm. "Take your seat." He gestured to the seat four places to his left.

The table was oval and long, and organized alphabetically. The *septons* voted in that same order, and only four *septons* came after Tarverro, which had worked well when the Tarverros were Kings themselves. Now, according to both Hiri and Arien, it gave the *sept* a great deal of power, as one of the last to vote and the only one of the last five not firmly welded to a faction.

Erik returned his King's nod and started toward his seat, which was directly next to Hiri's. He'd reached the chair and was about to sit when a voice rang through the chamber.

"I object!" Korand *septon* Jaras bellowed into the air.

"You have no right to object," Adelnis said calmly. "A *septon* is chosen by his *ept* and *kep*, and approved by his King. This Council has no authority over those decisions."

"I have *every* right," Jaras replied. "Only *sept* can be *septon*, and I say that this *bastard* is no *sept*."

Erik stared at the man, frozen in shock. He'd been prepared to debate and vote in a normal political forum, not to face a vicious personal attack.

"A *sept* must be born of a formal marriage before our gods and laws, not the ungodly coupling of a high-bred fool and a human *whore*!" Jaras spat.

Rage flashed through Erik's mind and veins and shattered his paralysis. His hand dove for his sword, but Hiri had been listening as well. The older *septon* moved with an incredible speed for such a fat man, his hand slamming Erik's back onto the chair.

The slapping sound of the two hands hitting the wood echoed through the chamber, and the sudden silence following it showed that every man there knew *just* what had happened.

"Speak of my mother again," Erik said slowly, flatly, desperately trying to control his rage as Hiri's fingers held his like a steel vise, "and it will be your *heir* who pursues this path."

Silence reigned in the Chamber for a long moment, and then another *septon*, Demar, stood. Tall for an aeradi but enormously fat with it, Demar looked like a little round ball of lard to Erik's eyes, but he was a close ally of Jaras, and Erik knew what he was going to say almost before the aeraid opened his mouth.

"The *septon* Jaras has a point," he said in a voice that sounded hoarsely squeaky, as if he was a child recovering from a cold. "For the child of *sept* to be *sept*, the marriage must be formally bound before the gods of our people, the Masters of Wind and Wave."

"You can't speak, lad," Hiri hissed into Erik's ear, his fingers tightening their grip as Erik opened his mouth to retort. "It's *you* on trial here, and you can't speak on that."

"A motion has been made and seconded," Adelnis, King of Newport said slowly, clearly unwillingly. "Will anyone speak to it?"

It was Hiri everyone expected to speak, but it took the burly aeraid a moment to weigh whether Erik was calm enough to be released, and in that moment another—a most unexpected other—stood in his place.

"This is foolishness," Admiral Bor *septon* Alraeis said loudly into the surprised silence. "Lord Pemmar," he said, turning to the high priest of Hydra, the god of water.

Pemmar was known for his devotion to his god and his refusal to involve himself in politics as a *septon*. He attended these meetings only because he had to, and to speak on religious affairs when necessary.

"My Lord Alraeis," the priest replied, inclining his head in question.

"Hydra is our god, correct?" the Admiral asked.

"One of our gods, yes," Pemmar said, with a glance at the *septon* Idilmar, Newport's high priest of Aris.

"Could you tell me, your Excellency," Alraeis asked, "which Gods would have been called upon in a wedding in a Hellitian city?"

"Edril and Hydra, of course," Pemmar replied. The gods of earth and water, the bloodlines that ran strongest in the human peoples of Hellit.

"Would not a marriage before Hydra among our Hellitian allies count as a wedding in His eyes here as well?" Alraeis asked, the Admiral's voice silky smooth.

For a moment, the high priest glared at Alraeis for putting him in this position, but he answered. "It would, my lord Alraeis," he said.

Alraeis looked over at Jaras and smiled, a cold and dangerous thing to see. "I think that rather undercuts your case, does it not?" he asked softly.

"Would any other speak?" Adelnis asked, his voice ringing through the chamber, silencing any answer Jaras made.

While Hiri had released Erik by now, this time the old merchant merely leaned back and made a slight gesture. In seeming response to the gesture, Idilmar, priest of Aris, rose to his feet. Unlike his fellow high priest, Idilmar was involved in factional politics. He—like most of his predecessors—was firmly welded to the merchant faction in Newport politics—Hiri's faction.

"A wedding before any of the four gods," he stated quietly but firmly, "has always been viewed as a wedding before all of them. If, however, some see it necessary, I am willing to extend the approval of my church to the wedding, long belated as it may be."

He sat, and Adelnis eyed the assembled *septons*. Erik noted his monarch's gaze and followed it, appraising each of the members of the Council in turn. Those who would vote for him, Hiri's and—apparently—Alraeis's faction, were silent, knowing that their case had been made. Those who wouldn't, the purists, seemed to have run out of steam.

Adelnis seemed to make the same judgment. "Unless another would speak, we will vote."

No one objected, and the King gestured to the pages around the table. "For the interests of preventing acrimony in such a personal case, this will be a ballot vote," he said calmly.

Erik shifted slightly but did not object aloud. The Council had two forms of voting: voice and ballot. Voice was most commonly used, except in the resolution of personal conflicts between *septons*, where secret ballots were used to, as Adelnis said, prevent acrimony among the *septons*.

The royal pages handed each *septon* a piece of paper, on which they wrote either *yea* or *nay*. The pages then collected the ballots and returned them to the King, who would only cast a tie-breaker vote. With one of the thirty non-royal *septons* unable to vote, there would be no need.

Adelnis read the ballots, then eyed his *septons* calmly. "By a vote of twenty to five, with five abstentions, the motion is rejected. *Septon* Tarverro, take your seat," he ordered.

Erik did, with a small smile. From what he'd been told by Hiri and Arien, as a rule, the merchants could poll twelve *septons*, the war faction eight, and the purists nine. The other four *septons*, including the *septon* Tarverro, the High Priest of Hydra and the King himself, were traditionally neutral. At least three of the purist *septons* had abstained, while neither the King nor Erik had voted, leaving two of the neutrals —of which one must have abstained.

Which one was clear from Arien's briefing: Guildmaster Kirenis *septon* Mogan *always* abstained at *septon* meetings. He also met with the Council of Guilds and voted there, and refused—unlike Hiri, Erik knew—to vote in both. He would, Arien had told Erik, *speak* for Guild affairs in the Council of *Septons,* but he would not vote there.

Jaras's motion had failed, which should hurt both his prestige and confidence. Despite Erik's desire to refrain from making enemies, it appeared he had already found one. Whatever Erik wanted, Jaras seemed to hold him in unwavering disgust, and the feeling was rapidly becoming mutual.

THE CONVOY WAS A RELATIVELY NORMAL TRADING GROUP HEADED to the sky city of Newport. A dozen black dragons, with six greens and eight browns for an escort. Unlike most trade caravans to Newport, however, the crews of three of the dragons were *not* traders.

At least, only three of the dragons that Brane knew about. He had his suspicions about the rest of the convoy, but his thirty men were the only ones he knew were Red Dragons. The group had kept company for two days now, flying northward out of Seije, and had finally reached its destination.

The massive cloud-like shape of Newport's sky isle filled the air in front of them, its massive connecting pillars vanishing into the spring fog beneath them. A pair of sky frigates, medium warships, escorted the convoy in toward the massive pens on the southeastern side of the city.

Once the dragons had landed, the two warships peeled off, leaving the draconans to the not-so-tender mercies of the aeradi trade officials. They issued each member of the convoy a simple pass card.

"This card authorizes you to be in most sections of the city," the official dealing with Brane informed him. "Any sections you are not allowed in are guarded, so you won't have to worry about straying into them accidentally. If you *are* found in them, however, you will be imprisoned and likely banned from the city. Understand?"

Brane nodded his silent acceptance and took the pass, suppressing his anger. Who were these arrogant, condescending bureaucrats to tell him where he could and could not go? Not that they were likely to *catch* him, but the idea still rankled.

Finally getting away from the officials and entering the merchants' compound, Brane immediately began to look for the inn he'd instructed his men to stay at. Before he could find it, however, a voice spoke to him.

"Brane Kelsdaver?"

Brane turned to find a shortish draconan standing behind him. While the man towered over the aeradi, a portly build lent to the impression of lack of height. The Red Dragon eyed the strange man up and down, and then nodded.

"I am," he said shortly.

"I am Yardmaster Pensi Diricas," the short draconan told him. "Come with me."

Unwilling to expose himself by refusing to follow the man in charge of the merchants there, Brane followed the man into what appeared to be an office building. An attractive draconan woman held down a desk in the front of the office, but Diricas led Brane quickly into the back office.

"Have a seat," he instructed as Brane entered, closing the door behind him.

Brane remained standing, silently regarding the man. "Do you pull every trader leader in off the streets like this?" he asked.

"Enough that it's not out of place," Diricas replied. "But you're no trader leader, no matter what the Council says."

"Really," Brane said calmly.

"You're a Red Dragon," the merchant replied bluntly. "So are your men. I've seen your kind before but never in such numbers. What in Fires is going on, Kelsdaver?"

"That is my business and that of the Dragon Lords," Brane told him.

"Everything in this city is my business," Diricas replied. "Our people here are my responsibility."

"Our lords apparently disagree," Brane said calmly.

The yardmaster snorted. "They also apparently think I'm stupid. I know how many of your people are in the city. You're planning an attack."

Brane stiffened in his chair, his fingers tingling with the urge to grab his crys-rod.

Diricas laughed. "I am many things, *Captain* Kelsdaver," he told Brane, revealing he knew far more about the Red Dragon than he'd admitted, "but I am not a traitor. I just want to know why *now*. This conflict has lasted for centuries and could drag on for centuries more."

"To prevent it dragging on for centuries more," Brane replied. "We have the resources, the plan and the will *now*. So, we will strike *now*."

The merchant sighed. "And that is all the answer I will receive, isn't it?"

Brane was silent, and Diricas nodded. "I do not approve, Captain Kelsdaver," he said bluntly, "but our lords have made their decision. What aid I can give, I will."

"Good."

It took Erik two whole days to track down Ikeras. It appeared as though the noncom was almost avoiding him, which made no sense. They worked together in the company and were friends besides. But even at the single set of training drills in those days, though Erik's sense of something wrong with the men was reinforced, Ikeras seemed to be very busy for the whole drill, and vanished quickly afterwards.

Finally, frustrated by his failure, Erik simply turned up at the house of the *hept* Ikeras and knocked on the door. It opened promptly to reveal a young aeradi girl, who Erik recognized as Harmon's niece, Irenda, from the *kep* meeting so long before.

"Good afternoon, Irenda," he greeted her, inclining his head. "Is your uncle home?"

The girl squeaked at finding her *septon* standing on her front doorstep and nodded wordlessly before vanishing back into the house. Erik found himself standing on the front porch, waiting.

He didn't wait long before Ikeras arrived. The noncom just looked at him for a moment and then sighed. "Good afternoon, my lord."

"Good afternoon, Harmon," Erik replied. "Can we talk?"

The ex-wing lancer nodded and stepped inside, holding the door open for his *septon*. Wordlessly, the two men entered the living area, and Erik took the seat he was gestured to. Ikeras took another of the half-dozen or so chairs scattered around the two couches in the plainly decorated room. The furniture and art were sturdy and plain but of high quality. Pretty much what would be expected of a low-level *hept* family.

"I think I know what this is about," Ikeras admitted quietly. "I've been trying to avoid the issue. We were hoping to deal with it without bringing you in."

"Harmon, something is affecting the men of *my* company," Erik told him, equally quiet. "Too broadly, I think, for it to be related to their day jobs. It is therefore my responsibility to find out what it is and deal with it."

"Some wouldn't think so," the noncom replied. "Some would think it was the responsibility of your noncoms and junior officers to deal with it."

"Maybe," Erik conceded. "But whatever it is has gone on long enough. What in Fires is going *on*, Harmon?"

"You remember the incident with Corens, right, sir?" Ikeras asked.

"Of course," Erik confirmed. He couldn't *forget*. He just tried not to think about it, as it annoyed him every time.

"The men respected you for it," the noncom explained. "You probably did as much to cement your command in the company with that *stupid* fight than you could have with weeks of solid authority.

"Unfortunately, you pissed off Corens. And *his* company is Firesburnt loyal to him."

Ikeras looked away from Erik, eyeing one of the plain pieces of art decorating the room. He sighed. "I don't know if he's ordered it, though I think he has, but his men have been harassing ours for the last week. It's worse because our men *do* respect you. His men haven't even directly started all the fights, though they've been Waters-cursed insulting to our men. About you, most of the time."

"I see," Erik said calmly. "And you thought I shouldn't know about this *why?*"

"It started off relatively minor," Ikeras replied. "A few insults exchanged, nothing more. I figured it was leftover bad feelings from the fight. Then it began to grow out of hand and turned into fistfights and brawls."

"My men have been getting into fights, and I haven't heard about it?" Erik demanded. "Shouldn't I know?"

The militia companies were part time, usually only assembling one day in five, but he was still responsible for those soldiers.

"The Watch haven't caught them at it yet, so it wouldn't come to you officially," the noncom told him. "I've been trying to stamp it out unofficially, without bringing in higher authority."

"If it's coming to fistfights and isn't stopping, it's only a matter of time before tempers flare enough for steel," Erik said flatly. "I will *not* see that happen. Understood, Ikeras?"

"Yes, sir."

"Where is this happening?" Erik asked.

Ikeras sighed. "I'll show you."

DRAGONS, SKY-MAJOR EDRIN KOLANIS, BOND TO LALEN, reflected, were loud, loyal, obnoxious, strong and *messy*. Compacting two strike regiments' worth of the beasts—twelve hundred war dragons, give or take a handful—into an area of almost any size was a recipe for aggravation. Add another regiment's worth of just transport beasts, all of which were blacks, whose size made things even worse, and about ten thousand soldiers, *not* including support staff and the Skyborne riders themselves, made for a large, *noisy* encampment.

Which, the draconan officer reflected, wasn't exactly the best thing, given that nobody in Hellit even knew this army was *there*. If the Hellitians *had* known, they'd have moved Earth, Air and twenty or thirty thousand men to dislodge them.

Fortunately, the Major reflected, scratching Lalen's head spikes, they *didn't* know. Hopefully, the operation would be concluded before they did, too. If it wasn't, the result could be messy. *Very* messy.

Sensing his unease, the green dragon bumped his shoulder gently, and he looked up at her. Kolanis was a big man, even for a draconan, towering well over six feet. Lalen, however, was quite small, even for a green dragon. The last other dragon to mistake her lack of size for weakness, however, had spent three days being healed before he'd been fit to fly.

Continuing to scratch her head spikes, Kolanis turned back to survey *his* portion of the campsite. Green Battalion of the Third Black Mountain Strike Regiment was at full strength, two hundred Bonds of dragon and Skyborne rider. So were Black and Brown Battalions of the Third, and the First Black Mountain's three battalions were also at full strength.

These two hundred dragons and riders, however, were *his* command. His responsibility. And, thanks to his own insistence, their portion of the campsite was neatly organized and clean. Not, he admitted, that the rest of the campsite was any *less* organized, but the Green of Third was definitely up to the standard around them.

His thoughts were interrupted by the arrival of the battalion's senior noncom, Sergeant Major Delt Cerians Bond Het. Unlike Lalen, Het had already been taken down to the pens, and the Sergeant Major was alone.

"Sir," Cerians greeted him. "The Green of Third is set up and awaiting your orders."

"No orders," Kolanis told Cerians. "According to the General, we're still waiting for word from our agents in the city."

"Do we know what kind of word?" the noncom asked.

For a moment, Kolanis considered telling the noncom. He had, after all, worked with Cerians for years, first as the senior noncom in Kolanis's company, now as the sergeant major of the Green of Third. However, General Idinris's instructions were quite clear: none of the men were to be informed what the army was waiting for.

"They haven't said," he lied.

"Well, I hope it comes soon, whatever it is," Cerians told him. "Feeding two thousand or so dragons is going to be bad enough, even without the troops."

Kolanis nodded, smiling slightly to himself at how the noncom's view of the issues differed from his own. He worried about being found and attacked—Cerians worried about *feeding* everyone. Each, in its own way, was their most serious worry.

"We have the resources," he noted.

Cerians nodded. "Just borrowing trouble, sir," he replied. "You want me to take Lalen to the pens?"

With a last scratch of the green's head spikes, Kolanis nodded and touched the dragon's mind, instructing her to follow Cerians. The dragon rubbed her head against his hand and then followed the other man.

Kolanis watched her for a while, and then turned his gaze to the south, eyeing the wide-swept plains of northern Hellit. Only time would prove which of the worries, his or Cerians', truly was their worst.

Or, of course, the ridiculous plan would actually *work*, and neither would be important, because the draconans would be in Newport.

THE NONCOM LED ERIK THROUGH THE STREETS OF NEWPORT'S HIGH City in the fading light of the afternoon sun. The tavern Ikeras led him to was frequented by the men of several of the Militia companies, mainly those of the Third Newport. That meant that Dekker's men could be reasonably sure of finding some of Erik's men there.

As they clearly had. Erik stepped into the darkened room to find two groups of men surging up from their tables. None were in uniform, but he recognized all the men of one group from his own company, and the weapons the other group bore were sky steel, marking them as Wind Guard.

Clearly, Erik had been quite correct about tempers, for even as the men came to their feet, they were drawing their swords. There were five of Erik's men to three of the Wind Guard, but the Guards' weapons were sky steel. The fight was going to be ugly.

Erik had no intention of allowing there to be a fight.

"Put up your swords!" he bellowed, his voice echoing through the tavern and stopping both groups of soldiers in their tracks. When neither group seemed inclined to put away their weapons, Erik stalked into the tavern, turning his gaze on each group in turn.

"Did you not hear me?" he demanded. "Sheathe your swords!"

Finally, both groups slowly returned their weapons to their scabbards. Erik turned first to his men. The man in the lead he recognized as Keltin Ders, a Corporal in his Third Platoon.

"Corporal Ders," he greeted the man, his voice suddenly calm.

"Sir, these men—" the Corporal began, but Erik cut him off.

"I don't want to hear it," he snapped. "Take your men and get out. We will discuss this later."

The Corporal bobbed a hasty salute and led the others, most likely his lance, though Erik wasn't sure, out of the tavern. As they left, Erik turned toward the three Guardsmen.

"And just what on Water did you think you were doing?" he demanded.

"I do not answer to you, *Militiaman*," their leader, who, like Ders, appeared to be a Corporal.

Erik fingered the hilt of the sky-steel sword he wore—his father's sword, and mark of his rank as *septon*. "Do you know what this sword means?" he asked the man, his voice very, very quiet.

"Yes," the man replied, but he seemed uncowed.

"It means that you *do* answer to me," Erik told the man. Which was technically true—the Wind Guard answered to the King and the Councils, and Erik sat on the *septons'* Council.

"I only answer to *real septons*," the man replied contemptuously. "Not half-blood imposters."

"Watch your tongue, fool," Ikeras snapped from behind Erik. "You have no authority to speak so."

"Watch your *own* tongue," the Guardsman snapped back, his hand dropping to the sword he'd sheathed only moments before.

"Hold your blade," Erik ordered, his voice a whip-crack of command. "Before you do anything hasty," he continued in a silky voice as the man's hand remained on his sword hilt, "I would remind you that the man behind me is *kep* to my *sept*, which means if you draw steel in my presence, he has every right to kill you where you stand."

Erik held the Guardsman's gaze for a long moment. Then another. Then, finally, the Guardsman released his blade.

"Good," Erik said, his voice still silky soft. "Now get out. And tell your friends that the next Guardsman who comes in here to harass my men *will be broken*." He snarled the last words, and his hand tightened on his own sword hilt.

"Do I make myself clear?" he asked.

The Guardsman nodded stiffly, clearly unwilling to speak. For a moment more, the three men faced Erik and Ikeras in the dead silence of the tavern, until they finally turned and stalked out.

Erik sighed in relief and very nearly sagged around his bones. He glanced around the tavern, and his gaze came to rest on the barkeep, who looked distressed. Erik realized, horrified, that neither group had actually paid their tab before he'd kicked them out.

He crossed to the bar and laid a handful of gold crowns on the darkened wood. "This should cover the tabs...and the inconvenience," he told the man quietly. The barkeep began to shake his head, most likely because the crowns were probably four or five times the tab of both groups. "Take it," Erik insisted. "A token of my apologies for whatever other incidents have happened as well."

Finally, the barkeep took the coin. Erik gave the man a firm nod and then strode from the tavern, Ikeras at his heels.

BRANE KEPT HIS EYE GLUED TO THE EYEPIECE OF HIS TELESCOPE AS he surveyed the military docks of Newport. His lips thinned underneath it as he saw empty slip after empty slip, where warships should have rested in the dock's support fields. He'd *thought* they were sending out too many patrols, and not enough had been coming back, but he hadn't thought it was *this* major.

They'd sneaked their entire fleet off to their war games, and the draconan spies had almost missed it! If Brane hadn't found his little hideaway, high on the outside of one of the merchant houses' towers, he would never have known, and the opportunity would have slid away from his people.

It hadn't, however, and he descended the outside of the tower to the ground with a smile on his lips. The first part of the mission was complete. Of course, that left more than few pieces still to fall into place.

He'd been surprised at just *how* many infiltrator groups there were in the aeradi city, but their numbers made sense, from a certain point of view. While Brane didn't know them all, he knew the messengers who, by passing messages from one to another, would carry orders to all the groups in the city.

The men he'd entrusted with the knowledge of who *those* messengers were waited for him at the bottom of the tower. Brane looked around the group and nodded to the man who'd first noticed that more ships seemed to be leaving than coming back.

"You were right, Dari," he told him. "They snuck their entire fleet out, and we barely noticed."

"Most of the lancers are gone too," the junior agent observed quietly. "It's hard to tell visually—they're a lot smaller than warships— but if you get close to the pens, the noise level is too low. There's maybe a tenth of their normal numbers there."

Brane was impressed. He didn't think he'd have noticed that when he was that new to the Red. He gave the youth another nod and then turned to the rest.

"The time is now," he said bluntly. "Contact the messengers, inform all groups they are to begin placing the explosives. I'll send the message to the army immediately—the attack will commence in three days."

The men nodded, their faces blanking as they swiftly memorized his words. *These* orders could not be trusted to paper.

"Once you're done, meet at the rendezvous to confirm," Brane continued. The men scattered, each to find his own contacts, as Brane turned back to the walls of the military enclosure. The rendezvous was a tavern named the Black Moonbeam.

His lips twisted at the thought. Even the *tavern* names were pretentious there. Aeradi arrogance and pretensions oozed from every corner of the buildings and streets. It sickened him, but he knew the place would be in his people's hands soon enough.

The room he was renting and the cage with the small courier pigeon in it were only a few blocks from the tower he'd scaled. Everyone always raved about how they would soon have a method of communication by magic of one kind or another. The dwarves' engineers and alchemists talked about wires and Fire, the draconan and aeradi crystal Aligners and Melders talked about crystals that could speak across the Air. None worked.

The only method Brane knew to work was the Mages' mind-to-mind communication, but the draconans had few mages, and they, like Dracona's healers, were half-bloods. Respected for their talents but despised for their impure blood.

Certainly, while he had no Mage to communicate with the army on the shores of Hellit, he didn't need one. He caressed the head of the courier pigeon as she cooed at him and took the time to write the message out carefully before he tucked it into the bird's ankle tube. Once the message was in place, he carried her to the window and let her loose.

The bird flew faster than dragons or rocs, let alone skyships. She'd reach her mate, with the army, by nightfall. The army would leave those shores by dawn.

Two days after that, ten thousand Claws of the Dragon would descend on the undefended city of Newport.

AFTER ERIK'S DISPLAY IN THE TAVERN, THE BAR FIGHTS BETWEEN HIS men and Dekker *sept* Corens' stopped. Unfortunately, according to Ikeras—who had given up on hiding anything from Erik—that was only because they'd moved their harassment to more public locations, where steel could not be drawn.

The campaign of low-level harassment sickened Erik, but he was hard pressed to think of things to do. The only option he could come up with was to confront Dekker himself. Which, of course, was what led to him standing outside an upscale tavern named the Black Moonbeam in the fading spring light.

According to Ikeras, Dekker frequented this tavern often, most evenings in fact, and should be in there now. Confronting him would be simple: all Erik had to do was walk inside and find the man. It wasn't a big tavern.

There was no way Erik could allow the harassment of *his* men to continue. He'd refused Ikeras's company on this venture, in the hope that the lack of other presences would encourage Dekker to speak honestly, but only time would tell.

He entered the tavern. It was a small tavern, with only one major room with a bar and several tables. Quiet and upscale, the tables and bar were Sky Isle oak, well polished and kept clean, and the room was well, if dimly, lit by dozens of crystal lights. The Moonbeam was only about half-full, with a noticeable number of draconan traders enjoying a drink before the evening rush of aeradi pushed them out.

Dekker sat alone at a table off to the right-hand side of the room. He was out of uniform and didn't even appear to be armed. The Wind Guard wasn't facing the door, and his gaze appeared to be riveted to the rear of one of the tavern's serving girls. With a quick glance, Erik confirmed that this sight was likely to hold his attention for a while, and crossed to the aeraid's table.

"Dekker *sept* Corens," he said, just loudly enough to be heard over the dull murmur of conversation in the room. "We meet again."

"Well-a-now," Dekker drawled, his gaze returning to his own table, "isn't this a pleasure." Despite his words and the drawl, his voice was flat. "And just what would you be a-wanting, Tarverro?"

"I want your men to stop pushing mine," Erik said flatly, circling the table to the only other chair at it. His gaze locked on to Dekker's as he slowly sank into the chair, half-facing the aeraid, half-facing the tavern door.

"I wouldn't be having the slightest notion what you're on about," Dekker replied lazily. "Soldiers get rowdy, you know, and there's little man nor god can do about that."

"Like Fires you don't," Erik hissed. "You and I both know you put them up to it."

"Maybe I did, and maybe I didn't, but I don't see how it's my concern if you're not keeping your own discipline," Dekker told him, a slight grin on his face.

"Oh, I can keep discipline if I have to," Erik murmured. "Which half of your men do you want me to kill to make the other half behave?"

Dekker's lazy, relaxed stance vanished as he straightened hard in his chair. "You'll be a-finding I'm not taking well to threats," he said, equally quietly, his drawl suddenly hard. "To my men least of all."

Erik blinked at this sign, the *first* sign, of the man caring for more than his own bloated ego. "Keep your own discipline, then," he told the man, "so that I don't have to."

"I don't be seeing..."

Whatever it was Dekker wasn't planning to see, Erik never heard. Even as the aeraid spoke, his gaze drifted to the door of the tavern, just as another draconan merchant walked in. He casually glanced at the man's face, and froze.

It was the man from Black Mountain. The Red Dragon who'd hunted him across half of Cevran. In the moment Erik recognized the man, the Dragon clearly recognized him. A twisting motion of the assassin's wrist brought *something* into his hand, and Erik didn't stay still long enough to find out what it was.

"Corens, down!" he snapped, and dove across the table to drive the Wind Guard officer to the floor. As he did, a bolt of lightning struck the table, shattering it into a dozen pieces.

The smell of burning ozone in his nostrils, Erik surged back to his feet, shoving Dekker one way while he jumped the other. Another bolt of lightning flashed through where they'd been kneeling, and exploded against the back wall, showering the patrons with shrapnel.

This was *not* what he'd been expecting!

BRANE CURSED HORRIBLY IN THE PRIVACY OF HIS MIND. BY ALL THE gods and powers, Tarverro *there*? There was only one, perhaps two or three, people in this entire *city* who could recognize him for what he was, and he had run into the only one he was certain of. The one man he wanted above all else to kill but couldn't afford to be seen by.

Both of his bolts had missed, and his crys-rod was expended. He could run, but he wouldn't make it. Besides, Tarverro knew he was there, and Tarverro knew *what* he was. No matter what else, Tarverro had to die.

Flinging his cloak from his shoulders, Brane drew his sword, and his mind began cataloguing threats. Most of the patrons weren't a danger, but the man with Erik had come back to his feet too quickly and was surveying the room with too sharp an eye. He was a soldier, definitely.

Four of his own men were already in the tavern, and a fifth was with him. He had no choice. Tarverro *had* to die, and the soldier as well, just to be certain.

"*Take them!*" he shouted, and his men threw back cloaks and jackets, drawing the swords they'd carried concealed underneath them.

It wasn't the venue he'd have chosen, but it was the battle he had.

ERIK DIDN'T LIKE THE STILETTO DAGGERS HE'D FORGED MONTHS before for the Red Dragon Rade, but he was too aware of their usefulness to give them up. So, even when he'd hung the rapier on the wall, replacing it with his father's sword, he'd had a leather wrist-sheath made for one of them.

Now, with draconans far too close for him to draw his sword, he flicked it out of its sheath. In one fluid motion, he stepped inside the reach of the draconan nearest him and slid the tiny blade between the man's ribs.

The Red Dragon froze in shock, coughed up blood and began to fall, clearing Erik a space. Before the assassin hit the floor, Erik grabbed the shortsword he'd been wielding and brought it up against the man who'd been with his victim.

He was too close to use the blade, so he simply slammed the pommel of the weapon into the draconan's face. The man stumbled backward, over a stool, and Erik took advantage of the free moment to spin to Corens.

As he'd feared, the Wind Guard was unarmed and facing off with two of the Red Dragons. Unarmed, the man was doomed. Erik may have disliked the man, but he had no intention of allowing *that* to happen.

"Corens!" he bellowed. The Wind Guard's head snapped around to face him, and he smiled grimly. "Catch!" Erik shouted, and tossed the sword in his hand. Corens caught it one-handed and raised it in salute, quickly turning the gesture into a parry as the draconans closed in.

He'd done all he could for Corens, and his own sword whistled out of his sheath as he turned back to the draconan he'd distracted. The man was back up on his feet and charged at Erik, his sword out for a disemboweling slash.

Erik thrust his sword out and into the charging assassin, whose swing faltered as the sky-steel point punched into his gut, and Erik batted the shortsword aside with the flat of his hand and yanked his blade out.

The draconan crumpled to the ground, but a whistle of air warned Erik of another assassin. He dodged sideways, sliding to one knee on the gory wooden floorboards, and a shortsword stabbed through where he'd stood. He surged back to his feet, parrying another blow as he did, and retaliated with a backhand blow that opened the spy's throat in a spray of blood.

Then Brane, the draconan he'd *known* was a Red Dragon, was there, his sword driving for Erik's own throat. Erik slashed his sword violently in front of his face, knocking the Red Dragon's sword aside but unbalancing himself.

Erik slid almost uncontrollably on the gore, causing Brane's next blow to go wide. He stopped his slide and came to his feet in a lunge, but the Red Dragon nimbly dodged out of the way of Erik's blade, sending his own strike sweeping at Erik's head.

The two swords met with a clang as Erik knocked the strike aside and lunged. The tip of his tachi scored the draconan's side as Brane failed to dodge swiftly enough, and Erik grinned mockingly.

"Even Rade was better than this," he told the other man softly, watching to see if his judgment of the man's blood relation to that long-dead assassin was right.

A wordless snarl was his only answer, enough to confirm his thought. Erik had no time for further worry, however, as Brane came at him fast and dirty. Three times the draconan struck, trying to find a weakness in Erik's guard, and three times Erik parried. His focus on Brane's strikes was almost his undoing.

"Tarverro!" Corens' shout echoed across the tavern. "Look out!"

One of the Dragons attacking Corens had broken off and come to his leader's aid. He came in from Erik's flank, stabbing for the half-aeraid's thigh. Corens' warning was just enough, and Erik stepped backward.

The draconan slid into the space he'd occupied, and Erik grabbed the man's shoulder with his left hand. The muscles of years of black-smithing stood out along Erik's arm as he propelled the man across the slick wooden floorboards into Brane's weapon arm.

Brane was too well trained to accidentally hit his own man, but the other Red Dragon knocked the draconan's arm off for a deadly moment too long. In that single moment of distraction, Erik struck.

His father's sword lanced out in a deadly-perfect underarm stroke that punched clean through the assassin's ribcage and drove splinters of bone into the man's heart and lungs before punching out Brane's back, severing the draconan's spinal cord.

For an unimaginably long moment, Brane's and Erik's gazes locked. Then, wordlessly, the draconan assassin slid from Erik's blade onto the floor.

ERIK BARELY EVEN SAW CORENS DISPATCH THE LAST PAIR OF RED Dragons. Brane's death put the rest of the fight into shadow, and Erik slowly knelt by the assassin's body, ignoring the gore.

The man had chased him across half a continent and somehow managed to follow him even there, to Newport, where he'd assumed he was safe. So many had died for this man's pursuit of him, and now it was over. Erik wasn't quite sure how to take it.

"Red Dragons," he heard Corens say softly, interrupting his reverie.

Erik turned away from the body of his enemy and faced the other soldier stiffly. "Yes," he agreed. "That one," he indicated Brane, "and I have met before."

Corens eyed the body and nodded slowly. "If you hadn't spotted him, we both would be dead," he declared. "I would have died again had you not armed me. I owe you a life, Tarverro."

Erik shivered. The words somehow meant more for their quiet sincerity and terrified him. *That* was not a debt easily set aside among the aeradi *ept*. Nor was it one he felt deserved.

"You saved mine with your warning," he replied. "We're even."

"No, we're not," Corens said flatly, straightening to face Erik. "What was between us is over," he told Erik. "You have my word."

At that moment, the Watch began to arrive, stunned by the carnage in the middle of a high-class tavern. Even through the noise, however, Erik still managed to be heard.

"And you mine," he told Corens. "And you mine."

"DOWN, GIRL!" KOLANIS BELLOWED AS LALEN SUDDENLY REARED under his cleaning brush. Cleaning the giant beasts was relaxing for both dragon and rider, and also helped solidify the Bond. A dragon rearing while being cleaned was highly unusual, and he looked into the air to see what had attracted her attention.

His link to his dragon drew his eyes to a tiny speck in the sky that quickly grew into a dot, and then a courier pigeon, diving for the communications tent where, Kolanis knew, its mate awaited it. Since the communications officer for the army was a half-human Mage, running a mind relay back to Black Mountain, there was only one reason for a pigeon to be coming there.

Calmly, oh so calmly, Kolanis gave Lalen one last scratch, then carefully hung up the brush. As soon as the brush was solidly on its hook, however, he took off toward the tent.

One of his men was waiting for him, the Captain of his First Company. The officer was almost bouncing up and down, and only slowed slightly at the sight of his commander. "Is this it, sir? Are we go?"

"I don't know," Kolanis replied honestly. "It might be. Are you ready?"

"Yes, sir!" the officer bellowed.

"Are your men ready? Are the other companies ready? The rest of the regiment?" the Sky-Major demanded. "Find out!" he barked before the Captain could answer. "If it's the order, we fly at dawn!"

The company commander saluted and took off at a run. Shaking his head, Kolanis headed to the communication tent, at a slightly less tumultuous pace. As he neared the tent, he saw that the *rest* of the army's senior officers, of both the Skyborne and Claw contingents, had closed on the tent.

Twenty-seven Claw and twelve Skyborne officers had converged on the tent, and they all stopped, looking around at each other sheepishly. Before anything more could be said, however, General Adaelis, the army's commander, came out of the tent.

He surveyed the crowd of majors and colonels in front of him and grinned widely. "It's good to see that my officers are neither blind nor ignorant," he told them loudly.

Adaelis didn't continue, so Kolanis stepped forward out of the crowd. "Is this it, sir? Is it time?"

"Relax, Sky-Major," Adaelis told him. "We have indeed received a report from our Red Dragon agents in the sky city of Newport."

Kolanis found himself holding his breath for the general's next words, like the rest of the officers. Adaelis could clearly tell and was just as clearly taking pleasure in drawing out the moment.

"As of this morning, the aeradi's wargames have definitely commenced, leaving only a handful of skyships and wing lancers to defend the city," the general commanding the largest deployment of draconan troops in a generation informed his senior officers.

"While this normally only draws the Marine units out of the city, several of Newport's Regular units are also involved this year," he continued. "In addition, many of their Regular units are outside the city, involved in other duties."

"The city, however, is far from defenseless," Adaelis warned his men. "Several Regular regiments remain, as does their Wind Guard regiment and the entirety of their Militia. However, given our assets in the city and that those assets are moving to destroy the city's external anti-air defenses..." The General trailed off, eyeing his men, and then shrugged. "It has been decided to initiate the operation as planned," he finished.

A cheer rose from the assembled officers, and Kolanis cheered along with the rest. After years of dancing to the aeradi tune, playing to their economic rules, accepting their dictates and closed borders, Dracona was finally striking back.

"We fly at dawn," Adaelis told them once he finally had quiet. "Let the aeradi tremble!"

IT WAS LATE IN THE EVENING BY THE TIME THE WATCH LET ERIK go. Bloody battles in the middle of upscale taverns were disconcerting enough for them without having a *septon* mixed up the mess. As time passed, Erik began to grow more and more worried that rumor of the encounter would reach Arien before he did.

In the end, however, the witness of the bar's patrons had borne fruit, and the Watch had finally released him. Most of the Watchmen left then, with the wagon carrying the bodies of the Red Dragons who'd disturbed the peace the Watch was sworn to protect.

Their officer, however, Captain Tel Demeraid, the man who'd questioned Erik, remained behind. Erik paused at the door, in the process of leaving, at the sight of the man waiting for him under a crystal light on the street outside the club. The Watch Captain beckoned to him, and Erik sighed and crossed to meet him.

"I thought your questions were done," he murmured.

"They are, *septon*," Captain Demeraid said respectfully. "I just wanted to advise you of my conclusions."

"I see," Erik replied, nodding slowly. The Captain had no need to do so, but it was an appreciated courtesy.

The dark-haired police officer eyed the club behind him. "They couldn't have known that you were going to be in the Black Moonbeam," he told Erik. "I don't think they were hunting you—at that specific moment."

"At that moment?" Erik queried, and Demeraid nodded.

"At that moment," he confirmed. "I think, though further investigation will be carried out, of course, that they *were* looking for you. I can see no other reason for them to put a man they *knew* you'd recognize in the city."

"There are other operations Red Dragons could be used for," Erik guessed, "and they would not need half a dozen men to kill me."

"Agreed," the Watch Captain said instantly. "However, it might have taken a dozen or more men to *find* you, and Kelsdaver isn't known to just you. They wouldn't send a man they knew could be recognized here for normal operations—too much risk."

Erik nodded slowly. "Perhaps," he said, still unconvinced.

The Watchman shrugged. "I do not know for certain," he admitted, "but I do not see any other reason. After all, what *else* could he have been after?"

"I do not know," Erik admitted. "But I fear what it may have been nonetheless."

DARI HENDALL HUNG FROM THE SIDE OF THE TOWER BY HIS harness, his telescope surveying the clouds around him. With Kelsdaver's death, the junior Red Dragon now commanded the central cadre of infiltrators—what was left of them, at least.

He was sure there were more senior agents in place on the island, but he was the one who was senior in the central group—which meant he was the one at the center of the communication net and the one who'd have to give the order to act.

Which put him up on the side of this merchant house's tower, watching for the army. And spotting them, he realized, as a slight movement drew his eye. There, on the horizon, where the clouds met the sea, a blur of motion turned into a sea of dots as the massive wave of dragons and men of the draconan army came into view.

It was time. Hendall released the catches on his harness and plummeted to the ground. He hit on his feet, gently absorbing the impact, and turned to the messengers.

"They're here," he told them quietly. "Blow the charges."

THE NEXT TWO DAYS HAD PASSED IN QUIET, WITH IKERAS confirming to Erik that the harassment of his men had been stopped. In one case that the former wing lancer had seen himself, a pair of burly sergeants from Dekker's company had intervened, breaking up the argument with a few choice words and sharp orders to the Wind Guards.

With no political affairs for Arien to shepherd him to, Erik had found himself with little to do except stop in at the small office maintained for him in the main Militia compound, to brush up on the men under his command. Only Captains and above *had* such offices, as most Militia affairs took place at the battalion armories scattered through the city at muster points.

Erik had only visited the tiny office twice and was unimpressed. It had been a small-enough office before someone had lined the walls with eight filing cabinets and then crammed a small desk into the remaining space. Its sole good point was that it *did* contain all the information about his company, but it was more of a file repository than an actual *office*.

Which meant that the letter lying on the desk was a surprise— especially since Erik had made arrangements with Ikeras for any mail at this office to be delivered to him elsewhere, and he'd merely been intending to read through the files.

Upon opening the letter, however, he found a quick note from his battalion commander, Major Leo Champion, instructing him to drop by the Major's office in the Militia compound at his "earliest convenience."

Despite having been a member of the battalion for nearly a week, Erik had yet to meet the Major commanding the Third Newport Militia. Curiosity won out over established plans, and he abandoned his tiny office for the Major's slightly larger one just down the hall.

Champion greeted him at the door himself and ushered him quickly into the room. "Come in, come in, Captain," he ordered in quick, jerking words. The man was tall for an aeraid and lean even for that slim race, with an untidy shock of blond hair.

"Have a seat, have a seat," he instructed, gesturing to a chair.

Erik took it, glancing around the room. The only difference in size between this room and his own office was the lack of filing cabinets, and a small door behind Champion's desk gave away the secret to that: majors had a second room for their files.

"Apologies, apologies, for not meeting you sooner," Champion said once Erik had taken a seat. "I've been busy, busy, with my duties in the Regulars."

"You're in the Regulars as well?" Erik asked, surprised. Most officers holding Regular commissions had retired their Militia commissions on the receipt of the Regular ones. Few had the time to handle *both* jobs.

"Yes, yes," the major replied. "Nothing too major, not to worry, not to worry. Just logistics, so rather quiet, quiet."

"Why's logistics been busy?" Erik asked with frank curiosity.

"Well, the war games are on now, now," Champion told him. "Setting up the supplies for two-thirds of the Fleet and all the lancers to go to the Isles is quite a task, quite a task."

"*What?*" Erik hissed.

Champion blinked, clearly surprised at being asked to repeat himself. "The war games are on now," he said. "Most of the Fleet and all of the lancers are in the Isles. Why do you ask?"

"Sir," Erik said, surging to his feet. "Two days ago, I was attacked by Red Dragons *in this city*. We thought they were after me—I've had previous dealings with them, to nobody's pleasure. But if the *entire Fleet* is not *here*—who knows what they saw?"

Champion's face blanched as the thought visibly struck home in his mind.

"We have to warn everyone, everyone!" he snapped, coming to his own feet.

It was too late. Even as the Militia major stood up, they felt the entire city *rock*—for all of the power of its magic, for all of its unimaginable mass and size, the floating island *lurched*—and the sound of massive explosions ripped through the air.

ERIK KNEW why the Red Dragons had been in the city now. It had *nothing* to do with him at all. They'd been spies and saboteurs, and his encounter with them had been an unplanned accident. An accident that had cost them an entire attack team.

Clearly, Brane's team hadn't been the only one, even if Erik and Dekker had succeeded in wiping it out. And now the city's defenses were gone, and an attack was almost certainly on its way.

Erik cursed in the quiet of his own mind. All the pieces had been there to be seen. Why had no one put them together? They could have been *ready* for this! His mind quickly went to people he knew—Arien, Hiri, even Elysia flashed through his mind with a heavy tinge of fear.

With a deep breath, Erik controlled his fear and anger and turned to Champion, who had frozen when the explosions shook the building and seemed to be in a complete stupor.

"Sir," he said sharply, trying to rouse the man. Champion just sat there, ignoring him. "Sir!" Erik snapped, louder. When the man started, he continued more quietly. "We have to go, sir. The battalion will be waiting."

"Yes, yes!" Champion agreed, almost pathetically latching on to any idea for action. "We must—*must*—get to the battalion. They'll need us."

Erik's unspoken opinion of his superior rose somewhat as the aeraid picked up a sword from behind his desk, where he hadn't seen it, and belted it on. Clearly, the Major was ready to do his duty.

"Let's go," Champion ordered, and Erik could only agree.

HENDALL ROSE TO HIS FEET FROM WHERE THE EXPLOSIONS HAD thrown him, brushing dust off of his clothes. He'd cut the fuse on his own charge a little too short, it seemed, but that hardly mattered compared to what they'd achieved.

The vaunted outer defenses of the aeradi sky city were piles of debris and shattered crystal now, unable to stop so much as a determined pigeon. The dragons of Black Mountain's assault force were no pigeons, and they had determination to spare, he was sure.

The primary mission of the infiltrators was complete, and now was the time for them to carry out their other objectives. There were sufficient numbers in the city Militia and enough choke points in the city that they could slow, perhaps even stop the attack. The Militia had to be neutralized and the choke points held if the draconans were to break through.

Each of the infiltrated Red Dragons had two pieces of information they'd been told to memorize: the name and probable location of a Militia officer they were to kill, and a rendezvous point for them to meet up with other Dragons.

Hendall's target lived less than three blocks from where he stood.

KOLANIS HAD ONLY *JUST* LOCATED THE CITY WITH HIS TELESCOPE when it vanished into a blur of light and smoke for a moment. The light merely flashed and was gone, but the smoke remained, a silent beacon of war guiding the armies of Dracona to her foes.

He glanced behind him, at the black dragon that carried Adaelis, in case the commander decided to change his orders based on this. No new orders came from the General, suggesting that this had been planned all along.

Which made sense, the draconan Sky-Major realized, and his teeth bared in a grin as Green Battalion of the Third Regiment swept forward. His men and dragons had been granted the honor of leading the strike, and the destruction of the outer defenses made that far safer than he'd expected it to be.

The dragons sensed the excitement of their riders and threw their great hearts into their flight. The city grew rapidly, until Kolanis could make out the very defenses the explosions had torn apart.

Some of the weapons were still intact, but their crews *must* be more focused on retrieving their wounded comrades from the ruins than on manning their guns and crystal bows. No matter how much logic would warn them that an attack had to be coming, they wouldn't think of it. Not now.

It wouldn't have mattered, anyway. Kolanis made a sharp hand gesture, above his head where all of his people could see it, then kneed Lalen. Two hundred green dragons lunged downward at the forts, blazing fire as they came, and the war cries of both dragons and men rang through the air.

On the quarter of the city wall where they attacked, perhaps forty weapons remained intact, and Kolanis's strike silenced half of them before they could fire. Cannonballs and lightning bolts struck a handful of his Bonds from the air, but it was too late for the defenders.

Dragon fires and dragon claws ended the first phase of the battle, slaughtering the last of the gun crews and shattering their weapons. As the last crystal bow fell silent, Kolanis added his own voice to Lalen's keening victory roar.

The way into Newport was open!

When the blood-chilling war cries of dragons echoed over Newport, Erik merely nodded to himself grimly and kept walking, his hand caressing the hilt of his sword. He couldn't fight dragons, but he could sure as Fires fight the men they bore. They had to land to take the city, after all.

Champion was more affected. He stopped in the middle of the street. "What was *that,* that?" he demanded.

"Dragon cries," Erik replied shortly, stopping and turning back to his commander. "The draconans have begun their attack."

"Attack?!" Champion replied, his voice querulous. "They would never dare attack us! The outer defenses—"

"Are gone," Erik cut him off sharply. "That's what those explosions were. Anyone left alive in the forts died when the dragons hit them. That was the vanguard, battle dragons. What is *here* of Sky Fleet will soon occupy their attention. It's the ones that come *after* them *we* need to worry about."

"What, what? Why?"

Erik was forced to wonder if his commander knew *anything* about war. "Because they'll be carrying the soldiers," he guessed.

"Not all of them," Champion suddenly said.

"Why do you say that?" Erik demanded, but even as he spoke, he knew. He'd heard the distinctive sound of a crys-rod discharging before, and this time it was *behind* him.

The next thing he knew, his diminutive commanding officer hit him in the waist, bearing him to the ground and out of the way of the bolt. A second bolt cracked moments after the first, and Champion's body crumpled onto Erik.

For an eternal moment, the Major's eyes held Erik's as he smelt the reek of burning flesh.

"Our men..." Champion gasped, "the city...save them. Save them."

With that, the aeradi Major had repeated his last phrase, and died in Erik's arms. Before Erik's mind had truly processed what was happening, a *third* bolt hit the aeraid's body and flipped it clear of the Militia Captain, leaving Erik half-fried by the discharge.

Half-fried or not, Erik came up to his feet and his sword swung free. Unless the man had more than one rod, he *had* to have expended his shots. Indeed, as Erik's sword came up, he spotted two draconans headed toward him at a run, one of them shucking a piece of crystal from his wrist as he drew his sword.

The one drawing his sword was no threat for the moment, and Erik lunged to meet the other draconan. The assassin reacted swiftly, and Erik's lunge was interrupted by a smooth parry.

Unfortunately for the draconan, Erik held one of his stilettos in his *other* hand. He allowed the force of the parry to spin him around, using the force to drive the metal spike into the Red Dragon's throat.

The infiltrator crumpled to the ground, and Erik finished his turn to face the first man, who had now drawn his own sword. With the stiletto in the other draconan's throat, he had no surprises for this man. Nonetheless, he didn't have time to play games.

The Red Dragon attacked first, moving forward in the draconans' textbook belly-thrust. Eschewing subtlety for brute force, Erik grabbed the hilt of the dragonclaw sword and pulled the draconan forward.

Unfortunately, the man was too good to allow Erik to pull him off-balance, releasing the sword before he was pulled too far forward. The spy rocked back on his heels, still perfectly balanced as he went for what was presumably another weapon of some sort.

Perfectly balanced or not, he never made it. Even as Erik unbalanced himself, he used his own backward motion to propel his sword. He went backward, and his sword went up and across, opening the draconan up from waist to throat in one vicious cut.

The fight was over in a matter of moments, and Erik took a moment to regain his breath and cross to Champion's body. The aeradi soldier was very, very dead. Living men didn't have that much of their back and side burnt away.

Nonetheless, the major had saved Erik's life, and Erik intended to fulfill the man's dying order. The Third Militia was *his* unit now, and Newport was *his* city.

As Champion had ordered, he was going to save them. He was going to save them if it killed him.

THE SCREECH OF A DRAGON BEHIND HIM ROUSED KOLANIS'S attention from the shores of the sky island below. He turned in his seat to see Sergeant-Major Cerians waving to him. Once the noncom was sure he had his commander's attention, he made a series of hand signals.

Sky Fleet, attacking, transports, followed by a gesture behind him. Kolanis followed the gesture to where the transport regiments were closing in on the city, but he knew what he was going to see.

Clearly, their intelligence had been correct. There were far fewer skyships out there than there should have been. Whoever commanded the aeradi warships, however, had obviously decided to try to do as much as he could and was striking at the weak point of the draconan attack.

Six battleships and twelve frigates shook themselves out into an attack formation as he watched, cannon and crystal bows beginning to flare as they came into range of the transport dragons.

The transport dragons were blacks, with the notoriously weak flame of that kind. That, of course, was why *war* blacks carried weapons. As Kolanis watched, the convoy's escorts surged forward to meet the warships, their own cannon and crys-bows flaring in return fire.

It probably would have been enough, but Kolanis wasn't willing to take the chance. His own gesture toward the fleet was followed by a signal: *Take them.*

The skyships were distracted by their engagement with the escort dragons and were still doing their best to take as many of the transports out of the sky as they could. If someone had been watching for other attacks, they had failed at their task.

Sky-Major Kolanis led his battalion in a swooping attack, fire blazing from their mouths. A frigate died under their fire as a dragon's flame burnt through into its inner hull. It either hit the ship's powder magazine or its crystal rooms, as it blew apart into a green-tinged fireball, the blast wave knocking two more frigates out of formation and forcing Lalen to beat her wings sharply to keep herself and the Major in place.

With a wave of his lance, Kolanis sent two of his companies to focus on the separated frigates, while he led the other two against the battleships at the heart of the line. He was waiting for the wing lancers to rise up to meet him, to take their toll of his dragons before he closed as always, but they never did.

They never did. Which meant that the wing lancers weren't *there*, as the aeradi would never take battleships into battle with dragons without rocs to cover them. The Sky-Major's lips peeled back in a death's-head grin as he led a hundred dragons in against the battleships.

Uncovered or not, the firepower of an aeradi skyship of the line was nothing to be laughed at, and Bond after Bond fell under their fire —but he'd diverted their fire from the transports. In the end, that was all he was after.

He led the attack against the topmost battleship, focusing the fire of two companies of greens against it. The other warships lent their fire to its defense, but it wasn't enough. This time, Kolanis *knew* it was the crystal room that had been hit. He *saw* the first burst of dragon-flame rip the hull open, leaving the crystals exposed for the *second* burst that shattered them, releasing their pent-up energy in an ear-shattering explosion of green light.

The Sky-Major blinked, trying to clear the effects of the explosion, and turned to the other warships. At the sight of them, his cold grin returned. They were retreating, bloodied and beaten.

The battleship he'd just killed and three of their frigates didn't retreat with them.

Hendall calmly wiped the blood from his sword with the aeradi's cloak. The Regular officer, a Captain from his uniform, had been good. He'd also been smart—at the sight of the draconan, he'd clearly realized what was going on and gone for his sword to defend himself.

He'd failed, of course. It had taken Dari Hendall less than four blows to kill the man, leaving him spilling blood all over his fancy uniform and the smooth-paved street. Clearly, the civilians had sensed which way the wind was blowing, as the streets had emptied even before the fight was over.

His sword clean, Hendall sheathed it and let the rag fall to the ground. It was time to head to his rendezvous point, he judged. As leaderless as they were rapidly becoming, the Militia would be weak and disorganized, and the infiltrators would sweep them aside with ease.

Only his beginning to move down the street saved his life. The arrow that would have punched through his left eye instead ripped the top off of his ear. With a startled shout of pain, he dove to the ground, allowing a crystal rod to slip out of his sleeve.

Another arrow shot through where he'd stood as he came up to one knee. Three aeradi stood at the end of the street. All three were older men, their hair tinged with gray, but they appeared deadly competent with the weapons they held.

There was only one bow among them, however, and Hendall put a lightning bolt through the bowman even as he fired again. This time, the arrow flew true and drove deep into the Red Dragon's left shoulder.

The explosion of gore that had been the archer, however, would fire no more arrows. Snarling, the two other men, both carrying the typical tachi of an aeradi warrior, began to advance down the street.

Hendall's lips twisted in pain, but he raised the rod again and fired off a second bolt. This time, both of the swordsmen managed to dodge, and he tried to loose another bolt. The rod failed, however, and he threw it aside, cursing again.

Wincing against the pain, he drew his sword and rose to face the two aeradi. He didn't have time to deal with the arrow, so he simply ignored it as they closed. Both held their swords with the ease of long practice and began to circle him slowly.

They were old, though, he could tell. Each was just slightly too stiff, just slightly too slow. Even the pain did not prevent a cold smile forming on his face as he feinted toward the left warrior. He moved to parry with his sword as the other struck.

Ignoring the striking sword, Hendall shifted his lunge in mid-step, turning his entire body in a vicious slash that removed the right-hand aeraid's arm, sword and all, before gutting the man like a fish and sending his body sprawling onto the stones next to the Captain he'd been there to kill.

The other aeraid drew back but clearly had no intent of retreating. Hendall eyed the older, slower man calmly, then lunged, wincing at the pain as the arrow tore deeper into his off shoulder.

The aeraid easily parried Hendall's blow and flicked out a counter of his own. The Red Dragon twisted away, but the blow struck the shaft of the arrow in his shoulder, tearing inside Hendall's body.

The young draconan dropped to one knee, gasping in pain. The aeraid moved in, trying to finish the fight. Hendall was far from finished, though, and rose from his knees in one lethal motion that ran the older man clean through.

For a long moment, the Red Dragon simply stood there as his enemy slid off of his blade, gasping for breath. Finally, he reached into his pouch for the antiseptic powder he carried, and then grasped the arrow.

He still believed they were going to win this, but—officers or no officers—he wasn't so sure the Militia could just be counted out anymore.

ERIK WAS ATTACKED TWICE MORE BEFORE HE REACHED THE MUSTER point for the Newport Third. Knowing now that draconans roamed the city, he hadn't been surprised again, and the battles had been quite short.

Surprisingly short, in fact. Erik *septon* Tarverro had *fought* Red Dragons before, and these men, well trained as they were, did not match the calmly competent lethality of those assassins. Spies, infiltrators and saboteurs they clearly were, but Erik doubted they were true Red Dragons.

Which was why he was still alive and eight of them lay dead in Newport's streets behind him. Nonetheless, his arrival on the training field where the Third Militia had mustered showed that few were so lucky.

An aeradi battalion, such as the Newport Third Militia, mustered five hundred and twenty-two men under arms, including all officers and command staff. Erik estimated that *maybe* four hundred men were on the field, and most should have had less distance to travel than him.

Erik was only halfway to his company when Lieutenant Meday, his own second-in-command, saw him and almost ran to meet him. The older man came to a halt in front of Erik and saluted with palpable relief.

"Captain Tarverro, sir!" he snapped.

"Lieutenant," Erik greeted him quietly, returning the salute. "How bad is it?"

"We've got a hundred and ten men, sir," Meday said flatly. "I'm the only Lieutenant from Fire here, and Ikeras isn't here yet." He paused for a moment and then continued. "At that, none of the other companies have more than a hundred men, and I don't think *any* of Earth Company's officers are here."

"Which officers have made it?" Erik asked.

"Myself, two Lieutenants from Sea and one from Air," Meday replied.

Erik froze. "Just Lieutenants?" he asked, praying he was wrong.

"Yes, sir," the Lieutenant replied. Something of Erik's dismay must have shown on his face. "What's wrong, sir?"

"Major Champion is dead," Erik told him flatly. "If there are no other Captains..."

"You're in command, sir," Meday finished for him. "What are your orders, sir?"

Erik turned, eyeing the four hundred men on the field. He was in command. He was *in command*. He didn't know what to do. He'd only been a *Captain* for two weeks, and now he was in command of the battalion?

"Which other battalion musters are near us?" he asked.

"Fifth's just down the street, and Seventh's about ten blocks away. Why, sir?" Meday asked.

"Send messengers to...*whoever* is in command of them," Erik told him. "Suggest that they rendezvous on our position, and we'll move out as a body from there. We're going to need all the force concentration we can get."

"Yes, sir," Meday replied, clearly relieved that someone knew what they were doing.

Erik wished he could share the other man's confidence.

THE RENDEZVOUS POINT, HENDALL DISCOVERED, WAS A CONFUSED mass of draconan soldiers. None of them were in uniform, the only sign of rank the insignia they all wore. As even a junior agent, Hendall outranked everyone he saw.

Casualties must have been heavy, he realized. There were maybe four hundred men in the rendezvous area, and his estimate had been for half again that. If that wasn't enough, there were too few agents. The chain of command had been battered into oblivion.

One of the more senior soldiers spotted his agent's insignia and gestured for him to come over.

"Agent?" he asked.

"Yes, soldier?" he replied. The division between *real* agents and the infiltration-trained but freshly-recruited soldiers in the Red Dragons was quite clearly defined, and the agents were in charge.

"Thank the gods," the soldier replied sincerely. "Too few of you folks made it here. No one seems to have a clue what to do."

Hendall raised an eyebrow at the soldier. Just a glance at a *map* should tell anyone what needed to be done. There was only one real choke point.

"I won't speak against your brothers, sir," the soldier said, finally.

"Ah" was all Hendall said. "Who's in charge?"

"Chaos and the Fires," the soldier replied with a grin. "There's a bunch of agents staring at maps who may *think* they're in charge over there, though," he finished, gesturing to a small knot of people Hendall hadn't noticed.

"Thank you."

"If you've got half a clue what you're doing, thank *you*, sir," the soldier said flatly.

Hendall merely nodded to the man and crossed to the other agents. They were, as the soldier had said, gathered around a map. Arguing.

Over where to *take* the men. Apparently, they were completely oblivious to the fact that every minute they argued, a tiny amount of their authority over those same men slipped away.

A quick glance at the insignia confirmed that none of them were senior to him. Most were the same rank or only a little junior, but none were senior. Which made things a little easier.

He stepped between two of them and laid his finger on a block on the map. "Here," he swiftly, silencing the arguments. "We attack here."

"The Square of the Gods?" one of them replied. "Why?"

"It's the key to the whole gods-accursed city," Hendall said flatly, staring the man down. "They'll man the inner defenses soon, if they haven't already, and we couldn't touch those. As long as the inner defenses hold, the dragons can't attack the city. They can land troops, but they can't *support* those troops."

The other agent nodded, silently.

"If we *take* that Square, however, and hold it," Hendall told them, "we can either clear out the defenses ourselves or leave them to the Claws. Once that's done, it's all over bar the burning."

He met each agent's eyes in turn, holding their gazes until each one nodded, accepting both his plan and his authority. *He* was in command there now.

"All right. Muster the men. We leave immediately."

FORTUNATELY FOR ERIK'S SANITY, IKERAS ARRIVED BEFORE THE other battalions did. He found his way straight to Erik's command post, where Erik had mustered the handful of officers he had for the entire battalion and was distributing responsibilities.

He saw the noncom arrive at the edge of the group and made a *hold on a moment* gesture with his right hand to him. He needed to talk to Ikeras, but this was more important.

"Finally, Lieutenant Meday will command Fire Company, with Lieutenant Jenar as XO," he finished. He eyed the group, most of whom looked half-dazed with the sudden responsibility landing on them.

"Gentlemen, we are suffering from a severe lack of officers," he told them quietly. "You're all being thrust into positions you don't feel ready for. Rely on your sergeants, people. They can handle minute-to-minute. *Your* job is to make sure your units follow my orders and achieve their objectives. Understood?"

He waited for nods of confirmation, most of them appearing a little more confident than a moment before, from everyone before returning it. "Dismissed, people. Let's get to it."

The officers dispersed, and Erik turned to Ikeras. "Thank the gods you made it," he said to the older man. "I was worried they'd got you."

"Thank the gods *you* made it, sir," Ikeras replied.

"Arien?" Erik asked, terrified of the answer.

"She'll be fine," his friend and retainer assured him. "That old house is a fortress, and the *kep* will defend her to the end." Erik felt Ikeras's eyes on him for a moment and met the older man's gaze. "*All* the *sept* houses are like that. They won't want to hit them until this is over. Unless we fail entirely, they're safe."

Erik nodded slowly. So, his grandmother was fine. Hiri was fine. He found himself hoping that Elysia had made it to her father's house, and wondered why he was worried about *her* when so many were at risk.

"Where are the Regulars?" he asked softly. "I know they pulled most out for the war games, but they can't have left the city defenseless?"

"Many were on the outer defenses," Ikeras replied grimly. "Doctrine calls for the Wind Guard to dig in around the palace while the Regulars and Militia form the first line of defense. Whoever's left..." He trailed off. "It'll depend on who ends up in charge," he said finally. "The regiments I know are in town have a normal station at the shipyards. They'll go there first—if they go anywhere else after depends on the officers. And the draconans."

"What about the Militia?" Erik asked, trying to focus on the map in front of him.

"I passed through the Fifth's camp on the way here," Ikeras told him. "They're a mess. Bunch of green Lieutenants trying to work out which way to move the men."

"Fires," Erik cursed softly. "I was hoping to pull them in as reinforcements. No one senior?"

Ikeras shook his head. "None. The bastards knew *just* who to hit. I doubt one in twenty of the company-level or higher officers made it to their posts. Looks like you're it for us, sir."

Erik turned away silently. He wasn't ready to command this. Not now.

"If we want the Fifth, sir, we're going to have to pick them up on the way," Ikeras said bluntly. "You'll have to take command of them, too."

"What about the Seventh?" Erik asked. "I sent messengers to both."

"I don't know," Ikeras said, pausing as the first groups of men turned the corner of the road. All across the square, hands went to blades and men stiffened but slowly relaxed as they realized it was the Seventh.

"They made it," Erik sighed. "Thank the gods."

He turned back to Ikeras to find the older man looking at him oddly. "You're going to have to take command, Erik," Ikeras told him. "We can't rely on the Regulars left to save the city. You don't have a choice. You *have* to."

"We'll see," Erik said. "Come with me; we need to find out who's in command."

The closer Erik drew to the Seventh's men, however, the more he realized that while someone obviously *was* in command, they hadn't done a good job of it. The men had clumped together by unit, but it was obvious they'd done so on their own, and nobody had bothered to dress the ranks or try to organize the troops.

The officers, instead of being spread through the men, providing the leadership and organization the Seventh so clearly needed, were clumped together at the front of the battalion. Erik eyed that clump, then sighed and approached.

"Who is in charge here?" he asked.

A dark-haired and -skinned man, tall for an aeradi at only an inch shorter than Erik, stepped forward. "I am," he said bluntly, without even bothering to salute. "Lieutenant Jells Felsten."

"I see," Erik said calmly. He eyed the officers behind the man. All

Lieutenants. They were all junior Lieutenants, too. And not a single one of them looked pleased with the man in front of them.

"As none of your senior officers survived, I'm going to add you to my own men," Erik told them. "We'll pick up the Fifth on our way, but we're going to be operating as one consolidated force."

"I don't think so," Felsten replied haughtily. "The Seventh is mine, and I see no reason to give up command to a *boy*."

Irritation flared through Erik's mind, but he controlled it. "*Lieutenant* Felsten, I am the senior officer here. I am assuming command."

"I have ten *years* of seniority on you, you jumped-up little prick," Felsten snapped back.

Erik knew that if he didn't do *something*, Ikeras was going to kill the smarmy bastard where he stood, and he couldn't *afford* that, not now. This time, he didn't even bother to control his anger, allowing it to suffuse his voice and burn away the last of his uncertainty.

"Lieutenant Felsten," he snapped. "We have one mission and one objective. Do you know what that is?"

"I don't give a—" Felsten began to say, glaring at Erik in clear contempt.

"*Defend this city!*" Erik snarled, cutting off the fool's words. "I *will* fulfill that mission, Lieutenant. Your offended ego means less than nothing to me beside that mission. You *will* obey my orders, or I will kill you where you stand for insubordination in the face of the enemy. Do I make myself *clear*, Lieutenant?"

For a long moment, Felsten looked like he was going to continue, but then he dropped his gaze, and Militia Captain Erik *septon* Tarverro, acting Major in command of the Third and Seventh Newport Militia Battalions, nodded sharply and turned back to the rest of the officers.

"As I was saying," he said calmly, "we will move out as soon as possible to pick up the Fifth Militia. We will then proceed to the Square of the Gods."

"The Square of the Gods?" one of Felsten's Lieutenants queried.

"Yes," Erik replied. "Where dragons can reach, we cannot hold," he said bluntly. "We need to man the inner defenses—and I intend to detach troops from our battalions to be *certain* that they are manned. Once those defenses are manned, the draconans will only be able to land troops, not bring dragons in for support. They will have no choice but to take the forts out on the ground, to allow their dragons clear access to the city. To do that, they have to take the Square of the Gods."

"You're going to put us straight in the path of their *entire army!*" Felsten snapped, a crack of whimper in his voice preventing it sounding as strong as he'd likely hoped.

Erik turned on the man coldly. "Yes. Because that is our duty and the only way we can hold this city. Understood?!"

Ignoring the man, Erik turned to the other Lieutenants. Each of them nodded in sequence. Finally, Erik returned their nods. "Gentlemen, we will move out as soon as possible. However, the Seventh is a mess. Therefore, 'as soon as possible' will be as soon as your units are organized and ready to move. Get to it!"

KOLANIS WATCHED EACH WAVE OF TRANSPORT DRAGONS COME sweeping in to land on the edge of the city with satisfaction. The battle dragons swept patrols through the sky over the transports and the troops forming into their regiments.

His hand caressed Lalen's head spikes one last time and he dismounted. A Claw Lieutenant, with the crossed quill and sword of a staff officer, was waiting for him. The youth looked barely old enough to shave, but he snapped off a perfectly credible salute to the Sky-Major.

"Sky-Major Kolanis, sir?"

"That would be me, son," Kolanis replied. "At ease. Your message?"

"Sky-General Adaelis requests your presence at the command post immediately, sir!" the youth barked out, his eyes trained on a point six inches above and to the right of Kolanis's shoulder.

"Which is where?" the Sky-Major asked gently.

The youth flushed. "Follow me, sir," he said quickly.

Despite his perhaps-excessive formality, the youth wove his way through the chaos of the forming battle formation with ease, guiding Kolanis to a massive black dragon, Adaelis's own Shield.

In the shadow of Sheld's bulk, a dozen clerks and as many junior officers had set up folding tables and spread out maps, bustling around the general like planets attendant on the sun. Flat crystals were neatly lined up on one set of tables, and Kolanis raised an eyebrow at them. He didn't know what they were, but he doubted Adaelis had brought them for decoration.

He didn't have much time to look around the impromptu command post, as the other Skyborne officers arrived at much the same time as he did, and all of them were brought to the general.

Adaelis was short for a draconan and pudgy for a soldier. Yet when he faced his hard-bitten veteran officers, Kolanis and the others found themselves coming to attention automatically. The general eyed them for a moment and then spoke.

"Gentlemen, well begun. Well begun indeed," he complimented them. "But *well begun* is only *half-done*, and *half-done* is *far too early to relax*. It appears," he continued, gesturing at a map of the city on the table before him, "that our agents in the city failed to breach the inner defenses. While our information suggests that these forts are only lightly armed and are almost completely unmanned in any case, they still represent a real and present threat to our force."

With a jerk of his chin, Adaelis indicated the regiments forming up around them. "Our best guess is that between Militia, Regulars and the King's Wind Guard, we are outnumbered by almost three to two. While our men have been even more successful in eliminating the enemy's officers than we'd hoped, and it looks like the Regular regiments have clumped together nicely for us, that remain a significant force. We *must* have the ability to provide aerial support."

Kolanis was a draconan officer, a brave and valiant man sworn to the defense of his people. He hesitated not a second before stepping forward. "Sir, the Green of Third is prepared to assault the defenses in the name of Dracona!"

He was less than a moment ahead of the rest of the officers, and Adaelis nodded gratefully at them. "Thank you, gentlemen. You have reaffirmed my faith in our men and officers. I refuse, however, to send a single battalion—or even several battalions—to attack these defenses. The forts are weak but the losses would remain too heavy.

You will all move, in a strike we will coordinate from here."

"How?" Kolanis could not help but ask.

Adaelis gestured for one of his staff to bring him one of the flat crystals Kolanis had noticed. "These, gentlemen. Tablets. Once broken in half, what is written on one will appear on the other instantly."

Kolanis whistled silently. Magical communication, something only water mages had ever managed before, and *theirs* was mind-to-mind.

The General raised a finger. "Be warned, the tablets are limited in both range and endurance; otherwise, we would have issued them before we left. They'll be active for barely an hour after they are broken.. Until then, however..."

He didn't need to finish the sentence. Twelve hungry grins finished it for him.

THE FIFTH, THANKFULLY, HADN'T GIVEN ERIK ANY OF THE TROUBLE the Seventh had. When he'd turned up and started issuing orders, even the officers present had been more than willing to obey. They were in complete disarray, with what had apparently been social cliques nearly dividing the unit without any outside influence.

Erik provided an outside influence senior to them all, and if that hadn't been enough, he'd brought nearly nine hundred armed men with him. If the Fifth's officers had defied him, he'd been willing to lock every single one of them in chains and put their Sergeants in charge. He was running out of time.

Now he led the Fifth and the Third toward the Square of the Gods at a full march. He'd have ordered them to double-time, but he *couldn't* —he needed these men fit and ready to engage in close action.

The Seventh, on the other hand, he'd sent on ahead with orders to *run* all the way to the inner defenses. The battalion had been the most intact of his three units, with almost five hundred men under arms, and five hundred men was the minimum Erik figured could man the defenses safely.

If they double-timed it all of the way there, Erik figured they'd make it in time to drive off the first major push. They'd be too exhausted to fight a close action, but they wouldn't *need* to, and enough of the guns and crys-bows would be pre-loaded and charged that they would have some time to get their breath back before having to reload the weapons.

With the Seventh gone, however, Erik only had eight and a half hundred men, and he'd had to send messengers to the Regulars and other Militia battalions. There were too many draconans in the city for him to feel comfortable sending men out in less than squads, so that pulled away another hundred and fifty men.

So, it was with a mere seven hundred men that Erik entered the Square of the Gods, to discover he was too late. A draconan force had already entered the square and was hot in the pursuit of what Erik presumed to be the Seventh.

He didn't have much time. He looked over at Ikeras and asked: "Archers and charge?"

"Only option," the noncom replied, equally quietly, then grabbed the signaler marching next to him. The aeraid raised his trumpet to his lips and blew a series of five notes, a specific signal.

The last note was buried in the noise as a quarter of the men in the aeradi force simultaneously came to a halt and drew their bows.

THE CHAIN OF COMMAND AMONG THE RED DRAGON AGENTS IN THE city had been all but nonexistent. What there had been of it had started to fragment when Brane had been murdered, and the losses after the attack began had shattered what was left of it.

There had been nobody to argue with Hendall taking command. At least, no one had been willing to try. He'd taken as long as he dared to organize the force around the noncoms among the infiltrators and the handful of agents he had to serve as officers, but the force was still a scratch-built mess.

Scratch-built or not, it was the only force this deep into the city, and after the troopers he'd collected on his way to the Square of the Gods, it was six hundred trained and armed men. If they could take the square, they should be able to prevent the aeradi from manning the inner defenses.

Or so Hendall thought, anyway. Until he entered the square, leading his troops from the front as draconan tradition commanded, and spotted the aeradi troops in the middle of it. They were moving fast and didn't look like they were stopping in the square.

"They're headed for the forts," Hendall snarled aloud, the venom in his voice startling those around him. All his efforts and it looked like he was going to fail *this* close to succeeding.

With a shake of his head, the Red Dragon drew his sword. They were *not* going to fail, not if he had anything to do with it. Fast the aeradi may have been, but they were still aeradi. They simply didn't have the legs to outrun his people.

"Take them!" he bellowed, pointing his sword at the aeradi soldiers almost running out of the square. With a rumbling growl, the entire Red Dragon force surged after them at a run.

The first few moments seemed to prove Hendall's belief. His people were gaining on the aeradi troops. They'd been clever, but they hadn't been clever enough. The city would be the draconans', and *he* would be the one who'd opened the way.

He didn't realize there was another aeradi force until the first volley of arrows dropped out of the sky like messengers of death.

THE SHIPYARDS BURNED BEHIND THE GREEN OF THIRD. THEY'D been too close to the landing zones to be left alone, and the presence of most of the aeradi Regulars clumped together had proven too tempting for General Adaelis.

Kolanis's orders had been clear, though—he was to make one pass through the Newport Shipyards with the rest of the Third Strike Regiment to break up the aeradi defenses, then move on to the inner-city fortifications.

He'd counted roughly four thousand Regulars in the defenses around the shipyards, but the Strike Regiments had ripped them apart. Fortifications were shattered and support weapons burned to ash.

Behind the aeradi's lines, they'd set dozens of under-construction ships —including ten *battleships*—ablaze.

Further aerial support for the assault would require Kolanis to succeed in his *next* mission, but with five thousand Claws of the Dragon descending on the shattered defenders, the Sky-Major didn't expect the Newport Regulars to last another twenty minutes.

Even if they held on by some miracle, the dragons had already destroyed every vessel under construction and every yard they were building. It would be years before Newport could repair the damage his people had done.

Kolanis's attention was distracted by one of his scout dragons screaming. He glanced over at the dragon, and its Skyborne rider gave a hand signal and gestured down, toward the city.

The Sky-Major looked down and saw what the scout was gesturing toward. A battle was rapidly taking shape on the ground below. He cursed horribly and felt Lalen scream her sense of his frustration.

His greens *couldn't* bombard ground forces. Their flame was too narrow, too focused. Their maneuverability made them good against fortifications, but they didn't have a wide-enough spread to make strafing worth their while.

Then his lips split in a feral grin as he recalled the tablet resting in his saddlebag. He pulled it out and grabbed the stylus they'd given to go with it. It took a moment for him to locate the battle on his mental map of the city, but he'd memorized enough maps of Newport that it was only a moment.

Enemy forces engaging infiltrators in Square of the Gods, he scrawled on the tablet. *Request Blacks for ground support.*

The letters rested on the tablet for several seconds and then faded. A moment later, more letters appeared, a response. *Adaelis agrees. Black of Ninth is en route. Maintain surveillance. If the square is contested, the forts should be unmanned.*

Kolanis flashed over his mental map of the city and nodded with a cold grin. The square was a choke point between the outer and inner cities. If there was a battle there, the infiltrators had probably stopped the defenses being manned.

Which meant the Black of Ninth was about to do what the Fifth had just done to the shipyards to the only troops who could man those forts.

~

ARROWS POUNDED THE DRACONAN FORCE TWICE MORE BEFORE Erik's men hit it like a hammer striking glass. Neither force was heavily armored, but the aeradi had the impetus of the attack. The Red Dragons shattered, the Militia driving deep into them.

Erik stood in the first rank of his men, using his greater strength and size to help push the draconans back. There was no time for tactics, simply the hammering of men against men.

Even as the draconan lines broke, Erik found himself cutting down a Red Dragon attacking Ikeras, who stood by his side. A moment later, the *kep* noncom returned the favor, casually gutting another draconan before he reached Erik.

The aeradi held their formations, and the archers continued to fire, carefully aiming at the back of the draconan troops, breaking their cohesion even more. Without any apparent organization, the Red Dragon force was doomed.

Even as Erik came to that realization, he came face to face with what *had* to be a real Red Dragon. Four aeradi troopers lay dead at the man's feet, and Erik's hindbrain catalogued several other such knots of resistance—where the *real* assassins were just barely managing to hold together groups of troops.

Erik drove forward without hesitation, lunging toward the assassin. His attack was parried, and the draconan slashed at him, only to be blocked by Ikeras. Erik shared a quick glance with his noncom, and then the pair began to circle the assassin.

For a moment, the Red Dragon tried to keep his eyes on both of them. Quickly realizing he couldn't guard against two men, he began to retreat. With his eyes on his attackers, he wasn't paying enough attention to the ground, and he stumbled over an arrow-ridden draconan body.

In the instant of his stumble, both Erik and Ikeras attacked. The assassin was good enough to parry Ikeras's attack, sending the older aeraid stumbling to one side as the draconan spun toward Erik.

No one could have been good enough to block *both* attacks, however, and Erik's old sky-steel blade ripped into the man's side. The man's parry clattered uselessly off Erik's blade, and he crumpled to the ground.

A moment's reprieve allowed Erik to pull Ikeras back to his feet, but before either could say a word, the heart-wrenching sound of a dragon's shriek tore the air in two.

Both men wheeled to stare up in horror as dozens—no, *hundreds*— of dragons swept down on the Square of the Gods.

Hendall had never imagined the sort of carnage the coordinated aeradi arrow volleys were unleashing on his ranks. Any chance of them catching the first group shattered under that steel-tipped rain and was ground under when the aeradi infantry smashed into his men.

The Red Dragon found himself caught up in the motion of his men as they split around the aeradi assault. For a moment, he was helpless and could only watch as the soldiers—surely only Militia!—butchered his men like hapless sheep.

Then the line reached him and he found himself fighting for his life. One on one, he was far better trained than the aeradi. But the little sky-men fought in groups, splitting the draconans up and matching four or five of them, with their lighter shields and longer swords, against each of the larger men.

One of those groups came straight for him as others sliced apart the soldiers around him. Two soldiers managed to stick with Hendall in the chaos, and he faced the five aeradi with them at his sides.

With a snarl, the assassin lunged, dodging nimbly around the longer sword of the lead aeradi to gut the man with his dragonclaw short-sword. As he gutted the leader, though, two more attacked him. He dodged one blade, but the other slashed across his shoulder, opening the arrow wound even wider.

The other two had gone after the soldier on Hendall's left, who now lay on the ground, choking on his own blood with an aeradi sword through his lung. The owner of the sword, however, was silent on the ground, the draconan's blade having opened his throat.

Gritting his teeth against the pain in his shoulder, Hendall parried the attack of one of the remaining soldiers, only to have another get by his guard and draw blood across his chest. The soldier with him managed to fend off his own attacker, however, and ran through the aeraid who had sliced Hendall as that man finished his stroke.

There was a moment's pause, and then the two surviving aeradi attacked together, and before Hendall could react, the soldier with him was down in a flurry of blades. He took an aeraid with him, and Hendall cut the other down as he turned back to the assassin.

Wounded, bloody and battered, Hendall stared around him in horror. The battle was chaotic and disastrous. Even in the chaos, it was clear that the aeradi were driving his men back and slaughtering them in the process. Only where the full agents stood did any of the Red Dragons seem to be holding their own, and those knots of resistance were being overwhelmed.

Even as his horror overwhelmed him, though, he heard the cries of the dragons and looked to the sky with a feral grin. An entire *regiment* of blacks, the soldiers on their backs aiming cannon and crys-bows, swept down from the sky.

With a weary cheer, Hendall raised his sword in salute. For one glorious moment, he *knew* the battle was won. The aeradi had no weapons to strike at the dragons!

Then the roar of cannon fire rang over the battlefield. It took Hendall a moment to realize the dragons hadn't fired. By the end of that moment, the first dragons fell from the sky.

He spun in horror to watch the inner fortifications begin to light up with the red and white flashes of cannon and crys-bow fire. He'd forgotten the first group of aeradi they'd seen. The ones who had been headed to the forts.

For an eternal moment, the Red Dragon Hendall watched the forts rip dragons from the sky, knowing he'd failed. Then an aeradi tachi he never saw put an end to his failure.

~

KOLANIS AND THE GREEN OF THIRD HAD BEEN ORDERED TO A HIGH covering position over Black of Ninth, which meant he was in a perfect position to watch the entire battalion fly headlong into a hail of fire.

It started at the forts right next to the gate but rippled out from there, obviously as men reached and manned the forts. Blacks were big dragons, tough dragons, but *no* dragon was tough enough to stand up to the oversized cannonballs and lightning bolts flung by those defenses.

He grabbed the tablet he'd been given. *Attacking forts to relieve Black of Ninth. Kolanis.* he scrawled on it, and turned to gesture his commands to his men.

Even as Kolanis raised his hands to issue his commands, the tablet burnt hot and he looked down at it. *Negative*, it said flatly, in a script very different from the previous handwriting. *Withdraw*, the message continued, and then, in case he hadn't guessed who was giving these orders, the signature: *Adaelis*.

Gritting his teeth, Kolanis gave the gesture commands to withdraw.

Section by section, the Skyborne of his battalion peeled back. Below them, the massive dragons of the Black of Ninth were trying their best to do the same.

But someone *else* had been watching, and even as the first Blacks began to win free of the range of the guns, sudden crys-bow fire ripped them from the air.

Cursing aloud, Kolanis turned Lalen toward the source of the volley. He cursed again at the sight before him: the remaining battle-ships and frigates of the Newport Sky Fleet sweeping in from above toward the forts in attack formation, weapons blazing fire.

This time, the draconan didn't wait for orders. If those ships weren't driven back, *all* of the Black of Ninth would be wiped out. With one gesture of his spear, he sent all two hundred dragons of his battalion surging toward the aeradi skyships.

Whoever was in command had expected that, however, and all nine of the frigates turned to meet his battalion, and the wing lancers he'd thought the city didn't have came with them. There were only a handful of lancers, less than fifty, but Kolanis's hopes died with the sight of them.

Nonetheless, he led his Skyborne into the teeth of the skyships and their winged guardians, trying desperately to break through, to open a gap that would allow *any* of the Black of Ninth to escape.

After a moment, the battle narrowed itself down to himself and Lalen, and trying to stay alive. The wing lancers' rocs danced their way around his dragons, but he saw some of those dances end in fire and knew his men were giving their best.

Even as he saw rocs die, however, a lancer came plummeting in at Lalen. Before their joined mind could react, the aeraid threw a javelin, hard. The steel-tipped lance scored along Lalen's side, leaving black ichor to ooze out onto her scales.

The wound was minor, however, and didn't stop the Bond twisting in the air and burning the roc from the sky. Kolanis felt nothing but satisfaction as the great bird disintegrated under the fire and its rider's scream echoed through the air.

Another javelin slicing through the air interrupted his satisfaction as it sank deep into Lalen's back, barely missing his own leg. With a curse, Kolanis reached down and yanked the shaft free. The dragon's roar of pain echoed loudly in his ears, but the wound was less restrictive on her motions than the shaft would have been.

Which was good, for a moment later, one of the frigates came into range of the Bond and opened fire. The dragon only barely avoided the cannonball that shot through the air where she'd been a moment before.

Her scream now was of rage, and Kolanis let her rage flow through the Bond and into him. With a battle roar of his own, he kneed Lalen toward the offending frigate. He knew through her senses that other dragons had fallen in around him, and he led them in a spiraling attack on the frigate.

Fire tore along the ship's wooden sides, and its cannon roared back in reply. A single thought directed Lalen in closer, and she flamed the cannon all along one broadside. Explosions rocked the ship, tearing half of the ship away as the firepowder ignited.

The skyship turned away, but Kolanis spotted a glint of light off of crystal through the smoke and led Lalen in a swooping dive through the smoke. He only saw the crystals of the ship's lift rooms for a moment, but that was enough. Fire seared across the crystal, shattering the carefully aligned patterns and unleashing the energy pent up in them.

Green fire immolated the ship, turning its entire hull and crew into little more than fine ash on the wind. The same fire seared across Kolanis and Lalen, and this time the dragon screamed in real pain before the draconan brought her clear, breathing hard as he broke clear of the smoke.

As he did, his eye fell on another frigate drifting away, its deck aflame as its crew struggled to either bring the dying vessel to a safe landing or at least keep it from hitting the city. With a cold grin, he turned his attentions elsewhere, trying to find enemies to kill.

There were none. It was over. Even as he searched, all seven surviving frigates suddenly withdrew, and the remaining wing lancers pounced on and slaughtered the squadron of Skyborne that tried to follow.

It took Kolanis a long moment to realize why, and then his eyes were drawn to the sky close to the forts. The five battleships were moving away under the cover of the inner forts' guns, where no dragon could reach them.

Not a single dragon of the Black of Ninth remained in the air.

Erik surveyed the Square of the Gods with something akin to shock. The surviving draconan infiltrators had fled when the forts started blasting dragons from the sky, but hundreds had died, their bodies being hastily cleared aside by the aeradi soldiers as he watched.

Scattered across the square, however, were the bodies no human could easily move. At least forty, possibly even more, of the dragons that had been shot down had landed in the Square of the Gods. Some were even still alive, though likely not for long, given their injuries, and lashed out at anything that approached them in a pain-induced fog; but even dead black dragons were impressive obstacles.

"Can we move the dragons?" Ikeras asked quietly from behind Erik. "They're blocking our archers' lines of fire."

"Yes," Erik replied, "but not easily. We cannot afford the time. Besides"—he shrugged—"they'll break up the Claws' ranks, and that is not a gift I'll lightly decline."

He didn't even need to look at the older aeraid to feel the man's tension. "Ignore the dragons and form the men up," he instructed. "Keep the archers back to fire if we can, but we need a solid shield wall across the square."

"I don't know if we have enough men," the noncom admitted. "Soldiers are trickling in, and I'm shoving into the line as they do, but..."

"Most of these men have never trained together, let alone fought together," Erik finished. He finally turned to face Ikeras squarely. Doing so, he caught a glimpse of movement over the other aeraid's shoulder and gestured the noncom to silence.

Men came spilling into the square in relatively neat lines. Not what a fully functional battalion, even of Militia, should have managed, but still neat. Still better than most of the battalions Erik had seen today.

The handful of signal bearers bore the flag of the Second Kirmon battalion. Erik hesitated for a moment and then gestured to Ikeras. "Continue organizing the men. I'll meet them."

"Yes, sir," Ikeras said. "Good luck, sir," he continued. "You may need it. Kirmon follows Jaras, and the *sept* has tried to keep its regiment under officers of the family."

Erik said nothing.

KOLANIS BARELY WAITED UNTIL HIS DRAGONS WERE CLEAR OF THE forts before dragging the crystal tablet out again. He took a moment to breathe and regain control of his temper, and then wrote on it.

We have to move against those forts, he wrote swiftly. *As long as they're intact, we can't deal with the inner city.*

Patience, Major, came the almost instant reply, again in the general's own hand. *Wait*.

The Skyborne waited with bad grace for the several moments until more writing appeared, this time in a clerk's hand, suggesting that the general was having it sent to all of the Skyborne commanders.

We have suffered a setback, but it is far from over, the words said plainly. *While we can defeat the forts or the skyships with ease on their own, the price of defeating them in combination is far too high for us to accept*.

The tablet stayed the same for a moment, allowing the General's words to sink in. *While the price for taking the forts by dragon could be paid, there is no need*, Kolanis's commander finally continued. *The defenders at the shipyards are almost finished. Detachments of the Claws of the Dragon are already being deployed against the handful of soldiers who bar our way. Once they have dealt with sufficient of the forts to clear us a way into the city, Newport will be ours!*

It was with bared teeth and a far better mood that Kolanis swung Lalen around, allowing him to look down at the neat and deadly columns of soldiers moving into the city.

THE MAN IN CHARGE OF THE SECOND KIRMON TURNED OUT TO BE A Lieutenant. Despite the situation, he was impeccably turned out in the dress uniform of a Regular officer. Everything about the man, from the perfect uniform to the hair, *exactly* the length of the current style, set Erik's teeth on edge. On the other hand, the man had several hundred *Regulars* with him, so Erik swallowed his annoyance and stepped forward to meet the man.

Before Erik could say a word, the Lieutenant came to attention and saluted. "Lieutenant Natan *sept* Kirmon, reporting with the Second Kirmon, sir!" he snapped off.

"I don't think that's entirely necessary, Lieutenant," Erik said drily. Especially as, technically, the Regular Lieutenant outranked his own Militia Captaincy.

The man only half-relaxed at Erik's words, still remaining stiff. "I brought my men as soon as your messengers reached us. Where do you want us?" he asked simply.

Realizing to his surprise that the Lieutenant was accepting his authority, Erik was taken aback for a moment. "Hold your archers back with the others in the center of the square. Move the rest of your men to"—he paused, turning to survey his own formation—"the left flank."

"They'll be facing the largest stretch of open ground, where the draconan formations will be most intact, and you're the only Regulars we've got," he explained.

"Understood," Natan said calmly. "Thank you, sir."

The Lieutenant turned away and gestured to the other men with him, passing on Erik's orders quickly and efficiently. As his couriers and subordinates scattered, the Lieutenant turned back to Erik.

"We are on the opposite sides of politics, my lord *septon,*" he murmured. "I won't pretend otherwise. But today, the outer forts are gone. The shipyards are burned. My men may be the only intact Regular formation *left.* Our politics do not matter."

"The *shipyards?*" Erik asked in shock.

"Most of the Regulars had muster point there," Natan replied quietly. "We were heading there when your messenger intercepted us, but from the smoke, we weren't going to make it in time to help."

Erik inclined his head to the aeraid. "You did the right thing coming here," he told the junior man softly. "We can worry about politics after we've thrown the draconans back into the sea."

IT TOOK THE DRACONANS FIFTEEN PRICELESS MINUTES TO GET THE first wave converged on the square. Erik took full advantage of that time, pulling together his formations and throwing up what crude fortifications they could. The scattering of trenches and berms wasn't much, but it would hopefully help slow down the formations the dragons' bodies would break up.

Finally, however, his scouts came running back into the square, passing through narrow lanes to reach Erik's position, gasping for breath. They didn't need to report, however, as their very presence said everything that needed to be said.

"Form up," he bellowed from where he stood, roughly halfway between the shield line and the archers. The command echoed down the line as sergeants and junior officers repeated it, and the men who'd been out of the line digging quickly fell back into formation.

An eerie silence descended over the square, through which could be heard dragon cries and the crackling sound of burning houses. Then, cutting through the silence, came a steady *thud-thud*, like a drum. No one in the Square of the Gods thought it was any such thing, and Erik could *feel* the tension as the men's hands shifted on their sword hilts.

Finally, the first even and glittering lines of the Claws of the Dragon came into view. Easily a hundred and ten men abreast and five deep, they advanced in even step, their feet hitting the ground simultaneously with a horrifying *thud*.

"Present arms," Erik ordered, and again the order echoed down the line. There was something viscerally disturbing about the sound of almost a thousand swords being drawn simultaneously, and Erik shivered as he turned to the archers.

In their case, however, he'd delegated the command to Ikeras, and he simply nodded to the noncom before turning back to face the oncoming Claws.

The first block of five hundred and fifty draconans was followed by three more, making their attackers a full regiment of over two thousand Claws. The sight of that many soldiers moving in step was awe-inspiring. On the other hand, so were aeradi archers.

"Ready!" Erik heard Ikeras bellow behind him as he judged the distance to the draconan regiments himself.

"Aim!" the noncom continued as the even ranks entered the square, and the aeradi soldiers lifted their own shields and swords.

"Loose!"

Even before Ikeras had finished bellowing, six hundred arrows were in the air. Three seconds later, before the first salvo even landed, six hundred more followed. The first salvo struck like a hammer, and the lead draconan battalion staggered in its tracks as dozens of men went down, wounded or dead.

Erik pursed his lips in a silent whistle as the regiment continued to advance toward the solid line of the aeradi defenders. Arrows pounded them, but they came on anyway. The bodies of the dragons forced them to split their ranks, but still they advanced.

"Swords ready!" Erik finally ordered as the draconans began to pick up the pace. Not quite a charge yet, as only the utterly battered lead battalion was in range for that, but close. With an almost-inaudible noise, nine hundred shields lifted and sword arms extended as the aeradi troops readied.

Then, finally, the draconan soldiers broke into a trot, burdened by their armor, and then finally charged. "Archers hold arrows!" Erik bellowed. "Aeradi, hold hard!"

"Hold hard!" echoed up and down the line as the lead draconans hit. They'd charged across nearly two hundred yards of open field, their formations scattered by dead dragons and by trenches and walls, under fire the whole way, and they *still* had intact companies in their charge.

It didn't matter. Single companies may have been intact, but the total organization of the draconan charge was gone. Only junior officers had control of their units, and it wasn't enough. The draconans had started with twice as many troops as Erik had in his line, but what reached them was a roughly equal number to the defenders.

For a moment, Erik stood, watching silently as he tried to assess where to deploy his limited reserve, two companies of Regulars composed of troops that had drifted in after the Second Kirmon. The exchange of battle cries rippled back and forth: "Newport!" from the aeradi troops, and "Dracona!" from the draconans.

The aeradi cries were clearly dominant on the left flank, where the soldiers of the Second Kirmon were proving the deadly competence of aeradi Regulars on the shattered bodies of their enemies. The right flank was less certain, and Erik grabbed a signal flag, preparing to send one of his reserve companies to help hold the line.

Before he could act, the draconans facing the Second Kirmon broke, running from their opponents. For a moment, the center and right-hand draconan troops continued to hold, but Erik made a signal with the flag. Not the one he'd intended to make, but it was enough.

Natan *sept* Kirmon either saw the signal or was intending the move anyway. As one body, the Second Kirmon and the Militia with it began to march, rotating on the central portion of the aeradi line as they swung to catch the rest of the draconan regiment.

The Claws of the Dragon were loyal, highly disciplined soldiers willing to die for their country. They weren't prepared to die for nothing, however, and the remaining soldiers disengaged, fleeing to avoid being caught by Kirmon's troops.

"Archers, see them off," Erik heard Ikeras bellow. Moments later, the archers resumed fire on the running soldiers. Every soldier they killed wouldn't come back to try again.

No one was foolish enough to think they wouldn't try again.

KOLANIS HADN'T BOTHERED TO WITHDRAW THE GREEN OF THIRD very far, on the presumption that even the distraction factor of the Claws attacking the forts might allow him to get a decent strike in, opening any gap the ground-pounders opened even further.

The real end result was that the Sky-Major was in the perfect position to watch when Colonel Dai Aerens obviously decided that his Fifteenth Regiment was more than enough to deal with a bunch of aeradi Militia.

He also had a ringside seat for the demonstration of what happens when a full twenty-two-hundred-man regiment charges a prepared aeradi position supported by archers. The Fifteenth had been shattered by the time they'd reached the aeradi lines, and only the sheer brutality of draconan discipline had kept the Claws fighting for as long as they did before breaking.

Which wouldn't keep General Adaelis from potentially decimating what was left of the regiment—literally killing every tenth man—and almost certainly *impaling* Colonel Dai Aerens. Which wasn't, thank Fiehr, his problem.

With a sigh, Kolanis picked up his communication tablet. *Fifteenth attacked unsupported*, he wrote, the words a silent condemnation without any further explanation. *Aeradi defenses intact, remnants of Fifteenth withdrawn.*

Understood, came the single-word reply after a moment, in the General's own hand. *Make certain*—the word underlined twice—*that the Ninth, Twentieth and Twenty-second move together. If they do not, you are ordered to use your Skyborne to change their mind.*

Had the orders come in the hand of the clerk who'd been relaying communications for Kolanis, he would have demanded clarification, but the words were in Adaelis's own hand. If any of the commanders of the three regiments moving against the square tried to repeat Aerens' folly, the Green of Third would convince them otherwise.

THE AERADI'S LOSSES DRIVING BACK THE FIRST ATTACK HAD BEEN light, in comparison to what they'd faced. That didn't make Erik feel any better about the hundred-plus bodies lying still and silent where their comrades had dragged them.

More troops had trickled in from around the city, making up the losses and a little more, but none had come in for too long. Which meant, Erik knew, that the draconans had probably cut off the approaches, and that the defenders' time was growing very short.

They'd used what time they had to finish the trenches across the square wherever they could, using the dirt and torn-up cobblestones to build impromptu barricades across the paved areas. The fortifications were still only a step or so up from nothing, but they would give the aeradi with their longer swords a few extra moments with which to strike at their enemies.

Every preparation they could make made, Erik stood on an observation mound they'd thrown together from extra dirt and watched in silence. He heard Ikeras behind him and gestured the older man forward.

"How much chance do we really have?" he asked his *kep* retainer quietly.

"These are good men, and we've probably pulled together as many as we could," Ikeras replied, equally quietly.

"That wasn't the question," Erik told him.

Ikeras sighed. "They won't mess up again. They've got enough troops to ram their way straight through us."

"That's what I thought," Erik said grimly. "We'll need every sword we can get on the lines."

"Yes, sir," the noncom replied.

"When the Claws have closed, have the archers leave their bows and reinforce the lines," Erik ordered. "They may be able to walk over us, but we can bloody well make them *pay* for the privilege."

"Yes, sir!" Ikeras snapped firmly, his voice suddenly stronger. Then his voice weakened. "Look," he told Erik.

Erik raised his gaze from the aeradi troops in front of him to the main entrance into the square. In the distance, just barely in sight, the sun had begun to glint off armor as the Claws of the Dragon came into sight.

"Get back to the archers," he ordered. "Do everything you can."

THE CLAWS MOVED IN THEIR FIVE-HUNDRED-AND-FIFTY-MAN battalions, advancing down the Royal Boulevard toward the square in battle formation, five men deep and a hundred and ten men abreast. Three more battalions followed, their lines neatly spaced in deadly parade-ground perfection.

Erik blinked at the sight and then checked the entrance again. Four battalions were all he saw, and that made no sense. They'd already tried to take the square with a single regiment, and the draconans were far from new to the art of war. If one failed, they should have sent several.

"Sir," one of the messengers standing near him shouted, "look."

Erik followed the man's gesture to one of the *other* two entrances into the square, and his breath stopped. The secondary avenues into the square weren't as large as the Royal Boulevard, but they were enough for the draconans to advance their battalions fifty men abreast and eleven deep.

He didn't even need to count to know the draconans had sent a regiment down each of them. It was the simplest way to apply the maximum force. Three routes into the square, so they'd sent three regiments. Three regiments was the better part of seven thousand men.

There were less than two thousand aeradi left.

FOR AN ETERNAL MOMENT, ERIK GAVE IN TO DESPAIR, *KNOWING* THAT he could not hold against this enemy. The Claws were better armored and better trained than his own men. The fortifications were almost worthless; certainly, they couldn't make up *those* odds.

Behind him, he heard Ikeras bellowing, "Archers ready!" and breathed deeply. He could not *afford* to believe that they would fail. They were defending their homes, their people, their city—*his* home, his family and his city.

"Aim!" Ikeras bellowed, and Erik felt his despair flake away. Whatever came to pass, he was *there*, in a place he could call his own, as a noble among these people and a leader among these soldiers. It was a far cry from being an oppressed blacksmith in a place he'd never felt was home.

"Loose!"

KOLANIS HAD THOUGHT HE'D SEEN THE WORST AERADI ARCHERS could do when they'd shattered the Fifteenth, but now he realized he was wrong. However unconsciously, the aeradi had been conserving ammunition when fighting the Fifteenth, keeping to a trained pattern.

Now they were firing as fast as they could, and even from above, the sky seemed filled with arrows. They fell on the shields and armor and bare flesh of the advancing Regiments, and draconans died.

The Sky-Major bared his teeth in a snarl, desiring nothing more than to lead his battalion sweeping down upon those archers, burning and tearing and stopping them from killing his countrymen.

As if to punctuate why, the cannon in several of the nearer forts began to boom, dropping red-hot cannonballs into the lead ranks. *Any dragon trying to intervene in the Square of the Gods would die under the guns of those forts.*

~

GRUDGING ADMIRATION FILLED ERIK AS HE WATCHED THE draconans advance. Even under the fire of his archers, they marched forward evenly, taking their losses to enter the square and close up the three regiments, creating one formation that now advanced upon his people like a giant hammer.

It was costing them—*gods*, was it costing them—but they came on anyway. Hundreds of them fell, wounded or dead, and their comrades merely split and reformed ranks around them, closing up as they came on.

The commanders of the last regiment to attack had lost control, Erik knew, and the men had simply charged. Whoever was in command *here* was still in full control, and proved it when the entire draconan forced slowed fifty yards from the aeradi force, exposing itself to continued arrow fire.

"Prepare for enemy missiles!" Erik bellowed, knowing full well what that slowdown meant.

Almost as one monstrous creature, the Claws drew back their right arms and lashed forward, loosing their javelins upon the aeradi defenders. Thousands of the weapons cascaded down upon the Militiamen, and only the warnings of the men who knew what was coming saved any of them.

Shields were thrown up and men ducked behind barricades all along the aeradi line, and still men died. Shields were fouled by the weapons and thrown aside, and Erik knew that all too many of his men would now face the draconan Claws with no defense but the fortifications they hid behind and whatever armor they'd managed to put on.

The draconans began to speed up again, but as they did, they launched a second javelin salvo. By now, however, most of the soldiers in the line had found something to hide behind, and only a few were injured.

The point, however, hadn't been to hurt anyone. It had been to make them keep their heads down, and it had done just that. With the aeradi behind their berms, the draconans burst into a full-scale charge.

There was no way the aeradi could have reacted in time, had the charge gone home as it should have, but the draconans had discounted the archers. There was a gap, several seconds long, after the second javelin salvo, as every archer made ready, and then they fired. The range was short enough that they were firing almost flat across the square, and aeradi longbows could go clean through a man and kill another at that distance.

The front rank of the draconan formation simply vanished, destroyed by the lethally accurate fire, and the aeradi kept shooting. They couldn't *stop* the draconans, and they didn't, but they slowed them down.

Slowed them down enough that when the Claws of the Dragon hit the line of trenches and earthen berms, the aeradi were waiting for them with drawn steel.

FOR THE FIRST FEW MOMENTS, IT DIDN'T MATTER HOW MANY MORE soldiers the draconans had. The square was wide, but not *that* wide. The aeradi had dug their line straight across it, but only about five hundred men held the front, with another thousand or so doubling up the line behind them.

Of course, the equivalent draconan formation was far deeper and provided the pressure that began to force the aeradi back off their positions. Whoever was in command of the draconans had clearly taken some of the time before the attack to interrogate the survivors of the first assault, as his heaviest pressure came against the aeradi's right flank, the opposite flank from where the Second Kirmon provided a steady resistance to the draconan attack.

Mere Militia couldn't hold against the pressure for long, and Erik gestured to his signalers, sending both of his reserve companies to reinforce the right flank. They got to the position just in time, as a company of Claws pierced the aeradi lines, coming up over the berm.

The two Regular companies slammed into the penetration like the hammer of the gods and drove the draconans back into the ditch. The immediate threat contained, they spread out to reinforce the soldiers there, assuring the aeradi's right flank for the moment.

A shift in the pattern of war cries now drew Erik's attention to the *left* flank. An increased pressure from the draconans, soldiers shifting from the center to the flank, was threatening to break through even the Second, and Erik had no reserves left.

Before he could curse, he felt a hand grasp his shoulder and looked back at Ikeras standing behind him. "The archers are armed and ready to go," the noncom said flatly. "Five companies. Where do you want them?"

The Militia Captain blinked and remembered. "Leave two companies with me," he ordered. "Take the other three and reinforce the left!"

Ikeras simply nodded and gestured to the men behind him. "Sorris, Telman," he bellowed, "keep your companies with Lord Tarverro. Kelm, Tukli and Aret, bring your companies and follow me!"

Somewhere in the back of his mind, Erik was aware that a noncom had no business ordering around the commanders of companies. The *front* of his mind, however, was well aware that only two of the five men were even Lieutenants, and other three were merely senior sergeants, and Harmon *hept* Ikeras had more experience than all five put together.

Even with the reinforcements on the way, Erik was forced to watch the left flank in horror as the companies guarding it gave way before Ikeras could reach them. At least two hundred men of the Second Kirmon were simply ground under, and two full draconan companies came over the berm and started to turn to roll up the line.

Then Ikeras reached them, sending the three companies swirling up in waves that hammered into the gaps between the two companies and shattering their cohesion. The four hundred archers, now rearmed with swords and shields, shattered the two companies and drove them back against their own compatriots.

The pressure of the oncoming draconan troops was too great, and the Claw companies couldn't retreat. When the survivors of the Second joined Ikeras in his attack, the draconans simply died.

Even as Erik began to relax, thinking that both flanks were under control, an eerie sound from in front of him drew his eyes inexorably. *Someone* on the other side was playing games and had brought several full-size brown dragons to the party.

They must have kept them out of sight until the troops had closed to hand-to-hand combat, as the only *real* threat to a grounded dragon was archers or artillery, and with the archers gone, the dragons were mostly safe. The only other weapons that might be able to hurt it were sky steel, and there were only a handful of those among the defenders.

The only sky-steel blade that Erik could reliably locate, in fact, was the one at his belt. He *had* to stay there, though. He couldn't rely on the security of his flanks, and the two companies of former archers with him were the only reserve he had left.

Then the lead brown lifted its head and launched a fireball, which arced over the draconans to explode messily in the center of the aeradi lines. He didn't think it did too much damage, but it scattered the men, and they only barely closed the gap in time to prevent the draconans pushing through.

With a curse, Erik gestured for his last reserve, the two archer companies, to follow him, and drew his sword.

ERIK AND HIS RESERVES REACHED THE BERM WHERE THE AERADI LINE barely held on, just in time. The brown had closed the range and chose the moment before they reached the line to hose the aeradi with flame, driving the soldiers back off of the berm. The heat from the flame beat against Erik's face as he drove forward furiously, leading his men into the fire to block the gap.

The draconans came surging up out of the ditch, taking advantage of the momentary distraction, but Erik's two companies arrived before they did it. With a snarl, Erik led them into the fray, using his greater strength and body weight to spearhead the aeradi counterattack.

For a moment, Erik began to appreciate just what the draconans had been facing all day, as they tried to attack up even the slight height difference of the berm. The draconan shields covered everything he could reach, and their shorter swords stabbed down.

A man next to Erik went down, a draconan blade in his guts, and Erik lunged forward into the moment of distraction on the part of his killer. The sky-steel blade of his father's sword punched clean through the draconan's heavy shield to run through the man behind it.

Erik yanked his sword free and shoved the suddenly heavy corpse and shield backward. The heavily armored soldier knocked several of his compatriots back as he fell, and Erik leapt into the gap opened.

For a moment, he laid about himself almost blindly, cutting down draconans too distracted by the enemy in front of them to pay attention to the one aeraid in their midst. Then, just as the draconans started to focus on him, more aeradi forced their way into the gap he'd opened, driving the wedge wider.

The draconan line wavered, and the aeradi swordsmen pressed their advantage, shoving their way back onto the earthen berm. A fragile balance teetered on the top of the berm as both sides tried to push the other off.

Erik prepared to drive forward again, but some inner instinct warned him to drop. Obeying without a thought, he only barely avoided the razor-sharp dragon claws that swept through where his head had been.

The brown dragons and their Bonded riders had finally reached the lines and, instead of bothering to use the fire that would have killed their own men as well, had fallen back on teeth, claws and ten meters of nearly unkillable dragon. Even as Erik ducked under the claws, the spiked tail flicked out, scything through several of their own troops but smashing half a squad of aeradi to paste.

The claws came back toward Erik, and this time, he lashed out with his sword as he ducked under them. The sky steel scored along the dragon hide, drawing a blood-red line as it cut through the steel-hard scales.

The dragon screeched, nearly deafening Erik as it rose up on its hind legs, wings flapping as it lashed at him. Erik ducked under the claws, noting with grim humor that the wings had driven back an entire draconan company.

Evading the creature's lethally sharp tail, Erik lunged in, closing the distance and stabbing his sword into the dragon's right leg. For a moment, it seemed as though the great beast hadn't noticed, then he yanked the blade out and *heard* the hamstring pop.

Before the dragon could fall, however, the great wings beat harder and lifted its massive bulk from the ground. It rose into the air and twisted around, bringing its flame-dealing jaws to bear on Erik. The jaws yawned open, a small spark flickering in their depths, and for one instant of horrific clarity, Captain Lord Erik *septon* Tarverro *knew* he was going to die.

Then the dragon exploded in a shower of gore as six crys-bow lightning bolts converged on it, burning it out of the air.

KOLANIS'S LIPS TWISTED IN DISGUST AT THE SIGHT OF THE DRAGONS among the ground troops. He could see the value of the great beasts in a ground fight, but he still had to wonder what Skyborne had been convinced to humiliate their dragon so.

He knew, intellectually, that hundreds—if not thousands—of dragons back in the citadels had their wings clipped and spent their entire lives in one place, driving machinery. That was vastly different, in his mind, from forcing a war dragon, a creature trained to fly and kill in the air, to walk on all fours like an animal, simply because it was convenient.

Inevitably, the dragons rebelled and took to the air, and died under the guns of the forts. All they'd really achieved had been to lose dragons that could have been far more useful in the air.

It wasn't like they were losing the battle, anyway. Even as the Sky-Major watched, two more regiments entered the square, moving to reinforce the attackers. The battle would soon be over and the aeradi crushed.

Even as he thought that, however, a glint of sunlight caught his eye.

He glanced over toward the inner city and swallowed, hard. A moment later, he was scrabbling for his communication tablet.

There had to be *some* way to warn the Claws of what was coming!

~

THE DAMAGE THE DRAGON HAD DONE TO ITS OWN RANKS OPENED A gap in the solid draconan line standing atop the berm. The Claws stood in shock for a moment, staring up as the gory remnants of the dragon rained down on them.

Erik brought his focus back to the surface before they did, and saw the opening. "Newport!" he bellowed, drawing the attention of the aeradi to him. "Aeradi to me! Push them! Newport!"

He lunged forward into the gap, and the aeradi around him followed him unhesitatingly. The survivors in the gap the dragon had opened were thrown back onto their own rear ranks, and the gap widened as the aeradi troops pushed their way back into the formations.

For a moment, Erik was lost in the force of the battle. The rear ranks that should have already closed the gap pushed in hard when they realized what was happening, and Erik and his men met them with glittering steel. The battle wavered for a moment on the top of the berm, the two sides locked in mortal combat.

Finally, slowly, the aeradi pushed the more heavily armed and armored draconans back, shoving them off the berm by sheer passionate fury. Erik almost *felt* the line solidify around him as the aeradi retook the position.

Somewhere along the way, he'd fallen behind the front line, and he paused, breathing heavily as he surveyed the line across the Square of the Gods. All along, the draconans were pressing against the aeradi lines, and pressing hard. He had no reserves left to send, and he wouldn't have known where to send them if he did—*everywhere* needed them.

Movement attracted his eyes, and he looked across the square at the avenues where the draconans had originally entered the square. The sight of two more regiments, another four thousand Claws of the

Dragon, entering the square caused his heart to fall. There were too many draconans. His handful of Militia and Regulars could *never* hold.

Then a voice bellowed across the square, at parade-ground volumes and tones that could cut through any noise, any battle. Ikeras had mastered the skill, Erik knew, but few others had. Only the best noncoms and the better officers could do it.

"Archers ready!" the voice bellowed, but that made no *sense*. Erik *knew* he'd brought all of his archers forward to use as reserves.

"Loose!" the voice bellowed again, cutting through the din of the battle, and Erik's disbelief vanished as a storm of arrows passed over his head to hammer the regiments entering the square. Another volley followed, and another, and Erik turned in place to look behind him.

He was nearly blinded by the glitter of the sun on silver chain mail. No! *Sky-steel* chain mail! Neat, ordered lines of soldiers advanced into the square, leaving a detachment of over eight hundred archers behind to hammer the draconans.

"Wind Guard!" the voice bellowed. "Advance!"

And the three-thousand-strong personal bodyguard of the King of Newport advanced to defend their city.

"Split the ranks," Erik ordered his signaler immediately.

"Sir?" the man queried.

"They can't charge *through* us!" Erik snapped. "Order them to split the ranks!"

The message passed up and down the line, and slowly, stubbornly, the aeradi Militia and Regulars slowly withdrew off of the berm they'd shed so much blood to hold. As they withdrew, they opened gaps in their lines. They weren't large gaps, but Erik hoped they'd be wide enough.

The Claws of the Dragon, many of whom weren't even aware of the arrows hammering their reinforcements behind them, only saw that the aeradi were retreating, and charged over the berm to follow.

They reached the flat ground on the other side of the berm just in time to meet the Wind Guard coming the other way. Despite everything, the draconans still had more soldiers than the two thousand Wind Guard swordsmen, and it didn't matter.

The Wind Guard was armored in sky steel, and every man of them was as well trained as the King's money could make them. All of them were veterans of real wars, real battles as marines and Regulars of their city.

For all the skill and numbers of the draconans, they couldn't penetrate the Guards' armor, and the Guards were even more skilled. Slowly at first, but then faster and faster, the Wind Guard drove the draconans, until the regiments broke into a full-scale rout.

Then Erik led his lighter-armored men, who were much faster than the Wind Guard, back in to finish the job. Encumbered by their own heavy armor, the draconans could never have run fast enough to escape.

Only a handful left the Square of the Gods alive.

SOMEHOW, GIVEN THE WAY THE DAY HAD GONE, ERIK WAS FAR FROM surprised to see Captain Dekker *sept* Corens picking his way across the battlefield toward him, followed by the Wind Guard command group. While the Wind Guard was barracked inside the palace itself, their officers lived in the main city.

"Erik," Corens greeted him. "You're in command here, I'm told?"

"I am," Erik replied. "And you?"

"I was officer on duty," the Wind Guard Captain said simply. "So far as I can tell, not a single Wind Guard officer made it into the Inner City."

"It was much the same for the Regulars and Militia," Erik told him. "They planned this *very* well."

"I'm sorry it took us so long to get here," Dekker apologized, "but we'd only barely finished organizing when your officer warned us."

"My officer?" Erik asked.

"A Lieutenant Felsten," Dekker told him as he turned to survey the field, where his men, mixed in with the survivors of Erik's, were now clearing the bodies and renewing the defenses.

"He got us here just in time, and the draconans are done," he said with quiet pride. "We'll hold them here."

A day before, even knowing all that would happen, Erik would have agreed. Today, he'd seen what a single dragon could do to the best troops on the ground.

"And if they bring up dragons on the ground?" he asked.

The Wind Guard's acting commander was silent for a long moment. "We'll stand a better chance than Regular troops," he noted grimly. "But you're right. We could probably take down three or four, perhaps more with the cannon, but if they send in enough, all we can do is die bravely."

"I dislike any plan that involves dying, bravely or otherwise," Erik observed. His gaze was resting on one of the great corpses mounding the field, where the forts had shattered an entire *regiment* of dragons. "We need bait," he muttered to himself.

"What?" Dekker asked, perplexed.

"Even the inner forts have enough firepower to take on the entire invasion force," Erik said slowly, "but the draconans *know* that and won't enter range of the guns. Sky Fleet, even just the squadron here, can pin them against the forts once they're *in* range, but we have to get them into range. We need bait," he repeated.

"They'll just bring dragons in on the ground for us," Dekker objected. "That won't lure them into range of the guns."

"We need a ship," Erik figured aloud. "But the shipyards are gone, I don't think we can reach the civilian docks, and the military docks are empty."

"A ship?" Dekker said slowly.

"Yes."

"There's one," the Wind Guard told him. "The *Tarverro.*"

"The *what?*" Erik demanded, turning to look at the other man.

"The royal yacht," Dekker explained. "It's old; they named her for the first ruling clan—your ancestors. But she's got crys-bows, and she can fly."

"The crew?"

Dekker shook his head. "They live outside the palace. They may be alive, but we won't be able to find them."

Erik nodded, and turned to one of his messengers. "Torin, fetch Harmon *hept* Ikeras," he instructed the man.

"Yes, sir!" the messenger replied, and took off.

"What are you thinking?" Dekker asked.

"Most of the Militia have day jobs as crew or marines on merchant ships," Erik told him. "If we can find enough..."

Ikeras's arrival cut off Dekker's answer. He wasn't even out of breath, but then, the square wasn't big enough for him to have been too far away.

"What is it?" the noncom asked.

"Harmon, can we pull together enough men to man a skyship?" Erik asked simply.

"Just fly her or fight her?" Ikeras asked.

"Fight her."

"Maybe," the noncom said slowly. "I can find ten, maybe twelve, men I know can help me *fly* it, but fighting it... We sent everyone with artillery experience to the forts."

"I didn't," Dekker said flatly. "If you can find the men to fly it, I can find the men to man the 'bows."

"I think we may just have a plan," Erik agreed.

"To do what?" Ikeras asked cautiously.

THE NEWPORT ROYAL YACHT *TARVERRO* FLOATED IN WHAT WOULD have been a decorative pond in the grounds of any other palace. Nearly two hundred feet from bow to stern, she was even larger than a war frigate, though not nearly as large as most battleships. She lacked the *weapons* of even a frigate, but the ones she did have would be enough. Should be enough.

The palace grounds around her were eerily quiet. Every time Erik had been there before, the place had bustled with servants and people, living the life of court. Now the only people within sight were the sixty soldiers they'd pulled from the Militia and the Wind Guard.

"You're sure you can fly her with fifteen men?" Erik asked Ikeras, eyeing the length of the ship.

"She can be flown entirely by changing crystal power levels," the noncom told him quietly. "It puts a lot of strain on the crystals, but it takes only a handful. I wouldn't want to make any long voyages with this few, but we can fight her for a short while."

"Good," Erik said flatly, and turned to Dekker. "What about you?"

The Wind Guard Captain shrugged. "We have forty-five men for forty crys-bows," he replied. "They're older 'bows, too. We'll get one shot from all of them to start, but we're only going to be able to keep nine, maybe ten, of them firing at a time."

Erik considered.

"It should be enough," he conceded. "We're not planning to fight the entire draconan host on our own."

"No," Ikeras agreed morosely. "Just piss them off on our own."

Pointedly ignoring his *kep's* complaint, Erik stepped onto the ramp leading up to the ship, carefully balancing as the wood sprang under him. A few steps and he stood on the deck of the ship named for his clan.

He didn't stay at the top of the ramp for long, as the rest of the *Tarverro's* impromptu crew came surging up it. They didn't have a great deal of time.

"Get her ready to fly as quickly as possible," he instructed curtly. "We'll only have one shot at this."

DISCIPLINE WAS FRAYING AMONG THE SKYBORNE PORTION OF THE draconan attack force. Kolanis could *feel* it. Skyborne warriors were the elite of Dracona's armies; they were *far* from used to impotence, and impotent was what they were today.

Hundreds of dragons clustered in the sky, providing "air cover" that couldn't extend to where they were truly needed. Resistance on the perimeter of the city had been effectively crushed. Stands by a platoon of Regulars here, a company of Militia there, had been burnt to death by dragons or crushed by Claws.

Outside the reach of the forts, the draconans controlled Newport

—but whenever a dragon strayed too close to the forts, a cannonball or a bolt of lightning reminded them of the limits to their ability.

The dragons didn't even need to get into actual range of the forts, either. The gunners were perfectly prepared to take risky long shots at targets outside their normal range. Every so often, they got lucky, swatting a dragon from the sky.

Kolanis felt control slipping from the fingers of the men who commanded the host. The Skyborne were linked with the minds of their dragons, and much of the dragons' impatient and hungry nature entered the men who rode them. Much of the reason for the iron discipline of the draconan military was that its brutality was practically *required* to keep men with dragons in their heads in check.

If they didn't find something for the Skyborne to kill soon, the commanders were going to lose control.

The only question that remained was would they lose control of the men—or of themselves?

Apparently, the *Tarverro* was kept ready in case the King needed to be evacuated on short or no notice. It took the sixty soldiers barely ten minutes to ready the ship for flight. With everything set, Erik joined Ikeras and Dekker on the bridge.

"Are we ready?" he asked.

"Yes, sir," Ikeras replied, his eyes firmly locked on the pattern of crystals before him, the central control matrix. He couldn't fly the ship from *just* there but, combined with hand gestures to the men positioned at central links, he could fly it almost as well as someone with a full crew to back them up. For a little while, anyway.

"Let's go," Erik told him.

Nodding abstractly, the older aeraid thrust his gloved hands into the crystals, twisting them into contact in a certain pattern. Raising his hands, he gestured, and two of his helpers moved larger crystals into alignment.

Shuddering with the effort, the old yacht slowly lifted out of the water, shedding droplets and pondweed across the gardens like rain. She gained speed, picking up energy as the crystal pathways energized.

"We're good," Ikeras announced, his eyes still on the matrix. "How do we want to do this?"

"Loop us around to the east and bring us in from the north," Erik instructed. "Most of them are concentrated on the southwest side, where they came from."

The noncom said nothing, but the ship curved around and began to pick up speed, rising away from the Square of the Gods and the host of dragons watching it.

FROM THE SKY ABOVE NEWPORT, THE EXTENT OF THE DAMAGE THE draconan invasion had wreaked was clear. The outer fortifications, dozens of mighty stone bastions built of solid stone, were now jagged ruins. The shipyards that had churned out dozens of skyships a year were smoldering embers. The city streets were empty, and a fire flickered its way through one of the outer neighborhoods, with no one attempting to stop it.

The draconans had apparently spread out a network of scouts, though how those scouts were communicating with their leaders was beyond Erik, and they were barely clear of the inner city before the yacht encountered the first one.

One of Ikeras's helpers was halfway up the mainmast, focusing one of the lift crystals from there. He spotted the dragon, a brown, before its rider spotted the *Tarverro*, and shouted down.

"Dragon!"

Erik jerked around at the shout and then followed the soldier's pointing arm. Either the brown dragon's rider or the dragon itself had heard something, quite possibly the warning shout, as the dragon began to turn toward the *Tarverro*.

"Gunners!" Erik bellowed. "*Take him!*"

While all the crys-bows on the ship had been charged and aligned, they'd only manned a handful in each broadside to begin with. The three manned 'bows in the broadside facing the dragon rotated and fired.

Perhaps two seconds elapsed between the first bow firing and the last, but the third bolt passed through empty air. The first two had converged on the beast and scattered its remains across the sky.

Erik breathed a sigh of relief. Unless there'd been a mage on the dragon with its rider, he couldn't have informed his commanders. Even if there had been, the dragon had been killed too fast for *any* communication.

"We're probably at their scout perimeter," he guessed, and Dekker nodded in agreement. "We should probably swing in now and head for their main body."

"All right," Ikeras replied, shifting crystals and making the gestures.

As the ship began to swing toward the southwest, Erik turned to Dekker. "It only takes one of your men to fire the 'bow if it's charged, right?"

"Aiming might be an issue, but yeah," the Wind Guard officer agreed. "Why?"

"Split them up," Erik told him. "Put one man on each 'bow. We'll get one good salvo in from all of them that way. Then we can man whichever broadside faces toward the enemy as we run."

"Makes sense," Dekker acknowledged with a small nod. He crossed the deck to his own men and started to give orders.

KOLANIS FELT LALEN TENSE UNDER HIM, THE DRAGON REACTING TO his own emotions as he watched the Claws attempt to assault the Square of the Gods again. His own feelings of impotence and rage were transmitting to the great beast, fueling her own fury, which she transmitted back. Their emotions were in a feedback loop, and only years of discipline allowed the draconan officer to maintain control of himself and his dragon.

Beneath them, the Claws doggedly advanced into an unending storm of arrows and cannon fire, rending formations and leaving bodies scattered behind them. Finally, the soldiers managed to close and charge the crude fortifications.

They may as well have charged the stone walls behind the square. The Claws of the Dragon were universally acknowledged as the best *Regular* troops around, but the Wind Guard was an *elite* unit. No Regular troops, however good, had any business charging them in prepared positions, but that was just what the Claws had to do.

The Wind Guardsmen's armor shrugged aside all but the strongest or luckiest of blows, and their own weapons ripped through the Claws' armor like it wasn't even there. Wind Guards died, but far more draconans died. The Claws were paying easily five or ten to one to take down their more heavily armored opponents.

Kolanis almost *felt* his own impotent fury spread through the Skyborne force as the Claws were forced to stubbornly retreat, leaving almost a third of their numbers behind. The dragons shifted, moving toward the square.

The Sky-Major almost lost control himself, but a flash of heat grabbed his attention, and he picked up the crystal tablet strapped to his leg as the heat faded. The command was simple and yet edging toward impossible:

All Skyborne, it read, *control your men!*

Kolanis focused on the message, using its importance to help him control his own emotions. Once his rage was quelled, he turned his attention to Lalen, calming her down. Finally, with his dragon and himself both under control, he turned to give orders to his men. Orders that, no matter how far they'd gone, he *knew* they would obey.

His turn meant he was looking out to the sea to the northwest and was in a perfect position to see the skyship arrive. The back of his mind acknowledged the intelligence of the maneuver, but his forebrain simply went into shock as the ship, clearly a battleship from its size, came swooping up from under the level of the city, emerging almost directly into the rear of the dragon host.

For a moment, he thought he was wrong and it was simply an unarmed merchantman trying to rattle the Skyborne host. Then the ship passed into the dragon formations and its crys-bows fired.

Forty separate bolts of lightning lashed out at forty separate dragons, and the war-dragons died under the skyship's fire. Any chance of controlling the host was lost as the psychic shock of their deaths rippled between the dragons and into their already-antsy riders.

The Skyborne needed to kill something, and this skyship, whoever she was, had just volunteered.

～

"FORM UP!" DEKKER BELLOWED TO HIS MEN. "MAN AS MANY 'BOWS as you can on each side."

Erik watched the dragons as the *Tarverro* whipped into their ranks. "Take us right through them, Harmon," he ordered. "Let's get their attention."

Almost as he spoke, fire flashed across the side of the ship, leaving visible scorch marks in the wood.

"I think we've got their attention," Ikeras replied, his hands busy inside the control matrix. A moment later, the ship suddenly shifted left as control paths changed. Fire blazed through the air where the *Tarverro* would have flown if she hadn't dodged.

Erik blanched as he looked over the side of the ship and saw just *how* many dragons were coming at them. He'd expected to get some, possibly even a lot, of dragons to come after them. He hadn't expected to get *all* of them.

"Dekker, where are those 'bow crews?" he demanded.

"Forming up!" the Wind Guard officer replied. A moment later, two of the crys-bows on the port broadside fired, blazing a black from the sky moments before *its* crys-bows fired into the yacht's hull.

In a spattering of lightning, the starboard broadside opened up again, five bolts lashing out in a staggered sequence at three dragons. Two died, and the third fell toward the ocean, one of its wings crippled.

Three more bows opened up on the port side, taking down another dragon, and then the first two fired again. That was all the weapons they had the hands for, Erik realized, and he hoped it would be enough.

~

SKY-MAJOR KOLANIS WAS A TRAINED WARRIOR, TAUGHT FROM THE day he'd Bonded with Lalen to control both his own emotions and his dragon's. His skill at that training, even more than his ability to lead or his skill at arms, was what had made him an officer.

But under strain of the long grinding stalemate and the provocation of that single foolish battleship, his training had failed. Now he led not just his men but almost *all* of the Skyborne armada in an insane attack on the single skyship. Fire ripped at its masts and hull, and still the ship flew onward.

Somewhere in the back of his mind, that tiny part of him that was still in control screamed a warning. They'd crossed into the range of the forts' guns and crys-bows. But no cannonballs or lightning bolts struck down the dragons, and the warning was lost in the tumult of his dragon's rage.

~

"WHY DON'T THEY FIRE?" IKERAS DEMANDED, HIS VOICE SCRATCHY from the smoke of the *Tarverro*'s slowly burning hull. "The Fires-burnt lizards are in range; why don't they fire?"

Even as the noncom spoke, a fireball tore the central mast clear off of the skyship, taking the man who'd been spotting from there with it. Lightning bolts from one broadside answered, and the screams of the man were lost in the roar of dying dragons.

"They can't," Erik gasped, holding on to a rail as the ship *bucked* beneath them. "We need warships to drive them against the guns. We have to lure them deeper!"

"This ship isn't going to hold together much longer," Dekker snapped as another series of fireballs seared across the decks. Despite what the fire had to be doing under the decks, the crys-bows continued to fire, answering the fireballs with their lightning bolts.

"She'll hold together long enough," Erik replied. "She *has* to."

"There!" one of the men switching crystals shouted, gesturing to the south. "The ships!"

Erik turned and knew what had happened. Whoever was in command of the ships had taken the time to circle around, outside the range of the forts' weapons, and hit the dragons from behind. It may have cost the *Tarverro* and her impromptu crew damage, even lives, but it gave them the best chance of inflicting critical losses on the draconans.

Even as he began to cheer, another salvo of fireballs hit home, and this time, even *he* knew something had gone wrong.

THE FIRST THING KOLANIS KNEW OF THE APPROACHING WARSHIPS was when a cannonball blew Sergeant-Major Cerians out of the sky less than thirty yards from where he flew. He turned Lalen in the air, forcing her away from her prey as he finally, slowly regained control of himself.

He saw the remaining battleships of the aeradi squadron formed into a neat line, their broadsides blazing fire and lightning as their formation wrapped around behind the Skyborne host. Even as he began to turn to give orders to his own people, the forts behind them finally opened up, catching the draconans between two fires.

Enough of the mindless rage remained that he wasted precious seconds finding the skyship that had lured them into this trap. He grinned coldly as he saw it, remaining masts ablaze, descending toward the city.

The last of his rage faded under the rush of cold fear as he saw another green dragon come diving *through* the fire from the forts, desperately trying to signal something. Kolanis didn't manage to catch the signals before one of the battleships blew the dragon away, but he wondered why the man was signaling by hand. The scouts had tablets, after all.

He knew, then, how bad the mess they were in was, but it took him a moment to drag out his own tablet to confirm it. As he feared, the crystal was dead and cold. The length of the battle had stolen the draconan communication advantage, and the solitary scout's warning, whatever it was, was in vain.

~

A HORRIFIC WHINING NOISE RESOUNDED ACROSS THE BURNING DECK of the royal yacht *Tarverro*, ignored now by her erstwhile opponents as the forts and warships gave them more pressing concerns.

The whine and the crackle of fire gave an eerie backdrop to the sight of the city beneath them, growing only closer as the ship slowly began to drift downward, gaining speed as she got lower.

"Harmon," Erik noted grimly, "we're falling."

"No shit," the noncom said flatly. "That's not our problem. You hear that whine?"

"Yes."

"*That's* our problem," Ikeras told him. "*That* is the primary crystals overloading, because those Fires-burnt dragons fused the connector crystals. I no longer have control. We are going to fall. We are going to hit the city. And *then* we're going to *blow up*." The last two words were screamed aloud to the winds, and Erik took a step backward at the force of Ikeras's fear.

His own fear tried to take control, and he used it to sharpen his voice as he stepped closer to Ikeras. "Harmon *hept* Ikeras *kep* Tarverro!" he snapped. "Control yourself, or we all *will* die!"

Ikeras stared at him, his gaze half-blank but no longer paralyzed with fear. Finally, the older aeraid nodded his control.

"You said the crystals were fused," Erik said patiently. "Can we break the connection from here?"

"Maybe..." Ikeras said in a whisper, as if he was thinking of something else. He turned back to the crystal matrix behind him and began twisting crystals.

He gave up after only a moment and looked at Erik. His eyes were calm, far calmer than they had been before. "I can't break it here, Erik," he whispered, his voice deathly soft. "There's only one way I know of that I can."

"What's that?" Erik demanded.

Ikeras only shook his head. "I'm sorry, Erik," he told his young lord, then turned and headed for the trapdoor into the depths of the ship, leaving Erik standing stunned behind him.

By the time Kolanis broke free of the melee developing around the forts, he'd lost his entire command. He had no idea where *any* of the Skyborne in his battalion were. He'd managed to gather a small group of green flyers around him, but they were far from free yet.

The forts' guns ignored the small group of dragons in favor of larger concentrations of targets, but a solitary frigate caught the group as they cleared the forts' range, bearing down on them with cannon and crys-bows blazing.

With a snarl on his lips, Kolanis led his dragons against it. With no choice but to destroy the ship or die, he drove Lalen harder than he'd ever driven the dragon before. The green somehow managed to avoid the lightning bolts to come within feet of the frigate's deck.

He touched her with his heels, and she spewed fire across the deck, scattering men and supplies until it hit a keg of firepower. Just one. The explosion ripped the top off the skyship's deck, exposing the ship's crystal rooms.

A single fireball, and the crystals fused, overloading with sparks and explosions. Lalen lifted away from the dying ship, and as she did, Kolanis got a good glimpse at the flag flying from the ship's mast.

That glimpse froze his heart, for it wasn't the winged ship of Newport's banner, but the crowned cloud of Sky Hame. No Sky Hame warship was supposed to be there. Indeed, he could only think of one reason for *any* Sky Hame warship to be at Newport, and as he turned his gaze to the northwest, his fears were confirmed.

To an untrained eye, the smudges along the horizon would have been nothing more than dark clouds. Kolanis's eyes, however, had been trained by the best Dracona had to offer. To him those smudges were sails and hulls—*hundreds* of sails and hulls.

The Grand Fleet of the Realm of the Sky, the one that gathered only once every year for immense war games, was coming to Newport, bringing with it death for all the hopes of her draconan attackers.

ERIK STARED AFTER IKERAS IN CONFUSED SHOCK. THE WHINE around him increased in pitch, but the fires were fading as Dekker's men beat them back. The Wind Guard commander himself returned to Erik's side just in time to see Ikeras vanish through the trapdoor belowdecks.

"Where is he going?" Dekker asked.

"I don't know," Erik admitted. "He said that the crystals were fused and had to be broken. He couldn't do it from up here."

"No, he couldn't," Dekker realized aloud, and Erik realized that, while he had ridden on aeradi skyships, he didn't know as much about them as would someone raised among the aeradi. Someone like Captain Dekker *sept* Corens.

"What?" he demanded of the Wind Guard.

"He can only break them physically," Dekker replied. "Which would..."

"Release the energy stored in them into the breaker," Erik breathed in horror. Leaving Dekker standing on the deck, he lunged toward the trapdoor himself.

"No! Erik, wait!" the other aeraid bellowed after him, but Erik ignored him as he plunged into the fire-stricken depths of the *Tarverro*.

Smoke and heat greeted him in the darkness as he dropped to the deck. Coughing, he tried to orient himself, forcing himself to remember where the crystal rooms were. All his memory of his time on other skyships told him was that there was one fore and one aft; nothing said which one Ikeras would have gone to.

The sound of the crystals whining intensified, and Erik realized the answer. The whining was coming from the aft, and he ran backward through the smoke.

"Ikeras," he yelled. "Harmon, wait!"

He didn't hear a response, but it was possible he couldn't have. His ears ached as he grew closer to the whining, and he wasn't sure he could hear anything *other* than the sound of the crystals dying.

Finally, he broke through the smoke and saw the open door to the crystal room. Fire and smoke billowed around it, but he could see a figure inside.

"Harmon!" he bellowed again, as loud as he could, but he couldn't even hear *himself* over the crystals.

As if to mark the futility of his attempt, a burning plank from the deck above collapsed, shattering and setting the deck in front of Erik aflame. It also cleared the smoke away, and Erik could clearly see Harmon standing in front of the painfully bright crystals with his sword drawn.

"Harmon!" he bellowed again, and ran forward, heedless of the fire cutting him off from his mentor and friend.

Before he could enter the flames, arms grabbed him from behind and dragged him back. As they did, and long before Erik could ever have reached him, Ikeras spun and struck the crystals with all his might.

The fused mass of crystal and slagged glass shattered into a million pieces. For a moment, it looked like that was all that was going to happen, but every single piece glowed with the same brightness as the original for a moment.

Then the moment faded, and the crystals flared blindingly bright as they voided their energy, ripping through the crystals around them, the hull of the *Tarverro* and the body of Harmon *hept* Ikeras *kep* Tarverro.

The last thing Erik remembered was the dark silhouette of the man who'd brought him to Newport, framed against a backdrop of brilliant light.

KOLANIS LED THE HANDFUL OF GREENS AROUND HIM IN FLEEING THE battle. Once that fleet arrived, there was no way any of the draconans could survive. They had to get out of Newport. If they didn't, they were going to die.

He felt guilty about it; both his honor and his sense of responsibility said he had to go back and fight, had to at least attempt find and extract his *own* men. His mind, however, knew that if they went back, they would die.

When the screams of another group of dragons sounded above them, Kolanis was stunned. He looked up and saw ten black dragons descending on his handful of greens. The man on the lead dragon gestured to the ground.

For a moment, Kolanis considered running, but he knew it was foolish. The crys-bows mounted on the blacks would annihilate his small group before they could escape. Unwilling to die just yet, he led his men to the ground and dismounted on the cobbled street of the aeradi's floating island.

To his surprise, all of the blacks followed them down, leaving no one to prevent them leaving, and the leader dismounted. As the Skyborne approached him, Kolanis realized with a shock that it was General Adaelis.

"Sky-Major," Adaelis said quietly, "you are very lucky."

"Sir," Kolanis said flatly, straightening to attention.

The draconan general shook his head. "I'm not here to censure you, Major," he told Kolanis. "One of the scouts managed to warn the command group. We can't fight that fleet."

"What do we do now?" Kolanis asked. If there was any solution, any way that they could retrieve anything from this situation, he trusted Adaelis to know it. The general *had* to know it.

"The blacks and browns aren't fast enough to escape," Adaelis said bluntly. "The greens are. The scouts and the greens of the command group are waiting at the southwestern edge of the city. You're the only officer not tied up in that accursed battle who rides a green."

"Your orders, sir?" the Major asked, unwilling to accept what he knew had to be coming.

"I've already issued orders to the Claws to surrender once the Fleet begins landing Marines," Adaelis told him. "By that point, it will all be over. I'm going to take the blacks and browns of the command group into that melee and try to organize things. I'm going to send the greens back to you and take the blacks and browns against the Grand Fleet."

"To me, sir?"

"Yes, to you," Adaelis confirmed. "I want you to rendezvous with the command-group greens and lead them and your own survivors back to the base on the Hellitian shore. I want you to wait there for two days, to collect any others who manage to make it out of this *fire-fuck*, and then head back to Black Mountain."

"We can't abandon you, sir!" Kolanis objected. He may have been prepared to run before, but that didn't mean he was ready to leave Adaelis behind.

"Someone has to tell the greens to run, and their riders will only obey me," Adaelis told him gently. "I'll buy you as much time as I can, Edrin," he continued, surprising Kolanis by using his first name, "but I have to go. Besides," he said, almost bitterly, "your greens can't carry passengers. Just you."

Kolanis braced to full attention and saluted. "I'll do my best, sir."

"You'll succeed," the General told him. "I know you will."

With that, Adaelis turned away from Kolanis, turning back to his dragon. The major watched his back for a moment, and then spoke again.

"General Adaelis, sir!" he snapped off, and the general turned back to look at him. "It's been an honor," he told the man who'd led them all to this defeat.

"Indeed it has, Major," the General replied sadly. "Indeed it has."

ERIK CAME TO ON THE FOREDECK OF THE *TARVERRO*. NEITHER THE whine of overcharging crystals nor the crackle of burning fires was audible, suggesting they were okay. Everything he could see was a blur, but finally one blur resolved itself into Dekker *sept* Corens.

"Harmon?" he asked the other aeraid as he struggled to a sitting position.

Dekker shook his head, offering his hand to help Erik to his feet. "He did break the crystals," he told Erik, an offering of what the man had to know was scant help. "The power surge was sufficient to lift us over the city, and it stopped the overload."

Erik looked behind the ship and saw the edge of the floating island only a few hundred yards away.

"How long was I out?" he asked.

"Only a couple of minutes," Dekker replied. "There's more, Erik," he said after a moment.

"What?" Erik asked, almost entirely unsurprised at the second shoe dropping.

"The aft crystal room is gone, entirely, and the fore room was damaged in the fight, though not so badly," the Wind Guard officer told him.

"We don't have enough lift?" Erik asked, knowing the answer.

"We don't have enough lift," Dekker confirmed. "Nor enough control to try to land. We're going down, gaining speed as we do. We'll hit with enough force to shatter the hull and kill us all."

Erik's lips twitched at the bitter irony. They'd turned the tide of the battle, saved everyone, from Arien to Elysia. *Then* they'd managed to prevent the ship blowing up over the city. Having done all that, they were *still* all going to die, and he'd woken up just in time to do so while awake.

KOLANIS TURNED LALEN BACK AS THEY REACHED THE EDGE OF THE city, watching the battle behind them. The Fleet hadn't reached the draconan host yet, but the ships that were already there were doing enough. The vast majority of the dragons were pinned, with no hope of escape.

Somewhere in that maelstrom of ships and dragons was the Green of Third, the battalion he'd led there. Some of them might even make it out alive; he didn't know. There was no way he could know.

Adaelis was in there too, sacrificing his life to buy as much time for those who could escape to do so. His life for his men's lives, the ancient code of the draconan leader. A code that said Kolanis should be back among that melee, spending himself to bring his people home.

He couldn't do that. He'd been charged with a greater duty, to save as many lives as he could and to bear warning to his people. Now the passion of the moment had failed, every bone in his body strained to return to the battle, to die with his people if he couldn't save them.

His mind knew that dying was all he would do, and his death would gain nothing. Only his *life* would allow him to achieve anything. His life, for his men's. Today, he'd failed his men. He would spend the rest of his life repaying that debt.

They had done damage—damage that Newport would be years in the repairing. Thousands of Regulars had died and dozens of ships had been destroyed. The outer forts alone would be a decade or more in the reconstruction. The rebuilding would weaken Newport, which would be essential now.

The war was coming, and for the sake of the men under his command who'd died there today, Sky-Major Edrin Kolanis Bond Lalen would be part of it. There were all the reasons that had driven a man into the Skyborne, all the reasons he understood and agreed with for this war, and now there was one more. If it were within his power, none of those men and dragons would have died in vain.

His oath sworn, Kolanis turned his gaze back to the dragons and riders around him, the Bonds he *could* save from the insatiable cauldron of war.

"Let's go."

THE ONCOMING WATER HELD A TERRIBLE FASCINATION FOR ERIK. Partially, it was the knowledge that it was going to kill him in only a few moments, but mainly, it was the lifelong fascination of the half-human, half-aeradi boy raised by the sea.

Love of the sea and the sky had brought him to Newport, to his grandmother and his father's people. His own sense of duty had done the rest, and ended there, aboard this battered ship. He knew that most of the fires were out, but they hadn't even bothered on the lower decks. They'd be swallowed by the ocean soon enough.

Less than twenty aeradi, including himself and Dekker, still stood on the deck of the *Tarverro*. The rest had died in the nightmare that had led to this moment. The nightmare was over now for the crew of the *Tarverro*.

Somehow, knowing that death was inevitable made the moment more peaceful than it could ever have been otherwise. The breeze was cool on Erik's face, and the ocean he watched was calm. Nothing could change anything now, and he accepted his fate with an odd calm.

Then the war scream of a wing lancer's roc cut through the air and shattered his reverie.

∾

ERIK ROSE TO HIS FEET, GAZING AROUND HIM IN WONDER. OVER twenty rocs had descended out of the sky onto the yacht, and they hovered around her, their great wings beating. The aeraid Erik guessed to be their leader waved at Erik with an odd spear, then gestured to his wing lancers with it.

Each roc and its rider swept over the ship in sequence, hanging down ropes from the bird's talons. Several birds hovered over the central deck, where the *Tarverro*'s impromptu crew had been taking care of the wounded, as soldiers tied their wounded comrades into the rope harnesses hanging down.

No orders were necessary; if they didn't go, they would die. Each roc acquired its passengers in turn, until finally the leader swept in to pick up Erik. The rope slipped by Erik quite quickly, but he managed to grab it and pull himself up into the crude harness.

"Hold on!" the wing lancer yelled down, and Erik almost laughed. Hysteria, he suspected, but he was going to hold on no matter what.

He was one of the last lifted off, and just in time. The lancers had only just pulled the last of the yacht's crew clear when she finally hit the waves. She entered at an angle, the rear of the ship hitting first with a tremendous *CRACK*.

A second later, the latter third of the vessel was torn off by the force of the waves and sank in moments. Erik found himself weeping as he watched it go under, knowing that it bore the body of Harmon *hept* Ikeras to the old soldier's final resting place under the sea.

The rest of the ship almost looked like it was going to lift away. It rose into the air, the lift of the one crystal room almost enough with only half of a ship. Too many lift crystals and foci points had been lost, however, and she merely described a long arc from where the aft half went under to where the rest hit.

She hit with more force this time, and the last remnants of the yacht *Tarverro* shattered into splinters and debris, bearing the bodies of those who died aboard her in her first—and final—battle to the watery depths.

～

AFTER A SHORT ETERNITY OF HANGING ON ONLY BY HIS ARMS, THE lancers delivered Erik and the rest of the late *Tarverro's* impromptu crew to the decks of a large battleship flying the winged-ship flag of Newport.

On closer inspection as they approached, Erik realized that the ship's flag also bore the numeral two, with a small star above it, marking her as the flagship of Newport Sky Fleet's Second Squadron.

The rider of the roc who'd borne Erik to the ship swung down from his bird to join Erik on the skyship's deck. Wordlessly, he offered Erik his hand. Erik took it, and the man shook it firmly.

"Wing-Master Stels *hept* Kelnar," he introduced himself. "I cannot begin to say how much we owe you."

"You know what happened?" Erik asked.

"We had Mages scrying all the way in," an older, deeper voice said from behind Erik. The *septon* Tarverro turned to find Admiral Bor *septon* Alraeis, commander of the Second Squadron of Newport Sky Fleet, standing behind him.

"We saw it all," the Admiral continued. "You managed to do our job for us and make our panicked rush entirely unnecessary."

"I wouldn't say *entirely* unnecessary," Erik pointed out.

"When I heard the reports of the attack on you, Lord Tarverro, I *knew* that the assassins weren't in Newport for you," Alraeis told him, ignoring Erik's comment. "Given the man in question, you probably *were* a target but not the sole target. I *knew* there was a real attack coming."

"And he managed to convince the rest of the Realm of the Sky to have their ships ready to fly at a moment's notice," Kelnar observed. "And had Mages quietly scrying the city, so the instant the first explosions occurred, we knew. We were probably on our way before you even left your house."

"I don't think *anyone* has ever made that long a flight on pure crystal power before," Alraeis told Erik, his voice suffused with pride for his ships and men. "It got us here in half the time the draconans expected, and we knew long before they expected us to. Nonetheless," he continued softly, "we would have been too late. They'd brought heavy anti-air weapons, Erik, ready to set up their own defenses around Newport."

Erik looked at him in surprise and he nodded. "Oh, yes. We could have taken them," the Admiral said coldly, "but the price would have been high, especially with dragons around to repeat what Fifth Squadron did to the bastards themselves. Your stand at the square, however, sucked down the manpower they needed to assemble the guns.

"And then you lured the bastards into the perfect trap," he finished with a cold smile. "All that is left for me and the rest of the Fleet to do is turn a defeat into an outright rout, which our people are doing right now."

Alraeis took Erik's hand and shook it firmly, then turned to Dekker and shook the Wind Guard's hand. "Thank you," he said simply. "Between the two of you, Newport is saved."

"And the draconans?" Erik asked.

The Admiral's faced almost seemed to turn to stone. "This will not go unpunished," he said flatly. "I am afraid, Lord Tarverro, that you have returned to your people only in time to join us at war."

6

"A LANCE of rocs followed the last group in, sir," the Skyborne officer, once General Adaelis's aide, now Major *Kolanis's* aide, reported to Kolanis. "They broke off before we could engage them, but they definitely know at least the general area where we are now."

Kolanis said nothing for a long moment, surveying the encampment where, not so long before, the vast host of the draconans had been encamped. Now a bare handful of dragons, mostly greens with a handful of browns, and their riders occupied it. Thousands had ridden forth, and barely two hundred would return.

The tents and huts of the camp would be given over to fire now. They'd been borne there by blacks, and the smaller dragons that had survived couldn't carry them. Not for the weeks-long journey home.

This was but the latest in the long series of wars between the draconans and the aeradi, Kolanis knew, but he didn't think either side had ever scored such a crushing victory—and certainly not when the other had come so close to winning a total victory of their own and inflicted so much damage along the way.

But that was how it had turned out. Adaelis was dead, along with the vast majority of the army he had commanded. It was left to Sky-Major Kolanis now to command the survivors of the host.

Adaelis had told him to wait at the camp for stragglers for two days. They'd now waited four, and the aeradi were getting closer. Another day, perhaps even only a few more hours, and the lancers would find them.

The skyships would follow, with the cannon and the crys-bows and the landing parties, and Kolanis's meager army would not survive the battle. He'd waited as long as he could, and now he had no choice.

"Tell the men to pack up," he instructed, his voice hoarse with suppressed grief. "Take only what we need for the trip home. Burn the rest."

The aide nodded and silently withdrew. The man was competent—otherwise, Adaelis would have long since broken him out of the military, Skyborne or no—so Kolanis would trust him to do his job.

For himself, he simply turned his gaze to the sky to the west, the sky that would bear him to the mountains of his home.

THE FIRST THREE DAYS AFTER THE BATTLE WERE DEDICATED TO cleaning up and repairing the damage, and even that was only enough to make a beginning on the wreckage the draconan attack had left behind.

On the fourth day, however, the King had decreed a day of rest, of remembrance for those who had died and to honor those who had defended the city in her darkest hour. Those like Erik *septon* Tarverro, who had spent most of the last three days either in meetings of the Council of *Septons* or coordinating relief efforts, or Dekker *sept* Corens, who had spent *all* of the last three days up to his elbows in repair work.

They stood in the Square of the Gods, where most of the damage *had* been cleared up, and faced a silent crowd of their people. A single line of carpet, guarded on both sides by deadly-neat files of an odd mix of Wind Guards and Militia, drawn not from any formal unit but from the soldiers who mere days earlier had held this square against all odds.

Erik and Dekker had paused at the start of the carpet, looking across the square at where Lokar *septon* Adelnis, King of Newport, waited for them. Both men were dressed in uniform, with black ribbons to mark mourning.

There should have been four people there that morning, Erik reflected as they started down the corridor of men toward the King. But Harmon *hept* Ikeras had died aboard the *Tarverro*, and while the half-wrecked flagship of Sub-Admiral the Mage Lady Desira *sept* Mogan, commander of the Fifth Battle Squadron, had survived the desperate sky battle over Newport, the Admiral who had inflicted such stunning losses on their enemy had not.

So, only the two men who'd first held this very square and then used the *Tarverro* as bait to lure the draconans into the deadliest trap in years were to be honored as living heroes. Most of the other honors of the day would be posthumous.

The King himself had fought in the battle, Erik reflected, holed up in a private residence in the outer city with a number of Wind Guards and senior officers. Most of the officers had likely never expected to use their swords again in their lives, but when Lokar had taken up his own blade to fight the draconans, they'd followed suit, barricading the residence's entrances first with furniture and then with the dead bodies of their enemies.

Somehow, that image reassured Erik far more than if the man had simply remained safe in the Palace while the battle was fought. His King had fought against the same enemy as him; he understood what had been asked.

Finally, the two "heroes" reached the dais where Lokar stood, and knelt before their King.

"Get up," Lokar told them quietly so no one else could hear. "Both of you. Neither of you has any need to kneel before me. If not for you, I would not have a city. Now stand."

Obedient to their King's command, the two soldiers rose to their feet, and Lokar stepped backward.

"People of Newport," he said aloud, his voice echoing across the square, "these two who stand here are, more than any other still alive" —the qualification was bitter in everyone's ears, but too many others had died to leave it out—"responsible for the salvation of our city.

"Should they be rewarded?" the King of Newport asked his people.

"AYE!" the crowd bellowed back, echoing off the buildings around them. At the front of the crowd, her eyes gleaming, Erik spotted Elysia *sept* Kirmon. For a moment, their eyes met, and then she glanced aside and Erik's attention returned to his King.

Lokar bowed his head to the crowd. "My people have spoken, and the only choice that remains to me is how to reward such deserving servants of our city."

He turned to Dekker. "Captain Dekker *sept* Corens of my own Wind Guard, what reward would you ask of me?"

Despite the King's previous words, Dekker sank to his knees at Erik's side. "Sire, I would ask no reward, of you or of Newport," he declared. "I did only my duty."

"I disagree, *Major* Dekker," Lokar told him, and reached down to remove the Wind Guard's Captain's stars and replace them with the Major's insignia he'd carried hidden in his hand, "commander of the First Battalion of my Wind Guard. I expect only the best from you and your men, Major."

Still on his knees, Dekker barely managed to salute. "Thank you, sire," he said.

Lokar raised his hand, forestalling the Wind Guard. "That promotion is within my power to give without thought," he told both Dekker and the crowd. "Others are beyond my power on my own, but I am not alone.

"I speak in this," he continued, "not as your King but as *septon* Adelnis, for the Council of *Septons*."

The King left a pause, winking at Erik as he allowed his words to sink in. Erik remained stolidly silent. He knew what the Council had decided—he'd both voted and argued for it.

"Major Dekker *sept* Corens, it is rare for the Council to approve the creation of a new *sept*," Lokar told Dekker. "In this case, however, given the nature of your service to the city of Newport, our decision was unanimous.

"No longer," the King told the kneeling and stunned man, "are you Dekker *sept* Corens. Rise, Dekker *septon* Deks, First Father of *sept* Deks."

The new *septon* rose to his feet jerkily, as if someone else controlled his limbs. "Thank you," he said, his voice choked.

Lokar gave him a firm nod and then turned to Erik. "Lord Tarverro," he said aloud, letting his voice carry once more, "what reward would *you* ask of me?"

"Nothing," Erik told him. "You have nothing to reward me with that I do not possess."

"Indeed," Lokar agreed. "I cannot reward you with social rank, for you are among the highest of us. I cannot reward you with wealth, for you are wealthy beyond need. There is, indeed, nothing *I* can reward you with."

Erik waited silently. He'd come to know his King well enough to realize there was another shoe coming.

"Fortunately, I am not limited to my own resources," Lokar said, and then stepped back.

Another man, who Erik hadn't noticed before, stepped forward. He wore the yellow uniform of a wing lancer with a single golden wing on his collar.

"Do you know who I am, Lord Tarverro?" the man asked.

Erik simply shook his head.

"My name is Joset *sept* Tukli," the man said simply. "I am the Wing Lord of Newport, commander of the wing lancers of our city in the name of our King. Kneel, Erik *septon* Tarverro."

Stunned, Erik sank to his knees, and Tukli drew his sword and laid its point on the ground before Erik's eyes.

"Do you, Erik *septon* Tarverro, willingly take upon yourself the ranks, duties, privileges and responsibilities of a wing lancer of the city of Newport?" he demanded.

Still in shock, Erik was frozen for a moment, before the new *septon* Deks kicked him in the heel.

"I do," he confirmed, loudly.

"Do you, Erik *septon* Tarverro," Tukli continued, as if the gap hadn't happened, "swear your service and your honor to our great city?"

"I do."

"Do you, Erik *septon* Tarverro, swear to serve so that others may not; to fight so that others are free; and to die so that others may live?"

"I do."

"Then rise," Tulki commanded, "Erik *septon* Tarverro, Wing-Leader of the city of Newport."

As Erik rose, the Wing Lord offered him the traditional two weapons of the wing lancer: the short-blade, identical to the normal tachi of an aeradi warrior, and the spear-like long-blade only the lancers used.

He accepted the weapons and breathed deeply of the air of the city of his home.

GLOSSARY

The following terms are used within the book:

aeradi: Short and slight in build, the aeradi are those who were drawn to the sea by the call of air and water. Using the magic of water and air, they forged the great sky cities of the Realm of the Sky and raised themselves as a people apart.

Bond: The linked pair of a draconan and a dragon. Also used to describe the link itself.

draconans: Tall and lithe, the draconans are a race set apart not so much by blood as by mind. This race has the ability to communicate with dragons mind-to-mind. Much of both their economic and military systems are based around this ability.

duredine: Tall, fair and long-lived, the duredine sit outside many of the affairs of the world. Their distaste for the use of metals leads them to produce fantastic woods in great demand outside their borders.

dwarves: Artificers, alchemists and miners without peer, dwarves are a low-set, burly race, unmatched technologically on the world of Cevran.

ept: The clans of the aeradi aristocracy. Can be used either as a reference to the members of the clans or to the clans themselves. Also *epti* or *epts.*

hept: A junior clan of the aeradi aristocracy.

hept: The honorific granted to a member of a *hept.*

heptel: The senior female of the line who is not the *hepton's* wife. This is usually the *hepton's* mother.

hepti: The primary male heir of the *hept.*

heptol: The senior female of the line. Either the *hepton's* wife or the guardian of the *hept's* wealth and titles if there is no senior male.

hepton: The senior male and patriarch of the *hept*. The *hepton* is the holder of all titles and privileges granted to the *hept.*

human: Of middling height and build among the races, humans are the most widespread of the people of Cevran, ruling most of the flatlands of the continent.

kep: *Kep* families are those bound to the major *hept* and *sept* by interwoven oaths of fealty and protection.

mermen: Dusky skin and hidden gills mark the sentient inhabitants of Cevran's oceans. They are a reclusive race, and only a handful are ever seen above the waves.

sept: A senior clan of the aeradi aristocracy.

sept: The honorific granted to a member of a *sept.*

septel: The senior female of the line who is not the *septon's* wife. This is usually the *septon's* mother.

septi: The primary male heir of the *sept.*

septol: The senior female of the line. Either the *septon's* wife or the guardian of the *sept's* wealth and titles if there is no senior male.

septon: The senior male and patriarch of the *sept*. The *septon* is the holder of all titles and privileges granted to the *sept.*

JOIN THE MAILING LIST

Love Glynn Stewart's books? To know as soon as new books are released, special announcements, join the mailing list at:

glynnstewart.com/mailing-list/

ABOUT THE AUTHOR

Glynn Stewart is the author of *Starship's Mage*, a bestselling science fiction and fantasy series where faster-than-light travel is possible–but only because of magic. His other works include science fiction series *Duchy of Terra, Castle Federation* and *Vigilante*, as well as the urban fantasy series *ONSET* and *Changeling Blood*.

Writing managed to liberate Glynn from a bleak future as an accountant. With his personality and hope for a high-tech future intact, he lives in Southern Ontario with his partner, their cats, and an unstoppable writing habit.

VISIT GLYNNSTEWART.COM FOR NEW RELEASE UPDATES

CREDITS

The following people were involved in making this book:
Copyeditor: Richard Shealy
Cover art: Jeff Brown
Typo Hunter Team
Faolan's Pen Publishing team: Jack, Kate, and Robin.

facebook.com/glynnstewartauthor

OTHER BOOKS
BY GLYNN STEWART

For release announcements join the
mailing list or visit **GlynnStewart.com**

STARSHIP'S MAGE
Starship's Mage
Hand of Mars
Voice of Mars
Alien Arcana
Judgment of Mars
UnArcana Stars
Sword of Mars
Mountain of Mars
The Service of Mars
A Darker Magic
Mage-Commander
Beyond the Eyes of Mars

Starship's Mage: Red Falcon
Interstellar Mage
Mage-Provocateur
Agents of Mars

Pulsar Race: A Starship's Mage Universe Novella

DUCHY OF TERRA
The Terran Privateer
Duchess of Terra
Terra and Imperium
Darkness Beyond
Shield of Terra
Imperium Defiant
Relics of Eternity
Shadows of the Fall
Eyes of Tomorrow

VIGILANTE
(WITH TERRY MIXON)
Heart of Vengeance
Oath of Vengeance

**Bound By Stars: A Vigilante Series
(With Terry Mixon)**
Bound By Law
Bound by Honor
Bound by Blood

TEER AND KARD
Wardtown
Blood Ward

CHANGELING BLOOD
Changeling's Fealty
Hunter's Oath
Noble's Honor
Fae, Flames & Fedoras: A Changeling Blood Novella

ONSET
ONSET: To Serve and Protect
ONSET: My Enemy's Enemy
ONSET: Blood of the Innocent
ONSET: Stay of Execution
Murder by Magic: An ONSET Novella

STAND ALONE NOVELS & NOVELLAS
Children of Prophecy
City in the Sky
Excalibur Lost: A Space Opera Novella
Balefire: A Dark Fantasy Novella

Made in the USA
Monee, IL
11 June 2023

35633235R00184